Praise for Ronald Malfi and His Novels

"Malfi is a master at horror."
—**RT Book Reviews**

"Malfi is a skillful storyteller."
—**New York Journal of Books**

"Malfi is truly gifted when it comes to writing . . . I am going to eagerly devour all the books from Mr. Malfi that I can get my chubby fingers on." —**Haunted Bookcase**

"Ronald Malfi has for years been a rising star in the horror genre. His lyricism and sense of character stand with the very best of the genre, and though I am hesitant to make comparisons, one cannot help but think of writers like Peter Straub, Chet Williamson, F. Paul Wilson, and Stephen King when reading . . . The sense of dread and tension are palpable, recalling another great writer, Charles L. Grant. His language is stirring and evocative." —**FearNet**

"Malfi continues to astound."
—**Horror Buzz**

The Night Parade

"The destruction or ending of the world as we know it is a common backdrop for examining the elements of humanity . . . Terrifying and fascinating. Malfi adds an interesting new angle to the mix by placing the story in a world infected by the Wanderer's Folly, a disease that blurs the lines between dreams and reality . . . Interesting, moving, and effective." —**Booklist**

"A highly recommended novel which, like everything Malfi writes, transcends genre and is a powerful story about love, family, and sacrifice." —**Cemetery Dance**

"A novel to savor and devour at the same time."
—**Catherine Cavendish**, author of *The Malan Witch*

"[A] beautiful and ultimately terrifying story that shows us
the incredible lengths a father will go to in an effort to
protect his daughter." —**Shotgun Logic**

Little Girls

"Terrifying."
—*Publishers Weekly*

"Malfi builds incredible levels of tension using the
psychological impacts of the secrets lurking within the pages
of *Little Girls* and by balancing the supernatural with the
ordinary. Weaving together the horror, mystery, and
psychological thriller genres, Malfi's *Little Girls* is a complex
and richly layered ghost story that slowly but surely creeps
under your skin." —**The Horror Bookshelf**

"*Little Girls* is much more than a haunted house or a ghost
story. It's a literary horror tale filled with lovely prose. The
story itself is a slow build, giving up its secrets sparingly,
providing plenty of questions. Recommended for fans of
literary horror and ghost stories." —*Cemetery Dance*

"A must for Malfi fans and a great read for those of
you who love classically told ghost stories."
—**iHorror**

"The perfect ghost story, with just the right amount of
psychological thriller added in for good measure."
—**HorrorBuzz**

"As always, Mr. Malfi has written a fantastic story."
—**Erik Smith, vlogger,
The Low Budget Review Show**

"Accelerates towards a relentless and twist-filled climax. As much about the darkness and deceit in human hearts as the supernatural, *Little Girls* promises to be a genuine chiller and another must-read from Malfi." —**This Is Horror**

"It takes these well-known tropes and completely turns them around . . . [which] results in a story that is highly entertaining and scary at the same time." —**IHeartReading**

Bone White

"Malfi's latest is a brilliantly weird, haunting blend of folklore, murder-mystery, and gothic terror that draws readers into an unsettling world filled with the kind of detail and insight that evoke early Stephen King. There is plenty of material here to prey on the most basic of human terrors, beneath the fear and the eeriness is an understated but no less effective story about the hollowing effect of loss on those left behind. The result is an elegant, twisted, gripping slow-burn of a novel that burrows under the skin and nestles deep."
—**RT Book Reviews, 4.5 Stars Top Pick**

"Creepy prose . . . with plentiful hair-raising enigmas and copious gore." —***Publishers Weekly***

"Ronald Malfi masterfully blends psychological terror and traditional gothic horror into dark delight." —***Dark Realms***

"Malfi's florid descriptiveness and taut writing style grip the reader right from the get-go." —***Rue Morgue***

"Malfi is an incredibly talented writer." —**Horror World**

Also by Ronald Malfi

Novels

Come with Me
Bone White
The Night Parade
December Park
The Narrows
Floating Staircase
Cradle Lake
The Ascent
Snow
Shamrock Alley
Passenger
Via Dolorosa
The Nature of Monsters
The Fall of Never
The Space Between

Novellas

Borealis
The Stranger
The Separation
Skullbelly
After the Fade
The Mourning House
A Shrill Keening
Mr. Cables

Collections

They Lurk: 4 Novellas
We Should Have Left Well Enough Alone: Short Stories

THE
NIGHT
PARADE

RONALD
MALFI

KENSINGTON
PUBLISHING CORP.

www.kensingtonbooks.com

For Maddie and Hayden.
Big smiles, Little Spoons.

"Five seconds; and what's happened in the wide world?"

—GEORGE SEFERIS, "Slowly You Spoke"

1

David Arlen's daughter woke up ten miles outside Fredericksburg. She had begun to stir just as the lights of the city receded in the Oldsmobile's rearview mirror, intermittently whining and sobbing in her sleep from the backseat. But now she sat up, almost too abruptly, and the image of her eclipsing the distant city lights in the rearview mirror caused David's heart to jump. It was as if he'd forgotten she was back there.

"Where are we?" She sounded hoarse.

He raked a set of fingers down the left side of his face and neck, feeling the fresh stubble there. He wondered if he should grow a beard. Maybe dye his hair. "I'm not sure. Heading south right now."

"I want my mom."

He had no response for that. He wanted her, too.

"Where *are* we?" she insisted.

"Please," he said, shaking his head and briefly closing his eyes.

"I want to sit up front with you," she said.

"Not just yet."

"Why?"

"Just sit back. Please. Try to go back to sleep."

"I'm not tired anymore."

"Please, Ellie," he said.

She sat back, her silhouette sinking below the rearview mirror. The lights of Fredericksburg were gone now, obscured by black trees along the sloping road and the heavy drapery of night.

David glanced at the Oldsmobile's dashboard clock. It was just after midnight. He tried to do the math and figure out how long he'd been awake, but found even the simplest brain work next to impossible. Two days? Longer? In his exhaustion, even his vision threatened mutiny: The sodium lamps that flanked the shoulder of the highway occasionally blurred into smeary arcs of colorless light.

For what seemed like the millionth time since they'd hit the road, he took mental inventory of the items he'd managed to squirrel away in the trunk: extra clothes, some food, approximately six hundred dollars in cash, some books and board games to keep Ellie's mind off the whole thing. There was a handgun and two boxes of ammo back there, too, in a stolen pink suitcase. He'd never fired a gun in his life. When he had come across it in Burt Langstrom's bedroom, he'd felt the world tilt slightly and time seemed to freeze. The weapon had seemed unreal. Until that moment, it had never occurred to him that he might need a weapon, a firearm. But there it had been, like a sign from God, and its mere presence was enough to drive home the gravity of their situation. He'd picked it up, surprised to find that much of it was made of plastic—he had always just assumed handguns were cast from iron or steel or something—and for some reason that made it seem all the more deadly. Quiet and unassuming, like a sleek black snake weaving through a flower bed. And for the first time he had wondered, *Could I kill a person? If it comes down to it, could I do it? Could I point this thing at someone, pull the trigger, bring them down?*

Now, gripping the steering wheel of the Olds with both hands, he thought of what was at stake and imagined that he could.

When he motored past a police cruiser tucked along a dirt passage between the trees just beyond the shoulder, he swore under his breath, then stared at the speedometer. He was cruising at just below seventy miles per hour. What was the speed limit on this particular stretch of highway? He racked his brain but couldn't remember the last time he'd spotted a speed limit sign. Goddamn careless. His eyes flicked back up to the rearview mirror. Holding his breath, he waited to see if the cruiser would pull out onto the highway in pursuit. Any second, those headlights would blink on, growing in size as the cruiser drew closer until the rack lights came alive and doused the world in alternating blue and red flashers.

But the cop car never slid out onto the highway.

It wasn't until a good ten minutes later that he allowed himself to relax. With any luck, they weren't even looking for him yet.

"I'm hungry."

Her voice startled him. He had assumed she had fallen back asleep. But she sounded clear, lucid.

"Can't it wait?" he asked her.

"Wait for what?"

That was a good question. He had no answer for her. No plan. Not yet, anyway.

"Listen," he said. "I've got some food in the trunk. Let me pull over and I'll get some out for you."

"Food in the trunk," she said. It wasn't a question, though he could tell by her tone that she was marveling over the peculiarity of it all.

David's eyes kept skirting to the shoulder of the road. With the exception of the police car, they hadn't passed another vehicle in over fifteen minutes. Desolate. Nonetheless, he wondered if he'd draw more attention to himself parked along the shoulder rifling through his trunk than if he just went to a rest stop where they could blend in more easily. What if the cop had decided to follow him after all, and happened to drive up as he stood rifling through the Oldsmobile's trunk? A *stolen* Oldsmobile.

Prior to tonight, and if he'd ever given the matter any serious consideration, he would have said that there were certain things you did when you were on the run: You headed out at night, avoided large cities while sticking to secondary roads, and, to paraphrase Chuck Berry, simply kept on motorvatin' over the hill. But now that he was in the thick of it, he second-guessed each move, finding the flaws in every single decision, the weaknesses in every plan. It was all cracks in a dam. Heading out at night meant you had the cover of darkness beneath which you could travel . . . but it also meant there were less people on the roads, and fewer souls among which you could hide. You attracted eyes; those eyes watched you. That held true for the secondary roads, too; it unnerved him that he hadn't seen any other vehicles for the past fifteen or twenty minutes or so. The odds that he would get pulled over out here were greatly increased. A bored cop might decide to pull him over for lack of anything better to do. For all he knew, the goddamn Olds might even have a taillight out. Had he cut through all the major cities, he could lose himself among the crowd.

"Dad," she said from the backseat. There was no pleading quality to her voice, no whining about it. She simply said it and let it hang in the air between them, as if to remind him that she was still there, and to remind him of who he was.

"I know. Gimme a sec, hon."

He noticed that, according to the gas gauge, the tank was nearly three-quarters empty. How had he not noticed this before? It was careless. But it made up his mind for him.

When they passed a sign that read REST STOP 1 MILE, David said, "We'll stop there. I'll park and get the food out of the trunk. You stay in the car."

"I gotta go pee," she said.

"Yeah, okay."

He glanced down and noticed a stringy dark smear on his left shirtsleeve. Even in the dark he recognized it as blood. He absently cuffed the sleeve past the elbow.

Jesus, he thought.

2

When they came upon the lights of the rest stop, David took the exit. His nerves vibrated; his hands shook. It wasn't a busy rest stop, probably due to the ungodly hour, with only a few scattered cars in the parking lot. Eighteen-wheelers were parked at the far end of the tarmac, their lights off, as motionless as great slumbering beasts. He and Ellie could get lost here, stay anonymous.

David parked the car but left the engine running. He popped the trunk with a button on the dash, then turned around to face Ellie in the backseat.

She was only a week shy of her ninth birthday, but at that moment, tucked into a darkened corner of the Oldsmobile's backseat, her knees pulled up to her chest, her eyes large and frightened, her clothes rumpled, she looked to David like the small child she'd once been. Helpless, with a face full of wonder and fear. The first few weeks after her birth, he'd paced the floorboards of the house in Arnold cradling her in his arms. She never slept, only stared at him with those wide, intelligent eyes, so wise and thoughtful for a thing that had been alive for such a brief time. Often, she would furrow her brow in some mimicry of contemplation, those murky seawater eyes focusing in on him like camera lenses, and David would wonder what thoughts could possibly be passing through her beautiful infant brain.

He shook the thought from his mind.

"Stay here," he told her. Then he got out of the car.

It was early September and the air was cool. He could smell gasoline and could hear the buzzing cadence of insects in the surrounding trees. A group of kids in their late teens stood huddled around a nearby trash can, smoking cigarettes and talking loudly. They had plastic dime-store Halloween masks propped on their heads, a trend that had become increasingly popular since the first reports of the outbreak. They shifted their gaze over to David and, somewhat distrustfully, pulled the masks down over their faces.

In the trunk, David popped open the plastic pink suitcase and dug through some clothes until he retrieved a handful of Nature Valley granola bars. There were a few warm cans of Coke in the suitcase, as well—the only thing he'd been able to get his hands on at the time—and so he grabbed one of those, too.

When he shut the trunk, he was startled to find Ellie standing beside the car's rear bumper. She was watching the smoking teenagers in the cheap Halloween masks, her hands limp at her sides. Her hair, sleek auburn strands that had been a carroty red when she was just a toddler, billowed gently in the breeze.

"Hey." He reached out and grabbed her shoulder. Firmly. "What'd I say? Stay in the car until I came and got you, remember?"

She turned and looked up at him. Her face was pale, her mouth drawn and nearly lipless. A spray of light brown freckles peppered the saddle of her nose. There was some strange determination in her eyes, and David suddenly felt weakened in the presence of her. It wasn't the first time she had made him feel this way.

David took a breath and caressed the side of her face with his knuckles. "Go back in the car, Little Spoon," he told her.

"But I gotta go to the bathroom, remember?"

No, he hadn't remembered. His brain felt like a rusted hamster wheel clacking around in his skull. He glanced around until he saw a brick outhouse with the word WOMEN on one door, MEN on the other.

"Okay," he said, and went back around to the driver's side of the Oldsmobile. He tossed the granola bars and the Coke on the seat, then pulled the key from the ignition. The Oldsmobile shuddered and died. Abruptly, he wondered what he would do if the car wouldn't start again. Steal another car? Would he even know how to do it? People in movies always seemed to know how to hot-wire a car—it was like tying your shoes, apparently—but he had no clue.

He placed a hand against the small of Ellie's back and ushered her forward. "Go on," he told her. "Be quick. And don't talk to anyone. I'll wait right out here for you."

He thought he heard her sob, so he stopped her, crouched down, and looked her in the eyes. They were glassy, but she still wasn't crying. She didn't even look all that frightened. In fact, it looked like she was studying him. Scrutinizing him.

"Don't cry, hon," he told her anyway. It sounded like the right thing to say, and it was certainly important. "Okay?"

"I don't understand this," she told him.

"Little Spoon," he said, squeezing her shoulder more tightly. He didn't want attention drawn to them, and an eight-year-old girl becoming upset in the parking lot of a rest stop at this hour would surely do the trick.

"I'm worried about Mom," she said. "When can I see her?"

"Hon," he said . . . and he wanted to hug her, but the last thing he wanted to do was make a scene, even if it was only in front of the masked teenagers smoking by the trash can. He could risk doing nothing that would cause someone to remember them at a later date. Of course, Ellie didn't know the truth of it, so he couldn't expect her to act accordingly.

That will have to change very soon, he thought. *If we're going to survive this, she'll need to know the score. If not the whole truth, she'll need to know something very close to it.*

Now wasn't the time, however.

In the end, Ellie turned away from him, his hand dropping from her shoulder. She wended around the group of teenagers with her head down and vanished into the women's restroom.

I'll tell her later, he promised himself, while simultaneously wondering if there would *be* a later.

When he found himself gnawing at his lower lip, he realized that he craved a cigarette. He'd smoked his last one . . . how many hours ago? It had still been daylight. There was a full carton of Marlboros on the top shelf of his bedroom closet, but they could have been on the moon for all their accessibility now. He glanced around, spotted a vending machine beyond the brick outhouse, but saw only columns of potato chips, chocolate bars, pretzels, and the like. Vaguely, he wondered if they still sold cigarettes in vending machines anymore.

In the quiet, his mind slipped back to earlier that evening and to the inexplicable thing that had happened in the car as they left their hometown in Maryland. He had been a rattled mess, his heart slamming in his chest, his mind spinning uncontrollably . . . until Ellie had reached over to him, her hand cool against his burning flesh . . .

He shook the notion from his mind. It was impossible.

After another minute passed and Ellie didn't come out of the restroom, David began to panic. His arms still crossed, he began pacing back and forth in front of the door to the women's room like a warden. The concrete walkway was covered in beetles; they crunched beneath his feet like potato chips. If she didn't come out in the next thirty seconds—and he was now counting silently to himself—he would go in after her.

But what if she's gone in there and started crying? he thought. *What if some woman is already in there, and she stops her and asks her what's wrong, and Ellie tells her that her father tucked her into the backseat of a strange car and spirited her away like a thief in the night? Isn't that a possibility?*

Christ, yes.

His hand was already clutching the door handle to the women's room when the door shushed open and Ellie came out. She looked up at him with an expression of consternation on her face. David glanced into the restroom and saw that the remaining stalls were empty. The single bulb at the center of the ceiling flickered.

"Come on," he said, rubbing the back of her head as he led her back to the car. He was reminded of the gas tank when he turned the ignition over, so he pulled around to the farthest set of pumps. A few tractor trailers stood like gathered cattle at the far end of the lot. David climbed out of the car, discovered that the gas tank was on the other side of the vehicle, swore under his breath, then got back in and repositioned the car. In the backseat, Ellie sat motionless and wide-eyed, staring at him and not touching any of the snacks he'd tossed back there for her. He could feel the heaviness of her eyes on him. "Go on," he told her. "Eat something. It's okay." The smile he offered her felt as false as a stick-on moustache.

At the pump, he pulled his wallet from his pants and had already slid his credit card through the slot when he realized what he had done. It seemed every muscle in his body tensed at once. Even his teeth clenched. Nearly in disbelief, he stared at the tiny digital screen as it processed his credit card, then stared down at the card itself, as if skeptical of its very existence.

"Shit, shit," he hissed through his teeth.

The screen prompted him to enter his zip code before processing the card. It also gave him the option to cancel the sale. Which he did immediately.

There was the cash in the trunk, but he also had a wad of tens and fives in his wallet. He held up one finger to Ellie, who watched him, emotionless, from the backseat, then he went to the attendant's booth, where he forked over thirty bucks to the ancient dark-skinned woman seated behind a sheet of bulletproof glass.

Three minutes later, they were back on the highway. When he saw a white van in the far right lane, David felt a cool sweat prickle his scalp. It looked identical to the one that had been parked across the street from their house on Columbus Court for the past few weeks. David couldn't decide if he should slow down or speed up. Finally, he decided to take an exit that dumped them onto a secondary roadway.

Despite her proclamation of hunger, Ellie never touched the granola bars, never cracked open the Coke. He could use the caffeine himself, but he didn't ask her to pass the soda up to him. She had been quiet since leaving the gas station, and he presumed she had fallen back asleep. So when she spoke up and asked him to turn on the radio, he nearly launched out of his skin.

And the radio was nothing but static.

3

After some careful deliberation, he decided to stop at a roadside motel for the night. Prior to this, he had considered parking behind a billboard off the main highway or something like that, catching some z's behind the wheel of the Olds like he'd done in his old road-tripping days during breaks from college, but he thought there would be time for that soon enough. Moreover, sleeping in the car would only prompt additional questions from Ellie, questions he wasn't yet prepared to answer. He was amazed she'd been so compliant thus far, but he wasn't willing to push his luck. Besides, he could use a hot shower. In fact, that sounded like heaven to him.

It was one of those motor lodges where all the rooms had doors that opened onto the parking lot. He counted only two other vehicles in the front lot and, after driving around the building, two more in the rear. He told Ellie to wait in the car while he went in and got them a room.

The lobby was dressed in outdated wallpaper and threadbare aquamarine carpeting. The lights in the ceiling seemed impossibly bright and were orbited by a cloud of gnats. The guy behind the counter, grizzled and rheumy-eyed, looked no more lifelike than the half-dozen taxidermy animals adorning the wooden shelves behind him. Pressing a handkerchief to his mouth, he looked up as David approached.

"I'd like a room please," David said to the fellow.

"Last name?" the guy asked through the handkerchief, swiveling on a stool so that he could tap out a few keys on an old PC.

"Arlen." It was out of his mouth before he knew what he was saying. Just like back at the gas station with the credit card. How long did he really expect to last being this careless?

"Ireland?" the old man said.

David went with it. "Yes."

The man tapped a few more keys on the computer.

David wasn't sure if it was possible to get a room anymore without a credit card or an ID, but he took his chances. "My cards are all maxed out," he said. "Do you take cash?"

"It's still legal tender, ain't it?" said the old-timer. Then something akin to suspicion glinted in his reptilian eyes, and he made no attempt at subtlety when he leaned forward and peered out the glass door toward the parking lot. He kept the handkerchief firmly in place against his mouth and nose. "It's just you?" the man said.

"Just me."

"No lady friend with you?"

"No, sir."

" 'Cause this ain't no brothel. Won't put up with no hanky-panky. Just 'cause the world's goin' to shit don't mean I surrender my morals. You catch what I'm saying?"

"Of course. It's just me. No worries."

Apparently contented, the old man retracted back behind the counter and completed the transaction. Blessedly, he did not ask to see David's ID. David forked over sixty bucks for the room and another hundred for a security deposit since he wasn't using a credit card.

"Kinda steep for a security deposit," David said.

"What's it to you, so long as you don't burn the place down," said the old man through his handkerchief.

David handed over the money. First night on the road and he'd already made a sizable dent in their meager account.

The man gave him a plastic key card with the number 118 printed on it in permanent marker. Back in the parking lot, David drove around to the rear of the motel and parked right outside the door to their room. Ellie was still wide awake in the backseat, glaring at him.

"Come on," he told her, leaving the car running as he got out. "I'll let you in, then I'm going to park the car somewhere else."

"Why?"

"Because this place looks shady and I don't want someone breaking in to the car," he lied.

"It isn't ours, anyway," she said as she climbed out of the Oldsmobile's backseat.

He was quick opening the motel room door and ushering Ellie inside. Glancing around, he took inventory: a single twin-size bed with a paisley coverlet; a wooden dresser on which sat an old tubed television set plugged in to a digital converter; a closet whose door stood open to reveal a horizontal wooden post from which a few metal coat hangers hung; brownish water stains on the ceiling and walls; a telephone and an alarm clock atop a gouge-ridden nightstand. There was a single window beside the front door, the drapes already pulled closed. David went to a lamp on a rickety-looking table, switched it on, then went back to the door, leaving Ellie to stand in the middle of the room, looking around in silence.

"I'll be right back," he told her.

She sat on the edge of the bed and stared at the TV. In her lap was the cardboard shoe box with the Nike logo on its lid. Over the past several weeks the shoe box—or, rather, the items *inside* the shoe box—had become something of a security blanket for the girl.

Outside, David got back in the car and parked it behind two enormous Dumpsters at the far corner of the lot. From the trunk, he gathered up his duffel bag, as well as the small pink suitcase he'd packed with clothes for Ellie, along with some board games to keep her occupied. The only item that actually belonged to Ellie was the stuffed elephant, and he had that now only because Ellie had given it to Kathy. It had been Ellie's favorite toy when she was no more than two, a gray plush pachyderm she'd named, in her pragmatic way, simply Elephant. He debated whether or not he should leave in it the trunk—his fear was that it might spark more questions about Kathy if he brought it into the motel—but in the end he shoved that into the duffel bag, as well.

Back in the room, he set the bags down on the bed, then stretched so that the tendons in his back popped. Ellie hadn't moved from her perch at the edge of the bed, her eyes still glued to the television set that she hadn't turned on. She was gripping the shoe box so tightly that her fingertips were white.

"You can watch something, if you want," he told her.

"The TV looks funny," she said.

"What do you mean?"

"Well, look at it."

"It's just old."

"Why's it so big?"

"This is how TVs looked before they were flat."

"Does it work the same?"

"Sure." He found the remote Velcro'd to the top of the set. "Here," he said, switching it on. The TV hummed, crackled, then came to life with a bleary image. Some sitcom with canned laughter. The color looked a bit off, the actors' skin a sour yellow.

He handed the remote to Ellie—he had to pry one hand away from the shoe box and shove the remote into it—then opened the pink suitcase. He snatched up the gun and ammo that were buried inside and quickly tucked them into his own duffel bag, then proceeded to empty some of the contents of the suitcase onto the bed. An old Chutes and Ladders game, some Harry Potter and Shel Silverstein books, a drawing set with colored pencils and graph paper. They weren't Ellie's belongings, but they would suffice. He took out a pair of pink pajamas, suddenly wondering if they would fit the girl. What the hell, it didn't matter. This wasn't a fashion show.

"The clicker doesn't work," she said, examining the TV remote, which she clutched in one reddened hand. David noticed that her fingernails had been gnawed down to nubs.

"Maybe the batteries are dead. You can change it manually."

"What does that mean?"

"You can . . ." he began, then leaned forward and punched one of the channel buttons on the front of the set several times. The image on the screen bounced from sitcom to news program to QVC to a tampon commercial. "See?"

"Oh."

"There's some pajamas for you." He nodded toward the bed, where he'd laid them out. "Why don't you go into the bathroom, wash up, and change?"

She peered at the folded pink pajamas over her shoulder. Then at the books and games. After a moment, she said, "Those aren't mine."

"I know that, hon. It's all we've got."

"Why?"

"It's just . . . it's what we've got."

"Where'd they come from?"

"It doesn't matter," he said.

"That house?"

"Yes, Ellie."

"What about a toothbrush?"

He hadn't thought of that. "We'll have to skip it for tonight. I'll buy us some toothbrushes tomorrow."

"I don't want to wear those pajamas."

"You'll be more comfortable. We can get new pajamas tomorrow, along with the toothbrushes. It's just for one night."

"I'd rather sleep in my clothes."

He sighed. There was no fight left in him. It didn't matter, anyway. "Okay. Fine. In the meantime, why don't you go wash up best you can in the bathroom. There should be some soap in there."

Wordlessly, she set the shoe box on the bed, then got up and made her way to the bathroom. She closed the door, watching him through the narrowing sliver as it closed until the latch caught and he heard the lock turn. A few seconds later he heard the water clunk on in the sink—a snake-like hiss.

All of a sudden, he thought he would throw up. There was a plastic ice bucket on the floor beside the nightstand and he snatched it up while he simultaneously dropped down on the edge of the bed. The mattress springs squealed as if in pain. Clenching the bucket between his knees, he hung his head over it, salivating, waiting for the wave of nausea to either pass or for a burble of acid to come rushing up and out of his throat.

It was the thought of Kathy that eventually had him gagging and vomiting into the receptacle. He did it as quietly as he could, for fear Ellie might hear him, and when he was done he set the bucket outside the door next to a concrete ashtray. In such a short period of time, the night had grown considerably colder.

Ellie eventually came out of the bathroom, her auburn hair damp and down around her shoulders, her face looking fresh and clean. She wore only her undershirt and panties, and she clutched her clothes to her chest. He considered saying that she might be too cold without the pajamas, but in the end, he decided to let it go. He was spent.

Ellie folded her clothes and set them atop the dresser as David grabbed his duffel bag and headed toward the bathroom. "I'm going to take a shower. Don't open the door for anyone. Understand?"

She nodded.

"If anyone knocks, you come and get me."

"Who would knock?"

"No one," he said.

"When you come out, can we call Mom?"

"No, honey. Not right now."

"How come?"

He considered this. "Because it's very late," he said in the end. "She's probably asleep."

"Tomorrow, then?"

"Yes," he said, feeling the word sting his tongue like battery acid. His throat suddenly felt very thick. "Tomorrow." He blew her a kiss and went into the bathroom, shutting and locking the door behind him.

The water came out of the showerhead steaming hot, which both surprised and pleased him. Leaning toward the mirror, he tugged down one lower eyelid and then the other. The skin underneath looked pink and moist, marbled with a delicate network of blood vessels. He turned on the ceiling vent, checked the lock on the door a second time, then set the duffel bag on the counter and opened it.

Shoving aside articles of clothing, he located the gun and both boxes of ammunition. As he had done back in Burt Langstrom's bedroom, he lifted it out of the bag almost too gingerly, turning it over with abundant care in both hands. It was a Glock, though he did not know the model. There was a single magazine in the hilt, and it took him only a few seconds to release it by pressing a lever on the side of the weapon. Aside from the trigger, it was the only other lever, and he marveled at the terrible and dangerous *simplicity* of the instrument. In the movies, it seemed like someone was always cocking back hammers or switching levers. A child could use this.

I'm an idiot, he thought. *What am I doing with this thing?*

He had hoped to find some instructions for loading the gun on the boxes of ammo, but that was not the case. He opened one of the boxes and pried out the little plastic tray. Each bullet was housed in its own circular well, bottom-up. They gleamed in the fluorescent lights above the bathroom mirror.

The back of the gun's magazine had little numbered holes running in two columns, so he was able to discern that the mag held just thirteen rounds. There was a spring-loaded mechanism at the top of the mag, which gave under the weight of his thumb when he pushed on it. One by one, he loaded thirteen rounds into the magazine, the spring becoming more resistant with each round, until he had capped it off. Then he slammed it back into the hilt of the gun and heard it click into place.

The one move he had seen countless times on television that *did* prove useful was charging the weapon—pulling back the slide in order to chamber a round. It clanked solidly, and all of a sudden he could feel nothing but the weight of the thing in his hand. It was heavier with the bullets in it. When he glanced up at his reflection in the steamy mirror, he hardly recognized himself. Yet that had very little to do with the gun; he'd stopped recognizing himself weeks ago, when this whole thing had started to get ugly.

He tucked the loaded gun back inside his duffel bag, then checked his cell phone. He'd kept it powered off during the drive, mostly to conserve the battery because he had forgotten to bring his charger—another stupid oversight—but also because he'd once heard that people could be tracked to a specific location by GPS just by pinging their cell phone. He didn't know whether this was true or not, but he thought it was better to be safe than sorry.

The phone powered up, searched for a signal, then chimed repeatedly to let him know he had unread text messages. He checked the log and saw there were five missed calls with an equal number of voice mails. There were twice as many text messages, too, each one sent from the same person, the most recent sent only an hour earlier. They were from Sanjay Kapoor. And although a white-hot rage rose up through him as he looked at Kapoor's name, he couldn't bring himself to delete the messages. Instead, he clicked on the most recent and read it.

Please reconsider your actions, David.
You hold the key that could save us all.

His eyes burned. Without giving the message another thought, he deleted it, then powered down his phone.

He stripped out of his clothes. They were sour with per-spiration and fell to the floor in a stiff and smelly heap. When he climbed beneath the spray of hot water, he tried hard to erase the past several hours from his mind—the past several days, several weeks, several months—but they haunted him. He couldn't scald those images away.

4

He showered for a good fifteen minutes. When he was done, he toweled off, pulled on a fresh pair of underwear, sweatpants, and an old Pearl Jam T-shirt. Unlike Ellie, he happened to have his own clothes with him, already packed. He had anticipated a longer stay at the hospital.

Back in the room, Ellie was already curled up on the bedspread, asleep. *My God, she looks so old.* He felt a pang of sadness in his chest. Looking at her reminded him of Kathy, and that hurt, too. It had all happened so quickly, his grief was still confused with disbelief, with anger, with helplessness. He had to keep reminding himself that it wasn't a nightmare and that it had all actually happened—was *still* happening. When he closed his eyes, it was Kathy's face that materialized through the darkness; only his urgency to *keep moving* was enough to bump her from his thoughts for small periods of time, allowing him to function. Well, his urgency . . . and what had happened earlier that night in the car, that unsettling and inexplicable thing that Ellie had done to him when they first set out on the road . . .

Ellie had one arm draped around the shoe box. David considered attempting to remove it, to set it on the nightstand, but in the end he decided to let it be. What was the harm?

Despite the squealing bedsprings, Ellie didn't stir when he eased down on the other side of the bed. Thank God for small miracles. He dreaded any discussion with her about the truth of what had happened. But she was a smart kid. A September baby—their Miracle Baby—they had petitioned to have her advance a grade early on, and it was a decision they never regretted. Sometimes, he knew, the kid was *too* smart.

She knows I've been lying to her, he realized now, the notion striking him like a terrible epiphany. *Jesus, she's just been humoring me, hasn't she? Yes, of course she has. I don't give her enough credit. She gives me too much.*

He turned off the bedside lamp, then reclined on his back, listening to the soft sounds of his daughter's respiration. As tired and defeated as he was, he thought he would have crashed the second his head hit the pillow, but that was not the case. He stared at the black ceiling, at the border of cold sodium light framing the closed drapes over the window. He counted the seconds between each flash of the smoke alarm's cyclopean eye.

His thoughts returned, not to Kathy and his final moments with her, but of what had occurred only hours earlier back in the Oldsmobile, as he drove frantically down the highway, his mind a kaleidoscope of nightmarish thoughts, his heart speed-racing in his chest. Ellie had been in the backseat, and had leaned forward at one point and placed a cool hand against the nape of his neck. She had—

It gave him chills.

After a time, he got up and fumbled around in the darkness until he located what he was looking for: Ellie's stuffed elephant. He crawled back into bed with it, pressing his face against it. There was Ellie's smell on it, a soft and breathy smell he associated with summer mornings spent lazing in bed. But there was another smell on it now, too—the stink of Kathy's hospital room, and all the horribleness that had happened there. It was a harsher and more specific smell than Ellie's, rounded and full in its terribleness.

I should sleep with the gun instead, he thought, burying his face in the stuffed toy.

After a time, sleep claimed him.

5

Twenty-one months earlier

"**W**ell," said Kathy, rolling off of him. They were slick with sweat and David's heartbeat thumped in his ears. He grazed his wife's buttocks with one hand as she rolled off her side of the bed. "I'm going to the kitchen for some water. Want some?"

"Yes, please." He smiled demurely at her from his side of the bed.

Kathy folded her arms over her bare breasts, cocked a hip. "What?" she said.

"You're pretty."

"Charmer. But you're supposed to say those things *before* getting lucky. You know that, right?"

"I've been out of practice."

"Making love?"

"Being charming."

She laughed as she tugged on her robe and went out into the hall.

David got up and went to the bathroom. He urinated, washed his face and hands at the sink, then returned to bed with a Robert Ludlum paperback. He was readjusting the pillows against the headboard when Kathy returned. She handed him a glass of ice water, then climbed into bed beside him.

"Ellie did the strangest thing today," Kathy said, fluffing up her own pillows against the headboard. "We were walking through Target, picking up a few things, when she disappeared down one of the aisles. You know how she does."

David nodded, smiling to himself. Ellie was prone to wandering off when something interesting caught her eye.

"She came running up to me at one point and asked for some money. She said she'd pay me back with her allowance when we got home, but that she saw something and had to get it right then and there. When I asked her what it was, she said she couldn't tell me, and that it was a surprise."

"Oh boy," he said, sliding an index finger between the pages of his book. "Did you give her the money?"

"Yes. It was only five bucks, and she was true to her word, paying me back as soon as we got home."

"What'd she buy?"

"You'll never guess. Not in a million years."

"So tell me."

"She said it was a present for the baby."

"Whose baby?"

"Ours," Kathy said.

"We don't have a baby." But then he looked at her, leaning over on one elbow. "Or is this your way of telling me something?"

Kathy's eyes went wide and she shook her head, laughing. "Christ, no. I'm not pregnant."

"So what's the deal?"

"I don't know. Maybe it was wishful thinking on her part. Or maybe she was trying to tell us something."

David sat up straighter in bed. He set the book down on the nightstand. "Are you saying you want to have another kid?"

She looked at him, the sweat from their lovemaking still glistening on her face, and smiled. "You know, I just don't know. I mean, I think about it from time to time, but never really seriously. And it's not like we've talked about it or anything."

"Is that what we're doing now?" he asked. "Talking about it?"

"Would you want another baby?"

He thought about it for a second. "I'm forty years old," he said. "And not to point out the obvious, your highness, but you're just a few years younger than me. Is it even safe?"

"Women are having babies later in life now," she said. "There are risks, but then there are risks with any pregnancy. There were complications with Ellie at the end, remember?"

The umbilical cord had gotten wrapped around Ellie's neck during labor. They'd had a monitor on her, and with each contraction and subsequent push, David had watched his un-born daughter's blood pressure drop on the computer screen beside Kathy's bed. In the end, the doctor had to take Ellie out via emergency cesarean. Even more terrifying was that she came out in silence, not making a sound. It wasn't until she was aspirated that she started to cry, but even then it had been a few short bleats, and she quieted right up to the moment she was placed in Kathy's arms, those deep obsidian eyes survey-ing them both from beneath a pink and furrowed brow.

But those complications hadn't just been at the end. They'd spent nearly two years trying to get pregnant, had visited countless fertility doctors. Kathy had been on a strict regimen of prenatal vitamins. There had been no medical reason why they shouldn't be able to conceive, yet conception eluded them for the longest time . . . until that one morning when both pregnancy tests turned up positive and a visit to the ob-stetrician confirmed it. Ellie—their Miracle Baby.

"Sounds like you've given this more than just a passing thought," he said.

"What about you?" she said. "Will you give it more than just a passing thought, too?"

He chewed his lower lip for a moment. "Yeah, okay. I will."

Kathy's smile widened. David admired the sweat at her temples, dampening her hair. When she eased back down into her pillows, he could smell the sex on her, wafting over to his side of the bed.

"So, do you want to see it?" Kathy said.

"See what?"

"What she *bought.*"

"I thought she didn't tell you."

"Not right away. But when we got home, she wrapped it in construction paper and gave it to me as a gift." Kathy rolled over and opened the drawer to her nightstand. When she turned back toward him, she was cupping a small, shiny sliver of metal in the palm of her hand.

David leaned forward for a better look. "It's a spoon," he said.

"Well, it's a charm," Kathy said. "Like for a bracelet. But yeah, it's a spoon. It was the sweetest thing."

David smiled and shook his head.

Kathy returned the tiny spoon to the nightstand, then made a sleepy purring sound while her cool foot found one of his sweaty legs beneath the sheet. David opened the book and skimmed the same sentence several times, not really paying attention to it. Deep inside the belly of the house, the furnace kicked on.

"Hey." Kathy sat up on one elbow. "Do you hear that?"

"Hear what?"

"Shhh," she said. "Listen."

He listened but heard nothing.

"Sounds like music," Kathy said.

"Music? I don't—" But he cut himself off as he heard it, too: the faint and discordant jangle of chimes set to some familiar tune. It took David just a few seconds to place it— "Yankee Doodle." But it wasn't the music itself that he found most peculiar; it was that he recognized where it was coming from, that prerecorded jangling melody, incongruous in the middle of a December night.

"Oh," Kathy said, sitting up in bed fully now. "That's eerie as hell." Which meant she recognized it, too.

The music grew louder, louder, until it was right outside the house in the street. In the summertime, that jocular little melody would send the neighborhood kids flooding into Columbus Court, anxious for a Rocket Pop or an Italian ice. But now, in the dead of winter and in the middle of the night—David glanced at the alarm clock on the nightstand and saw that it was well after midnight—the sound of that tune unnerved him.

"That's the strangest damn thing," he said, and climbed out of bed. He tugged on a pair of sweatpants and an undershirt, then went to one of the bedroom windows. He lifted the blinds and peered out into the night.

"What?" Kathy said.

"Yeah," he said. "It's the freakin' ice cream man."

Much of his view was blocked by the Walkers' house next door, but he was able to make out the rear bumper of the Freez-E-Friend ice cream truck with perfect clarity. It sat idling in the middle of the cul-de-sac, its tailpipe expelling clouds of vapor into the cold night air. The brake lights were on.

Kathy joined him at the window. "Is this some kind of joke?" she said, her breath fogging up the glass.

"Well, as far as jokes go, it's the creepiest one I've ever seen."

"What's he doing?"

"Just sitting there, it looks like. I don't know. I can't really see."

When he turned and headed out into the hall, Kathy said, "Where are you going?" There was a level of trepidation in his wife's voice he found strangely endearing.

"To go check it out."

"Outside?" She said this with incredulity, as if he'd just suggested he walk blindfolded into traffic.

"Why not?"

"Because it's weird," she said. "I don't like it."

"It's fine. Just wait here."

In the foyer, he shoved his feet into a pair of ratty moccasins, unlocked the front door, and, sans jacket, stepped out into the night.

It was bitterly cold, causing the sweat that still clung to his exposed flesh to freeze. From the front porch, he had a perfect view of the Freez-E-Friend truck, idling right there in the middle of Columbus Court. It was a quaint little cul-de-sac that served eight homes. The lampposts cast pale white light onto the white-paneled truck, giving it an otherworldly appearance. There were Christmas lights on all the houses, but at this hour, they had all been turned off. David hesitated for just a moment before stepping down off the porch, hearing Kathy's words echoing in his ears: *Because it's weird. I don't like it.* But then he was crossing the lawn and stepping down off the curb into the street, his shadow stretching disproportionately out in front of him in a halo of lamplight.

It was a typical ice cream truck, done up in white panels with decals of everyone's favorite flavors pasted onto the side. Cartoon clowns capered among the flavors, pulling cartwheels and somersaults. The truck's engine sounded like an uncooperative lawn mower, but it was barely audible over the sound of "Yankee Doodle" emanating from the roof-mounted speakers.

A figure sat behind the wheel—a dark form whose slouched silhouette suggested some level of distress, though David could not immediately identify why. Yet the sight of this figure caused him to pause once again. Despite the cold, he found he was suddenly perspiring.

Across the street, porch lights came on. Another light blinked on in Deke Carmody's front windows farther up the block. A second later, Deke was beneath the awning of his front porch, cinching a bulky white robe around his thick frame.

"What is it?" It was Tom Walker from next door, coming up beside David. "What's going on?"

David shook his head. "I have no idea." Then he proceeded to walk around to the driver's side of the truck.

Tom Walker grabbed him by the bicep. David paused and looked at his neighbor, noting the dark, sunken, sleep-weary eyes, the stubble on Tom Walker's chin. In the cold light of the street lamps, Tom looked like the newly risen dead.

"What?" David said.

"Nothing," Tom said, as if changing his mind, and released

David's arm. Then he shook his head and uttered a nervous laugh. "I'm right behind you."

Yet despite Tom's proclamation, David walked around the front of the truck by himself. Only when he passed in front of the truck's headlights, their startling white glow casting heat along the exposed flesh of David's arms, did he realize that he was suddenly vulnerable—that if the figure behind the wheel decided to floor the accelerator at that moment, he'd be a goner. Thinking this, he glanced over his shoulder and saw that there was a light on in one of the front windows of his own house. Kathy's silhouette stood behind the glass.

He crossed to the driver's side without incident. The truck's door was higher than a regular vehicle's, so David had to take a few steps back to see in the window. But even then, the window was rolled up, and there was nothing but glare from the streetlights at the opposite end of the court splashed across it.

"Hello?" he called to the driver. He waved his hands over his head, like someone signaling an aircraft.

Tom Walker came around the side of the truck. He looked spooked, his knobby knees poking from below a pair of lacrosse shorts, his big feet stuffed into what looked like his wife's fuzzy pink slippers.

"He's in there," Tom said. "He's watching us."

"He's not moving," David said.

Deke Carmody materialized out of the darkness, his bald head gleaming in the lamplight. He was staring at the truck as if the thing were an alien spacecraft just descended from the sky. "It's friggin' one in the morning," Deke said, as if this needed to be stated. "Somebody order some Rocky Road or what?"

And let's not forget that it's the dead of winter, David thought, but did not add. Instead, he reached out—

"Hey, now," Tom uttered.

—and popped the handle on the door. The door eased open, exposing the darkened cab and the oddly bent figure behind the steering wheel.

David took a step back. He couldn't make out the man's face, but from what he could tell, he was dressed in his starched white uniform and pin-striped apron. The Freez-E-Friend hat was perched on his head, a thing that always reminded David of an old milkman's hat. It was when the hat seemed to reposition itself in the darkness of the truck's interior that David realized the ice cream man had turned and was looking straight at him.

"Are you all right?" David called to the man over the din of "Yankee Doodle."

The man inside the truck said nothing. A starched white knee came into the light, ghost-white, and David could see the man wore shiny white shoes, too.

He's in full uniform. Which means he must be a lunatic. As if driving an ice cream truck around at night in the middle of winter wasn't enough proof of this.

The man's hand came up and brushed against the steering wheel column. David heard the jangling of keys. A moment later, both the truck's engine and the music died. The silence that replaced it was almost deafening.

"You okay, pal?" David said, taking a step closer to the open door.

"I don't . . ." the man began, then stopped. David heard him clear his throat—a raw, guttural sound, wet with phlegm toward the end. "I don't think I'm . . . doing this right," said the man.

"Doing what right?"

The man said nothing.

"What's your name?" David asked him.

"Uh," said the man. "It's Gary. My name's Gary."

"What are you doing out here, Gary?" He tried to put some jocularity in his voice, a bit of humor that might serve as the right amount of magic to dispel this whole uncomfortable scene. Yet his voice cracked, and David thought it had the opposite effect.

"Making the rounds," said the man. "Isn't that right?" He

added that last part with undeniable uncertainty, as if he was hoping David might be able to instruct him whether or not this was, in fact, what he was doing.

"Do you know where you are?" David asked.

The man said something that sounded like, "Pistachio."

David licked his upper lip. "Why don't you come on down, come out here with us? If you're lost, we can help you."

"I've got all this *work* to do," said the man. David still could not see his face. "If I don't do it, who's going to . . . going to do all this work?"

"I don't understand," David said. "What work?"

"All this . . . all this work," the man said, and motioned with one hand toward the back of the truck, presumably to indicate all the ice cream and frozen pops back there.

"We'll figure it out," David said.

"Mint chocolate chip," said the man.

"Is he delusional?" David heard Deke whisper at his back. David shushed him, unable to pull his eyes from the ice cream man.

"Butter pecan," the man said. "Strawberry cheesecake."

"Come on," David said, waving the man down from the truck. "Why don't you come on down. I'll give you a hand."

"Blueberry Surprise," said the man, a ball of phlegm clotting up the final syllable. Then he leaned forward so that the lower half of his face—the part not obscured by the shadow of the hat's brim—glowed white and garish in the moonlight.

Something dark was trickling from the man's left nostril. It appeared to lengthen, albeit almost imperceptibly, as David watched. For a moment, it almost looked like the man's face was splitting down the middle, a crack forming at the center of his skull.

He's had a stroke. It was the first thought to come into David's mind. This put him somewhat at ease, since strokes, while awful, were *comprehensible.* It stripped some of the mystery, the lunacy, from this whole thing and made him feel somewhat more at ease.

"That's it," David said, aware that he was talking to the man like he would to a child. "Come on down."

The man didn't so much climb down from the cab as slide down in a disjointed and ungainly fashion. When his white shoes hit the pavement, David thought the man's legs would buckle and give out, so he rushed to the man's side and quickly gripped him about the shoulders for support. That was when David caught a whiff of him—the stench of fresh feces clinging to him like a shroud. It was enough to nearly make him gag, and he quickly recoiled from the man.

It was then that he heard a police siren coming up the street. Relief washed over him. He found his feet and took several steps away from the man. As if sensing David's apprehension, the man turned and faced him with his whole body—a disconcertingly robotic adjustment of shoulders, torso, head—and that was when David noticed the dark splotches running down the front of the man's white uniform toward the hem of the pin-striped apron. More blood.

"Sweet Jesus," Deke muttered.

"It's important things get done!" the man roared, flecks of spittle launching from his lips. He balled up one hand and slammed it against the side of the truck, creating a resounding gonglike crash that caused David to jump. "None of you have any idea! You don't have any clue! Marybeth."

David took another step back from the man. He wasn't sure if he'd heard the man correctly until the name was uttered again.

"Marybeth?" It came out as a query this time, the man's voice laced with a terrible combination of grief and fear. How quickly his demeanor had changed.

David saw the lights of the police cars against the houses at the far end of the street before he saw the actual vehicles. Someone—Deke again?—said, "It's the police," and there was a grave finality to the voice.

The ice cream man whipped his head around and stared toward the opposite end of Columbus Court as two police cars appeared. The cars slowed down and came to a stop in front of the Fosters' house, their rack lights dousing the night in strobes of blue and red.

"Who's this?" the ice cream man muttered. The confusion was back in his voice. He turned and stared at David again, a crease forming between his eyebrows. The man's jowls quivered. He looked like a trapped animal. "Why would you do this to me?"

"Me?" David said. "I didn't do anything."

"You need help, pal," said Deke Carmody.

The man did not turn and look at Deke; his eyes remained locked on David. A hand came up and David flinched. "Marybeth, why would you do this to me?"

David shook his head.

The ice cream man removed his hat, revealing a mat of close-cropped dark hair that looked spongy with perspiration. His cheeks continued to quiver, and when he next spoke, he did so through clenched teeth with a voice drenched in fury.

"Why would you do this to me?"

"Hey, now," David said, holding up both his hands.

The police approached. There were two of them, young-faced and distrustful. One of them looked at the ice cream truck in utter disbelief before turning his attention to the man in the apron.

"Sir," said the officer. "Hello?"

"He's bleeding from his nose," David said, pointing. "I think he's hurt. And he doesn't seem to know where he—"

The man lunged at David, so quick that David didn't have time to react. He was driven backward and lost his balance, falling to the pavement. The ice cream man came down on top of him, the force of a meteor crashing to earth, and David felt the wind punched out of him.

The man made a hissing sound and David felt wetness speckle his face. He wanted to shriek but thought better of opening his mouth for fear that whatever—

(blood)

—was dripping off the man might spill into his own throat.

David bucked his hips, then reached out to clutch the man's head, seeking leverage to shove him off. But before he could, the man was yanked from him by the police officers. Deke and Tom Walker appeared beside David, each gripping him under an armpit and hoisting him to his feet.

The cops had the ice cream man pressed against the side of his truck while they cuffed his hands behind his back. But it seemed that the fight had left the man now, the anger and rage fleeing just as quickly as it had come. There was a perceptible slump to his shoulders, and his feet, clad in those ridiculous white patent-leather shoes, were positioned at odd angles.

"He said his name's Gary," David offered, smearing the splotches of blood along his undershirt in an effort to rid himself of them.

"Did someone hit him?" asked one of the officers.

"No," said David. "He came out of the truck like that."

"He came out of the truck like that!" Deke echoed, jabbing a finger in the ice cream man's direction.

The officer cocked an eyebrow at David. "How come he attacked you?"

"Beats me," David said.

"Gary," the cop said, pulling the cuffed man off the side of the truck. "That your name?"

The ice cream man craned his neck so that he could look at the officer. His eyes blazed with some lunatic fever.

"Do you need to go to the hospital?" the other cop asked.

"Mocha almond pecan," said the ice cream man.

6

The clock on the motel nightstand read 8:49 A.M. and there was a frame of silver light around the drapes. David rolled over, wincing at the stiffness of his body but careful not to make a sound. He couldn't remember his dreams, but he found both his pillow and the stuffed elephant damp and his eyelids puffy. Ellie was still asleep beside him, her back to him, her legs tucked up beneath her so that the heels of her feet nearly rested against her buttocks. She still hugged the shoe box against her. David wondered what dreams were currently shuttling through his daughter's head.

In the bathroom he hid the stuffed elephant back inside the duffel bag, washed his face and hands, changed into a pair of jeans, then carefully tucked the Glock into his rear waistband. His Pearl Jam T-shirt was long enough to cover the handgun, but he still felt conspicuous. If someone happened to see the bulge, it might draw unwelcome attention. It was safer to leave the gun behind, so he stowed it back inside the duffel bag. Lastly, he removed the wad of cash from the bag and stashed it in his pocket.

Before leaving, he wrote Ellie a note on the back of an old receipt he found in his wallet and stuck it to the door with a gob of chewing gum; she would see it if she went for the door. Then he slipped out into the harsh daylight, wincing.

In the car, he drove not in the direction of the highway, but down a narrow whip of unnamed blacktop that wound be-hind the motel and ultimately ran through a rural downtown area. Most of the shops here were closed—permanently, it seemed, given their state of disrepair, the blackened shop windows, the fans of unruly blond weeds bursting from cracks in the sidewalks—and even the scant few cars flanking the curb looked like they had been deserted a long time ago. The only living soul was a homeless man in tattered clothing huddled in the doorway of an abandoned building. There was a sandwich board propped up beside him, the words on it printed in accusatory black capitals—THIS TERRIBLE FATE IS YOURS ALONE.

Just when he considered turning around and heading back to the motel, David discovered a convenience store on the corner of an otherwise empty intersection. There were lights on inside, and the door was propped halfway open with a brick.

As he negotiated the Olds into one of several empty parking spaces along the curb, a lone dog, ruinous with mange, trotted across the intersection. It paused in the middle of the street as David climbed out of the car, perhaps alerted to the movement, and stared at him, its tongue unfurled from its mouth, its wolfish ears twitching. The thing did not have a tail, so David couldn't tell if it was simply curious or meant him harm. Judging by the look of the thing, it didn't seem like it would have very much to wag about.

David entered the convenience store, dodging between curling strips of flypaper that hummed audibly. His arrival triggered an electronic chime that sounded like a doorbell. The place was empty, without even a clerk behind the counter. Despite the chill in the air, large black flies thumped lazily against the light fixtures. The aisles looked like they hadn't been restocked in a decade, and indeed, there was the distinct aroma of spoiled meat hanging thickly in the air. He wondered if the place had been abandoned.

It was less like a 7-Eleven and more like one of those sundry gift shops that populated the boardwalks of beach towns, with novelty T-shirts, souvenirs, and stuffed animals hanging from wire carousels. There was a food aisle, comprised mostly of canned goods, bags of chips, and dry, packaged noodles; a clothing aisle, with gaudy summer clothes and silly hats on display; a hardware section; and a rack of magazines—mostly pornographic—against one wall.

David crossed up and down the aisles, grabbing items at random. When he came upon a Cinderella toothbrush, he pried it from the wall peg. Yet a moment later he wondered if perhaps Ellie would think it silly, childish, and if he should opt for a simple adult toothbrush for the girl instead. *These are the decisions that plague my mind now?* He nearly laughed aloud at the thought. And in the end, he decided to buy both the adult toothbrush *and* the Cinderella one. Just in case.

He went to the magazine rack, too. Aside from the porno rags, there were celebrity tabloids, teen magazines, automotive catalogues, and even a booklet with a marijuana leaf on the cover. No newspapers, though, which was what he really wanted. It occurred to him that he had no idea if his daughter read any of this stuff—the teen mags, the tabloids, comic books. She wasn't that type of girl. He didn't think so, anyway. In the end, he decided to bypass the magazine rack altogether.

It could have been a shopping trip just like any he'd made in his lifetime . . . until he paused beside a hat rack, a plan forming in his head. He selected a nondescript blue baseball cap from the rack—emblem-free and just about as unmemorable as a hat could get—and realized that he would have to explain much of this to Ellie upon his return back to the motel. If he was going to do this, to put this plan into action, then she would have questions. He couldn't lie to her forever.

He decided to buy the hat.

That settles that.

By the time he took everything to the front of the store, there was a sullen-looking man grazing behind the counter. His comb-over was thin and greasy and his eyes were denim blue. He wore a paper carpenter's mask over his nose and mouth, a trend that had gained popularity after the CDC suggested Wanderer's Folly might be airborne. At one time, David had tried to purchase some of the N95 masks that were initially recommended by the World Health Organization, but

that was before it became known that the masks were virtu-
ally useless in protecting against the virus. (One WHO
spokesperson suggested it was the equivalent of taping up your
doors and windows during a nuclear fallout.) The virus was in
the blood—not in a sneeze, not in a cough—but many theo-
rized that it was transmitted when the airborne virus gained
access to the body by osmosis through the flesh. Those who
still wore the masks did so out of fear or a false sense of security.

David's gaze lingered on the man just long enough for the
man to draw his eyebrows together in consternation. Without
a word, he proceeded to ring up David's items.

"You have any books?"

"Books?" the man said, his voice muffled through the
mask.

"Like, YA books."

"What's that?"

"Books for young adults. Like, for preteens."

"Ain't a library."

"That thing really work?" David asked him, nodding at the
mask.

"Couldn't hurt," the man said.

"Do you have any more?"

The man pointed to a wall of mismatched items—plungers,
automotive air filters, toilet paper, picture frames. There were
several paper masks hanging from a peg. David retrieved two
of them and added them to his purchase. It had nothing to do
with protection against the Folly; he thought the masks might
help hide their faces, if it came to that.

"I need a charger for an iPhone, too. I didn't see any on the
shelves."

The man reached beneath the counter and set one beside
David's other purchases. "Kids tend to steal 'em," the man
said.

"There are still kids around here?"

The man eyeballed him but said nothing.

"And a few packs of Marlboros," David said.

"We're all out."

"What other brands do you have?"

"None."

"None? No cigarettes?"

The man's milky eyes narrowed. "No cigarettes," he repeated.

"How about a place to eat around here? A diner or something?"

The man shook his head as he bagged David's items. He moved with a zombie's lethargy. "Not 'round here."

"What about off the highway?"

The man hoisted a disinterested shoulder. "Wouldn't know."

"Where *is* everybody?"

"You with the Census Bureau?"

David laughed—a forced whip-crack of a sound that sounded false to his own ears.

"That'll be forty-nine ninety-five," said the man.

David handed him fifty bucks, considered telling him to keep the change, but decided to hang around for it in the end. From here on out, every penny would count.

Back outside, the homeless man with the sandwich board was gone. So was the dog.

7

Ellie was awake when he returned to the motel. She was propped up against the headboard, her long hair in uncombed tangles. She was watching a cartoon on the TV. She had the shoe box in her lap, the lid open, and was gently running a finger along the bird eggs inside. There were three of them, small, speckled things that looked impossibly delicate to David, like porcelain. They were fitted snugly in a nest of twig-bits and leaves. Ellie swung her legs off the side of the bed and, setting the shoe box aside, studied the shopping bag he hauled into the room and set down on the table.

"Did you find my note?"

"Yes," she said.

"I got some stuff for us. Some food, but some clothes, too. And toothbrushes." He offered her a conciliatory smile.

"I want to call Mom."

"It's still early."

"She wakes up early."

"There are some things we need to do first," he said. From the shopping bag he withdrew a T-shirt with silk-screened trucks on it, the nondescript baseball hat, some other items. "Also, we need to talk, Little Spoon."

"Is it about Mom?"

It was, but he didn't need to go there just yet. He still needed some time to figure out how he was going to explain what had happened to Kathy, and now certainly wasn't the time. Right now, they needed to get back on the road and keep moving. Which meant, for the time being, he would lie to her. It was a lie he had begun last night when they traded the Bronco for the Olds, and he'd had several hours to build upon that story in his head so that it sounded plausible.

David pulled a chair out from the table and sat opposite her. "I want to explain to you a little bit about what's going on back home. Do you know what a quarantine is?"

"It's when they keep you in one place and they don't let you leave. Like jail."

"Yes, that's right. I'm surprised you knew that."

"They've been talking about it on the news for a long time. Some towns are being quarantined if too many people have the disease."

"That's right," he said. "Well, that's what's going on at home right now. Our neighborhood has been quarantined."

"That means we shouldn't have left," she said.

"But then we wouldn't be able to see Mom."

Her eyes narrowed the slightest bit, and David could read her thoughts: *We aren't able to see Mom now, so what's the difference?*

"It's like you said," he went on. "It's like being in jail. But I didn't want that for us. So I took you away before they locked everybody down."

Ellie said nothing.

"Because of that," he said, "there's a good chance people will start looking for us, Ellie. These are people who think they're doing the right thing and will want to make us go back."

"Back home?"

"Yes. But you don't want to be locked in your house without being able to leave, do you?"

"And we wouldn't be able to see Mom?"

"No," he said. "We wouldn't."

"Okay."

"It's important we don't let these people find us," he said.

"What will they do if they find us?"

He chewed at his lower lip. When he spoke, his voice

sounded paper-thin and intangible to his own ears. "We don't need to worry about that, sweetheart, because they won't find us."

"But what about Mom?"

"Mom is safe. You know that."

"Do you promise?"

He felt something toward the back of his throat click. "Yes," he said, the word tasting funny. Poisonous. "Yes, hon. She's safe. You know she is."

"Okay."

"Because I want us to be as safe as possible, too, there are a few things we need to do today before we get back on the road."

For the first time, he saw Ellie's gaze shift to just over his shoulder, to the items he had placed on the table behind him. The T-shirt, the baseball hat. The scissors, comb, hair dye . . .

"They'll be looking for a father and daughter," he said, his voice level, unemotional. When he realized that his hands were fidgeting between his knees, he forced them apart. "We need to change that."

Ellie had always been a perceptive child. Even as a toddler—heck, as an *infant*—it seemed her demeanor reflected the emotions of her parents. On more than one occasion, Kathy had commented that Ellie was special, and not just in the way all parents thought their children were special. Kathy was convinced that sometimes their baby daughter was able to *know* things. Emotions. Feelings. David had always presumed this was a trait all young children shared—that they were mirrors of their parents' emotions and fundamentally more perceptive than their adult counterparts—but now, looking at his daughter and seeing the wheels working behind her eyes, he wondered if Kathy might not have been on to something.

The corners of Ellie's mouth turned downward. Her chin wrinkled.

"Hey. It'll be okay," he promised her.

"I don't understand. If we can't go back home, where will we live?"

"It's just temporary," he said. "Things will work themselves out soon enough. This isn't permanent."

She had grabbed a lock of her auburn hair and tugged it down over her shoulder. She wound a finger in it now, as if feeling it for the last time. She was perceptive, all right.

"Things are going to be okay," he said again.

But her expression told him that she knew he was lying.

8

David cut off Ellie's auburn locks in the motel bathroom. They went through it together, without ceremony, the whole thing as somber as an execution. Ellie sat there with a look of horror on her face the entire time, but never once did she complain or cry or put up a fuss. He could be grateful for that, at least.

David was no barber, but he did the best he could, and in the end his daughter wore the approximation of a young boy's modest if clumsy haircut. When he finished, he came up behind her and they both looked at the mirror together to examine his work. Tears threatened to spill down her face, but she still did not make a sound. She no longer looked like his daughter. David kissed the side of her face. Her skin felt hot against his lips.

"Put on the T-shirt and hat I bought," he told her as he cleaned up the curls of auburn hair from the bathroom floor. He was careful to get every strand, every scrap, which he tucked away inside the plastic shopping bag. He'd take the hair with them and dump the bag somewhere along the way.

"Boy clothes," she intoned, leaving the bathroom.

"You're a boy now," he called after her.

Once he was done cleaning up the hair, he trimmed some of his own, then opened up the box of hair dye. His was a natural tawny brown, the sorrel hue of a deer's hide. The hair dye would turn him Superman black. He hoped it would be enough to suitably alter his appearance. He wondered, *Should*

I dye my eyebrows, too? Best to do the hair first and see how things looked.

Ellie appeared in the bathroom doorway as he was midway through the coloring process, his dripping head hanging over the bathroom sink, muddy tracks of dye sliding down his forehead.

"Are we in trouble?" she asked him. She had obliged, and was wearing the T-shirt with the trucks on it, the blue baseball cap. She looked alien to him. Some stranger's little boy.

"No," he said.

"Are *you?*" she said.

He looked at her sideways. "I said no, didn't I?"

Ellie shrugged. "What's my boy name?"

"Huh?"

"If I'm a boy now, you can't call me Ellie. Or Eleanor."

"I'll just call you Little Spoon." He grinned at her while he combed the dye through his damp hair.

"I don't like that," she said. "Not anymore."

"I've called you that since you were a little kid."

"Not anymore." She looked at the bag of hair clippings that sat on the sink counter. "I don't like it anymore."

"Since when?"

She rolled her slight shoulders. The T-shirt was a tad too big. "For a while now, I guess."

"How come?"

"I just don't. Stop calling me that. I'm not a baby anymore."

He straightened up, wiping the inky droplets off his forehead with a hand towel. He'd have to take the towel with them, too. No evidence left behind. "Okay. Okay. I won't call you that anymore. Sorry."

"Where are we going when we leave here?"

"To get something to eat. Aren't you hungry?"

"I mean, we can't just keep staying in hotels. Where are we going to go if we can't go home?"

"I'll figure that out after we eat. I'm starving. Aren't you starving?" He was desperate to change the subject.

"Are you telling me the truth?" she asked him. "About why we can't go home, I mean."

The question jarred him. And it wasn't just the question itself, but the confident and suspicious tone Ellie used when asking it. As if she knew the truth and was testing his honesty. It caused him to pause before answering, and she seemed to pick up on that, too.

"Of course," he said.

"And about Mom, too?"

"Yes," he said.

Her gaze hung on him.

She's special, Kathy's ghost-voice spoke up in his head then. *A special child.*

"I'll only be a few more minutes," he said, and eased the bathroom door closed with his toe.

9

Nineteen months earlier

It was one of the rare evenings he stayed late at the university grading papers. Walking across the quad, the night was a cold, wet soup. Late-winter snow swirled around the lampposts, weightless as dandelion fluff, and never touched the ground. He took the footpath to the parking lot, slowing in his progress when he noticed something small and dark flapping about on the path. He came within two feet of it and saw that it was a small brown bird. It was still alive, its twig-like feet scrambling for purchase on the stamped concrete. As David watched, one of its wings flared open and fluttered maniacally to no avail.

David crouched down and watched the bird die. It took less than a minute. By the time he stood, a chevron of geese was honking across the sky just above the treetops. He thought it odd that they were there in February. Didn't geese fly south in the winter?

He coughed into a fist as he continued along the footpath toward the parking lot. There were still a number of cars in the lot, even at this hour. His Bronco was parked at the far end of the lot, since he'd misplaced his faculty pass earlier that month and didn't want to risk being towed by parking in any of the faculty spots without it. The tow-truck drivers fished the campus parking lots day and night and were ruthless.

He was halfway across the lot to his car when something exploded off to his left. It was very close, the sound of its detonation causing him to drop his briefcase. He looked around but could not see what might have caused it. The lampposts were spaced too far apart, and it was too dark to make out any real—

He caught movement out of the corner of his eye, a large object bulleting down from the sky at such an alarming speed, David drew his arms up to cover his head despite the fact that the object was crashing down several yards away. It struck the hood of a Volkswagen with a sickening solidity, rolled up over the windshield, then toppled to the asphalt. It took David only a second to realize what it was, but by that point, more and more had begun to rain from the sky, a mortar attack. Only instead of bombs, they were geese.

A car alarm went off. Windshields imploded. Most of the geese were killed upon impact, but a few of them survived, albeit mortally wounded, and their shrill cries were more like the agonizing shrieks of a child than any bird he'd ever heard. Some of them screamed just a few feet from him, their massive, twisted wings sliding cruelly along the pavement.

The whole thing lasted thirty seconds, maybe less. When it was over, the parking lot was a minefield of dead fowl, the occasional spastic jerk of a massive black wing, the incessant trilling of a chorus of car alarms.

David gathered up his briefcase and ran for the Bronco, thankful that he'd misplaced the parking pass, which had left his own vehicle, parked so far away, unscathed.

He felt the urge to call someone on the drive home, but who would that be? The police? The fire department? The goddamn ASPCA?

It was generally a thirty-minute commute home, but an accident on the beltway had knotted up traffic near Baltimore, and David found himself staring at a wall of taillights for over an hour. Rain began to fall. To make matters worse, someone thumped against his rear bumper, and David had to get out and examine the damage. There was only a faint white scuff on the Bronco's rear bumper, but it was enough to cause him greater unease. He couldn't stop hearing the shriek of those birds, the terrible sounds they made as they smashed through windshields and caved in the hoods and roofs of those cars.

By the time he turned onto Columbus Court, it was just after ten o'clock. He was starving—the last thing he'd eaten was an apple with peanut butter around noon—and his mood hadn't changed much since getting his bumper nudged on the beltway. When he heard his cell phone chime, he groaned and fumbled it out of his jacket pocket. It was a text from Kathy, asking where he was. When he glanced back up, the pale shape of a man, illuminated by the Bronco's headlights, filled his windshield.

David simultaneously jerked the wheel and jumped on the brake. Had he been driving a less weighty vehicle, the thing would have fishtailed or simply plowed into the man. But the Bronco was a sturdy ride, and it shuddered to a stop in the middle of the street.

"Holy shit." The words wheezed out of him in sour notes, as if he were a punctured accordion. He spun around in his seat, craning his neck to glimpse the pale figure through the side window. David didn't think he'd struck the man—he was still standing, after all—but he couldn't be positive. The damn fool had appeared out of nowhere.

David climbed out of the Bronco, his sweat-dampened shirt growing chill in the cold night. He hustled around to the rear of the Bronco and saw the man still standing there, now tinted red in the glow of the Bronco's taillights.

It was Deke Carmody, clad in nothing but a pair of threadbare boxer shorts. Deke's ample gut spilled over the boxers' waistband, a runway of black hair rising from his navel and fanning out across his heavy, sagging breasts. His feet were bare, and as David stared at him, Deke took a shuffling step toward him through a puddle of black water.

"Deke, what the hell are you *doing* out here?"

"That you, David?"

"Look at you." David approached him, touched the man on one shoulder. Deke's flesh was cold, wet, and knobby with goose bumps. The feel of it made David recoil, and he was quick to withdraw his hand. "What's going on here, Deke?"

Deke blinked at him, as if to clear his vision. There was muddled confusion in his eyes. David wondered if Deke was in shock from having nearly been run over.

"Hey, David." Deke broke into a wide smile. The sight of it chilled David further. "How you been?"

"Deke, man, why are you standing out here in the middle of the night in your underwear?"

Deke glanced down. His bare feet shuffled around in the puddle. His toes were practically blue. When he looked up and met David's eyes again, there was still no clarity there.

"Come on," David said, grasping Deke high on one forearm; it seemed his fingers sank too easily into the pliable flesh. "First thing, let's get you inside."

"Oh," Deke said. "Okay, David."

David led Deke up the walk of the man's house. When he reached out and grasped the doorknob, he found the knob wouldn't turn.

"Christ. Door's locked, Deke. You locked yourself out. In your undies, no less."

"Side door's unlocked, I think," Deke said.

"Let's go see," David said. Still clutching Deke's forearm, he went around the side of the house and found the side door was, in fact, unlocked. And not just unlocked—*open*. David glanced at Deke again, hoping to ascertain some semblance of normalcy behind the man's eerie, vacuous stare. But Deke Carmody's eyes were like two dead headlamps. It was like some vital fuse had burned out inside of him.

"Go on," David said, urging him toward the doorway. "Get in."

Deke shuffled inside and David followed. The lights were off, and David felt along one wall for the switch. When he found it, he flipped it on, and the single bulb over the kitchen sink winked on. Deke quit shuffling and stared up at the naked bulb as if in awe.

Unmarried and without children, Deke Carmody lived alone. The house was the domicile of a lifelong bachelor, complete with dirty dishes stacked in the sink and the smell of burnt coffee in the air. But as David looked around, he saw that things had been changed, and in a way that set him on alert. David's first thought was that Deke's house had been burglarized . . . but on closer inspection, he realized that no burglar would bother doing the things to Deke's house that David was observing. Kitchen chairs, for instance, hadn't simply been knocked to the floor; instead, they were stacked on the kitchen table. The sight of them was jarring. When he turned around, he saw that all the cupboard doors stood open. Boxes of cereal and canned goods had been arranged in careful pyramids on the countertops. David couldn't help himself—he thought of poltergeists and exorcisms.

"What's been going on here, Deke?"

"You know," Deke muttered, shuffling out of the kitchen and into the living room. He said no more.

David heard noises in the adjoining room. It was the TV, showing the rerun of some eighties sitcom.

"Sit down," David said, beckoning Deke over to an upholstered armchair.

Deke sat without protest. In fact, he was smiling at David. Practically *beaming*.

That smile is worse than the blank look in his eyes, David thought. *What the hell is wrong with him?*

"I'll be right back," David said, and hurried down the hall. In the bathroom, he found a towel on a hook behind the door. He brought it to Deke, draping it over the big man's broad shoulders.

"Thanks, David."

"You want to tell me what the heck you were doing out there?"

Deke laughed. It was a nervous, tittering sound that should have come from a smaller person. "Damnedest thing. I guess I was sleepwalking."

"Sleepwalking."

"Used to do it a lot when I was a boy," Deke said. "And again in my early twenties. It's brought on by stress, you know. Doctors told me so."

Ellie had suffered the occasional bout of somnambulism when she was four or five. It was eerie—David had once caught her ambling past him in the hallway in the middle of the night, which had scared the shit out of him but hadn't woken the girl—but as eerie as it was, it seemed a quirk befitting of a young child. Deke was in his fifties. The thought of him roving around his house—Christ, the goddamn *street*—in his sleep was more than just unnerving.

"Is this a common occurrence?" David asked.

"The sleepwalking?"

"You wander around outside in your underwear regularly, or is this a special occasion?"

"For me?"

"Of course for you. Who else would I be talking about?"

"I don't know." Deke's eyebrows arched and his mouth curled into what could only be described as a playful frown. "There could be other things here, too."

David frowned. "What do you mean?" He looked around, noting that the walls were all bare and there were picture frames on the floor. A rug had been rolled up into a tube and set against the jamb of the front door in the foyer. The gauzy curtains hanging over the windows were all tied together in knots.

"What have you been up to in here, Deke?"

"I don't know if it's something new," Deke said, and it took David a moment or two to realize he was answering David's previous question. "If I've been doing it for a while, I've been asleep and wouldn't know." And then he laughed—a great bassoon blast that caused David's toes to curl in his shoes.

"Are you on any medication?"

"Cholesterol meds," Deke said. "Nexium for my 'flux."

"Anything heavier?"

This time, Deke's scowl was genuine. "I look like a drug addict to you, David?"

"I'm just trying to help. I almost ran you over out there. I can't say I like the idea of you wandering around the neighborhood in a daze every night. And your house . . ."

"What about it?" Deke said, glancing around. If he recognized the unusualness of the place, his face did not register it. "You got any liquor in the house?"

"You want a drink, buddy?"

"No," David said. There was a credenza against one wall, a few bottles of vodka and bourbon on it. None were open, and he couldn't see any used glasses. "I mean, have you been drinking?"

Deke waved a hand at him. *Don't be silly,* his expression said. Some of the old Deke was filtering back into his features now. His eyes looked less dead than they had just moments ago.

"Why don't you get to bed and I'll lock up on my way out," David suggested. For some reason, he was growing increasingly uncomfortable about being in Deke's house. Coupled with that discomfort was the feeling that he was overlooking something very obvious—and very important—and that feeling was setting him on edge.

"Okay, boss. Whatever you say." Deke got up from the armchair in a huff—it seemed to take great effort—and handed David the towel. His rounded gut glistened with rainwater. "I got some long johns around here someplace," he said, pausing to peer behind the TV.

"You keep your long johns behind the television?" David said.

Deke stood upright, as if suddenly considering the absurdity of it all. When he turned to look at David, his eyes were unfocused again.

"Maybe I should call for an ambulance," David suggested.

"Do it and I'll brain you. I'm no invalid." Deke's voice had gone deadly serious.

"Something's off with you."

"Who the hell asked you to come in here, anyway?" There was real malice behind Deke's words, enough to make David consider bolting from the house right then and there. It was as if some switch had been flipped, instantly altering Deke's personality.

Drugs, David thought . . . although he had never known Deke Carmody to abuse narcotics. Alcohol, maybe, but not drugs. *What else could it be?*

Deke slammed a palm against the TV and the screen went dead. Then he turned and grinned idiotically at David. The large man opened his mouth, presumably to say something, but nothing came out. Instead, he liberated a fart that sounded like a trumpet blare, sustaining it for a good five seconds.

"Jesus Christ," David said, too stunned to show emotion.

"Go home," Deke said, turning around. "You shouldn't be here." He ambled down the darkened hallway toward his bedroom, his hands dangling limply at his sides, the canvas of his broad, pallid back speckled with pimples and reddish striations. Like a ghost fading into a fog bank, Deke Carmody vanished into the darkness at the far end of the hallway.

David stood there in the living room for perhaps thirty seconds, listening to the grunting sounds of Deke climbing into his bed. Almost instantly the man began snoring.

David went to one of the windows and untied the curtains. They fell away from the pane, only to reveal a series of carpentry nails that had been pounded into the sill. The sight caused a thick lump to form at the back of David's throat. He went to the next window, untied the curtains, and found a similar display of carpentry nails there, too.

Go home. You shouldn't be here.

David returned to the bathroom, hung the towel back on the hook, and was about to turn and leave when he happened to glance down into the toilet. What he saw there caused him to freeze—and not solely in a halt of his movements, but he could literally feel his entire body suddenly grow cold.

The toilet bowl was filled with blood.

Not just a little bit, and not the superficial hue of a flesh wound or a nosebleed diluted in water. The blood in the bowl was the startling Christmas red of arterial blood, and as David stared at it, he thought he could see small clumps of fibrous material in it. There were spatters on the seat and some red-dish spray down the side of the toilet tank. A few bright stars stood out sharply on the ecru tiles. One particular spill had been smeared by David's own shoe, most likely when he had first come in here to get the towel; he had inadvertently left a shoe print of blood on the pale green bath mat. His gaze lev-itated until he saw splotches of blood in the sink, too. Crim-son droplets littered the countertop. The mirror was speckled with red teardrops.

How had he missed all this just moments ago? Had he been so focused on helping Deke that he had just overlooked it all? Given the condition of the bathroom, it seemed impossible.

He wanted to wash his face and hands—just looking at all that blood, not to mention the blackish clumps floating in it, made him feel unclean—but he wouldn't touch this sink. In-stead, he went down the hall, into the kitchen, and scrubbed himself at the kitchen sink, where there was nothing more ominous than dirty dishes and empty glasses in the basin.

He considered going against Deke's wishes and calling 911 after all. He could request paramedics come out and take a look at Deke. Would they examine the blood, too? Deke hadn't looked hurt—he certainly hadn't been bleeding from anywhere that David could see—but that blood had come from *somewhere.*

In the end, he decided not to call. Instead, he checked in on Deke before leaving the house. The big man lay like a beached whale on his mattress, one pasty leg dangling over the side of the bed. His snores were immense, thunderous rum-blings. For a moment, David considered flipping on the lights . . . but he feared what that light might reveal of Deke's bedroom. Before he could chase the thought away, he imag-ined Deke sprawled out across a mattress sodden and black with blood, carpentry nails driven into the hardwood floor like booby traps.

"Deke?" It came out in a whisper.

Deke's only response was a guttural snort.

"Okay," David said. "Good night."

He left the house, thumbing the lock on the side door before pulling it closed behind him. The hunger he'd felt for hours had fled, leaving in its wake a sickening hollowness. He knew that when he went to sleep that night, he would see that bloody stew floating in Deke's toilet behind his eyelids. All of a sudden, the thing with the geese seemed trivial.

When he got home, Kathy met him in the foyer. In a pair of gold silk pajamas and her hair pulled back in a ponytail, she was already made up for bed.

"Where've you been?"

"I stopped at Deke Carmody's house," he said, stepping out of his shoes. "I caught him wandering around outside in his underwear."

"*What?*"

She followed him into the bedroom, and he told her what had happened as he undressed. Once he finished, he said, "What do you think? Should I call someone? Paramedics?"

"Maybe it's cancer."

"What is?"

"All the blood," Kathy said. "He could be sick."

"Maybe. But what about the other stuff? The condition of his house and the nails in the windowsills?"

"Early stages of dementia?" Kathy suggested.

"Since when?"

"It's just a guess."

"I don't feel good about this. Not at all. I should call an ambulance or something."

"If he asked you not to call, then you should respect that."

He considered this for perhaps five seconds.

Kathy said, "Maybe he's going through some medical issue and doesn't want anyone to know. You just happened to find him—"

"Standing outside in his underwear, yeah," David finished.

"Does he have any family that you know of? Someone we could call?"

"I have no idea. Even if I knew that he did, I wouldn't know how to get in touch with anyone."

Kathy sighed. "I'm just not sure what to tell you except that, for now, you should respect his wishes and not call anyone."

"Yeah," David said, though he wasn't sure he actually agreed.

"It's probably an illness. When was the last time you were over at his house?"

"Not for a while."

"Isn't he on disability?"

"For falling off scaffolding at a construction site," David said. "Nothing to do with cancer. Or dementia or anything like that." *Or with a bowlful of blood,* was what he wanted to say. "It was so weird, Kath."

"Then go check on him first thing in the morning. But if the man doesn't want you prying into his private business, you have to respect that."

"Do I? I've got no responsibility beyond that?"

"No."

"Even if it *is* dementia and he doesn't know what's good for him? And that he might be putting himself in harm and not even realizing it?"

"You're hypothesizing. Talk to him tomorrow and figure things out then. He might have a clearer head by then and be ready to talk to you. You'll have a better picture of what you're dealing with, too, and can make an informed decision."

"Spoken like a true therapist," he said, exhausted.

"That's what I am," she said. "Wait till you get my bill."

He smiled at her. "Okay. You're right."

"Are you hungry?"

"I was," he said. "Now, not so much."

"I was going to go to bed. Would you rather I stay up with you for a while?"

"No, hon. Get some sleep." He kissed her forehead.

In the kitchen, he began to fix himself a turkey sandwich, but then thought of the geese, and decided to go for some ham and cheese on white bread. It wasn't that he was hungry, but he knew he had to eat something. After the first bite, his hunger returned, and he not only devoured the whole sandwich, but a handful of Doritos and a Coke, too. Just as he finished, Ellie appeared in the kitchen doorway.

"Hey, Little Spoon," he said, getting up from the table. "What are you doing up so late?"

"Bad dream," she said.

"Monsters?"

Solemnly, Ellie nodded.

"Come on," he said. "Let's tuck you back in."

The bedsheets were in a ball at the foot of the bed, the comforter on the floor. As Ellie climbed into bed, David gathered up the blankets, then tucked Ellie beneath them. He smoothed back the hair from her forehead, then planted a kiss there.

"You were there," she said. "In my nightmare."

"Was I the hero who saved the day?"

She shook her head. "No. You were crying. You were screaming, Daddy."

He frowned and said, "Hon—"

"You were pulling on my arm and it hurt. But I didn't want you to stop. I didn't want you to let go. Because then the monsters would get me."

He kissed her forehead a second time, then said, "There's no such thing as monsters, Ellie. You know that."

"Yeah, I know. Come on." She smiled, and he thought—strangely—that it was solely for his sake.

"Yeah," he said. "Come on."

When he stood, she said, "Good night, Dad."

"Good night, Little Spoon. I love you."

"Love you, too."

For the next hour or so, he sat on the couch watching an old movie, though he really wasn't paying much attention to it. He couldn't relax. A few times, his gaze drifted away from the TV, settling instead on some dark corner of the room. He saw the blood in Deke's toilet, watched those tiny bits of blackened fibers in Deke's sink take on life and begin twisting and jerking furtively in the thick pool of blood. After a while, he found he was sweating profusely.

He got up, shut off the TV, and locked the front door. The gauzy curtains over the bay windows were drawn, but a strange, dancing light beyond them was enough to attract his attention. He went to the windows and swept aside the curtains.

Deke Carmody's house was on fire. Pillars of flame belched from the windows, and there were black columns of smoke rising up in front of the moon. A number of neighbors stood outside on their lawns, watching. As David stared, two fire trucks turned onto Columbus, sirens wailing.

David was out of the house and running down the street a moment later, the cool night air speckled with rain freezing against his skin. But the soft rain did little to staunch the flames blooming from Deke's house. A wall of heat struck David halfway down the block, causing his eyes to water as he approached.

"Where is he?" he asked the neighbors who had gathered on the lawns across the street. "Where's Deke?"

"No one's seen him," said Lucy Cartwright, holding her silk robe closed with two hands. She couldn't peel her eyes off the burning house across the street.

There were police officers here, too, and they waved away the more curious onlookers. David rushed over to one of them and shouted, "The owner of that house—has he been—"

"Step back," directed the officer.

"There's a man inside that house!"

"Sir," said the officer, placing a hand against David's chest. "I said to step back. Everyone's doing their job."

"You don't—" David began, but was silenced as something exploded inside Deke's house. It was a deep-bellied *whump*, followed by a rolling wave of thick, hot air. One whole side of Deke's house blew out, spraying debris across the lawn and against the Bannisters' house next door. A ball of flame roiled out, casting the faces of the nearest onlookers in a pale yellow light. Cops and firemen quickly motioned for people to *get back, get back.*

After a time, it began to rain harder, but it did little to douse the flames. When the roof caved in, a second fireball belched up into the night sky. A few people cried out, and many more sobbed. By morning, Deke Carmody's house was nothing but a charred frame of struts and smoldering black boards, and it took firefighters much of the afternoon to locate Deke's remains.

10

The stranger staring back at him in the mirror had his eyes. Beyond that, there were no other similarities. His hair was freshly cropped and dyed black, his complexion sallow and seamed with hairline creases around the eyes, mouth, and nose. It was like staring at himself wearing the mask of another.

He cleaned up the dye and the shorn bits of hair, collecting them in the plastic shopping bag where he'd previously stowed Ellie's hair clippings. He cleaned the dye from the sink, a task that proved more monumental than he would have thought. He kept dumping wet globs of dye-blackened tissues down the toilet. He had gotten some dye on one of the bath towels, so he tucked that into the shopping bag, as well. After he finished, his fingertips looked as if he'd been printed at a police station.

When he stepped back into the room, he said, "So, what do you think of the new 'do?" He was grinning like a fool, trying to mitigate the seriousness of it all, but he stopped when he saw Ellie peeking through a part in the drapes. The smile fell from his face. "What are you doing?"

"There's people fighting outside, I think," she said, quickly pulling her face away from the drapes. "A lady's out there crying."

"Get away from there."

He went to the window himself and peeled back a section of drapery. At first he could see nothing but the shiny chrome of the Oldsmobile's front grille, and he realized that he had parked it right out front out of habit instead of behind the Dumpsters as he had done the night before. He could see no one outside, and he was just about to turn away from the window when he heard the strong baritone of a man's voice barking some indecipherable order, followed by the pained mewl of a woman David could not see. The man's voice had sounded very close—possibly even in the room next door— but the woman had sounded even closer, and less muffled. David pressed his forehead against the glass and craned his neck. A shadow moved along the walkway outside his door. He heard scuffling along the tiny bits of sand and gravel that had collected in the cracks between the stamped pavers. David felt his bowels clench. For a moment, he couldn't remember where he'd hidden the handgun.

Then he saw the woman. She came ambling into his line of sight, moving in a defeated stagger behind the Oldsmobile and across the parking lot. She wore a plain white T-shirt that fell to midthigh and nothing else, as far as David could determine. Her hair was short, spiky, the color of pennies. She was sobbing. The lower half of her face was a slick and blotchy mess, and something dark had dribbled down the front of her T-shirt. It looked like blood.

The man with the baritone voice barked again, though his words remained indecipherable. This time, David caught a glimpse of him along the walkway, too—a robust fellow with a meaty forearm braided with wiry black hair. A bluish tattoo near his shoulder. Indeed, the man was standing in the doorway of the room right next door. His thick voice reverberated behind the wall of their room.

The woman paused beside the Oldsmobile's rear bumper and seemed to sway momentarily on her feet. As David watched, she brought up a hand and touched her mouth. When she looked at her fingers, she whined like some injured animal.

David jerked away from the window, letting the drapes swing back in place.

Ellie was standing on the far side of the room, as if determined to get as far away from the commotion outside as humanly possible. Her eyes were wide, staring, terrified. Somehow inquisitive, too. "Is that lady okay?" she asked. Despite the fear in her eyes, her voice was remarkably calm.

"It's not our business," David said. "Let's just get our stuff and get out of here."

"Right now?"

"Yes. Before the police show up."

"But I haven't showered."

"You'll have to go without."

"But I didn't shower last night, either."

"We don't have time for this, Ellie."

In the bathroom, David took the Glock from the duffel bag and jammed it down the back of his pants. He shouldered the bag, then glanced at himself in the mirror. His hair was still wet, the dye job looking too dark and suspiciously artificial. Yet he wouldn't risk hanging around here, in the event someone called the cops on the sobbing woman in the parking lot.

He hurried back into the room. Ellie was standing by the front door clutching the suitcase handle in one hand, cradling the shoe box of bird eggs to her chest with the other.

"We go straight to the car," David said, gripping the doorknob. He already had the car keys in his other hand at the ready. "Go to the driver's side and then slide over. You understand? I don't want you separated from me and going around to the other side of the car. Not for a second."

Ellie nodded, her expressive eyes mostly shaded by the brim of her ball cap.

"Okay," he said, licking his lips. "Okay. Okay."

He swung the door wide and charged out into the daylight. Somewhere off to his right, the sobbing woman made a hitching sound, then went instantly silent. David didn't want to look, but he couldn't help himself—he stole a quick glance over his shoulder just as the woman was turning to look at him. The back of her T-shirt had ridden up, exposing a single pale buttock. There was an ugly bruise there, mean and purple with a greenish border. Glancing up at her face, David could see the blood spilling from her nose and mouth, black as motor oil. Her eyes possessed the distant gaze of the legally blind.

David yanked the car door open. "Go," he said to Ellie, shoving her forward with one hand. "Get in."

Ellie quickly got into the car, the suitcase banging against the door frame, careful not to crush her shoe box.

"Hey," the woman said, her voice so unexpectedly calm, almost childlike, that it caused David to look in her direction again.

She stood facing him, her head cocked curiously at an angle now. Despite the blood that trickled from both nostrils and spilled down over her chin, hers was an expression of utmost serenity. Yet there was the foggy detachment in her eyes that immediately chilled David to the core, reminding him of Deke Carmody's similarly detached stare. It was as if she was looking right through him and at something visible only to her on the horizon.

"Hey," she said again . . . and took a step in his direction. A bare foot scrudded over blacktop gravel. In the motel room behind her, the drapes over the window twitched.

"Daddy," Ellie said from inside the car.

"Please," the woman said. "Wait a minute. Please . . ." There was agony in her voice now.

David shook his head. "I'm sorry," he said.

"I need help." She took another step toward him. "I'm hurt. I need help. He won't . . . he won't . . ." She glanced briefly over one shoulder, at the window where the drapes continued to twitch and move. For a second, a man's wide, ghost-white face peered out before receding back into the darkness a moment later. David had time to glimpse a brutish, Cro-Magnon forehead and dark rodent eyes.

David switched his gaze back to the woman. He shook his head. "I'm sorry."

"Daddy," Ellie said again. She was leaning halfway out of the open door, watching the woman.

"*Please,*" the woman said, the word whining out of her as she proceeded to sob again.

David quickly got into the car and immediately slammed the door.

"Daddy, what's—"

The woman was at his window before he got the key in the ignition. Ellie cried out, startled.

"Please!" the woman shouted on the other side of the glass. When she slammed one palm against the window, David jumped and Ellie let out a strangled whimper. "I need help! Why won't you help me?"

"Daddy—"

"*Please!*"

David threw the car in Reverse and stomped on the accelerator. The Olds lurched backward, jerking David's head on his neck. Sharp, hot pain blossomed at the base of his head. David spun the wheel until the tires squealed and the whole car seemed to groan in protest. Then he dropped it into Drive. The car shuddered before its tires found purchase on the asphalt. David sped straight across the parking lot, daring to glance up at the rearview mirror only once. The woman had collapsed to the pavement and was rapidly shrinking as he put distance between them.

11

They had driven several miles before David realized he had the duffel bag in his lap, wedged between himself and the steering wheel, making it difficult to steer.

"Help me with this," he said, shoving the duffel bag over his shoulder and into the backseat. Ellie reached over and lent some assistance without uttering a sound. Once his heartbeat slowed, David eased up on the accelerator and glanced over at his daughter.

She was staring at him, her face emotionless. Based on the whimpering sound she had made as they fled the parking lot, he assumed she'd been crying, but she wasn't. She was stoic. Unmovable. He felt colder for looking at her.

"Are you okay?" he said.

Her eyebrows ticked together, a movement so subtle it was nearly undetectable. She glanced toward the windshield.

"Ellie?" he said.

"Why didn't you help that woman?" She was sitting ramrod-straight in the passenger seat, which looked very unnatural to David. As if she might launch herself at the windshield at any moment.

"There was nothing I could do."

"She was hurt. She was bleeding."

"I saw, Ellie."

They merged onto the highway. David felt about as conspicuous as someone driving around with a missile strapped to the roof of his car, even with so few vehicles on the road.

When he looked to his left, he noticed the woman's bloody handprint on his window, stark as an accusation. He quickly rolled the window down, flooding the car with a cool wind.

"She was crying," Ellie said.

"It's none of our business."

"She was hurt."

"No," David corrected. "She was sick. It's different."

"How?"

He shook his head. It was all too much to explain. "Cut me some slack, will you, please?" he managed.

"We could have driven her to the hospital."

"You don't understand," he said. "The hospital won't do her any good." He glanced at her. Those deep, searchlight eyes. "That's probably the first time you've seen it," he said. "Up close like that, I mean."

Ellie turned away from him, facing forward to watch the horizon. "No," she said, quite matter-of-fact. She had the suitcase down at her feet, but was picking at the plastic handle with her thumbnail.

"No?" he said.

"The first one was a girl at school," she said. "There were others, too. But the girl at school was the worst." She added, "Up close like that," as if to turn his own words back around on him.

As she said it, he recalled the incident with the girl at school. It had happened during recess, out on the playground. But other than that, he hadn't been aware of any other occasions Ellie would have witnessed such horror.

"What others?" It seemed impossible. In fact, it seemed as if he had failed her in some way. He and Kathy had done their best to sequester her from it all, and until that moment, he had thought they'd done a commendable job.

Ellie shrugged. "Doesn't matter," she said.

"Well, I want to talk about it with you."

"I don't."

He continued to stare at her until someone blared a horn at him. He jerked the wheel, centering the car back in its lane.

His whole body felt prickly with perspiration. When he glanced up at his reflection in the rearview mirror, he was dismayed to see streaks of black sweat spilling down his forehead from his hairline. Goddamn hair dye.

"Okay," he said after a time. "That's okay. We don't have to talk about it right now if you don't want to."

"How 'bout the radio?" she said, still not looking at him.

"Have at it."

She switched it on and scrolled through the dial. Most of the stations were nothing but static. She paused when she came upon an evangelist orating on the sins of mankind. "Many will tell you that the time for repentance is now, brothers and sisters," he rallied amidst washes of static and crackling audio. "They'll tell you to repent, repent! But what if we are faced with some greater truth? What if the magic has turned black? Perhaps repentance is no longer an option, children. Perhaps we are the marching doomed, a parade of devils, the hopeless dregs paying for the sins of a world that has gotten so out of control, so repulsively foul with sin—"

"Find something else," David said.

She was staring at the radio dial, unmoving.

"Find something else," he repeated.

Ellie reached out and spun the dial, eventually stopping on a station playing old swing music. She finally settled back in the passenger seat, her posture seemingly more relaxed. Yet her eyes remained alert.

12

They drove for another two hours before David decided to stop for lunch. With no destination in mind, he had fled the main highway to the back roads that wound and twisted and looped through a gray September wilderness. He guessed they were somewhere in the southwest corridor of Virginia by now, though he couldn't be sure. For all he knew, he'd spent most of last night driving in circles.

"I'm not hungry," Ellie said as he pulled into the parking lot of a diner. There was a large handwritten sign over the entrance that said, simply, WE ARE OPEN.

"We should really eat something," he said, pulling into a parking space. The parking lot was comprised of white gravel, the tiny stones popping beneath the Oldsmobile's tires and raising a cloud of white powder. When he turned off the engine, the whole chassis seemed to shudder and die. He resisted the urge to crank the ignition again, just to make sure the engine hadn't seized up on them for good.

Ellie did not move. She stared at the diner through the windshield, as if trying to divine some great secret hidden within the 1950s-style design of its chrome-and-glass construction. Her forehead glistened with sweat. She looked like a stranger sitting beside him, her long tresses shorn away, her face stoic and impassive.

"Put the hat back on," he told her.

She only stared at it, turning it over in her hands.

"Ellie," he said.

"Back at the motel," she said. "Were you telling me the truth? About what's going on back home? The quarantine, I mean."

He felt the skin across his face grow tight. "Yes," he said.

"If we're not sick, then why would people be after us and wanting us to go back home? Why would they want to keep us locked up if we're okay?"

"It's just how they do things now, Ellie. They don't know who's okay and who's not."

"But we've been doing our blood tests," she said. "They should know."

"I don't make the rules," he said. "Now, put your hat back on."

She tugged the ball cap onto her head.

Before climbing out of the car, David blotted the inky runnels of sweat from his forehead with a wad of Kleenex. Then he offered Ellie a sad little smile, hoping the girl would give him one in return.

She didn't.

"You're my son, not my daughter," he reminded her before stepping out into the sunshine.

David was relieved to find that they were the only patrons in the place. The hostess, who also turned out to be their waitress, was middle-aged and portly. She sported a dismal expression that made David limit his eye contact with her. Which was for the best, anyway. She had a paper mask hanging from her neck, similar to the kind David had purchased earlier that morning from the sundries store, and a photograph of two small children pinned where her name tag should be. She led them to a booth and set two laminated menus on the table before departing, quite unceremoniously.

David picked his up, thumbed through its sticky pages. After a time, he glanced up at Ellie in the seat opposite him, who hadn't moved a muscle since sitting down.

"They've got bacon cheeseburgers," he told her.

"Don't really care."

"Honey, you've got to eat."

"I told you I'm not hungry."

"You'll be hungry later."

"Then I'll eat later."

There might not be time for that, he thought but did not say. Their situation was still too unreal to him: his daughter seated across from him with a short haircut, wearing a monster truck T-shirt and a blue baseball cap. Not to mention the hilt of the Glock poking into the small of his back. *Yes, my friend, it is all too unreal. Like the plot of a movie. Or walking through a dream.* For whatever reason, he realized at that moment that he was out the hundred bucks he'd left with the motel proprietor as a security deposit the night before. *Shit.*

"How about a salad, then?" he suggested. "Something light."

"I'll eat if I can call Mom first."

David scratched a fingernail along a paper place mat. "The cell phone is in the car," he said. He held his hands out, palms up—*what can we do about it now?* "We can call her later."

"I won't eat unless I can talk to her."

His thumbnail scratched so hard he tore the place mat. Smoothing over the tear with his palm, he said, "Okay. I'll get the phone and call. You wait here."

"I want to talk to her myself," she said.

"Yes, I know," he said, sliding out of the booth. "I know, Ellie. Just wait here."

He walked out of the diner at a quick clip and with his head down. Outside, the daylight seemed overly bright, and he shielded the sun from his eyes with one arm. *Sunglasses would have been a good idea, too,* he thought. *Even better to hide my face.* The Olds was parked across the lot, but as he climbed into the driver's seat, he could see Ellie intently watching him through the diner's plate-glass window. He waved at her, then held up the cell phone to show her that he was dialing.

He didn't dial. Instead, he faked it, then held the phone up to his ear. It wasn't even powered on; it was a cold black brick of plastic pressed against the side of his head. He thought about all the intricate little bits and pieces that made a cell phone work. When he inhaled, he could smell the plastic of the thing. For some strange reason, it brought tears to his eyes.

When he saw that Ellie's gaze was still on him, he feigned a conversation with someone on the other end of the line. He found it impossible to know how to express himself while speaking nonsense—should he frown, smile, look concerned? He was a horrible actor. He recited a few lines from an old Bruce Springsteen song, then set the phone back down on the console and returned to the diner. Before he could sit down at the booth, Ellie was frowning at him.

"What's the matter?" she said. "What about Mom? I wanted to talk to her."

"She's in treatment right now," David said, sliding into his seat opposite her. The waitress had returned in his absence, leaving behind two tall plastic cups of ice water with accordion straws.

He thought Ellie's eyes narrowed just the slightest bit.

"You folks made up your mind?" the waitress said, returning to the table. Her expression was no more pleasant than it had been when she had first shown them to their table. She held the paper mask up over her mouth as she spoke.

"Two bacon cheeseburgers," David said, ordering for the both of them.

Without another word, the waitress collected the menus and performed her disappearing act once again.

Ellie turned her gaze from him. She plucked the straw from her ice water, her thumb pressed against the straw's opening at the top. She proceeded to release droplets of water onto her place mat, lifting her thumb in quick little jerks. Whenever she looked up, it wasn't to address David, but to glance at the television set mounted to the wall over his shoulder.

"You haven't told me what you think of my new look," he said.

"What do you want me to say?"

"Do you like it?"

"Not really."

"Does it at least look natural?"

"No."

"No?"

"I don't know." She still wouldn't look at him.

When their food arrived, David went overboard saying how delicious the burgers looked, then proceeded to douse his in ketchup. Ellie said nothing, though he was pleased to see that after the first bite it didn't take any coaxing to get her to finish her meal.

"Does Mom know about the quarantine back home?" Ellie asked.

He hesitated too long on the question, causing the girl's eyes to narrow again. "I don't know," he said.

"Have you told her?"

"No, not yet. We can tell her when we talk to her."

"Or maybe she saw it on the news," Ellie said.

"Maybe," David said.

Ellie opened her mouth to say something more, but no words came out. Instead, her mouth just widened as her chin sank lower. She had her gaze fixed on the TV above David's head.

"What?" he said. "What is it?"

When she didn't respond, he turned around and looked up at the TV.

There were two photos on the screen—one of him, one of Ellie. He recognized the photo of himself from a vacation in Ocean City two summers ago. Kathy had taken the picture. Beneath the photo was his full name, David James Arlen. They did that with criminals and presidential assassins—used their first, middle, and last names. So there would be no confusing him with all the other David Arlens there might be in the world.

The photo of Ellie was more recent. A school photo, with a fake woodsy backdrop. In it, she was bright, vivacious, and somehow cunning. Her smile was a thing of beauty. Beneath her photo was her own name, Eleanor Arlen. She was an innocent, so there would be no need for her middle name, which was Elizabeth.

The first thing that hit him was a jarring sense of disbelief. He was sitting here, looking at himself smiling in a photograph on a TV news broadcast. The second emotion that struck him, nearly instantaneous with the first, was pure fury at having been violated in such a fashion. Because they would have had to break in to their house to obtain those photos. There was no other way. Which also meant they had started looking for them sooner than he would have thought. Or hoped.

That white van . . .

He caught the final few words of the male newscaster, whose voice was superimposed over the photos: ". . . have issued an AMBER Alert for the pair, who are assumed to be driving a black Ford Bronco with Maryland tag number M-one-five-nine-seven-two. Arlen is being sought for questioning following the death of his wife, Kathleen Arlen. Police also advised that Arlen's daughter, eight-year-old Eleanor Arlen, is in dire need of medical assistance. If anyone knows the whereabouts of David Arlen, police are requesting you contact . . ."

David turned back to face his daughter. Briefly, the whole diner seemed to tip to one side. His skin prickled with heat, yet at the very core of his body it felt like a solid rod of ice had formed, restricting his movement and freezing his guts.

A single tear spilled from Ellie's eye. When she looked away from the broadcast and found her father's face, David saw that his own vision had grown blurry and threatened to break apart.

Ellie mouthed, "*Dad . . .*" But only the slightest whisper of sound escaped her. Ellie's lower lip quivered. A second tear burned down her cheek and pattered onto her plate.

He was already digging his wallet out of his pants before he knew what he was doing. He tossed a handful of bills onto the table, not bothering to count them, then reached out to his daughter with one hand. She did not move, did not recoil from him as he feared she might, and he was able to grasp her around one wrist. With his other hand, he stuffed the wallet back into the rear pocket of his jeans. Distantly—or seemingly so—there sounded a muted *thunk,* and it took him several seconds to realize that it was the sound of the handgun coming loose from his waistband and landing on the cushioned seat behind him.

"Shhhh," he said. It was somewhere between a whisper and a moan. "Look at me, Ellie. Look at me. Don't take your eyes from me."

He released her wrist just long enough to tug the bill of the ball cap lower so that it obscured her eyes. With his other hand, he felt around the seat until he located the handgun. When he did, he stuffed it down the back of his pants again. The gun's cool metal slid freely along the sweaty pocket of flesh at the small of his back.

Ellie groaned. It was a tiny sound, and it approximated the word *"Mom."*

"Come on," he whispered. "Let's go. Let's get up and go."

He took her by the wrist and gave her a gentle yank out of the booth. She went limp and he caught her with an arm around her shoulders. He whispered nonsense into the side of her face, then begged her to keep it together, keep it together, they needed to get out of here without making a scene . . .

Their waitress studied them with a puzzled expression. She was wedged between two vinyl bar stools at the counter and thankfully didn't approach.

"He doesn't feel well," David said.

His hand atop her head, he kept her facing the floor as he ushered her through the diner and out into the parking lot. He felt her go limp again and threaten to collapse to the ground, but he held her upright by the forearm and refused to let her go. He never slowed in his trek across the parking lot to the car. His shoes stirred up dusty white clouds.

"Shhhh," he said.

"No, no, no," she said, her voice choked with tears.

His grip on her arm tightened. "Let's get to the car."

She uttered something—a sound so pathetic and alien to

him that it seemed impossible it had come from another human being, let alone his daughter.

He directed her around to the passenger side. It seemed to take forever to get the door open. And when he did, Ellie refused to move.

"Get in." He squeezed the sweaty nape of her neck, though gently. "Please, baby. Get in the car. Get in the car."

She turned and looked up at him. Beneath the brim of her ball cap, a faint crease formed between her eyebrows. Catching her breath, she said, "You're a liar."

"Honey . . ."

"You lied to me."

"Ellie," he said. He attempted to turn her around and shove her through the open door.

"No." She pulled away from him.

"It's not safe." He looked back at the diner. The waitress was watching them through the glass now.

"You're a *liar!*" she screamed at him . . . and then collapsed to the ground.

He dropped quickly to his knees and raised her head with a thumb beneath her chin. The pain on her face wounded him, but he refused to look away. Instead, he embraced her, squeezed her tight. She tensed up within his arms . . . but then sobbed against him as her whole body went limp.

"Shhh," he said. "It's okay. But we need to get in the car now. We need to get out of here, Ellie. Do you understand? It's important we get out of here right now." He kissed the hot, damp side of her face, and repeated the question in her ear: *"Do you understand?"*

She withdrew from his arms and slouched against the side of the car.

The waitress was still watching them from behind the diner's plate-glass windows.

David said, "If you don't get in the car, Ellie, I'm going to smash those bird eggs. Do you understand me?"

"No," she sobbed. Then she hugged him again. He hugged

her back with one arm, not taking his gaze from the waitress in the window.

Someone is going to call the police. This must look too fucked up not to call the police.

"I want to know what's going on," she cried.

Briefly, David closed his eyes. "Okay. I'll tell you. I'll explain it all. Just get in the car first so we can get out of here and get someplace safe. We need to get someplace safe first, Ellie. And then I'll tell you."

In the end, he wasn't sure how long they remained like that, kneeling in the gravel parking lot of the 1950s-style diner, the waitress watching them through the wall of plate-glass windows, but by the time they ultimately climbed into the car and drove away, it seemed like an eternity had passed. His only hope was that the scene they had inadvertently caused had kept the waitress's eyes off the television broadcast.

13

Sixteen months earlier

David poked his head into Ellie's bedroom. Kathy and Ellie were propped up against a mountain of pillows, Ellie's head in Kathy's lap. David leaned against the door frame and watched them both in silence. After a time, Kathy looked up, found his eyes on her, and smiled wearily at him. She mouthed the words "*Is she asleep?*" to him, because she couldn't see their daughter's face. David nodded.

Without waking her, Kathy maneuvered Ellie's head off her lap. She pulled the sheet up over the girl, kissed the side of her head, then joined David out in the hallway.

"How is she?" he asked.

"As good as she can be," Kathy said. "Better than most, I would suspect."

"She's always been tough."

"She has," Kathy agreed. "She didn't even want to talk about it. Do you think that's bad?"

"Bad?"

"Like, should we be concerned?"

"I don't know."

Kathy began to cry, quietly and with a hand covering her mouth.

It was something she did so rarely that it was unexpected, and he stood there staring at her for several seconds before drawing her into an embrace. They hugged each other in the dark hallway for a time. He could feel her heartbeat against his chest.

"I think she should talk to a therapist," Kathy said once she dried her eyes on his chest and separated herself from him. "A counselor or whatever."

"If you think that's best."

"I'm just worried what she saw . . . what's been going on . . . I don't like that she's not talking about it."

"It just happened today, Kath. Let's talk about it with her tomorrow. Maybe she'll be ready tomorrow."

Kathy nodded, swiping a thumb under one eye.

David reached out and quietly closed Ellie's bedroom door. Then he nodded his head in the direction of the living room, where the TV was on with the volume turned low. Kathy followed him, her bare feet shushing along the floor. David suddenly felt exhausted, like he could shut his eyes and not open them for a month.

"I need a drink," Kathy said, going through the living room and into the kitchen. "You want one?"

"All right," he said, easing down onto the sofa. Anything to soothe his nerves. He glanced at the TV but had no interest in whatever was on.

Kathy returned with two glasses of white wine. She handed one to him.

"Come here," he said, patting the cushion beside him.

Kathy sat. She took a sip of her wine, made a smacking sound with her lips, then leaned her head against David's shoulder.

"How much did she actually see?" he asked after a while.

"I'm not exactly sure. Her teacher said she was right there when it happened."

"Any word on the girl?"

"None yet," Kathy said. "The last bit of news was that she was still in critical condition. They took her to Hopkins." She glanced up at him, her breath warm and already smelling of wine. "It's the same thing that happened to those students of yours, isn't it?"

"They weren't my students," he said. "They just attended the college. I didn't even know them."

"But it's the same thing, isn't it?"

"I'm not a doctor, Kath."

"It's what happened to Deke, too." It wasn't a question this time. She was running through all the incidents in her head now, he could tell, replaying them as if their sum would now total the blueprint to some terrible plan unleashed.

David had thought about Deke every day since that night he'd found him wandering down Columbus Court in his underwear. It was impossible not to, since Deke's house—or what remained of Deke's house, following the fire—could be seen from their front windows. Two days after the fire, David had spoken with a police detective about the incident—he told the detective about finding Deke in his underwear in the middle of the street, and about ushering him back into his home. He spoke of the disruptive condition of the house, the strange, detached way Deke had been speaking, and about the massive amounts of blood he'd discovered in Deke's bathroom. The detective, a pock-faced fellow in his late thirties, jotted down notes without the slightest inkling of emotion. When David had finished his story, the detective set down his notepad and asked if anyone else on Columbus Court had exhibited any strange behavior lately. David said no, and asked what that had to do with anything. The detective shrugged and commented that he had been getting a lot of reports concerning strange behavior lately. More than the usual stuff, he'd said. When David asked him to elaborate, the detective was reluctant. When David pushed the issue, the detective told him it was nothing and that he shouldn't have brought it up. It hadn't been until later that evening, after speaking with the detective, as he'd lain in bed staring at the darkened ceiling while Kathy snored gently beside him, that David's mind had returned to the ice cream man. It occurred to him that no one on Columbus Court had ever learned exactly what had happened to Gary, the ice cream man. The police had taken him away, the Freez-E-Friend truck had been towed, and that had been the end of it. As if it had never happened.

David considered mentioning this to Kathy now, adding

one more piece to the peculiar and morbid puzzle that she was now so obviously assembling in her head, but he ultimately decided against it. A young girl had fallen ill at Ellie's school today, coughing up blood while staggering around the playground during recess as if lost, before collapsing on the ground in a series of convulsions. Ellie's teacher had told Kathy that a handful of students, including their daughter, had witnessed the whole thing. He didn't need to frighten Kathy any further, augmenting her fear with reminders of all the strange events that had been happening over the past nine months. As it was, he could feel her trembling against him now.

"Ellie's teacher said Ellie wasn't even that scared," Kathy said. She was staring off into the distance. "In fact, she said Ellie even helped calm some of the other kids down."

"Well, that's a good sign," he said, trying to sound upbeat.

In the kitchen, the telephone rang.

"Jesus," he said, startled.

"I'm not in the mood," Kathy sighed, not moving.

"I'll get it."

"No, I'll get it," she said, patting his thigh and getting up from the sofa. She disappeared into the kitchen and answered the phone with an exhausted, "Hello?"

David turned his attention to the TV. It was an episode of *The Big Bang Theory,* one he and Kathy had seen half a dozen times. The show's canned laughter irritated him, so he found the remote wedged between two sofa cushions and muted the volume. A scroll at the bottom of the screen read, *Officials at the U.S. Fish and Wildlife Service are still puzzled over bird deaths and disappearances following unusual migratory patterns.*

He thought now of the students from the college, two of whom had exhibited symptoms similar to the girl in Ellie's class. He hadn't witnessed either episode, but had learned about them both from Burt Langstrom later in the English department's office. Burt hadn't witnessed the incidents either, but he had always been a veritable font of subversive knowledge on campus, and David had no reason to doubt the sto-ries' authenticity.

Some girl, a freshman, had doubled over in the quad be-tween the humanities building and the cafeteria and had be-gun convulsing on the ground. When blood started gushing from her mouth, witnesses assumed that she had bitten her tongue while having a seizure. But then the blood had spilled out of her nose, and people started to shout for campus secu-rity.

A similar incident had occurred to a frat boy as he sat in class—he simply stiffened and tipped over, crashing to the floor. His legs began to jerk spasmodically, and when he coughed, blood sprayed along the linoleum floor tiles. Both students died at the hospital within days of their collapse. As far as David was aware, no cause of death had ever been stated.

"It's an illness," Burt Langstrom had suggested over lunch. Just talking about it had stemmed David's appetite, but Burt tore into his roast beef sandwich as if they'd been talking about nothing more gruesome than the upcoming Orioles game. "Probably some strain of meningitis or something like that."

"You'd think they'd notify the school if it was meningitis," David had said. "Besides, what about the Sandoval kid? That certainly wasn't meningitis."

Patrick Sandoval had been the third student to fall ill. He had been a junior, a basketball player, a good-looking kid who'd been in David's literary criticism class the year before. As far as David was aware, and unlike what had happened with the two previous students, there hadn't been any clear signs of a physical illness with Sandoval. There was no blood, no convulsing—only that he was spotted by a number of students wandering around campus in the middle of the night com-pletely naked, and with a broad, sleepy smile stretched across his face. Someone even spotted Sandoval holding a conversa-tion with thin air. Campus security showed up, approached him, and assumed he was intoxicated. They took him to the security office, where an officer administered a breathalyzer test. Yet despite his slurred speech and increasingly perplexing statements to the officers, Patrick Sandoval was stone-sober. Assuming he was under the influence of narcotics, he was taken to Mercy Medical Center in Baltimore. Whether or not a toxicology test was done at the hospital, David didn't know, but the boy had returned to school the next day, apparently fine. Two days later, he found his way to the roof of his dormitory—a twenty-story tower at the east end of campus that everyone called the Fortress—where he walked right over the ledge to his death on the pavement below.

Meningitis, David knew, most likely wouldn't cause someone to do something like that. In fact, it was even possible that the thing with Sandoval was unrelated to what had happened to the two other students. Yet David couldn't forget the bewildered look in Deke's eyes that night, and how the poor guy must have, for some reason that would never be explained, set fire to his own house, where he had died in the inferno. How Sandoval had been wandering around campus naked, while Deke had been doing the same in his underwear outside in the street. Moreover, and even more disturbing to David, Patrick Sandoval had dropped right out of the sky like those geese that had rained down on the parking lot at the college the very night Deke died.

This realization was chilling.

David set his wineglass on the coffee table. His hands were trembling.

"Jesus Christ," he heard Kathy utter from the kitchen. "No. Oh *no*, Carly!"

Carly Monroe's daughter, Phoebe, went to Arnold Elementary with Ellie. The girls had been friends since preschool. David leaned forward on the couch, feeling sweat prickle the small hairs on the nape of his neck.

"Okay, okay," Kathy was saying in the kitchen.

David stood. He was halfway across the living room when Kathy appeared in the entranceway, the portable phone still to her ear. The look on her face was enough to cause David to freeze in midstep. He knew right then and there that the little girl from Ellie's school was dead.

"Okay," Kathy said into the phone. Her voice wavered, unsteady. "Yes, hon. You, too. Please. Okay. Okay. Thank you, Carly. Good night." She lowered the phone and stared at him, her eyes impossibly wide. David had never seen her look more fearful, more terrified in her life.

"It's not good," he said.

"That was Carly Monroe. She just got a call and wanted to pass along the info. Jesus, David, she died," Kathy said. "The poor kid died."

"God." David went to her, hugged her. She shuddered against him. "Did Carly say what caused it? Was the girl sick?"

"No one knows anything yet," Kathy said, not sobbing now, but just resting against his chest. David smelled her hair, fresh with lavender shampoo, and savored the warmth of her face against the crook of his collarbone. "Mostly rumors. But she's *dead,* David. That poor kid. And Eleanor . . ."

"Ellie's fine. Let's not overreact. It's a horrible thing that's happened, but let's not lose sight of the fact that our daughter is absolutely fine."

She pulled away from him, stared up at him. There was a hint of conspiracy behind her eyes now. "What if she's not?"

"Hon—"

"What if it's contagious?"

"No one knows *what* it is," he told her.

"Which means," she said, "that no one knows whether it's contagious or not."

"We'll take Ellie to see the pediatrician, if it'll ease your mind."

"I don't know if it will. I don't know if anyone even knows what to look for. Don't you watch the news? This is happening all over."

"I think we just need to stay calm."

"I'm scared to death, David."

He nodded, then told her things would be all right. But in

his head, all he could hear was Burt's final comment from that afternoon in the teachers' lounge, clanging now like a death knell: *"It's some epidemic, some new disease, David. That's my take, anyway. And the reason no one's got answers is because it's like the first appearance of the Black Plague—no one's ever seen it before."*

14

He pulled off the road and bumped along the uneven shoulder until he spun the wheel and cut across a swath of grass. A large billboard advertising new homes stood in the weeds and faced the highway; some joker had spray-painted END-OF-TIMES PLAGUE SALE—ALL HOUSES ARE FREE! across the billboard in bloody red letters. David pulled the Olds directly behind the billboard, hoping that he'd angled it in a way that would make it invisible to any passing traffic, and shut it down.

In the passenger seat, Ellie continued to sob. He stared at her profile for a while, watching the tears stream down her cheeks, unsure what he could possibly do to comfort her. Her face was a mottled red. He reached over and removed the ball cap from her head. With her freshly cut hair, she still looked like someone else beneath the hat, and David couldn't help but marvel at how much someone's haircut defined their entire look.

When he reached out to caress her face, she slapped his hand away. Her eyes blazed on him.

"What'd you do?" she shrieked at him. "What'd you do? What'd you do?"

"Baby," he said, and reached out for her again.

This time she grabbed his wrist. Her eyes flared . . . and David felt a sudden tingling sensation radiate up his arm and flood through his body. A moment later, something like a surge of electricity rocketed through his body, so powerful he jerked in his seat and yanked his wrist from his daughter's grasp.

"You're a *liar!*" She gritted her teeth and threw her head back against the headrest. A solitary sob ratcheted up her throat before she turned and stared at him again, her face blotchy and red but radiant, her eyes both angry and imploring. "Is she dead? Is it true?"

"Ellie . . ."

"Tell me!" She slammed one small, pink hand against the console.

"Yes," he said. "Mom's dead."

A high-pitched keening sounded from her. But then she quickly regained control of herself. "On the news . . . they said . . ." She fought back another sob. "What did you do to her?"

"I didn't do anything, baby."

"It was on the news! The news wouldn't lie! *You're* the liar! What did you do?"

"I didn't do anything to her. I would never hurt your mother in a million years, Ellie. It was the doctors. They said she would be okay, and that they would take care of her, but they were wrong—Ellie, *they* were the liars—and now she's gone. They killed her." And now he was crying freely, too. His grief was suddenly so great he was unable to keep it together, even for the sake of his daughter.

Ellie just stared at him, her whole body shaking as her eyes welled up with fresh tears. "Those doctors wouldn't kill Mom. They said she was special. They said her blood . . . what she had inside her . . . that she might even be able to cure what's happening . . ."

"They broke her, Ellie. There were tests and they worked her too hard. Your mother got weak. That's why I stopped taking you to see her. She got so *weak*, Ellie, and I didn't want you to see her like that. And those doctors, they never stopped, they never let up. They wanted your mom to be the cure for this thing so badly that they used her up until there was nothing left."

"But the police are looking for you," she said. "It has nothing to do with back home, does it? There is no quarantine back home, is there?"

"No," he said.

"If you didn't do anything, then why are the police looking for you?"

He cradled the back of her head, rubbed his thumb through her hair.

"They're not looking for me, baby," he said. "They're looking for you. That special thing about your mom, that one-in-a-trillion resistance she had against the disease that made her immune . . . you've got it, too. It's in you, too. You're immune, Ellie." He pulled her close to him so that their foreheads touched. "But I'm not going to let them take you. I'm not going to let them find you."

Trembling, she pushed him away from her.

"Wait," he said.

"I'm gonna be sick." She shoved open the passenger door and staggered out into the grass. She braced herself against the back of the billboard with one hand and bent at the waist.

"Honey." He slid across the seats and got out the passenger side. He reached her, rubbed her back, bent down to her level. She didn't get sick; she just stared absently at the ground, at the incongruous bursts of wildflowers that surrounded them, spitting occasionally into the weeds. Gnats orbited around their heads.

After a time, she straightened herself. She wiped the tears from her eyes as her chest hitched one last time. Then she looked up at him, wincing in the blaze of the sun that was at his back.

He grabbed her, held her tight against him. He inhaled the scent of her hair, her clothes, her skin. He felt the gentle undulation of her ribs as he rubbed his hands along her sides. Faintly, he was aware of insects chirping in the trees, of the heat from the sun baking the nape of his neck, of the occasional shush of a vehicle trolling down the highway on the other side of the billboard.

He squeezed her more tightly.

"I love you," he whispered in her ear.

"What do we do now?"

"I don't know," he said, letting her go. "For now, let's get back in the car."

Wordlessly, she crawled back into the car, her shadow rippling across the overgrown grass behind the billboard.

That news broadcast had punched him in the gut, and he knew he would have to shift things into a higher gear from here on out. *I can't believe they've started looking for us so soon,* he thought as he pulled back out onto the highway. They were the only car straight out to either horizon. *They reported that we're driving the Bronco. That's something, at least. It may take them a while to realize we're in a different car. Hell, they may never figure that out.*

So all hope wasn't lost.

"Put your hat back on," he instructed her.

She did so without uttering a word. Then she turned and stared out the window. This time, she cried in silence.

15

David drove for about an hour, piloted by the foolish compulsion that the more distance he created between themselves and the diner, the safer they were. The highway was eerily empty, and they were joined by only a few cars every once in a while. David did his best to avoid running alongside them, leaving a wide berth of glistening pavement between them, but occasionally a car would sidle up beside the Olds and trot there for a minute or two. When this happened, David couldn't help but glance at the vehicle's occupants, terrified that they might look at him and recognize him. But these people—these strangers—possessed the expressionless faces of alien life forms, and rarely did someone even return his glance through the barrier of windows that separated them.

When a police cruiser appeared in the rearview mirror, David felt a tightening in his chest. He wondered if the waitress had been paying too close attention in the diner after all. He decided to take the next exit and see if the cruiser followed him before he started to panic. When the ramp appeared on the right-hand shoulder, David turned on his blinker and took it. Holding his breath, he kept his eyes trained on the cruiser in the rearview mirror. Ellie's crying had eventually lulled her to sleep, but the car's quick movements jolted her awake. Startled, she looked at him, then turned around in her seat to peer through the rear windshield.

"Don't do that," he said sharply. "Turn around."

Without a word, she turned around.

The cruiser followed them down the exit ramp.

Christ, no.

Still, he wouldn't panic. Suddenly, the bulge of the Glock against the small of his back was all he could feel. Yet he wondered if he'd actually be able to use it on another person.

I won't let them take her from me, he thought, slowing down as he approached the first in a series of traffic lights. The light was red, and so he stopped, the only car at the intersection. Up ahead was a grid of urban streets, a few people bustling up and down the sidewalks. There were a few other cars at the next intersection, too.

The cop pulled up alongside them in the right-hand lane.

He was grateful that Ellie didn't turn to look at the cop. He did, however—a casual glance just to see if the cop was staring back at him.

The cop was.

The guy had a meaty face with ruddy cheeks and dark hair buzzed to bristles atop his head.

David averted his gaze, staring once again at the traffic lights that lined the boulevard ahead of them. He reminded himself that the cops were still searching for the Bronco— according to the news report, anyway—and that they were safe in the Olds. *For now,* he thought. *How long until someone goes to the Langstroms' house and finds the Bronco in their garage? How long before they realize I swapped cars and there's an APB out on Burt's Oldsmobile? How long before authorities enter his house and find—*

A car horn blared. David blinked his eyes, then peered over at the police car. But the police car was already cruising through the intersection. David glanced over his shoulder and saw the chrome grille of a large pickup truck filling the Oldsmobile's rear windshield. The pickup's horn sounded a second time.

Ellie said, "Daddy?"

David took his foot off the brake and eased through the intersection. Behind him, the truck cut over to the next lane, sped up, and swerved in front of them. The driver's window rolled down, and then there was a meaty forearm with its middle finger extended.

David slowed the car, letting the pickup truck and the police car collect some distance. He managed to blend in with traffic as they passed through the next several intersections, thankful that the lights held green and there was no more stopping.

"It wasn't just a bad dream, was it?" Ellie said quietly. "About Mom."

"No, hon."

There were still a few businesses open along this road, though many others looked dark and deserted. Placards containing biblical quotes had been erected in some of the darkened windows. When they drove past a grove of condominiums, David could see yellow police tape over many of the doors and windows. Trash cans lay strewn about on the sidewalk. The few pedestrians who meandered up and down these blocks looked like extras in a George Romero film.

Because he felt too conspicuous—and too uneasy—driving down what appeared to be the main street of this run-down urban area, David took a turn onto a tree-studded secondary road that was mostly deserted. A few houses stood a distance from the road, mostly shaded behind pin oaks and corralled behind fences made of pine logs. There were large red X's painted on each of the front doors of the houses, something that chilled David on sight. He had heard about such places on the news and had even seen pictures in newspapers back when neighborhoods were first being evacuated, but until now he hadn't witnessed it in person. It was like coming face-to-face with a mythological creature.

"Did I hurt you?" Ellie said, looking at him. She glanced at his wrist.

"It's okay now," he said. The jolt of electricity he'd felt shoot up his arm and radiate through the marrow in his bones had faded just as he'd pulled his wrist free of Ellie's grasp. "What was that, Ellie? What did you do?"

"I don't really know," she said. "It's never happened like that before."

"What's never happened like that before? What are we talking about?"

"The touching thing," she said.

"Like what you did to me last night," he said. "In the car." She nodded.

He had all but convinced himself that he had imagined the whole thing—how he had been driving like an erratic mess when they first lit out in the Oldsmobile, his body a jumble of live wires, Kathy's death like a lead weight in the center of his chest. That small hand had touched the nape of his neck, her palm as cold as ice, and in that instant he had been flooded by an overwhelming serenity that quickly staunched his grief and panic and let him regain focus and composure. It was like being injected with some kind of narcotic, something ten times more potent than morphine—yet it had been a morphine that calmed only his nerves while leaving him at a level of alertness that made the world around him clear and comprehensible again. She had kept her hand on his neck for a while, until she had fallen asleep and the hand had dropped away. As her hand left him, the fear and anxiety and grief returned to him, but in a more manageable dosage. By the time they had reached the motel last night, he had all but convinced himself it had been his imagination.

This had been different, though—not the lulling serenity of Ellie's cool touch, but the fiery *zap* of a Taser. It had resonated through his molars and burst like fireworks behind his eyes. Thank God it had only lasted for a second or two.

"How do you do that?" he asked.

"I don't know. It just sort of started."

"When?"

"A while ago," she said. "I don't really remember. I used to do it just to sort of calm you and Mom down when you were upset."

"Me and your mom," he said. "You've done that to us before?"

She nodded again. "You didn't used to notice. But last night you did." She seemed to consider this. "I think it's getting stronger."

"But how do you *do* it?"

"I don't know. I just think about it. I think about taking your sadness away. Your worries and the things that make you scared."

He was staring at her, unsure if he was hearing this conversation correctly. Or perhaps he just wasn't comprehending what she was telling him. His mind seemed cluttered and confused at the moment, making it difficult to concentrate.

"I never did it the other way before," Ellie went on. "The bad way, I mean. I guess I was just scared and angry earlier. I didn't mean to hurt you."

"You didn't hurt me." He considered this. "Did it hurt you?"

"No."

"Not at all?"

"No."

"And you can do it whenever you want?"

"I'm not sure."

He held out his right arm. "Do it again," he said.

She just stared at him, not moving.

"Go on," he said. "Just a little shock, okay? I'll be ready for it this time."

Hesitantly, she reached out and closed her small, cold fingers around his wrist. Her gaze hung on him, unblinking. She remained that way for several seconds.

"Nothing's happening," he said.

"I don't know how to shock you," she said. "It's never happened before, like I said. That was the first time."

"Then do the other thing," he said. "The thing you did last night."

She opened her fingers and slid the palm of her hand halfway up his arm. Other than his daughter's soft touch, there was nothing unusual about—

He felt it filter through his system like warm medicine,

coursing through his veins and arteries, networking through his body until the hairs along his arms stood at attention and his skin tightened into gooseflesh. In that moment, all the clutter and confusion in his head cleared. It was like a fog lifting and exposing a grand, lighted city against a dark horizon. He felt anesthetized.

"Holy shit," he said, and uttered a laugh. "Holy shit, Ellie."

Ellie smiled, though somewhat timidly. She removed her hand from his arm, and David felt the serenity quickly drain from him. That thick fog blew back into his brain and obscured the lighted city.

Grinning to himself like an idiot and shaking his head in disbelief, he said, "Jesus Christ, El. I don't understand."

"I don't understand it, either," she said. Then she turned in her seat and faced forward.

"And you're sure it's not . . . it's not doing anything to you? It doesn't hurt you to do it?"

"No."

"How did you learn . . . I mean, how'd you figure out . . ."

He couldn't even formulate the proper questions.

"I don't know," she said.

His smile fell away from his face. He could tell she was troubled by either this conversation or of her ability in general. He rubbed the back of her head. "What's wrong?"

"Nothing."

"Are you scared of it?" he asked. "What you can do?"

"I haven't been," she said. "Until I hurt you."

He put both hands back on the steering wheel. "You didn't hurt me, El. I'm fine. You didn't hurt me."

She said nothing.

They drove for several minutes in silence. David's head reeled. He had so many questions, but it was obvious that Ellie had no answers for him: She was just as perplexed by the whole thing as he was.

"What are those big white things?" Ellie asked, sitting forward in her seat.

At first, David didn't know what she was talking about. But

when they cleared a bend in the road and the trees opened up, he saw several large white tents set up on a grassy slope of lawn before a large schoolhouse constructed of white stone. Emergency vehicles were parked in the paved roundabout at one side of the school, and there was a single police car blocking the entrance. Sawhorses had been erected in front of the paved driveway.

"I don't know, hon," he said, slowing down. As they drove by, he could see people filtering back and forth between the tents, all of them wearing crisp white biohazard suits and faceplates.

"It's a school," Ellie said.

"Yes."

"Why are those people dressed like that?"

"The people inside that school must be sick."

"Kids?"

"I don't know."

She read the name she saw in large blue letters over the front doors of the building. "Morristown Elementary School. It's for little kids, Dad."

"Maybe they turned it into a hospital," David suggested, unable to pull his eyes from the community of tents that had been erected on the front lawn of the school. The people in the biohazard suits looked about as hospitable and familiar as alien invaders.

Beyond the school, there were a few more houses on either side of the road with red X's on their doors, as well. He was so busy scrutinizing these homes for some sign of life that he failed to see the roadblock up ahead until he was just a few yards from it.

"Shit," he uttered, and hit the brakes. The Olds growled to a stop, skidding on the gravelly pavement in front of a series of yellow sawhorses adorned with blinking orange emergency lights. On the other side of the roadblock stood another emergency vehicle, this one parked horizontally across the street as if to prevent passage to anyone who had inadvertently—or perhaps purposefully—gone through the roadblock. There were more tents set up here, as well, only these were of the camouflaged military variety. These troubled David more than the white tents back at the school.

A man in a hazmat suit hoisting an assault rifle approached the vehicle, seeming to materialize out of nowhere. There were insignias on his sleeves and a name sewn above the breast, though David couldn't make it out because it was partially obscured by the rifle's strap. The suit's plastic faceplate obscured the man's features.

"Shit," David muttered again. Then he glanced at Ellie. She was watching the man in the hazmat suit approach the car with something like awe in her eyes. "Stick that box under your seat," David instructed.

She didn't move.

"Do it now," he barked.

Ellie bent forward and stashed the shoe box containing the bird's nest beneath her seat. When she straightened back up, the figure in the hazmat suit was right outside David's window, motioning for him to roll it down.

"Hi," David said. "My son and I just got lost. I'm sorry."

"This is a restricted area," said the man. His voice was muffled on the other side of the clear plastic shield that covered his face. His breath caused little clouds of moisture to bloom on the plastic. "This road is closed. There were signs posted."

"Were there? I must have missed them. I apologize. We'll just turn around and go back—"

"You live around here?"

A second figure dressed in similar attire—and carrying his own rifle—appeared in the space between two of the camouflage tents. He approached the scene without hesitation, pausing just a few yards behind his comrade. The person was too far away for David to make out any features behind the plastic face shield.

"No, sir," David said.

The man bent slightly so that he could peer into the car. His hazmat suit crinkled like tarpaulin. His breath continued to fog the faceplate. David couldn't tell if he was checking the interior of the vehicle for anything in particular or if he wanted a better look at Ellie. David held his breath and found he couldn't take his eyes from the man's gun.

"You two need to turn around and get out of here," the man said finally, straightening up. He pointed with one gloved hand back in the direction they had come. "Don't stop until you're back on the main road."

"Yes, sir," David said, already rolling his window back up.

The man in the hazmat suit stepped backward onto the curb. He continued pointing in the direction they had come, one hand on the grip of his rifle.

David executed a clumsy three-point turn, his heart hammering in his chest the whole time, and found himself waving stupidly at the man in the hazmat suit as he drove past him at a quick clip.

What if he had asked to see my driver's license? he wondered, passing those darkened, eerie houses with the *X*'s on their doors again. *What if he had recognized my name and pulled me out of the car right then and there? What if—*

But he could *what if* himself to death. The important thing was that the man *hadn't* asked to see his driver's license. They were headed back the way they had come, no worse for wear. Couldn't he just leave it at that?

Also, that wasn't just a man. It was a soldier. National Guard, most likely.

This time, when they drove past the school and its assortment of antiseptic white tents, David saw what were undeniably body bags lined up in a tidy queue along the sloping lawn. A few of the people in hazmat suits paused to watch them go by. Ellie waved to them. To David's astonishment, a few waved back.

16

David bought a newspaper, two packs of Marlboros, and two sixteen-ounce bottles of Pepsi at a gas station just over the Kentucky border. The gas station was nothing more than a ramshackle clapboard structure with a few ancient pumps beneath a graffiti-laden portico and a murky front window as dark and uninviting as a panel of glass that looked down into the depths of a black sea. The blacktop had been defaced by graffiti, and straggly haylike weeds sprouted through its many cracks. Ellie waited in the car.

They were back on the road before anyone else pulled up to the gas station, and were motoring along with steady traffic—the most they had seen in several hours—a minute or so later.

In the passenger seat, Ellie had the shoe box back in her lap again. Its lid was open and she was absently stroking the three tiny eggs inside the nest while watching the ebb and flow of traffic. She had calmed since the incident at the diner and her subsequent breakdown behind the highway billboard. In fact, her face had grown tight, her eyes distant, with a look of contemplation. Grief at her mother's passing was normal, but David worried that she was regretting having spoken to him about her ability. He was anxious to bring it up again—to have her touch his arm or the back of his neck again—but he didn't want to make her uncomfortable. She looked frightened.

But she's strong, he thought. *She's strong.*

They drove until hunger growled deep in his belly. He knew better than to ask Ellie if she was hungry, so he simply turned off into a shopping center and drove around until he found a random burger joint that was open. Ellie said nothing as he read the items on the menu aloud, and David did not afford her the opportunity to rebuke any suggestions he made; he merely ordered a sack of cheeseburgers and two Cokes at the first window, avoiding the whole messy routine.

Across the plaza was a strip mall that had long been forsaken, judging by its appearance. Skeins of yellow weeds swayed among the broken shelves of asphalt. The windows of the shops were either soaped over or boarded up, the signs above each entranceway no longer in existence, save for the ghostly gray outline they left behind on the façade, like fingerprints at a crime scene. Someone had rolled a bunch of steel barrels beneath the awning of one shop, their arrangement somehow suspicious and off-putting to David, though there was no one around to cement his discomfort.

David drove along the ruined parking lot, the Oldsmobile bumping and thumping the whole way, until he pulled out of sight behind a row of Dumpsters, shielding them from the street traffic and the rest of the plaza.

Ravenous, he tore open the paper sack, yanked out a fistful of burgers, and tossed a couple into Ellie's lap.

"Not hungry," she intoned.

He rubbed the back of her head, then stripped away the greasy wax paper on his own burger and folded half of it into his mouth.

The newspaper was wedged between his seat and the console. He grabbed it now, a wad of burger swelling his right cheek as he chewed, and opened it up in his lap. He searched first for any mention of him and Ellie. There was none. That was good; it most likely meant they hadn't been looking for him by the time the paper went to press. Still, it was a small victory, what with their faces—their *old* faces—presumably on television screens across the country. Freshly dyed hair and a baseball cap would only get them so far. If some inquisitive police officer happened to stop them and ask for identification, they were screwed.

It's not just the police, he reminded himself, stuffing the rest of the burger into his mouth. *It's those people in the white vans and the black cars I've got to keep an eye out for, too.*

On the second page of the A Section, he found what he was looking for: a map of the United States. This map had become a staple in pretty much every newspaper throughout the country over the past few months. David had stopped looking at it many months ago, unnerved by the prospect of what the future held. Or whether or not there would even *be* a future. But he needed it now.

The map detailed a variety of things, from the diplomatically named "free zones," to the hot spots with their color-coded bull's-eyes, the coding disconcertingly similar to the Department of Homeland Security's terror alert levels. There were also a few areas designated by stark black *X*'s—only a few, but still, more than there had been the last time David had checked this map in the newspaper back home. The colored bull's-eyes were bad enough, signifying the estimated level of infection in any given area. There was a key in the lower right-hand corner of the map that explained, in very general terms, what was typically being done in these areas depending on the color level. But the black *X*'s were worse, because those were the places that had fallen early and fallen quickly. The key identified these locations as places of thorough evacuation, though there had been rumors back at the college that those *X*'s really meant that everyone there had died. Looking at the increased number of *X*'s on the map now—perhaps two dozen at a glance—David hoped that rumor was not true.

Whether it's true or not, that doesn't change the fact that those places are empty, he thought now, studying the map. He traced an index finger along the ridge of the Great Smoky Mountains. *Either those places have been evacuated or the people there are all dead. Either way, there will be no people. No cops.*

As if reading his mind, Ellie said, "Where will we go?" She

was staring out the window, the cheeseburgers in her lap untouched. On one slender thigh she balanced the shoe box. Its
lid was off, and she was absently petting the three speckled
eggs within.

"You know, I've been thinking about that. Do you remember Uncle Tim?"

"Your stepbrother," she said.

"We should get in touch with him, go to his place for a
while."

"I haven't seen him since I was little."

"Yeah, well, it's been a long time for me, too," David said.

"Mom says he's a slouch." Then she hung her head, as if
physically pained by the sheer mention of her mother. "Where
does he even live?"

"Missouri, last time we talked."

"That's far."

"It isn't so far," he said. "We can do it."

"In this car?" She glanced up and looked out the windshield, which appeared hazy behind a cloud of gravel dust.

"It's the only car we have, Little Spoon."

She looked back down at her lap and at the speckled eggs
in the bird's nest.

"I'm not going to let anything happen to you," he told her.

"I know." She turned over in the passenger seat so that he
was left staring at her back.

David went back to the newspaper's map. Yes—given their
situation, Tim was the only logical choice he had left.

It wasn't that he and Tim had left things on bad terms; despite Kathy's disapproval of his stepbrother's irresponsible
lifestyle, David had never expressed this to Tim, nor had he let
it sour anything between them. It was simply that they had
gone off in different directions in life, and their infrequent
conversations over the phone had eventually stopped altogether. He wondered now what kind of reception Tim might
show him, receiving a phone call out of the blue. Moreover,
what might he say or do if he'd already seen the news bulletin?
David couldn't imagine.

David's mother had married Tim's father when David and Tim were nine and eleven years old, respectively. Memories of David's stepfather, Emmitt Brody, were of a hulking lumberjack of a man, broad-shouldered and thick-nosed, with a deeply furrowed brow and hands as abrasive as the outer shell of a pineapple. He had been a physically intimidating man, a stern man, but also a fair and kind man, and he had always treated David and his mother with respect and, to the degree he was capable, love. As he grew up, Tim Brody had adopted some of his father's workmanlike attributes—he took to building things with his hands, for instance, to include an entire canoe that he carved from the bole of an enormous tree one summer—but he did not possess his father's work ethic. Time spent punching a clock, which Emmitt Brody had done his entire adult life in a Pennsylvania quarry up until he was whisked away by pancreatic cancer in his early seventies, was time wasted slaving away so some corporation could get rich, according to Tim. And while David had somewhat admired Tim's aloofness and free spirit, he couldn't quite bring himself to follow in his stepbrother's shoes. David had gone on to college, got his teaching certificate, fallen in love with and married Kathy, had a daughter. Tim had dropped out of high school his senior year, spent the next decade or so running around with various women—one of whom accidentally got pregnant and had a subsequent abortion, David had heard—and never worked the same job or stayed in the same place for long before his feet got itchy and, like a wonky compass needle, he switched direction. It occurred to David now that while Tim had been living in Kansas City the last time they had spoken, there was a good chance he had rolled up his carpets and headed someplace else—perhaps *many* other places—since then. For all David knew, Tim Brody could be anywhere in the world right now.

Or dead, he thought, the notion seizing him about the throat. *Maybe it's unlikely, but maybe it's true, too. Just look at that map. Look at all those colored bull's-eyes printed right there in front of you.*

There was also an ever-changing number printed below the map, maintained by the Social Security Administration, known morbidly as the Death Tally. The SSA and the CDC had stopped using actual numbers and had changed to percentages sometime last year, because 0.05 percent of the country's population dead or infected sounded a hell of a lot better than 17.5 million people. David folded the paper in half and tucked it down between his seat and the console.

He rubbed Ellie's shoulder. "I'm gonna step outside and check my phone, see if I can get reception out here."

Ellie didn't respond.

"Try to eat something," he said.

Leaning over the seat into the rear of the car, he dug around in his bag until he located his cell phone. Then he stepped outside, startled by the heat of the fading afternoon, and of the smells of gasoline and decay emanating from the deserted strip mall.

He turned on the phone. A series of chimes indicated that there were more text messages waiting for him. He ignored those. At least there weren't any additional voice mails; if there were, he might be tempted to listen to them this time.

He scrolled quickly through his contact list, distraught when he did not find Tim's number listed under the *T*'s or the *B*'s. It had been so long since they'd spoken that it wasn't out of the question that he'd deleted Tim's number or simply replaced his phone since then. Goddamn, that was foolish. He wondered if Tim had likewise deleted him at some point.

He executed a quick Google search on his phone for Tim's name, and was hastily assaulted with over five million results. He blinked and looked stupidly at the phone's screen, his greasy fingerprints smudging some of the lines of text. This would require more extensive searching, at a time and a place where he could sit down and do it properly without worrying about the federal government tracking his cell phone via GPS. As it was, he was beginning to feel conspicuous parked out here all alone in the middle of a run-down, deserted shopping center.

He was about to power the phone off again and get back in the car, when the phone suddenly rang in his hands. The number wasn't programmed into his phone, yet he recognized it nonetheless.

Anger twisted his guts. Suddenly, he was back in that horrible hospital room again, the smell of death clinging to everything, his wife's eyes on him at first . . . then gone, distant, emptied of life. The utter helplessness of it all. And it was bad enough that they had broken in to his family's house and stolen pictures of him and Ellie—goddamn *family vacation photos!*—to use for their bullshit news bulletin, but now they were calling him to goad him out of hiding . . .

Before he knew what he was doing, he answered the call.

"You sons of bitches," he growled into the phone.

"David." It was the heavily accented voice of Dr. Kapoor. He sounded surprised that David had answered the phone.

"You've got a lot of nerve," he said into the phone.

"Please, David, hear me out—"

"I saw the news report. That's some stunt."

"It wasn't my idea. I was against it."

"Bullshit."

"David, you must hear me out. You are acting out of impulse, and you are only causing greater harm. Believe me, I understand your grief, and I'm here to help you see things more clearly before you—"

"You're here to *help* me?"

"If you'll only listen—"

"Leave me and my daughter alone," he said.

"David, please—"

"Listen to me. You stay out of our way or you'll be sorry."

"David, it doesn't have to be this way. You have misunderstood the situation."

"Don't you fucking tell me what I—"

"Listen to me, David. You can't keep running."

"You'll never find us."

"You can't keep it up, David." There was a hitch in Dr. Kapoor's throat. "David, you're sick."

For a moment, Dr. Kapoor's voice faded out . . . then faded back in.

"You're sick, David. Your last blood test. You've got it."

"You're a liar," David said. "You're just trying to get me to come back. I won't do it."

"It's not a lie. It's no trick. David, please, think about your daught—"

"Fuck you," he said, and ended the call.

His hands shook. Sweat rolled down his forehead, though the rest of his body felt strangely cold. Through the center of his body, he felt as though an electrical current pulsed, causing every fiber of his being to vibrate with a surge of power— of anger—that threatened to shatter him into a billion microscopic pieces. He wondered if it was a residual effect of Ellie's touch or if it was generated internally, born of his own anger.

He closed his eyes, leaned against the car, and focused on controlling his respiration. The last thing he needed was for Ellie to see him upset. Things were already bad enough without that.

In his hand, the phone rang again.

He powered it off without a second thought.

17

For better or worse, he opted to drive to the nearest city identified as a black *X* on the newspaper's map. It was a town in Kentucky called Goodwin, and he liked the sound of it. Even when he turned the map on its side, making all the *X*'s look disconcertingly like little black crosses, he clung to the plan and didn't veer off in another direction.

While he smoked, he pulled up directions to Goodwin on his phone. He was fearful it might ring again in his hand—fearful he might actually answer it and scream at the person on the other end of the line right in front of his daughter—but the phone did not ring. He kept it on long enough to scribble the directions down on a slip of paper he found in the glove compartment, then shut it back off. He lit a fresh cigarette with a match and, for the first time since he was a little boy watching his mother smoke in the car, marveled at how there used to be cigarette lighters built into the dashboards of American automobiles.

As they drove, the horizon soured to the color of a bruise. The sun sizzled out like a dying fire. Ellie scrolled through the radio stations, hoping to find a broadcast that played music, but the reception was poor and there was nothing but static across the dial. Even the radio evangelists had disappeared. To keep her happy, he stopped at a gas station and bought a few used CDs from a bin, things he would never listen to in his real life—Roxette, Cyndi Lauper, Bananarama. They were only a dollar apiece. Ellie played them but remained unemotional. Detached. It concerned him.

That evening, they ate the remainder of the burgers from earlier, now cold, tasteless, the patties beginning to stiffen. Ellie kept the shoe box of bird eggs tucked between them on the console. As he drove, David kept glancing at her profile, desperate to decode her emotions. He didn't like how silent she was being, didn't like the distant look in her eyes. He knew it would only get worse tonight, when they arrived in Goodwin. He would have to put on a good face. He would have to somehow make it all palatable, them staying overnight in what promised to be a deserted ghost town.

But that proved more difficult than he had thought.

As he had assumed, based on the X that covered the town on the map, Goodwin had been evacuated. He was prepared for the empty streets, the darkened buildings, the ghostly nothingness left behind. What he wasn't prepared for was what greeted them a good five miles prior to reaching the town. Signs had been staked along the shoulder and the median, the handwriting done in harsh lettering with thick markers of varying colors, some signs so large they looked like billboards, others so small they were barely noticeable among the clutter. Snippets of phrases stood out as they drove by: THIS IS A DEAD TOWN; THE LORD GIVETH, THE LORD TAKETH; POPULATION ZERO; SODOM & GOMORRAH. One sign in particular caught David's attention, perhaps because it was decorated much like a poster for a high school pep rally, adorned with glitter and letters cut from brightly colored construction paper. It read:

Let the little children come to me,
and do not hinder them,
for the Kingdom of Heaven belongs to such as these.

As they drew closer to the town line, David saw small crosses erected in the grass on either side of the road, eerily similar to ones he sometimes noticed along the highway memorializing victims of automobile accidents. There were too many crosses here to count, blank white structures perhaps two feet in height, each one identical to the next. That was what he found most troubling—the sameness of all those crosses—for it spoke of some morbid unity that had taken place here, a ceremonial mourning of the collective dead.

"I don't like those things," Ellie said, gazing out at the crosses as they drove by.

"They're just crosses."

"Did all those people die here?"

"I don't think so," he said. It was a lie; he felt the wrongness of it on his tongue. "I think they put them here before they evacuated."

"Crosses mean someone's dead," Ellie said flatly.

David said nothing.

"Where did the rest of the people go?" she asked.

"Someplace else."

"Why are we here?"

"Because no one else is."

"So people left this place because of the disease," Ellie said. It wasn't a question.

"According to the newspaper, yeah," David said.

"That means the disease was worse here than in other places."

David nodded. The white crosses blurred together as he drove.

"What if it's still here?" she said.

"What's that?"

"The disease," she said. "The Folly. What if it's still around, hanging in the air or something?"

"I'm not sure it works that way."

"But it might."

He glanced at her. "You're immune, Ellie. You're safe."

"But what about you?"

He smiled wanly at her. "I'll be fine, too," he told her.

Thinking, *That son of a bitch Kapoor won't get inside my head with his lies and his tricks.*

They drove beneath an overpass. American flags hung from the ramparts, and there were stuffed animals tied to the chain-link fencing. A plastic doll's head dangled from a length of rope like some primitive trap. In startling white letters, someone had spray-painted across the roadway a single, blinding word:

CROATOAN

"What's that word mean?" Ellie asked.

"I don't know," he said, though he recalled a history lesson from his school days about a group of settlers who mysteriously vanished from Roanoke Island in the sixteenth century, leaving no trace behind, save for the word *croatoan* carved in the trunk of a tree. He thought it best not to mention this to his daughter.

"I don't like this place," she said. She had gathered her shoe box into her lap again and was now running her fingers along the three eggs inside the nest. "It's scary."

"It's just a town," he assured her, wondering just how confident his voice sounded. "It's roads and buildings and cars. There's nothing here to be afraid of."

"There's nothing," she said, and David couldn't be sure if she was repeating part of what he said or if she was making some observation of her own. Perhaps trying to convince herself. "It's not just a town," she added. David did not ask her to elaborate.

Just before the city line, they were greeted by a road sign welcoming them to Goodwin, Kentucky. It was incongruous, though, since it was posted on what remained of a chain-link fence outfitted in concertina wire. Several sections of the fence had been knocked down, including the part that should have run across the roadway. The place had been quarantined at some point, too. David drove through, feeling his skin prickle. There were more white crosses here, and someone had painted a crude biohazard symbol on a tree trunk in neon orange.

"Daddy!" Ellie shrieked and David slammed on the brakes.

There was a figure slumped over in the middle of the road, perhaps ten yards ahead of them. In the garish light of the car's headlamps, David could make out the awkward angle of the person's head, the stiff, unnatural way the figure was sitting upright in the middle of the road. A leg was bent at an aggressive angle off to one side, the foot seemingly absent and leaving behind the abrupt bone-white stump of an ankle.

But—

"Another one," Ellie said, pointing toward the shoulder of the road. This figure was standing, arms strangely akimbo, its body propped against the guardrail and leaning at an impossible angle. Its head was missing.

David felt a prickling sensation course down his chest and melt like steam off his body.

"It's okay," he said, touching Ellie's knee. "They aren't real."

She leaned forward, staring out the windshield.

David flicked on the high beams and said, "See? They're dummies. Mannequins."

"Oh," she said, still tense. David thought he could feel her heartbeat vibrating through the Oldsmobile's chassis. "Why?"

"I don't know."

"To scare us?"

"I don't think so."

"Like scarecrows," she said anyway. "But for people."

"No, hon. I don't think so." He pointed farther ahead, to a row of shops that flanked the main road. Several shop windows were broken, and there were items strewn about the sidewalk and street—clothing, furniture, household appliances, a shopping cart tipped on its side. A third mannequin leaned halfway out of a storefront's busted plate-glass window. The stores here had been ransacked.

David lifted his foot up off the brake and rolled down the street, carving a wide arc around the mannequin in the center of the road. As they went by, the headlights washed over its blank, emotionless features, its eyes dulled to tan orbs, the whole of its nose busted off like the nose of the Great Sphinx of Giza. They cruised through an intersection where the traffic lights were dark. Pages of newspaper whipped along the pavement in the breeze. There were no cars in sight, with the exception of a scorched black frame that sat on four rims, door-less and windshield-less against a curb. It looked like some great slaughtered beast that had been picked clean to the bone by vultures.

At the next intersection, someone had propped up a large white sandwich board in the center of the street. It read:

ATTENTION!
All EMERGENCY RESPONSE SERVICES to this area
have been suspended indefinitely.

"What's that mean?" Ellie asked.

"It means no cops," David said. He drove carefully around the sign.

When he spied a surplus shop on one corner, he pulled the Olds around the back and parked in a weedy lot. He shut down the engine and felt the car shudder, as if exhausted, all around him.

"Why did we stop?" Ellie asked.

"We need to rest. Just for a bit."

"Here?" She looked around the lot and at the scarred brickwork of the surrounding buildings, the sagging black telephone lines, the tumbledown collage of metal trash cans at the far end of the lot, the fizzing sodium street lamp—the only working light source—across the street. It seemed like every shadow moved, shifting almost imperceptibly, drawing the night closer to them.

"We'll try this store, see if the door's unlocked," he suggested. There was a metal door back here in the brickwork, situated at the top of some makeshift wooden stairs. Someone had spray-painted a Mr. Yuk face on it in neon green, as if the whole place was poison. "We can find some stuff to keep warm and maybe close our eyes for a bit. We can change our clothes, too, and use the bathroom." He was trying to sound upbeat, but by the look on his daughter's face, he could tell his suggestion had frightened her. He touched her shoulder and said, "Don't be afraid."

She looked toward the door with Mr. Yuk on it. "I'm not," she said. "I'm just worried that this isn't a good idea."

"Why do you say that?"

"Just a feeling."

"Should we try a different store?"

"It's not the store," she said, looking past him and out at the dark slip of roadway on the other side of the parking lot. The buildings there looked like the smokestacks of a sunken ocean liner. "It's this whole place. It feels wrong. Like something bad is gonna happen."

He squeezed her shoulder and said, "It just seems that way because it's empty. We'll be okay. I promise."

The look she gave him showed how little faith she had in his promises now. It was his own fault. He only hoped he could soon regain her trust.

He reached into the backseat and dragged the duffel bag into his lap. Without further protest, Ellie grabbed the pink suitcase and, tucking her shoe box beneath one arm, opened the passenger door.

The night was cold, and the air reeked of gasoline. David went up the wooden stairs and tried the door with the number seven on it. It was locked, and made of an industrial metal that would prove impossible to kick in.

"We'll try the front," he said, and they hurried around the side of the lot toward the street. Here, broken bits of glass glittered like jewels in the sidewalk cracks. A cardboard cup hopscotched down the center of the street on the breeze, briefly attracting their attention. At the street corner stood an old-fashioned arc lamppost, a massive spiderweb stretched inside the ninety-degree angle of its arm. Something large struggled in the web, and it wasn't until they drew closer that David saw it was a small mouse. The thing was partially cocooned in webbing, with only its head and tail exposed. Its tail whipped about frantically . . . then went still . . . then whipped about again.

"Jesus," David said, just as he caught movement along the lamppost directly above the web. A piece of darkness detached itself from the shadows and campaigned down the length of the post. When it reached the web and proceeded across it, moving at a steady clip now, David saw it was the spider it- self . . . though this thing was larger than any spider he had ever seen. It was nearly the size of a grown man's hand, its dark body and slender legs gleaming like armor in the moon- light. It advanced toward the struggling mouse, but not before it paused and seemed to scrutinize David and Ellie with inhu- man intelligence.

"Come on," David said, and ushered Ellie around the lamppost.

The door to the surplus shop was situated beneath a semi- circular cloth awning. It was locked, too, but the center of it was made of a single pane of smoked glass. A sign on the other side of the glass read CLOSED.

David pulled a T-shirt from his duffel bag, wrapped it around his knuckles, and punched a hole in the glass. Shards tinkled to the ground. He cleared away some jagged spears from the hole, then reached his hand inside to unlock the door.

"That's breaking in," Ellie said.

"No cops, remember?" He offered her a wan smile, but it did nothing to cool her stern reproach.

"Doesn't make it right," she said.

"Give your old man a break, will you?"

He shoved the door open and they went inside.

18

Thirteen months earlier

They stopped watching TV during dinner. It was a bad habit anyway, something they had just fallen into over the years, the three of them eating and talking but occasionally throwing glances at the shiny box atop the credenza in the living room. Kathy dressed it up like she was finally being responsible, and no responsible mother would allow their family to eat dinner with the TV on. But that wasn't the reason. Dinnertime was also news time, and Kathy had grown tired of the news. Tired . . . and frightened. As the death count mounted and pockets of newly infected cities cropped up, it was like watching the end of the world with the regularity of your favorite sitcom.

Kathy had replaced the noise of the TV by playing CDs on the stereo, usually some Miles Davis or John Coltrane from her jazz collection. But on this evening, when David came into the kitchen, there was nothing but silence as Kathy set the table. He glanced at the paper plates and the cans of Sprite that Kathy had set out. The scent of tomato sauce was in the air, but he was somewhat dismayed to see that she had only microwaved some cheap Celeste pizzas. She was sliding one of them out of the microwave when he came up behind her. She hissed, her finger burned, and she dumped the pizza onto the stove top.

"You okay?"

"Fine. Call Ellie. Dinner's ready."

"What's the matter?"

"Nothing's the matter." The frustration in her voice only confirmed for him that there was some problem. He had spent the afternoon cleaning out the garage and mowing the lawn— mechanical chores to keep his mind off more serious things— so he had been out of her hair for most of the day. It couldn't have been something he'd done.

Ellie was in her room, kneeling on a plush pink armchair and gazing out her bedroom window. She had long ago outgrown stuffed animals and baby dolls, her room a host now to science kits, books, a few board games, and a fairly expensive telescope David had gotten for her for Christmas two years earlier, despite Kathy's protestations that Ellie was too young for such a gift.

"Dinner's ready," he said, coming into the room. "Whatcha looking at?"

"I'm not looking," she said, not turning to face him. Her long auburn hair was woven into a braid that coursed down the slope of her back. "I'm waiting."

"Waiting for what?" he said, coming up behind her. He touched the back of her head and peered out the window with her. Instantly, David's eyes were drawn to Deke Car- mody's house—or, more appropriately, what *remained* of the house farther up the block. It had been approximately eight months since the fire and Deke's death, yet that smoldering black framework served as a constant and horrible reminder. On occasion, David still suffered nightmares about Deke, where he followed Deke through a house that was on fire all around them, choking on thick, black columns of smoke while pillars of white flame boiled out of the walls. In the nightmare, Deke was always a few steps ahead of him, his broad back covered in huge, weeping blisters, while the elas- tic band of his underwear burned. Whenever Deke would turn to look at David, which was blessedly infrequent in these dreams, the man's flesh had melted from his skull. Deke's eye sockets smoked. When Deke tried to speak, his larynx dropped from his throat and swung back and forth like a pendulum on fire.

"I'm waiting for the bird to come back," Ellie said, pulling him back into the present.

"What bird?"

"There," she said, pressing a finger to the windowpane.

It took David a moment to see what she was pointing at, but when he saw it, he smiled to himself. There was a wide hedgerow directly beneath Ellie's bedroom window. Tucked between some boughs was a bird's nest. Inside the nest were three pale eggs streaked with dark spots.

"Wow," he said. "Look at that."

"The mother hasn't come back," Ellie said. Her tone was grave, which always made her sound older than her years. "I'm worried she's abandoned them."

"She's probably out foraging for food," he said. "I bet she'll be back tonight."

"She didn't come back last night," said Ellie. "Or the night before that."

"Maybe she came when you were asleep."

She turned, studied his face. A vertical line formed between her eyebrows. "I wasn't," she said, quite matter-of-factly. "I was awake."

"Well, come on," he said. "Dinnertime." He paused in the doorway, then turned back. "Did you do something to upset your mother today?"

Ellie climbed down off the chair. "Nope," she said.

"You're sure? Mom seems angry."

"She's been like that since she came home from work yesterday."

Had she? David hadn't noticed.

In the living room, David switched on the stereo and inserted a Dave Brubeck album into the disc player. Once the music started, he adjusted the volume, then joined Ellie and Kathy in the kitchen.

"I'm feeling some wine," he said, going to the breakfront. He selected a bottle of cheap merlot. "You want some?"

"Sure," said Ellie.

"Ha," David said, retrieving two wineglasses from the shelf.

"No, thanks," Kathy said.

"Have some anyway," David said.

Kathy hardly spoke a word throughout dinner. David was thankful that Ellie was there to keep the conversation going. David did his best to keep things lively and ask questions of Ellie about summer vacation and her friends, but he kept glancing at Kathy across from him at the table. There were dark grooves beneath Kathy's eyes. Her mouth looked tight and drawn. Once, when she caught him staring at her, she didn't smile or even acknowledge him; she merely kept staring at him until it was he who looked away, an inexplicable feeling of shame causing his face to grow hot, as if he'd been caught spying on her doing something in private.

After dinner, Ellie went out back to play in the yard before it was fully dark. She said she wanted to look for more birds, in the event that those three abandoned eggs might need a surrogate.

"Where does she come up with this stuff?" he said, dumping the dirty paper plates into the trash. Kathy remained at the table. When he looked over his shoulder at her, he saw that she was refilling her wineglass.

He came up behind her, rubbed her back. "Tell me," he said. "What'd I do? If I'm going to sleep in the doghouse tonight, I'd at least like to know what I did that put me there."

She slid a hand up her shoulder and rested it atop one of his. "It isn't you," she said. Her voice was flat.

"Then tell me," he said. He pulled out the chair next to her and sat down. "What's wrong?"

"Three of the women in my office have gotten sick," Kathy said. She held the wineglass up in front of her face and stared at the bloodred wine as if she could discern some prophetic insight from it. "Two are already dead."

"Oh God . . ."

"And eleven patients."

"Jesus. *Dead?* Eleven? Was it—"

"Yes." She practically spat the word at him, exasperated. "What else would it be? Of course it's . . ." She didn't need to say it. Instead, she fluttered a hand at him.

"Are you worried you might be sick, too?"

She said nothing.

"Then make a doctor's appointment, Kath. Go see Bahethi. You can do it first thing on Monday."

"There's no need," Kathy said.

"Why?" He didn't like the defeat in her voice.

"The hospital has mandated that all remaining employees get blood tests to see who else might be infected."

He had heard about this on the news, but he wasn't sure how foolproof the blood tests were. It seemed the CDC didn't even know what they were dealing with yet, so how reliable could a blood test be?

"Okay," he said, digesting all of this. "Okay. Then get your blood test and you'll see. You'll see that everything's okay."

"I'm scared." She turned to him, her face pale, her eyes searching his.

"It's going to be all right," he said. He brought her close to him, hugged her.

She pushed him away and straightened up. "Have you seen the news? Have you read a newspaper? Jesus, David, they've started printing maps with all the cities where . . . where . . ." She shook her head, her thoughts too weighty for them to be spoken. "I don't know," she whispered, more to herself than to him, he thought. "I just don't know."

"There haven't been that many cases here," he said. "Not in Maryland. Not in this area."

She made a noise that sounded like part-laugh, part-cough. "Are you serious? Deke Carmody just down the street—"

"There was no proof he was sick."

"Of course he was! You said yourself you saw all that blood in his bathroom. The way he was acting, was talking . . . Don't you remember how worried you were about him when you came home that night? And then he sets fire to his own house . . ."

"That doesn't mean he had the disease," David said. Yet he knew right then and there that he was fighting a losing battle, and not just with Kathy, but with himself, too. Of *course* Deke had been sick. And not just Deke: All too clearly he was thinking of the ice cream man again, so long ago now, and so early in the game that none of them even knew about the illness that everyone was now calling Wanderer's Folly—a silly, almost innocuous name, which somehow also made it all the more terrifying.

"All right," Kathy said, calming down. She kissed his knuckles, then got up from the table with her wineglass. He listened to her footfalls move down the hallway. A moment later, he heard the tub's faucet clunk on.

Wanderer's Folly, he thought now, and it was suddenly impossible not to see what remained of Deke's house through the bay windows.

There was no certainty as to its origin, though many doctors, philosophers, and government officials reserved their own opinions. It was given a scientific name, some cryptic-sounding rubric cobbled from language in medical textbooks that proved a real tongue twister for newscasters, but it soon became known among the general public as Wanderer's Folly. Little was known about the illness, including its origin or exactly how it was contracted, except that it was a virus that apparently poisoned, attacked, and ultimately killed the brain. Early symptoms appeared harmless enough: a bit of brain fog, excessive daydreaming. More progressed symptoms were supposed to include mild hallucinatory stimulation—such as feeling cold when it was hot, or smelling things that were not there to be smelled—which only escalated as the virus grew stronger. In the middle stages, the infected supposedly found themselves more apt to act out their daydreams or even respond to the hallucinations as if they were real. Someone could spend hours wandering around a city park before realizing their lunch break was over and they were due back at work; someone might drive fifty or even a hundred miles off course of their destination before clearing their mind and wondering what had overtaken them; someone might believe they were standing in the middle of a beautiful orchard, a shiny bronze apple in each hand, when in reality they had wandered into their neighbor's garage.

Many of these symptoms were easy to overlook, even by someone who found themselves suffering from them. After all, how often did David zone out while grading papers? Wasn't it true that he could practically drive to the college on autopilot after all these years, paying no attention to road signs and exits?

It wasn't until the final stage that the disease made itself truly known. Instead of daydreaming through fields of sunflowers or apple orchards, several people took to meandering, terrified and confused, down an interstate and into oncoming traffic. Others walked off rooftops. Others—like Deke Carmody, David couldn't help but acknowledge—were found stumbling around outside in the middle of the night, often naked. Early in the game, a young mother in Nebraska set herself and her infant son on fire; witnesses observed her walking serenely from her house cradling the baby to her chest while both were engulfed in flames. A young man in Ohio became paranoid that there were tiny bugs under his flesh; he proceeded to shear the skin off his face with a steak knife while his wife stared at him in horror. It was reported that dozens and dozens of people would wake up one morning, get dressed, and drive to a job they hadn't held in years. In many ways the early stages of Wanderer's Folly mirrored Alzheimer's. Yet doctors were at a loss as to how to treat it. It was believed to be airborne, given how widespread it was, though epidemiologists were split on whether you had to breathe the disease into your body or if it simply gained access to the body through osmosis. Others went as far as suggesting that the virus itself wasn't alien to the human body, but was actually created within it, and functioned as some sort of built-in self-destruct button that, for reasons unknown, had suddenly been activated. But in truth, no one really knew anything for sure. For now, it was incurable. Incubation time varied. Once symptoms were exhibited, the person could last for hours or weeks, depending on what they might do to themselves during one of their hallucinatory spells. And in the end, the results were invariably the same as the brain ceased working altogether—death.

David rubbed absently at his chin, feeling the roughness of his two days' growth against his fingertips. Ellie always squealed when he kissed her while sporting beard stubble, and he would laugh and continue to rub his face against hers while she giggled and pretended to fight him off.

The sound of the back door closing jarred him from his reverie. Ellie stood there with dirt on her knees and her braid undone.

"What happened to you?"

"It's tough work," she said.

"What's that?"

"Looking for birds."

"You still worried about those eggs? You're being silly."

"They won't survive without a mother."

"Mama bird will come back."

"Not if someone touched the nest. Birds can smell if a human touches their nest. They won't come back, not even if there's babies in it."

"Did you touch the nest?"

"No way."

"Well, I certainly didn't. And I'm pretty sure Mom didn't, either. So you've got nothing to worry about. She'll come back."

"I don't think so," Ellie said. She went to the fridge, took an ice pop from the freezer, and proceeded to peel the wrapping off as she leaned against the dishwasher. "Haven't seen a bird all week."

"Yeah?" he said, still gazing at the charred struts and blackened brickwork of all that remained of Deke's house across the street.

"Nope. Not a single one," she said, and disappeared with her ice pop into the living room.

19

There was a staleness to the air, a gray moldiness that seemed to clot halfway along his nasal passageways. He thought about the events of the past several days, then stopped Ellie in her tracks with a single hand to her chest.

"Stay here," he said.

"Be careful." She sounded like an adult.

He crossed over to a display of camping gear, a trio of mannequins seated in camping chairs outside a bright orange pup tent, camouflaged knapsacks at their feet. He was alerted to a ghostly moan that started out low, then ascended through the octaves. He froze in place, looking around. The store looked empty; there was no movement from the rear of the shop, where darkness encroached upon racks of clothing and shelves laden with camping gear.

"There," Ellie said, pointing to a spot on the ceiling just above David's head.

He looked up and saw a set of bamboo wind chimes swaying from an acoustical tile; a gentle breeze was issuing in through the hole he'd punched in the glass and causing the bamboo chimes to howl.

In no time he was able to locate a battery-powered lantern, which he used to check out the rest of the shop before inviting Ellie to join him. Briefly, he fretted over the idea that the lantern's light would be visible to anyone who happened to stroll by the shop, but then he convinced himself he was being paranoid. Besides, it was important he execute a thorough

check of the place, lest he come across any undesirable sce-
nario at the end of one of the aisles or in one of the darkened
corners of the shop. He'd seen some in the past, and he didn't
want Ellie stumbling across anything perverse.

But there were no horrible scenes lying in wait for them.
The place hadn't even been ransacked, as far as David could
tell. He wondered if this was a good sign or a bad sign—why
hadn't the place been ransacked?—before convincing himself
that if he continued to overthink everything, he'd eventually
blow a gasket.

The only time he paused was when the lantern illuminated
a bright orange extension cord coiled like a cobra on a shelf.
The sight of it caused sweat to pop out on his forehead. The
hand holding the lantern began to tremble. He turned quickly
away from it.

"There's snacks," Ellie said, peering down into a glass display case. On the top shelf were boxes of protein bars.

"Grab a handful," David told her. He snatched two sleeping bags from a shelf and carried them over to a second tent
display set up in the center of the store. This tent was larger,
with a zippered flap at the front. He set down the lantern,
then unspooled each sleeping bag, tucking them partway into
the tent so that only their legs would poke out.

"I got a bunch," Ellie said, coming over with an armful of
protein bars. She set them down beside her suitcase and shoe
box, then examined David's setup.

"It'll be like camping," he said.

"Okay."

He took the baseball hat off her and rubbed a hand along
her head. Her short hair felt strange to him. "Make yourself
comfortable. I'll be back in a sec."

At the front of the store, there was a multitude of small items
by the register—little cylinders of Mace, a display of plastic
lighters, key chains, a rack of embroidered wallets, brightly
colored whistles, and slender metal canisters whose labels suggested the product was made with actual deer urine. David
stuffed several cans of Mace into his pockets, then grabbed

two fistfuls of lighters. He returned to the door, where broken javelins of glass sparkled in the moonlight across the floor. Meticulously, he went about placing the canisters of Mace and the plastic lighters in tidy little rows in front of the door.

"What's that for?" Ellie asked.

"In case someone comes in," he said. "They'll knock these over and we'll hear them."

"Like a trap?"

"More like an alarm system."

"Who would come in?" She was gazing out the window at the darkened street beyond.

"No one," he said. "It's just to be safe."

"Smart idea," she said.

"Yeah? Well, I got the idea from you, you know."

"From me? How?"

He stood up, his back aching. Wincing, he went over to a rack of hunting magazines and selected one. He nodded toward the counter and told Ellie to go back there and find him some tape or something. She returned with a spool of electrical tape.

"Perfect." David took the spool and tucked it under one arm while he tore the cover off the hunting magazine. He proceeded to tape the cover over the hole he'd knocked in the glass. "When you were around three years old," he said, "you used to set up some of your little toys in the front hall of the house, right by the front door. You did this every night before bed, without fail, for the longest time. One night I asked you why you did that, and you said it was in case someone ever tried to get in while we were asleep, they'd trip over the toys and we'd hear them and wake up. Do you remember?"

Ellie shook her head. Her eyes were huge in the semidarkness.

"Your mom and I called it the Night Parade—all those little toy figurines marching across the floor, keeping watch over us while we slept. Protecting us."

"Did anyone ever break in?"

"No. But I nearly broke my neck over them a few times,

stumbling around in the middle of the night for a glass of water or to go to the bathroom."

"What was I so afraid of?"

"I never thought of it that way. You were just a smart kid," he said. "You still are."

"Were you there when Mom died?"

He felt something stick in his throat. The question had caught him off guard.

"Dad?" she said when he didn't answer. "Were you with her?"

"Yes," he said.

"How did it happen? Did she get the disease?"

"No," he said. "Those doctors, they used her up, Ellie. They were . . . they were too hard on her, and her body, it just gave out. She had gotten so weak. But those doctors, they didn't listen." He could summon a picture of Dr. Sanjay Kapoor's face now, and all the anger, still fresh and boiling and very near the surface, welled up inside of him as quickly as if he were being inflated with air. He briefly closed his eyes.

"Did she hurt?" Ellie asked. A single tear slid down her cheek; it shimmered like a jewel in the moonlight.

"No, baby, she didn't hurt." Yet he was picturing Kathy's face now and knew that she had. Down deep.

"Those doctors should have listened to you. If they thought Mom was the cure, they should have been more careful with her."

"Yes. They should have."

She hugged him, her face pressed against his chest. "I'm sorry you had to be there," she said.

"It's okay," he said, rubbing her head. "It's okay. It's okay." Then he pawed at his eyes, cleared his throat, and smiled down at his daughter. "We'll be okay," he promised.

"Okay," Ellie said.

"Let's go lie down."

They returned to their little campsite in the middle of the store. Ellie pulled off her shoes, then crawled into the tent, carrying the shoe box of bird eggs with her.

David felt grimy, but his exhaustion made the little door with the word RESTROOM on it at the back of the store seem a million miles away. He stripped off his own shoes and pants, already feeling the chill in the air prick his bare thighs. After a moment of consideration, he wrapped the Glock in his jeans and tucked it beneath his sleeping bag. He bent down and parted the tent flaps. Ellie sniffled quietly in the gloom inside the tent.

"How 'bout a bedtime story?"

She sniffed again and said, "Okay. What story?"

He undid the clasps of the little pink suitcase and rifled through the items he'd taken from the Langstrom house. Without thinking, he had dumped a few books in there; looking at them now, he saw that many of them were probably too immature for Ellie. But then he saw the crinkled dust jacket and recognized a book from his own youth—a hardcover edition of *Where the Sidewalk Ends.*

"This," he said, climbing into the tent to join his daughter, "is a great book. I had a copy when I was about your age."

"Where'd you get this copy?"

"Just someplace. Hey, do you want me to read or what?"

"What's it about?" She snuggled closer to him as he turned on the electric lantern. Their shadows bloomed like great arching beasts on the walls and ceiling of the tent.

"Poems. Do you like poems?"

He felt her shrug against him. "Some, I guess."

"Well, you'll like these. They're pretty clever."

He opened the cover, and before he could turn to the title page, Ellie's hand was up, her fingers splayed across the book.

"Wait," she said. "What's that say?"

It was a handwritten inscription on the blank white page. David adjusted the book so that she could read it for herself in the lamplight.

To our little Moon-Bird,
Wishing you the happiest of birthdays!
Love, Mom & Dad

"Who wrote that?"

David had an idea, but he pretended like he didn't.

"Who's Moon-Bird?"

"Just someone's name, I guess," he said. His exhaustion was like a physical weight pressing down on him now. It was a struggle just to keep his eyelids open.

"Strange name," Ellie said.

"Probably a nickname. Like how I call you Little Spoon."

"But not anymore, remember?"

"That's right. I remember. Not anymore. So can we read a bit so we can get some sleep?"

She curled up against him. He could smell her sweet-sour breath, the odor of her unwashed hair, the heat radiating from her body. Again, Kathy's face flashed before his eyes, and it was all he could do not to groan in utter grief at the thought of her.

When his heartbeat slowed and the jitteriness of the day seemed to evaporate from him, he realized Ellie was touching his arm with both hands.

"Are you doing it now?" he asked.

"Yes. Is that okay?"

It was a level of peace, of comfort, that he hadn't experienced since he was a child. Yet something else invaded his thoughts. "What is it doing to you?"

"Nothing," she said.

"How does it happen?"

"I don't know. I'm just taking the badness out of you."

"So where does that badness go?"

"I don't know."

"Maybe it's doing something bad to you," he said.

"I don't think it is."

"But you don't know, do you?" he said. When she didn't respond, he said, "Do you, El?"

"No."

"Let's maybe not do it until we understand it better," he said. "Okay?"

"Okay." Her palms lifted from him. She encircled his arm

in an embrace. A moment later, he felt a tremor of anxiety pulse through him. The heaviness of it all was back, just as quickly as Ellie had chased it away.

"Okay," he said, turning to the first poem. "Let's read."

So they read, and David was halfway through the third poem when Ellie's breathing softened and she began to snore quietly against him. He paused in midverse and said her name aloud. When she didn't respond, he closed the book, turned off the lantern, and shut his eyes.

For a time, the whole world was comprised of the whooshing sound of his heartbeat in his ears. He focused on Ellie's gentle snoring, but after a while, it seemed that her snores grew more and more distant, as if some great expanse of space had gradually begun to separate them. He dreamt. And at some point, his dreams segued into a nightmare, which concluded when men in dark suits stuffed Ellie into a nondescript white van and drove her away.

20

Ten months earlier

After a number of other students and two teachers got sick at Ellie's elementary school, David and Kathy decided to pull their daughter out. Many other parents did the same, which made it difficult to find tutors. The few tutors Kathy was able to locate were already setting up mini-classrooms in their homes and tutoring anywhere from five to ten kids at the same time.

"That's no different from sending her to school," Kathy argued. "She's still around other kids who might be carrying something."

"Well, it's still less kids. The chances of exposure are much, much lower."

It was a pointless thing to say, and David recognized that the second the words were out of his mouth. To date, it was still not known how the illness was transferred from one host to another. There had been countless reports where only a single member of a family had contracted the illness; on the other hand, there were the nightly reports that told what U.S. cities had the highest rate of infection, though no one could understand what made those particular cities more susceptible. The National Guard had moved in to some of these areas to maintain control and to begin quarantine procedures. The images of quarantined suburban neighborhoods on the nightly news were disturbing—street corners and intersections no different from any other throughout the country patrolled by military vehicles; soldiers in fatigues wearing gas masks, assault rifles strapped to their chests; children with masks over their mouths playing soccer behind a fence capped in concertina wire surrounding the perimeter of the quarantined zone.

"What happens if someone wants to leave?" Kathy asked him on one of the rare nights she agreed to watch the news with him.

"I suppose they don't let them."

"But what if they *try* to leave?"

"They'll stop them."

"How?"

"However they can."

"Do you think they'd really shoot someone?"

"Probably not," he said, although he didn't know this for sure.

"Then what's with all the guns?"

"Intimidation factor," he suggested.

"What about kids?" she said, and for a split second David thought she was changing the subject. Back before this whole mess had started, they had contemplated having a second child. Wanderer's Folly had put their intentions on hold, but he wondered now if she had been thinking about it all along.

"What about them?" he said.

"If some kids tried to leave, do you think they'd shoot them?"

"Those guards?" he said, nodding at the TV. On the screen, a National Guardsman who looked no older than nineteen stood frowning at the camera. He was waving the cameraperson away and pointing toward something offscreen. David wondered if the news crew was actually attempting to get inside the quarantined perimeter. "I don't know, hon. Like I said, I think those guns are mostly for intimidation. They're probably not even loaded."

"Bullshit." Kathy got up and went into the kitchen.

Her blood test from work had come back clean, but in the time since, her attitude hadn't improved. She'd remained agitated, nervous, quick to bite his head off. Her behavior had caused an opposite reaction in him, as he felt responsible for maintaining some stability, some normalcy, in the household and not to spiral into panic. He kept trying to rationalize the situation, to present her with facts that might ease her mind. Maryland boasted some of the lowest numbers of infected persons. Things would be okay.

He got up and went to the kitchen in time to see Kathy throw a pill into her mouth and follow it up with a glass of water.

"What's that you're taking?"

"What's it matter to you?"

"Please," he said. "Please stop."

She set the glass down on the counter, then folded her arms over her chest. She was wearing just a tank top, and David could see the tiny braille knobs of gooseflesh pimpling up on her shoulders. He, too, felt a slight chill in the air.

He picked up the medicine bottle, read the label.

"Zoloft."

"So?"

"These aren't even prescribed to you. Who's Jeanette Vasquez?"

"A secretary at work."

"Are you kidding me? You're taking someone else's antidepressant meds?"

"I just wanted to see if they would take the edge off. I've got an appointment with Bahethi next week for my own prescription."

"You really need these?"

"I'm losing it, David. I'm a paranoid mess. Haven't you noticed?"

"You're overreacting, is what you're doing."

"How many students at your college have died?"

"I don't know," he said. He'd stopped counting after the first dozen. "But none of them were ever my students."

She made some snorting sound that approximated a laugh. "So? What does that mean? Tell me."

"I'm just saying that we're okay, that I haven't been exposed to anything, and that we're going to be just—"

"How can you say that? No one even knows what actual 'exposure' even is! It could be airborne. It could be in our drinking water, our food. We could both be breathing it in right now."

"Relax," he said.

"Don't tell me to relax. We've got a little girl in there who we've pulled out of school, and now we can't even get someone to tutor her because half the tutors are afraid to be around people, and the ones who are working are so overbooked we might as well send her right back to that goddamn school."

"Keep your voice down. You'll wake her."

Kathy dragged her hands down her face. Her fingernails left reddish tracks against her otherwise pale skin. Her eyes were sober, her mouth a perfect slit. Kathy had never been much of a crier; when she got frightened or upset, she got angry.

"I'm terrified of going back to work," she said.

"So quit."

"Just like that?"

"Why not?"

"What about the money? The mortgage?"

She made more as a therapist at a state hospital than he did as an untenured instructor at the college. They had discussed her cutting back some hours in the past, particularly when Ellie was younger, but in the end they had always agreed that their budget was tight enough already. Now, however, he was willing to give in. If it gave her peace of mind, he would make it work.

"Let me worry about that," he said. "We can make it work if we need to. And if you're home, then our tutor problems are solved. You can home-school her."

For some reason, Kathy found this deliciously funny. She barked laughter, but there was no humor in it. It left him cold.

"You're the teacher in the family," she said after her laughter subsided.

"Yeah, but you've got a Ph.D. You've *attended* more school than me."

"Fair enough."

. He kissed the side of her face. Then he went back into the living room, still feeling cold. He shut the TV off and just sat there on the sofa, staring out the windows at the night sky. Nervous, he chewed at the inside of his cheek. It was too quiet with the TV off, so he turned it back on and flipped it to some sitcom. After a time, the kitchen light went out. Kathy leaned out of the doorway and said she was going to bed.

"Good night," he said, and closed his eyes for a few seconds while fake laughter filtered through the TV. Outside, a light rain began to fall; he listened to it patter against the roof and sluice down the eaves. Soon enough, thunder announced its presence with a low, guttural growl that sounded like the banging of garage doors.

On his way to bed, he peeked in on Ellie. He was surprised—and a little startled—to find her silhouetted against the moonlit windowpane, staring out at the storm.

"Hey," he said.

She spun around, similarly startled by the sound of his voice. "Oh," she uttered, a squeaky half-sound. She leapt from the armchair and into bed.

"You should have been in bed already," he said, coming over and pulling the blanket up to her shoulders. He wondered if she had heard them arguing earlier.

"It's getting cold. They'll freeze."

"Who?"

"The eggs."

He'd forgotten about them. That first discussion about the abandoned eggs had been back in August. He went to the window and peered out, though he couldn't see the nest in the darkness.

"I'm not so sure it matters anymore, Little Spoon."

"It matters," she said.

It was less the substance of what she said than the tone in

which she said it that caused him to pause and consider his daughter. *It matters.* It wasn't the tone, the cadence, of a young girl playing or even declaring a statement of fact to her father. It was said as if he was a fool and blind to the reality of the things around him. Over time, David had grown accustomed to the premature adultness of his daughter, but this was something else. A conspiracy she was allowing him to glimpse, even if she couldn't come right out and tell him what it was. She wanted him to see something and he was too damn ignorant to open his eyes.

"No more bird-watching," he told her, kissing her nose.

"What birds?" she said. "The birds are all gone."

"Go to sleep."

"Good night, Dad."

"Good night, Little Spoon."

He left her room feeling like he had overlooked something. Something important.

21

He awoke in the morning to find Ellie gone.

He sat up sharply, only to have a shock wave of burning pain radiate across the right side of his neck. The top flap of Ellie's sleeping bag was flipped over. Her sneakers were gone.

"Ellie?" His voice echoed through the empty store. "Eleanor?"

He got up and went to the restroom door. It was closed. He knocked but Ellie did not answer. He opened the door and found the restroom empty.

At the front of the store, the door was still closed and locked. The magazine cover was still taped over the hole in the glass and it didn't appear as if the Night Parade of lighters and cans of Mace had been disturbed. No one had come into the store and no one had gone out.

"Eleanor!"

The only response was from the wind chimes above his head; they tinkled as they swayed in a soft breeze.

What breeze?

He thought simultaneously of the back door and the Glock wrapped up in his jeans, stuffed beneath his sleeping bag. He went quickly to their little campsite, fumbled the gun out onto the sleeping bag, then hastily climbed into his jeans. He headed straight to the back of the store toward the door. It was a fire exit, marked as such by a sign posted close to the ceiling, and it was propped open. A cone of daylight spilled across the scuffed linoleum floor.

David winced as he stepped outside. Aside from the Olds-mobile and a few trash cans strewn about, the parking lot was just as deserted as it had been the night before. Across the street, the storefronts looked empty. There was no movement anywhere. The only sounds came from the cicadas in the trees, emitting their mechanical buzzing.

Was this how the world was to end? Not with a bang and not even with a whimper, but with the slow deterioration of everything good and beautiful and kind? With a sky absent of birds, a world overrun by insects, of droning cicadas and kaiju spiders, and a daughter who simply vanished into thin air while he slept through a matinee of chilling nightmares?

He was losing it; that much was suddenly clear. *Get a grip, get a grip.* He realized that if he hadn't had Ellie to take care of, he might have done something terrible to himself long ago. He would have done it right after Kathy had died.

It seems like a hundred years ago that she died, but it's only been two days. Two goddamn days.

(get a grip get a grip)

He hopped down the steps and crossed the parking lot to the sidewalk. He held the gun out in front of him, but it suddenly seemed impossibly cumbersome, as if it had grown heavier while he slept. He paused in the middle of the side street, flanked on both sides by crumbling brick buildings, and considered shouting his daughter's name. But before he could make up his mind, he caught movement on the other side of the main street—a minute shift beneath the lee of a storefront awning.

He hurried across the street, his jog turning into a full sprint as he recognized Ellie's slight form beneath the awning. She had her back to him and was peering into the darkened windows of a defunct bistro, hands bracketing her eyes.

"Ellie," he said, rushing up to her and grabbing her by the wrist.

The girl spun around to face him . . . and for a moment, her face wasn't hers, it wasn't even a face at all, but a blank, featureless bulb of flesh, like unmolded putty. But then she was staring at him, perfectly normal, except for the terror in her eyes. His panic had distorted reality.

"What the hell are you doing out here?" he said.

"I thought I saw someone," she said, tugging her wrist free of his grip. Her gaze focused on the gun, which he quickly tucked into the rear waistband of his jeans.

"There's no one here," he told her. "Let's get back inside."

"No." She peered beyond him for a moment before meeting his eyes. "I saw someone. A man."

David scanned the block. Discarded newspapers waved in the cool breeze, and a few bits of trash bounded along the sidewalk. Other than that, the world was silent and motionless.

"All the more reason to get back inside," he said in the end, and reached out for Ellie's wrist again.

"Shit," Ellie said. She took a step back from him. Yet her eyes were no longer on him; they had refocused on something just over David's shoulder.

David spun around to see a man quickly crossing the street. He was maybe twenty yards away and closing fast. He held a shotgun in both hands, the barrel pointed at David's chest.

"Daddy," Ellie moaned.

"Shhh," he told her, and instinctively stepped in front of her. He raised both hands. "It's okay," he yelled to the approaching man; it was the first thing that came to his mind, and he hated the terrified, pleading quality of his voice. "We're not doing anything."

"You've got a gun," the man said. It was not a question. The man stopped less than five yards away, wedging himself between two parked cars. The barrel of the shotgun shook. David couldn't see the man's face behind it.

"Yes. For protection. Same as you."

"Put your hands on your head and turn around."

"Please, man. I've got my kid here. What do you want?"

"For you to put your hands on your head and turn around." The barrel of the shotgun lowered the slightest bit, but it was enough for David to make out a portion of the man's face. He had a gingery beard and a sunburned face. His eyes were pale blue and intense. The barrel came back up again as the man said, "Do what I say and I won't shoot you. I'm just going to take your gun for my own protection."

David placed his hands atop his head, then turned around. He looked down at Ellie, who looked more curious now than frightened. Her gaze volleyed between David and the man with the shotgun, finally settling on the shotgun man because, presumably, he was more interesting.

"You run if I tell you," David whispered to her.

Ellie nodded but did not take her eyes from the man with the gun.

David heard the man's footsteps approach. He saw the guy's shadow ahead of him on the sidewalk, which meant he saw when the gun was lowered, but he didn't feel right about turning on the guy and trying to fight. He doubted he'd be quick enough to knock the shotgun from his hands.

The Glock was yanked from his waistband. A second later, one of the man's hands began patting around his waist, his thighs, both his ankles.

"I've got no other weapons," he assured the man.

"Okay," the man said. "You can turn around."

David did. Slowly. He still held his hands atop his head, but when Ellie came up beside him, he reached down and stopped her with a hand across her chest.

"It's all right," said the man. "You can put your hands down."

"Can you lower your gun?"

"Shit. Sorry." The man lowered the shotgun. He looked to be about David's age, but in better shape: Pectoral muscles pulled taut the fabric of the plain blue T-shirt he wore. His head was shaved, though David could tell by the darkened widow's peak of stubble that he had already started losing his hair. Drops of sweat glistened in the man's beard. "What's your name?"

"David. This is Eleanor. My daughter." It was just after he said this that he realized his carelessness. Their names had been on the news. People were looking for them. If this guy made the connection, the game was over.

Ellie grabbed David's right hand. Squeezed.

"Where'd you folks come from?"

"Back East. We got a bit turned around on our way to see my brother. We didn't think . . ." He trailed off, unsure what to say.

"You didn't see the signs posted? The crosses and the what-have-you?" To David's surprise, the man laughed. It wasn't an aggressive or humorless laugh, but a good, hearty country laugh. "Jesus, boy, this place is a ghost town. Who's your brother? Maybe I know him."

"He doesn't live around here. We're headed to Texas." He thought up the state at the last second, reluctant to give this guy any additional information that might prove useful to the police or anyone else who might be looking for them later on.

"He's my stepuncle," Ellie volunteered.

"Is that right?" The man smiled at her. There was genuine goodness there, David decided . . . though he'd been wrong about people in the past. "My name's Turk." The smile fell from his lips as he looked up and down the street. "We should probably get back indoors. You folks hungry?"

"We're okay," David said.

"Nonsense. We got food back at the house. Seriously. That little gal of yours looks about famished."

"I'm supposed to be a boy," Ellie said, though low enough so that David didn't think the man had understood.

"We should really get on the road," David said.

"Just a bite," Turk said. Smiling.

"What if I asked for my gun back and for you to just leave us alone?"

Turk's smile faltered. "Well, now, this ain't a hostage situation, Dave. Can I call you Dave?"

"Sure."

"You're both welcome to leave. It's still a free country, last

I checked. A fucked-up one at the moment, but a free one. Oops." He covered his mouth and made bug eyes at Ellie. "Sorry for the profanity, darling."

Ellie just stared at him.

"Couldn't give you the gun back, though," Turk said. "Don't rightly know who you are or what you plan to do with it."

"I plan on leaving with it. That's all."

"Sure, sure. But, you see, we've got to protect our own. Ain't no one 'round to do it for us no more." He nodded at the sandwich board farther down the street, the sign that said there was no longer a police presence in Goodwin.

"So, I'm never going to get my gun back?"

"We'll let Solomon make that call. It's his to make, not mine. He's runnin' the show now. In the meantime, Pauline can whip you folks up some breakfast. I'm starved myself."

He's got my gun. I'm defenseless. Should we leave it with him and get out of here? Would he really just let us leave?

Just then, a chubby boy of about seven or eight appeared around the corner of the row of buildings at the end of the block. He wore a striped polo shirt and khaki shorts. He froze when he saw David and Ellie, his full cheeks flushed and red, his eyes squinting and piggish.

"Pop?" the kid said.

Turk turned and waved to the boy. "Get on back now, Sam. Tell Mom these nice folks will be joining us for breakfast."

There was no acknowledgment in the boy's expression; he simply pivoted right there on his heels and took off in a labored trot in the direction he had come.

He's got a son. Can this guy be that bad if he's got a son?

"Pancakes, bacon, and home fries," said Turk. "Yeah, boy." He winked at Ellie, then turned and sauntered up the block, the shotgun leaning on one broad shoulder. Before Turk turned the corner to join his son, David noticed his handgun poking up from the waistband of the man's pants.

22

Turk led them three or four blocks off the main thorough-fare, where the stores and traffic lights surrendered to a grid of single-family homes. The street was quaint and lined with oaks, their branches bare this late in the season. There were many cars parked along the street and in a number of the driveways, but David did not see another living soul, with the exception of Turk's chunky son, who traipsed ahead of them, wading through drifts of dead leaves and peering back at them every once in a while. There were no lights on in any of the houses, no blue flashes from TVs in the windows. Worse than that were the red *X*'s emblazoned on every single front door, like some curse had befallen this quiet suburban neighbor-hood. Looking at every door, David realized that was exactly what had happened—that a curse had befallen this community and all the people who'd once lived here. All the world, really.

"Newspapers said this place had been evacuated," David said, sidling up beside Turk as they followed his son through a yard.

"Yep."

"Is there anyone else here besides your family?"

Turk offered him a sidelong glance. "Absolutely," Turk said. "Some just ain't as friendly as me an' my family. Best to keep that in mind."

They followed Turk's boy onto the front lawn of a quaint bungalow with lime-colored siding and an American flag hanging from the porch. The name on the mailbox read POW-

ELL. There was a red X on the front door here, too, but Turk didn't bother mentioning it as he led them up the porch, opened the door, and waved both David and Ellie inside.

David took Ellie's hand and entered the house with some trepidation. The first thing that struck him was the smell of food cooking—bacon, toast, coffee—and he felt his stomach flip; he hadn't realized just how hungry he'd been until that moment. The smell of the food set him somewhat at ease, though he did not let go of Ellie's hand. When he glanced down at her, he saw her licking her lips. He laughed and ran a hand through her hair.

"Baby," Turk called down the hallway. "We got company. Break out the good china." Then he turned and winked at David, as if he'd just gotten off a good joke.

"I'm Sam," said Turk's boy. He'd inched closer to Ellie as they stood in the foyer, and now it looked like he might actually reach out and grasp her hand.

"I'm Ellie."

"Like the letters? L and E?"

"No. It's short for Eleanor."

"Oh." The tip of the boy's tongue poked out one corner of his mouth. There was a smudge of something on his forehead—grease or dirt. "Do you want to come see my room?"

"No," Ellie said flatly.

"Not just yet," David softened, grinning at the boy.

"C'mon," Turk said.

David and Ellie followed Turk down the hall. The smell of the food grew more substantial, causing David's stomach to clench painfully. It was a simple country kitchen with curtains over a wall of windows, a tidy kitchen table already set with plates and glasses, and wallpaper with little roosters on it. A woman stood before the stove, slim and pretty, with a plain face that needed no makeup. She looked up from a frying pan, a somewhat bemused expression on her face at the sight of David and Ellie. Her mouth opened, but she said nothing.

Turk made the introductions. "This is Dave. And that's his

daughter, Eleanor. Found them wandering along Bixby like they just fell from the sky or something." He leaned over the stove, inhaled, grinned. "Smells delicious." He pecked his wife's cheek. To David, he said, "This is my wife, Pauline."

"Hiya," she said. The surprised look had yet to leave her face.

"Hello," David said.

"Well, it's a good thing I made extra," she said. Then she swatted Turk on the rear end. "Show these nice folks where the washroom is, then set a couple more plates."

"Sammy," Turk said, opening the fridge and peering inside. "Go on, now."

"I'll show you," Sam said, slipping around the table and back out into the hall. David and Ellie followed him to a small bathroom. "Flush if you pee," Sam instructed, then left them to it.

David closed the bathroom door.

"Why did you have a gun?" Ellie said.

"For protection."

"Where did you get it?"

He sighed and rubbed at his forehead. "Hey. I'm the parent, remember?"

"I don't like it here. In this house."

"It'll be okay."

"It's the same feeling I had last night, when we first got here. It doesn't feel right."

"Let's just be polite, and then we can go after breakfast." He turned on the tap. "Wash up."

She went to the sink while he went to the toilet. He hadn't urinated since last night, and his bladder ached. "You okay stepping out in the hall while I go to the bathroom?"

"Don't want to," she said, shutting off the water.

"Well, turn your head. Look at the wall or something."

She turned her back to him as he unzipped his jeans. David stared up at the ceiling until he began to urinate. Midway through the process, Ellie said, "Wow. How long are you gonna pee?"

David tried to stifle a laugh, which only caused a bubble of snot to burst from his right nostril. "Keep quiet, will you?" he said, snatching a swath of toilet paper and blowing his nose.

Before they went back out in the hall, David said, "Just for the record, our last name is Smith. Okay?"

"That sounds phony-baloney."

"Yeah? Then what name should we use?"

"Monroe," she said. It was the last name of her best friend from school, David knew.

"Yeah, okay. Monroe. Just don't volunteer it. You get me?"

"Sure. Don't forget to wash your hands. You peed."

"Christ." He washed his hands, then opened the bathroom door.

Sam was standing there, waiting for them.

"Oh," David said. "Hello."

"Food's up," Sam said, and led them back to the kitchen.

23

David relaxed throughout the meal, which was delicious, and by the time his plate was clean, he was completely at ease with the Powells. Pauline was a wonderful cook, and she was more than happy to give both David and Ellie second helpings of everything. The pancakes were thick and fluffy, and there was a richness to the cooked meat that was both unusual and superb. David assumed he was just ravenous. By the third time David expressed how delicious the meal was, Pauline waved a hand at him and said, "Well, you're too kind, but it's darn hard to screw up premade pancake batter."

During the meal, and for the sake of the children, they kept the conversation light. The tone shifted only once, when a resounded trill of a distant Klaxon interrupted the meal. It sounded disconcertingly like an air-raid siren.

Turk sensed their discomfort. "That's the firehouse down on Cotton Road," he said. "There's some folks holed up there."

"People like you?" Ellie said.

"Unfortunately, little darling, that's not the case." He turned his attention to David. "Like I said before, there's some folks around here you gotta be careful of. The people down at the firehouse, well, they're sort of like a cult, I guess you'd say."

"Are they Worlders?" David said, referring to the burgeoning sect of people who believed that Wanderer's Folly was nature's way of cleaning the slate, a biological Noah's Ark.

They were opposed to any attempt to come up with a cure for the illness. David had read about them in the newspaper and a bit online. Their numbers were growing, their sects cropping up all throughout the United States and overseas.

"I don't think they're as crazy as all that, although they're probably pretty close," Turk said. "There were some rumors before the evac that some guy was healing the sick. Real sorcerer-type shit. He wound up gathering up himself a small congregation, too."

"False prophet," said Pauline.

Turk nodded. "They waited out the evac, same as we did, and now they're holed up in the firehouse. Got weapons, too, I've heard. They sound their alarm once a day to let people know they're still there."

"Did they heal someone who had the Folly?" Ellie asked.

"They ain't healed no one, sweetheart," Turk said. "Was just stories. They want you to believe in their witchcraft."

"Lord knows what they do to any poor soul who hears that siren and happens to follow it to them," Pauline said. She genuflected.

"What does he look like?" Ellie asked. "The false prophet."

Turk stared at her for a moment, then shook his head. "Ain't never seen him. Only hear his siren. That banshee call."

"Because I saw someone this morning," Ellie said. "Just before you found us on the street. I saw someone and I thought maybe he wanted us to follow him."

David placed a hand on Ellie's shoulder.

"Then you're lucky I found you both when I did," Turk said.

A moment later, the siren ceased. The silence that followed seemed preternatural.

Once Sam had finished his meal, he invited Ellie to go play in the yard. David nodded his approval and Ellie got up from her chair, albeit reluctantly. David was comfortable enough around this family to permit it, not to mention he had a perfect view of the backyard from the kitchen windows. He told her to stay within sight and she nodded obediently. She looked miserable. A moment later, Sam was sprinting across the back lawn while Ellie, almost cautiously, walked behind him.

"Why don't I clean up while you boys finish your coffee on the porch," Pauline suggested as she stood and gathered some plates.

"Sounds like a plan," Turk said. He practically rocketed out of his seat. Slapping David on the forearm, he said, "You smoke?"

"Sure."

"Let's do it."

It was more a mudroom than a porch, but it caught a good breeze and the day was warming up all around them, so sitting out there turned out to be pleasant enough. Turk offered him an unfiltered Camel, and they smoked and drank their coffee while, in the yard, Sam executed cartwheels as Ellie watched him with an expression of utter perplexity.

"So where you from exactly?" Turk asked him.

David took too much time thinking of an answer. By the time he spit out, "Outside D.C.," Turk was already smiling wryly to himself and shaking his head.

"Listen," Turk said, leaning closer to David over the armrest of his chair. "The world's a changed place, *amigo*. What's happened in the past is in the past, you dig? I'll only ask you one question and one question only." He nodded toward the yard. "That really your little girl out there?"

"Yes."

"All right. Then everything else is cake, my friend."

"What happened here?" David asked.

"Ain't it obvious? The Folly come through."

"Yeah, but why did Goodwin get hit so hard? Things weren't half this bad back home. There are still businesses open on the interstate and other cities seem like they're doing just fine. Why'd you guys get it so badly?"

"God's will," Turk said. "What else could it be? We've stopped thinking on the whys of it some time ago. Ain't no one we can blame. We just gotta make do." He pointed due east. "Half the whole neighborhood went in just three days—boom, boom, boom. Jus' like that. People got sick, started dying right in the streets. Most of 'em acting crazy when they went. That's when people started picking up and leaving, but then the National Guard moved in and quarantined the place. Couldn't get out and they weren't lettin' no one in."

"I saw places like that on the news."

"Yeah, well, what they don't tell you is them guardsmen, they was all too afraid to come in here and lay down the law. They just stood on the other side of that fence and made sure no one walked out. Heck, they was just a bunch of scared kids themselves. But in here, in the thick of it, it was every man for his self. Martial law turned anarchy. After a time, they forced the evac and sent whoever was left to . . . well, to hospitals, supposedly, but I don't believe that for a second."

"No?"

"Where you gonna put up a whole town? Nearest hospital is T.J. Samson over in Glasgow, and they ain't got the staff or the room for ever'body."

"So, what do you think happened to them?"

Turk sucked on his cigarette, then blew rings into the air. "You don't wanna know what I think, Dave."

"Sure I do."

He rubbed a hand across his shaved scalp. "Rounded up and sent to some test facility someplace, is my best guess. The evacuees were still healthy, or so they seemed, so I'm guessing the government's prob'ly interested in *why* they're still healthy. So now they're test subjects. Guinea pigs. Sounds paranoid, but it's what I believe."

"You're not the only one. I've read some articles about that recently." But he wasn't thinking about newspaper articles. He was thinking about Kathy.

"Yeah, well, I wasn't going to let that happen to my family."

"They didn't force you to leave?"

Again, Turk gave him that strange sidelong glance, which David interpreted as a suggestion not to delve too deeply into what Turk and his family had had to do to survive.

"You mentioned someone named Solomon," David said, redirecting the conversation. "How many other people stayed behind?"

"We've got three more staying with us," Turk said. "Four, if you include Solomon. Then there're those nutters down at the firehouse, like I mentioned earlier. Lord knows how many they've got in their ranks now. There're more out there besides them, too, but like I said, you'd best want to steer clear of 'em." Turk thumped an index finger against his cranium. "Some ain't right in the head. You dig?"

"What's your plan?"

Turk frowned. Behind the veil of cigarette smoke, he suddenly looked much older than he had when they'd first met out on the street. "Plan? What do you mean?"

"You can't stay here forever," David said.

"Why not?"

"Well—"

"We get everything we need from town. Don't cost nothin' 'cause there ain't nobody there to charge us. Anything else we might need, we get in a car and drive there. The rest of the world's still ticking. Mostly, anyways. Said so yourself."

"What about your son? What about school?"

"Pauline schools him."

"But those other people out there in town—the people at the firehouse and all the others. Heck, you stuck a gun in my face because you didn't know who I was. This environment can't be good for Sam in the long run."

Turk laughed. "The long run? Just how much time you think this world has got, boy?"

David just stared at him. It was by no means a unique notion, but it troubled him to hear Turk espouse it in such a flippant manner. Worse still was the man's apparent resignation to it—that they were all going to die in the end, and that no one would be spared this illness, so why fight it? They just sat there eating their hearty breakfasts and looted deserted stores and waited for the end.

"You can't think like that," David said. "We're still healthy. Our kids are still healthy. Maybe there's hope."

"Maybe. Maybe not. Could be many of us will be spared, and we'll just have to pick up the pieces once this thing . . . well, once it blows over, I guess. But, see, there comes a point when you got to take a look around and say, hey, what the heck am I livin' for? The world's gone to shit, most of my loved ones are dead, and things are just gonna get worse and worse. It's like them zombie apocalypse movies. You know the ones I'm talking about? Folks in those movies are always struggling to stay alive, to get from one place to the next place, to do whatever they got to do . . . but for what? You really want to live like that? For-fucking-*ever?* No, thanks."

Jesus, David thought. Yet what troubled him most was what Kathy had said to him on the last night in their home together, a thing that echoed almost verbatim Turk's sentiments . . .

"I've become quite the religious man, Dave," Turk said. He produced two more cigarettes and handed one to David. "Something like this, a man can't help but fall back on his faith. And you know what I figure? I figure this is the rapture. This is our penance. This is the final plague. We're talking real-life book of Revelation shit, my friend."

"You sound like a Worlder now," David said.

"No." Turk held up a finger. His expression was stern. "Those peckerheads, they're like Wiccans. They want to see Mother Nature drag things back to the Stone Age. That ain't got nothing to do with Jesus Christ." Turk cleared his throat. " 'And I saw heaven opened, and behold a white horse; and he that sat upon him was called Faithful and True, and in righteousness he doth judge and make war.' Now, Dave, I don't know about you, but it's my opinion that mankind as a whole ain't been faithful and true for some time now. And if we ain't in the middle of a war, then I don't know my head from my ass."

As a general rule, David reserved his own opinion about people who quoted the Good Book, but for some reason it seemed fitting coming from Turk. Or perhaps it was the current state of things.

"Mall shootings, school shootings, passenger jets blown out of the sky or slammin' into skyscrapers, those animals in the Middle East choppin' off heads and lobbing bombs at each other since the dawn of time—what we're doing now is paying the piper," Turk said. "Bill's come due. It's come down to the individual to confront his or her own sins, and to either make amends and appeal to God, or to go down with the rest of the lot in a crowd of screaming lunatics." With that, Turk bolted up from his chair and shouted out across the yard at his son, who was halfway up the tenuous branches of a magnolia tree. "Get down, you idiot! You'll break a leg and then where'll you be? I ain't fixin' to mend no broken bones, boy!"

The boy dropped down from the tree, slapping bits of bark away from his palms. Ellie stood beside him, still watching him as though he were something curious swimming around inside an aquarium.

Turk turned to him, grinning. "So in the meantime, I got this nice house, a pretty wife, a happy little yard where my kid can play, damn fool that he is. Nothing so bad about that, in my opinion." The cigarette jounced between his lips.

"Okay," David said. "I understand."

"Do you?"

He shrugged. "Even if I didn't, it's not my place. You've got a lovely family."

Turk sucked on his cigarette so hard that it looked like the insides of his cheeks touched. Then he tossed the ember into a ceramic flowerpot that had some soil and bottle caps in it. "You want to know why else I can't leave?" he said, his voice lower now.

"I don't know," David said. "Do I?"

"You gonna be cool?" Turk asked. "If you're cool, I'll show you."

"Sure. I'm cool."

"Come with me, you're so cool," Turk said, and went back into the house.

David stood, tossed his own cigarette into the flowerpot, then shouted to Ellie that he would be right back. She regarded him the way a puppy might, with a cocked head and no expression. He went inside and followed Turk through the house and up a flight of creaky stairs. The upstairs hallway was outfitted in the same rooster-patterned wallpaper as the kitchen. Doors lined the hall, each of them closed. Hanging in the center of each door was a crucifix. The sight of them all lined up like that gave David a chill.

Turk went to the end of the hall. He dug around in his pocket as they came to the last door, and ultimately produced a ring of keys. David noted that there was a dead bolt attached to the door frame, right above the knob.

"What's in there?"

"He won't hurt you. Just don't say nothing or move around a whole lot. Too much stimuli seems to set him off."

Turk unlocked the dead bolt, opened the door, and flipped on the light switch.

David recognized it as a child's room only because there was a child sitting cross-legged in the middle of the floor. It was a boy, perhaps Sam's age, though it was difficult to tell because the kid had his back to them. The walls were covered in quilts, the mismatched patterns nearly seizure-inducing, and there were smeary brownish-black handprints stamped on some of them. A mattress sat on the floor, soggy and yellowed with stains. Several white balls were scattered about the floor and atop the mattress; it took David a second or two to realize these were tufts of stuffing that had been torn out of stuffed animals, whose gutted carcasses lay strewn about the room. Lastly, he spotted what looked like some dog toys near the head of the bed—a short length of rope; a stuffed animal whose classification in the animal kingdom was no longer evident due to its missing limbs and mangled, threadbare face; a plastic Frisbee stamped with teeth marks; a few rubber balls.

There was also the distinct odor of shit in the air.

"Jimmy," Turk said.

The boy turned his head the way a ventriloquist's dummy

might. He had a face similar to Sam's, though less meaty, and there was dried blood crusted around each of his nostrils. His eyes looked like twin mirrors facing each other, with no comprehension behind them whatsoever. Just idiocy.

"He's sick," David said.

"Yeah," Turk said. "He's got the Folly, all right. Had it for nearly two months now."

"Two *months*?" It must have been a record.

"Far as we can tell, anyway," Turk said.

"There's butterflies in your hair, Sam," Jimmy said to Turk. The boy's voice was raspy, ruinous. Probably from screaming himself hoarse. Some of the infected screamed until their throats ruptured. Yet there was an eerie singsong quality to this boy's voice, and somehow that was worse.

"All right," Turk said.

Jimmy turned those dead eyes on David. "Your hair, too, Sam."

Turk put a hand on David's shoulder and said, "He knows, sport. You hungry?"

"No, Sam." An almost musical cadence.

"Okay. Good boy. Check on you later."

"Good boy, Sam," Jimmy intoned. A fresh trickle of blood began to seep from his left nostril.

"Jesus," David said once Turk had shut and locked the door.

"He's Sammy's twin. Been callin' everyone Sam for the past two weeks or so. Lord knows what delusion he's riding now. It's better than before. Used to be he'd scream himself raw, day and night, until his goddamn throat bled."

"He hasn't been to a doctor?"

"For what? So they can let him die in some hospital room? No, thank you. Besides, we've been taking care of him. His family. Ain't no one could do it better for him. You think he would have lasted this long in some hospital?"

"Trust me, I'm no fan of doctors," David said.

"Never have been, m'self," said Turk.

"And he's been like that for two months?"

"Give or take. Maybe been sick with it even longer than

that, though with kids, it's harder to tell. They're always half-stuck in some dream world as it is, am I right?"

Not Ellie, David thought. *Never Ellie. She has always been a practical child, a girl not prone to fancies or silliness. A pragmatic soul. Like her mother.*

"We feed him, clean him, take care of him best we can," Turk said. "We try to keep the end from coming." Turk shrugged. They could have been talking about baseball scores for all his casualness. "It's all we can do."

"And no one else who's been in contact with him has gotten sick?"

"No. Anyway, no one's sure how people even catch the damn thing to begin with. Some think it's airborne, others say it's in the water. Even the government's come out and said it might just be hanging in the air and absorbed through the skin. Heck, who's to say it ain't genetics? Who's to say some of us ain't just born with it and now it's coming active inside our brains?"

"You could be right. It's almost like—"

Something slammed against the other side of the door, causing them both to jump. The door bucked in its frame, and the crucifix fell from its nail and thudded to the carpet. David took a step back, but Turk remained planted to the spot, a look of consternation on his hardened, sun-reddened face. A muffled moan reverberated against the door, and then it bucked a second time against the frame. It was Jimmy, throwing himself against the door.

"Let's head on back downstairs," Turk suggested, his voice lowered now. "He don't like us standing out here jawin' about him, is all."

24

Pauline invited them to stay for dinner, and David accepted. He was aware that Turk had stashed the Glock somewhere and he didn't want to leave without it, so he thought it best to respond in a positive light to their hospitality. Hopefully he could earn Turk's trust and he'd give him back the gun. Despite the discomfort of knowing they kept their terminally ill son locked in a bedroom upstairs, handprints stamped in shit on the walls, there was still a level of trust and even comfort David felt around this family. He wondered if it was because his own family, over just the course of a handful of days, had essentially disintegrated.

Ellie had brightened a bit toward Sam, too, and after David came down from using their shower (dressed now in one of Turk's clean T-shirts, this one a Motörhead concert tee about two sizes too big), he found them both in the living room watching a DVD of Disney's *Beauty and the Beast*. David paused in the doorway and watched his daughter for several seconds. She had never been the type of girl to dress up like a princess or sing along with a movie's soundtrack, and even now she sat watching the movie cross-legged on the carpet, the look on her face one of studious incredulity at the sight of an animated anthropomorphic teapot lecturing like a British schoolmarm. Yet some fashion of levity had come into her countenance, some brand of innocence and awe that seemed more befitting of an eight-year-old girl than the dark suspicion that also hung just behind her eyes. David had always thought she was too smart for her own good, and too practical to maintain many friendships with girls who just wanted to play dress-up and house, so it did him some good to see a softness in her profile now. Beside her, Sam narrated the events of the film a few seconds ahead of the action, something that the old Ellie would have found annoying. But now she was actually *smiling* at the boy.

In the kitchen, Pauline was preparing a strange assortment of food on a single plate—chocolate chip cookies, a single slice of white bread slathered in peanut butter, apple slices, and a powdered doughnut.

"Healthy food for a healthy body," he joked.

Pauline smiled at him, but there was no humor in it. David couldn't help quell the feeling that whenever Pauline looked at him, it was with an odd mixture of appreciation and pity. She turned away from the plate and retrieved a plastic cup with Transformers on it from the cupboard. From the fridge, she pulled a jug of chocolate milk. She filled the cup with it.

"Turk says you met Jimmy."

"Yes. I'm sorry."

Pauline set the plate of food and the cup of chocolate milk on a tin tray with the NASCAR logo on it. "It happened after the evacuation, you know." She didn't look at him as she spoke. "Turk says there's no way to be completely sure, seein' how there could be an incubation period and all, but, well . . . a mother knows."

"So he was healthy after the evacuation? And he hadn't been around anyone else who was sick?"

"No one else," she said.

He heard Turk speaking in his head, the same words he'd said upstairs, on the other side of his son's locked door: *Some think it's airborne, others say it's in the water. Even the government's come out and said it might just be hanging in the air and absorbed through the skin. Heck, who's to say it ain't genetics?*

"Maybe the rest of us ain't gotten sick because we don't got the gene in us," Pauline said, eerily echoing her husband's sentiment. "Or maybe it's for other reasons." For the first time, she looked up at David and held him in the gaze of her dark, hypnotic, almost childlike eyes. "Turk thinks there could be other reasons. Like, maybe this ain't something science can explain. Turk's found religion." She fingered a tiny silver cross on a chain around her neck. "We all have."

"It's good to have faith," David said. "I wish I had something I could believe in."

"You can." She smiled at him, a gentle easing of her features that never quite reached her eyes. "Maybe you already have. It's been working for us."

"You mean with Jimmy," he said.

"Ain't no one else but God could keep Jimmy with us for this long," Pauline said. "That's my belief, anyway."

He returned her smile, but something about the falseness of it on his face made him feel cold.

"Turk's on the porch drinking a beer," she said, picking the tray up off the counter. "Help yourself to one. They're in the fridge."

When she left, he got a can of Budweiser from the refrigerator and joined Turk on the back porch.

"Hear that?" Turk said, not bothering to look at him.

David listened. He could hear nothing. After a time, he said, "What?"

"Bugs," said Turk. "Crickets. Cicadas. What-have-you. Millions of bugs out there. You know why?"

"Yes," David said. "I do."

Turk craned his head around to face him. His eyebrows arched.

"No birds," David said.

"It's the rapture," Turk said. "Signs of the plague. Birds die, bugs propagate, start growing, multiplying. Hell, they already had us outnumbered on the planet about a million to one. And that was *before* the Folly."

David thought about the monstrous spider that had crawled down the lamppost in town, the spider that was preparing to feast on a mouse. He could imagine the chain reaction such events would have—birds die, bugs propagate, just as Turk said. Bugs grow, eat larger prey. Mammals vanish. Larger bugs are eaten by fish—by serpents—and those terrible things grow in size, too. Meanwhile, people vanish from the planet, giving way to a whole new caste of creature that then inherits the earth.

"Where you think them birds went, anyway?" Turk said.

"I don't know." David sat in the empty chair beside Turk. "People have been asking that for some time now." He thought of the geese dropping like anchors out of the sky, pulverizing automobile windshields and leaving cracks on the asphalt.

"If they were dead—if they all got sick and died—their little bodies would be all over the place. But nope. Not a single bird. Not even a dead one. Not anymore, anyway." Turk swigged some beer. "For a while, U.S. Fish and Wildlife were tracking 'em, and you could pull up info on the Internet from the Department of the Interior. But then they stopped tracking."

"There were early reports of birds migrating out over the oceans," David said. "Some were being tracked. But then the tracker signals went dead. Scientists on TV and in the newspapers said they probably died during the migration and fell into the oceans."

"Could be," said Turk. "But you don't much hear about it anymore. Pauline says maybe they're focused on more important things, given all that's going on now, but I think maybe we don't got the people to do all these things anymore. Let me ask you—when was the last time you saw the president on TV? Or heard a live briefing on the radio?"

"It's been a long time."

"Sure, the White House releases statements to the media, and every once in a while there's some pencil-neck in a bow tie standing behind that podium with the seal on it to give us a rundown on the situation, make us feel like they're wrangling things under control, although even then they've got no real news for us. But nope, you don't see the president. Or even the vice president. Nobody of any importance, I mean.

They said they're holed up in some undisclosed location somewhere, healthy as thoroughbreds, but I ain't so sure about that. They'll play some old recordings of him to make us think that he's still there toiling away behind the scenes, but for my money, I think something bad has happened. Real bad."

"You think the president's dead."

"I do. Much of his cabinet, too. And Congress. Not that they've ever been too lively, you ask me. But everyone's been real quiet the past few months."

"Then who's running the country?"

"That," said Turk, holding up one finger, "is a very good question, Dave. A very good question, indeed."

"What about the statements that have been coming from the CDC?"

"I suppose there's always someone around to give a statement."

David thought of the roadblock near that elementary school, the soldiers in the biohazard suits with the assault rifles. Someone was certainly giving them orders.

Not to mention the people out there looking for Ellie and me, David thought. *They've got their orders, too.*

Once again, Turk craned his head around and looked at David. There was a smoothness to his face now, an expression akin to empathy. "Whatever you and that girl are running from, friend, you're most likely safe as milk. Ain't no one got the time or even the wherewithal to hunt down a father and his kid at the moment." Turk shrugged as he added, "Unless, of course, that ain't really your kid. But we already covered that, now, didn't we?"

"Yes," David said. "We did."

"Then you're just a daddy-o chillin' on the patio." Turk raised his can of Bud in a lazy salute before emptying its contents into his mouth.

You're wrong, my friend. What if my daughter is so goddamn important they can't not look for her? And thinking this made him think of the other thing, of Ellie's newfound ability, and what that might mean. It seemed impossible to believe someone could be exclusively blessed with both immunity to Wanderer's Folly and also possess the ability to do what she could do—to regulate her father's mood, was the clearest way he could define it for himself. It went beyond coincidence, which meant there was a connection there. She was immune because of her ability . . . or she had the ability because she was immune . . .

Turk snapped his fingers. "You zoning out on me, bud? I boring you?"

"Sorry, no. Was just thinking. You mentioned the Internet earlier. Are you still connected?"

"Yeah. There's a desktop off the living room. Long as we keep paying the bills, they keep the service active."

"How long will you be able to keep that up?" He knew this was treading close to their previous conversation about packing up and getting out of town, but Turk had mentioned over dinner that he had lost his job with the county's sanitation department, so David wondered how much extra money they actually had squirreled away.

"Long as I can," Turk said. "Got a generator out in the toolshed. I figure once the power goes out—whether they cut the service or everyone working at the plant keels over dead, whichever happens first—I'll hook that up. After that . . . well . . . I guess God will have to provide. You need to get online?"

"Is that okay?"

"Fine by me. Ask Pauline to boot it up for you. I'm not much of a PC jockey myself. And don't go lookin' at no dirty pictures." Turk winked at him. He pronounced it *pitchers*.

David entered the kitchen just as Pauline returned from upstairs with the food tray. She wore a haggard expression, and there was a thread of bright red blood high up on her cheekbone where she had apparently been scratched by something. It wasn't until that moment that the true horror of the situation dawned upon David—the daily maintenance of that brain-sick child up there, his mind mostly gone to rubble, his brain slowly rupturing, poisoned by madness—and he felt a sudden bolt of sadness for this tired-looking woman.

"Turk said I could use your computer?"

She set the tray on the counter. "Sure thing. Follow me."

It was an ancient PC filmed in dust, resting on a clapboard desktop in a tiny corner room. There was a single window that looked out on the neighbor's house and a bookshelf over-run by model cars. What dominated the room, however, was a three-foot crucifix hanging on the wall, the face of the miniature Jesus contorted in agony, His eyes rolled partway back to portray what looked to David like insanity. David had never been a religious person, but since Wanderer's Folly, it seemed many folks—including Turk and his brood—had found religion. Many zealots even believed they were in the throes of the Second Coming. Ordinarily such talk would have reduced David to grins and snide comments, but he found that the eyes of that plaster Jesus, which seemed to fol-low him around the room, gave him a chill. *Judging by the look on His face, forgiveness is probably the furthest thing from His mind,* David thought. *Those are the eyes of a lunatic driven crazy by tor-ture, a man reduced to a feral monster by a whole different kind of madness.*

"Neat cars," he said, opting to address the models on the shelf instead of the crucifix.

"The boys did those." Pauline sat at the desk and turned on the computer.

"That's impressive."

"Bronwyn helped. My sister. She's got an eye for projects."

"Oh." There was nothing else he could say, assuming the worst had befallen Bronwyn.

"Oh, she ain't dead," Pauline said, apparently able to read his thoughts. "She's out with the others."

"What others, exactly?"

"Cooper and Tre. Local boys. They stayed behind. Like us."

"And Solomon," he added.

"Yes," she said, a noticeable change coming over her face at the mention of the name. She grew darker, somehow. "That's right. And Solomon. They should be back by supper. You'll get to meet the whole crew."

The PC chimed as icons populated the screen. Pauline clicked on Firefox and the screen opened up.

"She's all yours," she said, getting up.

"Thank you."

"Do you want another beer?"

"No, thanks." He smiled at her, mainly because she hung in the doorway a little longer than necessary and he didn't know what else to do. After she left, her perfume lingered for a moment. Something sweet, like cinnamon.

She's nice. Terrified and a hostage to that poor boy upstairs, but nice.

After having no luck identifying his stepbrother's phone number online, he had recalled the receipt of an e-mail from him last Christmas, which he'd saved in his Yahoo! in-box. Knowing Tim, addresses and phone numbers changed frequently, but e-mail accounts typically remained the same. He'd shoot him an e-mail and hope to hear back from him. It was the best he could do.

He accessed his Yahoo! account and searched for Tim's e-mail. As he waited for the screen to reload, he wondered if his account was currently being monitored. Would they go that far?

They've already been in your house, gone through your personal items, and posted your photos on the TV news—is there really any line you think they won't cross?

No. But it was a chance he would just have to take.

He located the e-mail, opened it up, and clicked Reply. After taking a moment to collect his thoughts, he hammered out a quick message, telling Tim to either respond to this e-mail or, better yet, call him on his cell phone. He added that he was in trouble and needed Tim's help. He thought it best to keep the e-mail brief and ambiguous; he could explain in more detail over the phone when he had more time.

He could access his e-mail periodically through his phone

to see when—or if—Tim responded. The only problem was that he'd left his cell phone back at the surplus store with the rest of their stuff. He could go back and get it, but he'd have to take Ellie with him.

And what if they won't let you leave? whispered the head-voice. *What if their hospitality has been a ruse to keep you calm and docile until "the others" get here?*

Thinking this now, he realized that the thought had never been too far from his mind.

Chewing his lower lip, he typed his own name into the Google search engine. In less than three seconds, it returned enough hits to make his stomach sink. The first dozen hits looked to be an Associated Press article published in the on-line editions of various newspapers around the country. He clicked on the *Washington Post* link and read the following:

> Police have issued an AMBER Alert for Arnold, Maryland, resident David James Arlen, 42, and his 8-year-old daughter, Eleanor Elizabeth Arlen, who have purportedly fled a Centers for Disease Control facility in Prince George's County on September 9. Police said Arlen's wife, Kathleen DeMarco Arlen, was under observation at the facility when she was found dead of an apparent suicide on the evening of September 9. Arlen and his daughter were also under voluntary observation at the facility, but following Mrs. Arlen's untimely death, CDC officials issued a quarantine order for Arlen and his daughter. Local police also want to question Arlen regarding the details of his wife's death. Police said Arlen is most likely driving a 2010 black Ford Bronco, Maryland license plate number M15972.
>
> A spokesperson for the CDC, Dr. Sanjay Kapoor, said, "We are very concerned for the well-being of the little girl and her father."
>
> As to whether the Arlens had contracted Wanderer's

Folly and if they posed a potential threat to anyone they might come in contact with, Kapoor would not say.

"It is important to remember," said Dr. Kapoor, "that there is much about this illness that we still do not understand, including how it is contracted."

Police, however, are warning the public not to approach Arlen or attempt to apprehend him. "The best thing to do," said Anne Arundel County Chief of Police Martin J. Rasmussen, "is to notify the authorities if you happen to see David Arlen. Call 911. Let the police handle the situation."

He read the article a second time, his skin growing hot. The bastards had lied, covering up Kathy's murder at their hands as a suicide. It made David want to smash something.

He peered over at the agonized face of Jesus on the cross and grimaced. The Savior's eyes blazed with delirious insanity. And as David watched, those eyes rolled in his direction, the pupils small as pinpricks, the whites networked with ruptured blood vessels . . . and for one terrible, impossible moment, the face of the maniac on the cross was David's.

Out in the hallway, a floorboard creaked. David blinked. His skin felt prickly and hot, his breath coming in great, whooshing gasps. It was nothing more than the shifting of daylight coming in through the blinds that had caused the statue's face to . . . well, to change. Nothing more.

David quickly minimized the screen, then leaned back in the desk chair and peered out into the hall. No one was there. He could hear the TV on in the living room, but that was all.

When he returned to the kitchen, Turk and Pauline were talking in low voices.

"I'm sorry," David said. "I didn't mean to interrupt."

"Ain't interrupting," Turk said, clearing his throat. "Just discussing what's on the menu tonight."

"I guess we'll be having more mouths to feed once your friends show up," David said.

Turk gave him a wide smile. "That's right. It'll be a regular celebration."

"I just hope we're not intruding. If we are, we can—"

"Nonsense," Pauline said. "We're just gonna throw some burgers on the grill. You and your little girl like hamburgers?"

"Absolutely."

"And beer," Turk said. He sauntered over to the fridge and grabbed two more cans of Bud. He held one out to David.

"I think I'll pass. In fact, I left some stuff back at the place we're . . . well, where we stayed last night. I think I might head over and pick it up."

"Well, now, I can't say I'd recommend that." Turk popped the tab on the beer. "Remember what I said about wandering around out here? It ain't safe."

"Turk would drive you, but we try not to waste gas," Pauline added.

"It was only a few blocks," David said. "It won't take me long. And I know how to be careful."

"How 'bout this," Turk said. "You tell me where your stuff is and I'll see if I can raise ol' Coop on his cell, tell him to stop by and grab it for you."

"That isn't necessary."

"It's no bother. He'll be coming back into town within the next hour or so anyway."

Something—some twinge deep within the animal part of him—didn't feel right. This realization struck him all of a sudden, like a slap across the face, and despite the Powells' hospitality all morning and afternoon, David reminded himself that he'd met Turk staring down the business end of the man's shotgun. He recalled what Ellie had said to him earlier that morning, too, as they stood in the bathroom together—*I don't like it here. It's the same feeling I had last night, when we first got here.*

Suddenly, David didn't like it, either.

25

In the end, David decided it was best to try to sneak out of the house before the others arrived and while the rest of the Powell clan was busy, even without the gun. While Turk went outside to clean off the grill and Pauline was busy excavating a packet of ground beef from the freezer, David crept into the living room. The TV was still on, an encore performance of *Beauty and the Beast*. But Ellie had lost all interest in the film this time around, and was instead seated on the sofa with a book opened up in her lap. Sprawled out on the floor with a thumb jammed in his mouth was Sam, snoring like a locomotive in his sleep.

"We're getting out of here," David said.

Ellie closed the book, slid off the sofa, and followed him to the front door. David turned the knob and opened it, just as he heard the back door slap against its wooden frame at the far end of the house. Turk began whistling, then stopped and said something to Pauline in the kitchen. David couldn't make out a word of it.

"Let's go," he whispered, and shoved Ellie out onto the front steps.

"Are we going back to the car?"

"Yes."

"Good idea. I don't like this place. Something bad's gonna happen."

They were halfway across the front lawn when a gold Silverado appeared at the end of the block, its subwoofers thumping. David paused and watched it progress up the street. He felt his testicles retreat into his abdomen when it pulled up into the Powells' driveway. The truck looked too new, too expensive, for this area. The driver revved the engine, then laid on the horn.

"Ouch," Ellie said, covering her ears.

That must be Solomon and the rest of the gang. So either we run now, cut through the yards so they can't chase us in that monstrous truck, or we play along.

Instinct told him to run, and he would have if he'd been alone. But he knew Ellie wouldn't be able to keep up, and he certainly couldn't carry her all that way. Yet what truly prevented him from taking off was the fear that the people in that truck had guns, just as Turk had, and that they'd climb out and start firing at them before they even made it across the street.

The driver's door popped open just as the engine died. A lanky guy in his twenties got out. He had a clump of greasy hair that hung in his eyes and a face decimated by acne. He wore a ratty tank top and his boxer shorts mushroomed over the waistband of his cargo pants. There was some sort of strange, flat hat on his head.

"Heck," the guy said. He smiled and raised one hand. "Hi! You Dave?"

"Yes."

"I'm Cooper. Spoke to Turk on the phone earlier, said we had a couple visitors from outta town." He sauntered over to them, his hand extended in anticipation of a handshake the entire time. Cooper was maybe six-three or six-four, and skinny as a rail. He had the pinched, beaky face of a rodent. The thing on his head wasn't a hat, but a plastic dime-store Halloween mask, held in place by a band of elastic that cut into the flesh beneath his chin. From what David could tell, it was the Incredible Hulk.

David shook Cooper's hand. The shake was loose and clammy. The guy reeked of marijuana.

Two others came out the passenger side of the truck. The

man looked about thirty, tanned skin, dark hair, solid build. His forearms were intricately tattooed and the strap of a backpack hung from one shoulder. He wore a distrustful look that mirrored how David felt. The girl who was with him also looked about thirty, with a nearly nonexistent bosom beneath the drooping Kenny Chesney T-shirt she wore. She also had a straw cowboy hat perched back on her head and two long braids draped over her shoulders. Her face bore a striking resemblance to Pauline, so David assumed this was Bronwyn, her sister.

"Boy, you guys are in for a real treat," Cooper said. Then he bent down to address Ellie, even though he was still a bit taller than eye level with the girl. David could see sprigs of dark, oily hair purling out of the Hulk's eyeholes. "You like fireworks, sugar?"

"Not really," she said.

Cooper blinked in surprise. "You kiddin' me? What kid don't like fireworks?" He jerked a thumb over his shoulder. "My boy Tre there's got a whole backpack full."

"Is that such a good idea?" David said.

Cooper's gaze shifted toward him. His eyes were bloodshot and about as droopy as Bronwyn's oversized T-shirt.

"Turk mentioned there were . . . undesirables . . . still in the area," David finished.

Cooper stood. Behind him, Tre and Bronwyn cut a circuitous path toward the front door that took them partway around the front yard. David felt like they were circling before closing in on him and Ellie, the way hyenas might.

"Undesirables?" Cooper said. He pronounced it as if he'd never heard the word before, or was at least unfamiliar with its meaning. "Undesirables . . ."

"Bad guys," David clarified.

Cooper twisted his lips into a knot and looked skyward in a parody of contemplation. He even rubbed at his chin. David suddenly disliked him.

"No, no, I don't think so," said Cooper. "Nope. No one

that I can think of around here goes by that name. 'Course, this is Turk's neighborhood. He'd know better 'an me. I ain't from this side of town."

"Coop's from the *bad* side," Bronwyn chided, one leg up on the front step of the house. Her comment possessed the conspiratorial tone of an inside joke. "He's trouble, mister. Steer clear."

The guy with the backpack—*Tre*, David thought—flared his nostrils as he glanced at Bronwyn. He looked irritated. He had one hand on the doorknob, which he twisted apprehensively, but did not open the door. There was a joint tucked behind his left ear.

"Undesirables," Cooper repeated. There was a musical quality to his voice. Then he laughed and said, "I'm just fuckin' with you, mister. We're cool."

"Language, shit head," Bronwyn scolded, and jerked her head in Ellie's direction.

"My bad." Cooper grinned toothily at Ellie. "I got me a bit of a potty mouth."

"You smell awful, too," Ellie said.

"Ellie," David said.

Cooper just stared at Ellie. Then he crossed his eyes, lolled out his tongue, and made a clicking sound way back in his throat. A second later, he barked a single laugh—a high-pitched Pee-wee Herman honk—and said, "That's funny. You're funny, kid. Come on inside." He took a step toward the front door.

"We were just leaving," David said. He pushed Ellie toward the curb.

That goofy grin had yet to leave Cooper's face. "Yeah? Where you headed?"

"Just back on the road. This was only a pit stop. We got a little turned around last night."

Cooper frowned. It was as goofy an expression as his grin. And while David did not like the stern and distrustful look on Tre's face, he liked the goofy, playful façade on Cooper's even less. At least Tre was expressing his true feelings, whether he realized it or not. Cooper was putting on a show. A very poor one.

"Seriously," Cooper said. "Come on back inside."

"No, thanks. Take care." A hand against Ellie's back to usher her forward, he began walking toward the street. Yet he hadn't fully turned around, keeping Cooper and friends in the periphery of his vision.

"I doubt Turk will approve," Cooper called.

"Approve of what?" Turk said, and David froze. Turk came around the side of the house, a long brush with steel bristles in one hand. He must have heard the commotion while he was out back cleaning the barbecue. Turk turned toward David and looked instantly hurt. "Hey," he said. "Where you goin', Dave?"

"To get my stuff," David said. "Remember? I mentioned it to you earlier."

"And I told *you* that it wouldn't be safe," Turk said.

"Undesirables," Cooper said, and snickered.

"C'mon back to the house, Dave," Turk said. He waved him back.

"Listen," David said, "I appreciate the hospitality, but we really need to go."

"I'm afraid I can't let you." Turk took two steps in his direction. "As I said, it ain't for us to decide who goes and who stays."

"That's Solomon's call," Cooper said.

"Well, I don't think we can wait around for Solomon," David said. "Sorry."

"Oh, man, no need to worry about that." Turk smiled widely. Sharklike. "Solomon's here."

"Enough," David said. "Thank you, but no."

"Ain't up to you," said Turk. There was a forcefulness in his voice now. In that instant, David knew the man would physically try to stop him. Could he outrun him? Probably not. Especially not with Ellie in tow.

Cooper stepped forward. He withdrew a handgun from the rear of his pants and leveled it at David.

"You're making this messy," Turk said to David. It sounded like he was pleading with him now. "It ain't necessary, Dave. We've had a pleasant afternoon, haven't we? It don't have to be all fights and struggles, you know. We can have a nice dinner first."

Cooper walked down the length of the driveway, birdlike in the way his head bobbed, never taking the gun off David. That kiss-my-ass grin was still firmly seated on his ugly, pimple-ridden face. The gun looked too heavy for his broomstick arm with its knotty, bulging elbow.

"What do you mean 'first'?" David said.

Turk paused midway down the lawn. He lifted both arms in a *what-can-you-do?* gesture but said nothing.

"Ouch," Ellie said. David realized he was squeezing her shoulder.

"Get in the house," Cooper said. There was no trace of jocularity in his voice now. When David didn't respond, Cooper redirected the gun so that it pointed at Ellie and then repeated his request: "I said get in the *house,* man."

He'll kill you dead, David's head-voice whispered. *You and Ellie both. You can see it in his eyes. Hell, he'll even enjoy it.*

Briefly, David considered stepping between Ellie and the gun, shouting for her to run, to go, to get the hell out of here. But he'd no sooner get half the words out of his mouth before Cooper would drive a bullet into his gut. Or his head. David knew that with certainty. And a second or two after that, the lunatic would fire at Ellie, who probably wouldn't even make it across the street.

"Okay," David said, raising both hands. "I'll go inside. But, please, let my daughter go."

"No, Daddy," Ellie said. She gripped a handful of his T-shirt, which had formerly been Turk's T-shirt.

"Where would she go, Dave?" Turk said. "What good would that do? Besides, like I said, it ain't up to us."

"Right," David said. "Solomon. Where is this guy, anyway?"

"Shit," Cooper said, cracking that grin once more. "He's right here with us, dude. So let's go inside and meet him."

That was when David heard a high-pitched, tittering sound. It was so coarse that it hurt his ears. And his first thought upon hearing it was, *It's a bird, Jesus Christ, a goddamn bird. They're not all gone, not all dead. That is the sound of a bird shrieking nearby.*

But it wasn't.

It was Bronwyn.

She was laughing.

26

At Turk's instruction, they were led back inside and into the living room. The talking teapot was still on the television, but now Sam was sitting up and rubbing his eyes, a groggy expression on his chubby face. Pauline was here, too, and when she saw Cooper pointing the gun at David, she knelt down beside her son and said, "Go outside and play, Sammy."

"He's old enough to be here, Pauline," Turk said. Then he gestured toward the couch. "Sit."

David sat. Ellie remained standing a moment longer, gazing at Cooper's gun, then at her father. Then she sat beside him on the couch.

The rest of them crowded into the tight living room, the smell of them—stale perspiration mingled with marijuana—suddenly overpowering. The sight of Cooper's gun set against the Disney score coming from the TV made David feel like he was in a dream.

Cooper stood directly in front of David, the handgun pivoting between him and Ellie. David wanted to spring up from the couch and clobber the asshole. He still might; if it came down to Ellie's safety, he'd tackle the son of a bitch and hope for the best. It was all he could do.

"Don't point that thing at my daughter."

Smirking, Cooper let the gun hang on Ellie. Yet his eyes stayed with David.

Turk dug something out of his pants pocket as he stepped up beside Cooper. He looked down at David, his eyes full and brown and creased at the corners. A film of sweat glistened across the saddle of his nose.

"Roll it," Turk said, extending his hand to David. Pinched between Turk's thumb and forefinger was a die.

David shook his head.

"Don't be a fool," Turk said. "Do as I say and you've got a fifty-fifty chance the girl lives. Best odds in the house."

Against the far wall, Bronwyn tittered laughter again. She had her cowboy hat perched back far enough on her head so that David could see her sunburned scalp where her hair was parted.

"Take it," Turk said. He held the die three inches from David's face, pinched now between thumb and forefinger.

David took the die. It felt almost nonexistent as he closed his hand around it.

There was a scuffed coffee table beside the couch. Turk pointed to it now and said, "Roll it, David."

David didn't bother to shake it; he simple tossed the plastic die across the table, where it tap-danced along the lacquered surface and ultimately fell to the carpet.

"A six," both Bronwyn and Cooper said at the same time.

"Evens," Pauline said. She held her son against her, her hands draped like a harness over Sam's meaty chest. "He's evens." She began to pray softly under her breath.

"Which means you, little miss," Cooper said, cocking his head at Ellie, "are odds."

"*You're* odd," Ellie said.

"Nice." Cooper's cadaverous grin widened. "Real nice. Some mouth on this kid."

Turk clapped his hands, causing David to jump. "So," Turk said. "Let's meet Solomon, shall we?"

At first, it seemed like no one moved. But then David noticed Tre at the back of the room sliding the backpack strap from his shoulder. He stepped between Cooper and Turk and set the backpack down on the coffee table. When he unzipped it, David could see fireworks packaged in cellophane inside, along with a slender bottle of whiskey and what looked like a propane torch. David's eyes cut back toward Cooper, who was still staring down at him. The mouth of Cooper's gun looked about as big as the Harbor Tunnel.

Tre lifted something out of the backpack—grayish-yellow, somewhat circular, approximately the size of a bowling ball. It wasn't until Tre set it down on the table that David saw it for what it was . . . and even then, his mind was slow to compute what his eyes were seeing. He processed it in pieces rather than a single whole—the twin hollows of its eye sockets, the dual rows of yellowed teeth, the triangular nasal cavity. It was a skull. Printed in block letters just above its empty eye sockets in brownish-red was the name SOLOMON.

"Jesus," David breathed.

"We're all just pawns," Turk announced. "It's Solomon who decides who must be sacrificed."

"Sacrificed for what?" David managed. He looked to Ellie, who stared without emotion at the grinning skull on the coffee table.

"For the sake of my son," Turk said. "For Jimmy. It's why we've been able to keep him with us for so long, despite his worsening condition."

"Amen," Pauline said.

"Amen," murmured the rest of them.

"You're insane," David said. He reached over and grabbed Ellie's hand. Her skin was cool to the touch. "All of you."

"It's what we must do to keep my boy alive," Turk said.

It was then that the ultimate horror dawned on David—a blood sacrifice to appease a vengeful god. How many innocents had fallen victim to this archaic ritual already? What had *really* happened to those who ignored the evacuation and stayed behind in Goodwin? *Undesirables . . .*

As if in response to these unasked questions, two resounding *thumps* echoed from the floor above. Everyone glanced up at the ceiling. A second later, a pained sob filtered down through the air ducts and filled the room.

"Jimmy," Pauline said, her voice reverent.

Turk stepped up to the coffee table. He picked up the skull, then bent down and gathered the die up off the floor. When he stood again, he looked like a man who had suddenly realized he held the power of the whole world in his hands.

"Now Solomon will decide who lives and who dies," Turk said. He upended the skull so that it faced the ceiling. Then he dropped the die into the right eye socket. David heard a muted *click* as it dropped into the hollow cranium. Turk shook the skull gently, both of his big hands on either side of it as if to protect it from hearing something inappropriate. Then he extended his arms and rotated the skull so that those sightless eyeholes now faced the grubby carpet of the Powells' living room. David registered a single thought—*Whose skull is that, anyway?*—just moments before the die dropped from the eye socket and bounced to the carpet.

It tumbled, finally coming to rest against the leg of the coffee table.

Four black dots faced the ceiling.

"Evens," Turks said.

"Evens," Cooper echoed. He grinned around the room, though everyone else's face was somber.

"Amen," said Pauline.

"Amen," said the others.

Turk slipped his thumbs into the pockets of his pants and looked almost sympathetically down at David. "It's you, old hoss. Good news is, your daughter's safe. We'll keep her here with us for a time. No worries about that at all. Seems like she and Sam get along just fine, way I see it. And you're a big fella. Should hold us off for a while."

Bronwyn cleared her throat and said, "Should we—"

But she was cut off as another series of loud *thumps*—much more agitated than the previous two—reverberated down through the ceiling. This was followed by a piercing shriek that caused Turk's son, Sam, to slam both meaty hands over his ears.

"Jesus," Tre whispered, staring at the ceiling. It was the first thing David had heard him utter.

Jimmy's agonized howls funneled through the vents.

"He's worse, Turk," Pauline said, obviously concerned.

Turk held a hand up, silencing her. He cocked his head, as if to listen for the faintest sound, but there was no need to strain himself: Jimmy's cries came again, the wails of a banshee, causing Pauline's eyes to moisten and Sam to groan as if in pain himself.

Ellie's grip tightened around David's hand. She was staring at the vent in the ceiling directly above her head. Motes of dust spiraled down and powdered her hair. She didn't even blink her eyes.

Then—*whump!* The sound of a sledgehammer whacking against the trunk of a large tree. It came over and over again, steady as a heartbeat—*whump! whump! whump!*

"He'll hurt himself," Pauline said. Her voice was low and hardly audible over the sickening sound emanating from upstairs. Then she shouted it at Turk: "He's hurting himself!"

"Goddamn it," Turk growled. He spun around, charged out of the living room, and bounded up the stairs. Momentarily, his heavy footfalls competed with the throbbing heartbeat that shook the walls.

"What's he *doing*?" Bronwyn said. She stepped partway out into the hall and peered up the stairwell.

"He's slamming his head against the wall up there," David said. "If I had to guess, anyway, that's where I'd put my money."

Pauline glared at him, teeth clenched. "You don't know nothing," she growled at him.

"Probably smashing his face to pieces," David continued. His mouth was dry; his tongue felt like a fat sponge sticking to the roof of his mouth.

"You cut it out!" Pauline shouted. She pointed at Cooper. "You shut him up!"

"Mama!" Sam bawled. He still had his hands clamped to his ears.

"You shut your mouth, buddy," Cooper said, threatening David with the muzzle of the gun.

"Or what?" David said. "I'm dead anyway, right?"

"Just shut it." Flecks of spit sprang from Cooper's lips.

The banging upstairs reached a steady fever pitch—

whumpwhumpwhumpwhumpwhump

—until Pauline shrieked and covered her own ears. Bronwyn made a high-pitched whimpering that sounded like air hissing from a deflating car tire. The gun in Cooper's hand began to shake.

And then the banging stopped. The silence that followed was as loud as an explosion. Sam was sobbing against his mother while Pauline, fists still balled against her own ears, stared at the ceiling, wet tracks sliding down her cheeks.

"They're okay," Cooper said. He was staring right at David now. So was the gun. "They're okay, Pauline. Just relax."

"That *sound*," Pauline moaned. She dropped her hands and hugged her boy.

Bronwyn stepped over to the foot of the stairs; David could see her terrified expression from the living room doorway. She called, "Turk? Turk?" Then her face appeared to collapse. She brought a hand up to her mouth, which seemed to have come unhinged. A high-pitched whine escaped her.

Turk descended the stairs. Cradled in his arms was the limp body of his son Jimmy. When Turk reached the bottom of the stairs, he staggered into the doorway of the living room just as Pauline began to cry. The look on Turk's face was one of utter shock. The look on Jimmy's was worse—a slack, pale face, juxtaposed by streamers of dark red gore smeared across his nose and mouth. The boy's eyelids were open, but the eyes themselves were bright red Christmas balls filled with blood.

Turk surveyed them all, helpless and lost. There was a sound like cloth being slowly torn in half, which David realized was actually the sound of blood spilling from some orifice of the boy and pattering to the floor.

Pauline rushed to her husband, tried to wrangle the lifeless body from his arms. But Turk wouldn't let the boy go. Pauline wailed and pressed her face to Jimmy's, soaking her hair in his blood.

Only Cooper seemed fully aware of the situation; his stare

kept volleying between the terrible scene in the doorway and David's face, which was still only inches from the barrel of the gun. "What do I do here, Turk?" he asked.

Turk said nothing; he only gazed down at the dead child in his arms. Pauline had dropped to her knees and was sobbing against her husband's leg. She clutched at one of Jimmy's small, limp hands like someone groping for something in the dark.

Cooper cleared his throat and, more agitated, said, "Turk? What you want me to do here, man?"

Turk lifted his gaze. He surveyed the room with dead eyes, resting momentarily on David.

The gun shook in Cooper's hand.

"Kill them both," Turk said, turning back toward the stairs.

David sprang up from the couch, but Tre grabbed him and wrapped him in a bear hug. He was impossibly strong. From the couch, Ellie looked at him, then turned to Cooper. Cooper leveled the gun at her face.

"You motherfuckers!" David screamed.

Cooper eased the muzzle of the gun toward Ellie's forehead. The gun was nearly touching—

(touching)

—Ellie's forehead now. David struggled within Tre's grasp, but it was a futile attempt.

"I'll kill you!" he shouted at Cooper—at all of them. "I'll kill you all!"

Ellie glanced at him, then turned back to look at Cooper. She brought up a hand—slowly, so slowly—and let her fingers dance along the barrel of the gun. Cooper watched, mesmerized by the strangeness of it. Those lithe little fingers danced along the edge of the gun until they came to rest along the top side of Cooper's hand.

"Whatever you're trying to do, sweetheart," Cooper said, "it ain't gonna do you no good."

Ellie's hand closed around Cooper's wrist.

David stopped struggling.

Cooper grinned. Then his head cocked slightly to one side, the bewildered look of a dog overcoming his features, and the grin fell away from his face. A vertical crease appeared between Cooper's eyebrows. Cooper's lower lip began to tremble, to quiver, and it was soon obvious that he was muttering something just barely audible, like someone reciting the Lord's Prayer.

Then he screamed. It was a shrill, womanlike sound, raw enough to rupture his throat. His eyes grew wide, fearful, terrified, and his cheeks began to quiver. But not just his cheeks—his whole face began to quiver, his head shaking rapidly as if possessed by some force that was overtaxing his brain. And David wondered if that was exactly what was happening . . .

"Coop?" Tre said, his voice small and seemingly far away.

David felt Tre's arms loosen around his chest. He seized the opportunity, throwing Tre's arms off him and driving himself into Cooper's chest while simultaneously clutching at the hand that held the gun. Sharp pain blossomed in his nose and radiated along the contours of his skull. There was a deafening explosion as the gun went off. David drove Cooper back against the wall; he felt the air gust out of Cooper's lungs in one giant expulsion; a second after that, Cooper's legs went rubbery and they both crashed to the floor.

Someone screamed.

David was quick to his feet, and had already administered a swift kick to the side of Cooper's head before he realized he now held the gun in his hands. Cooper's head rebounded off the wall and his eyes went foggy. His mouth worked silently, like a fish hauled out of the water gasping for air.

When David glanced up, he saw Tre's thick, blocky silhouette rushing toward him, though seemingly in slow motion. It was as if the gun redirected itself and pulled its own trigger. The second gunshot seemed to suck all the air out of the room. Tre twisted in midleap; he spun away and crashed through the coffee table. In that millisecond, David was able to make out the look of utter shock on Tre's tanned face; he could see the tats on his forearms and biceps in stark and terrible clarity; he could see the shimmering beads of sweat spring from Tre's forehead and arc like cannon fire through the air in slow motion.

A moment later, the world caught up with itself. A grayish mist hung in the room, tangible as a spiderweb. David took a deep breath, and the acrid stench of gunpowder burned his sinuses. He tasted blood at the back of his throat, and when he touched his nose, he found his fingertips bloody. On the floor, Tre rolled over on the broken bits of the coffee table and moaned.

Turk reappeared in the doorway. He still held his son, but the look of shock had been wiped from his face. He now looked like a bull prepared to charge.

"Don't move," David said, swiveling the gun in Turk's direction. "I'll blow your goddamn head off."

No one moved.

"Ellie," he said, and motioned for her to get up off the couch. She did, but kept her eyes on Tre, who was clutching his abdomen as a dark, wet stain spread across the front of his shirt. David snared her around the wrist and pulled her close to him. Then he pointed the gun at Turk. "Get in here. Up against the wall with the others."

"You're a poison." Turk's voice was a low rumble. "You've come here and infected us all."

"Do it now or I'll shoot you in the face. Your wife, too."

Pauline sobbed into her hands. She was still kneeling on the floor, her hair, face, and arms slick with Jimmy's blood.

"I'll put a bullet in her head, Turk. I swear it."

Still cradling his dead son in his arms, Turk looked down at Pauline. "Get up," he told her. "Stop crying and get up. Do what he says."

She used Turk's leg as support, hoisting herself off the floor. Blood from Jimmy's mouth continued to spill onto the floor, black as oil. Blood had soaked Turk's pants legs.

Once they were all in the living room, David backed toward the front door. He clutched the gun in two hands, yet still it shook. His breath whistled up the stovepipe of his throat. Ellie clung to his hip. When his foot thumped against something, he glanced down and saw it was the skull. *Solomon.* It spun slowly on the carpet like a top winding down.

"Don't move and don't follow us." David opened the front door without taking his eyes from the roomful of people.

"Poison," Turk said.

And then they were outside, he and Ellie, wincing against the harsh white sunlight of late afternoon. He paused midway down the driveway and pulled Ellie against him, covering one of her ears with the palm of his sweaty hand. He fired the gun at one of the Silverado's tires, the gun bucking, the report like a whip crack. Then he shot out a second tire, hearing a faint metallic *zing!* as the bullet presumably rebounded off the rim.

"Run," David said, and shoved Ellie forward.

The girl stumbled, then righted herself before breaking into a full gallop. They were on the other side of the street when a shotgun blast sheared the limb off a nearby tree. Ellie screamed. Brown leaves and splinters of wood rained down on them. David shouted for her to keep going.

27

He wasn't sure whether they were being followed or not, but he wasn't taking any chances. They didn't slow down until they reached the main thoroughfare of town, and even then it was just to catch their bearings before taking off again. Ellie spotted the surplus store first, and they both sprinted across the street and around back, where the Olds was still tucked into its parking space. The car keys were in David's pocket, so the urge to just jump in and speed off was powerful, but he knew he'd regret not grabbing his phone and whatever else he could manage from inside the store, so he darted through the partially opened door and raced across the store, knocking over a display rack as he went, until he nearly tripped over one of their sleeping bags. He gathered their bags in his arms while Ellie grabbed the shoe box of bird eggs, then together they ran back outside.

He kept anticipating a second sonorous blast from the shotgun, or perhaps for his pursuers to appear around the next street corner. But neither of those things happened. He jammed the key in the ignition, revved the Oldsmobile's engine, and sped out onto the vacant street. Tires squealed as he gunned it toward the town limit.

The only peculiar thing he saw—or imagined he saw—was the wooden Jesus from the Powell house, now liberated from His cross, standing in a narrow alleyway between two buildings, staring at David with those mad eyes . . .

★ ★ ★

He was still speeding fifteen minutes later when a police car turned on its rack lights behind him.

Shit.

He looked over at Ellie, who sat ramrod-straight in the passenger seat. The expression on her face—or lack thereof, for she looked to him like a zombie freshly dragged from the grave—terrified him.

He glanced up at the rearview mirror.

Maybe it'll pass us.

But they were the only two cars on this desolate stretch of highway.

Shit. Shit.

The cruiser sped up until it was right on his bumper. David considered his options, which were practically nil, before clicking the directional and pulling over onto the shoulder.

Ellie turned around in her seat and stared through the rear windshield as the car came to a stop. "What are you doing?" There was panic in her voice.

"We have to stop," he said.

"No!"

"It's okay. Relax."

Cooper's gun lay on the console between their seats.

This is it, he thought. *It's showtime. What am I made of?*

He picked up the gun. It was still warm. The interior of the car reeked of gunpowder. Or maybe that was just in his head. Either way, the gun felt like it was forged from iron; it was impossible to hold it steady. At the last second, he shoved it under his seat.

The officer approached the vehicle and made a *roll-your-window-down* gesture when he came up to the door.

"Daddy," Ellie said.

"Shhh," he told her. "It'll be okay."

He rolled down the window.

"License and registration," the officer said automatically.

David leaned over onto one buttock and reached for his

back pocket, only to find nothing there. He felt like he'd been kicked in the chest. But then he remembered his wallet was in his bag, which was piled up in the backseat. He said as much to the officer, who responded by taking several steps back from the window.

"Sir," the officer said.

David looked at him. "What?"

"Sir. Sir." It seemed all the officer was able to say.

"My wallet is in the back, in my bag," David repeated. "If you want, I can get out and you can—"

"Are you sick, sir?"

He thought he'd misheard him. "What's that?"

"Are you . . . are you sick?" The cop's voice cracked. He took another step back from David's window, his shiny black boots stomping over a tangle of kudzu. He had a pale, drawn face, with a fair complexion and eyelids rimmed with red.

David said, "Sick? What do you mean?"

The cop pointed at him. "You're bleeding," he said, then clapped a hand over his own mouth.

"I'm . . . ?" David glanced at his reflection in the rearview mirror. Indeed, his nose was still gushing blood. He probably broke it when he slammed into Cooper back at the house. Blood trickled down over his lips and had spilled onto his shirt—*Turk's* shirt—too.

"Stay in the car." The officer held up a hand like a crossing guard.

"I'm not—"

"Please," said the cop. He peered in at Ellie, then took another step back. "Go. Just go."

The cop returned to his car, got in, and pulled back onto the road. The rack lights went dead as the cruiser sped by, leaving a cloud of exhaust in its wake. The cop didn't even glance at them as he drove away.

David stared at his bloodied reflection again, his heart thundering in his chest.

"Here," Ellie said. She had dug a Kleenex out of the glove compartment and handed it to him.

He cleaned up as best he could, which wasn't very good at all. When he pressed a finger to the tip of his nose, pain blossomed behind both his eyes, though he didn't think it was broken.

Yet for some reason he couldn't help but laugh.

28

They slept in the car that night, parked behind a row of Dumpsters in the parking lot of an abandoned bowling alley in southeastern Missouri. Ellie had already been asleep for some time when David parked the car. He was ravenous but he looked like shit and didn't want to risk stopping anywhere. He reclined his seat and rolled down the window, letting in the cool autumn air. Crickets chorused in a nearby field and a cloud of gnats orbited the single lamppost at the far end of the parking lot. There would be no birds on the prowl tonight. Once again, David wondered if this was how the world ended—in disease among a plague of insects. It wasn't just that the birds had disappeared; it was that the insects had begun to take over. Wasn't there something in the Bible about that?

Before closing his eyes, he powered up his phone and checked his e-mail. He knew it was wishful thinking, hoping that Tim had gotten back to him so quickly. And he was right—there was no message from Tim.

What if he's gone dark? Completely off the grid? It was only a matter of time before Tim vanished completely.

Tim had never trusted the government, the police, the politicians, the bureaucrats. He'd stopped carrying around a cell phone because he didn't want NSA listening in on his calls. He didn't own a TV. The last bit of correspondence David had received from Tim had been in the form of an e-mail, so that kept some hope alive that he was still connected to the World Wide Web . . . but even that knowledge was not very reassuring.

What will we do if I don't hear back from him? Where will we go? We can't run forever.

David turned his phone off and shut his eyes. He slept for a while, surprised at the ease with which he came upon it, only to awaken sometime later by the harsh, mechanized sound of a helicopter flying close to the ground. He opened his eyes, hearing nothing but the steady *chuh-chuh-chuh* sound of its rotors.

It passed directly overhead, a great black hornet against a smoky black sky. It had a single searchlight combing the ground below. For a moment, the light passed right across the hood of the car. David sat there holding his breath, watching as the helicopter continued on into the night, the massive pro-peller eating up the darkness.

They're looking for a black Ford Bronco, he reminded himself.

Once the helicopter was gone and the world settled, it was as if it never existed.

29

Six months earlier

In the weeks before his classes were discontinued, David would arrive at his classroom to find that a great number of his students had taken to wearing cheap plastic Halloween masks. The trend had begun months earlier, after fears that the virus might possibly be airborne and that any precautions that might keep exposure to germs at a minimum—to include the use of face masks—were recommended. When the sale of face masks could no longer keep up with the demand, people began rioting in the streets. It was then that the CDC revealed that the masks held little to no benefit. Nonetheless, people—mostly teenagers and young adults—who couldn't get ahold of the N95s and similar masks took to wearing plastic dime-store masks. After a time, wearing the masks became less about protecting yourself against the disease and more about the solidarity of the healthy. To wear a mask meant you were still "clean." In a way, it even became some sort of morbidly bizarre fashion statement. It wouldn't be unusual to see packs of teenagers roving through the streets in the early evenings, their faces adorned with the countenances of Wolverine, Spider-Man, Minnie Mouse, or Smurfette. At first, the college had tried to ban the wearing of masks in the classrooms, but they ultimately conceded that point when students, citing public health fears, threatened to withdraw from their classes altogether. And so it became typical for David to arrive at class and look out upon a sea of plastic cartoon faces.

Creepier than the cartoonish masks were the paper plates with eyeholes cut out that some people tied around their faces. The more imaginative individuals drew faces or designs on their plates, sometimes beautifully and skillfully rendered, though more often than not just downright eerie. The more practical individuals kept their plates untarnished, walking around with blank white ovals strapped to their faces like expressionless mutes in a hospital psych ward. In David's estimation, these were the creepiest.

It was one of these blank white plate-wearers who happened to remain standing near the back of the classroom when David entered. Most everyone else had dropped into their seats right away when he entered, with the exception of a few stragglers who felt entitled to finish their conversations first. David always gave them about a minute. He removed a stack of texts from his briefcase and waited for the murmurs to die down before looking up and out over the columns of masked faces.

The student in the plain white plate-mask was the only one who had not taken a seat. He wasn't even facing forward, but gazing across the classroom at the wall of windows that looked out onto the quad two stories below. In general, David had always been pretty good at learning his students' names, but since they'd started wearing masks, it seemed a futile and unreasonable task, so he had given up on it. It provided for anonymity when grading their papers, which alleviated implications that a low grade on an essay was because he disliked a particular student (though a slim few still attempted this, albeit unsuccessfully), yet the trade-off was that the masks made for rather antiseptic and emotionless discussions during class. In any case, because of the masks, David did not know the name of the student who stood at the back of the classroom.

"Take your seats, please," he said, flipping to one of the bookmarked pages in the Bible-size *Norton Anthology*. He briefly scanned the highlighted text before glancing back up at his students.

The student in the plain white mask remained standing at

the back of the classroom. The student was male and dark-skinned—that much David could determine—with hair buzzed nearly to the scalp. He wore a flimsy nylon jacket over a checkered flannel shirt. His motorcycle boots were covered in grime.

There was a roster somewhere in David's briefcase. He kept it handy whenever he felt the need to address a certain student by their name (as opposed to the corresponding character depicted on their mask), and he produced it now, scrutinized it. The empty seat belonged to Sandy Udell.

"Mr. Udell," David said, straightening his posture behind the desk. "Is there a problem?"

Udell ignored him; he just kept gazing out the window. David looked out into the quad to see what might be attracting the guy's attention, but save for a stamped concrete walkway papered in dead leaves and an overcast sky, there was nothing.

"Hey, Sandy," another guy in the class said to him. "Drop your ass, yo."

This comment elicited a few chuckles from the peanut gallery.

David came around his desk and stood at the front of the class. "Mr. Udell," he said, more sternly now. "Sandy. Hello, hello." He snapped his fingers.

The white mask gradually turned until the jagged eyeholes faced David. The plate was not a perfect circle, pulled in at the sides by the bit of elastic that held it to Udell's face, giving it a warped, oblong look. David was suddenly struck by the impression that, behind that mask, Sandy Udell's *face* was actually squished out of proportion, too. He imagined a narrow fish-face with eyes bulging on either side of a narrow, bladed head, and lips so distorted that they couldn't close all the way.

Udell pointed toward the wall of windows. "You see that?" he said, his voice muffled behind the mask.

Again, David looked out the windows. The other students did, too.

"I don't see anything," David said.

"Storm's coming," said one girl.

"Please sit down," David said to Udell.

"We a party to it," Udell said. Those blank eyeholes gazed at David. "All of us."

David said, "What?"

"It's right there, if you all want to see it," Udell went on. He still had his arm up, his finger pointing out the windows. "Just have to open your eyes."

"What is it?" David said.

"An angel," said Udell. He turned back to face out the windows. "Angel coming down from heaven, right through them black clouds. Has a key in one hand, big chain in the other."

The students closest to Udell scooted their desks away from him, the sound of the chair legs squealing across the floor like trumpet bleats. A girl in a plastic Barbie mask got up and, clutching her books to her chest, moved quickly to the opposite side of the room. Others started to get up from their desks, too.

"Everybody just stay calm," David told them.

"He's sick," someone said.

"It's the key to the abyss," Udell said, his voice rising as if to compete with the din of his classmates. "Here I am! I stand at the door and knock!"

"Holy shit," someone groaned.

The students began their evacuation, filing quickly out the door at the back of the classroom and into the hallway. A girl fell over a desk and someone else stepped right on top of her to get out the door. The girl cried out, then managed to hoist herself to her feet and flood out into the hallway with the others.

"Look at it," Udell said. He walked slowly toward the wall of windows. On the horizon, dark storm clouds crept closer and closer to the campus. But what was Sandy Udell seeing? When he reached the windows, Udell placed both palms flat against the glass.

Someone called David's name. He turned and saw Burt Langstrom standing in the doorway behind him, his face pale and stricken. Burt looked over at Udell, who appeared to be mumbling a prayer.

And then Udell screamed.

It was the bloodcurdling scream of someone in physical pain. Udell's hands balled into fists. He began pounding them against the glass.

"What do you want from me?" Udell shouted. "Tell me! Tell me!"

"Come on," Burt said, snatching ahold of David's arm and yanking him toward the door.

But David's feet felt glued to the floor. He couldn't pull his eyes from Udell, his pounding fists against the windowpanes like the thrum of a heartbeat.

"There is a monster coming out of the sky!" Udell screamed. Then he slammed his face against the glass. Again. Again.

David jerked his arm free of Burt's grasp and rushed over to the boy. He grabbed Udell around the waist and yanked him back, but the kid was too big and too determined. David slipped a hand around to the front of Udell's head and tried to prevent any subsequent blows to the glass, which had already begun to fracture, but the kid threw an elbow into David's ribs, knocking the wind from him. David buckled and dropped to the floor.

Someone out in the hallway screamed. Burt rushed over to David, scooped him up under both armpits, and dragged him toward the door. The heels of David's shoes left black streaks on the linoleum.

Udell rammed his head against the window a final time, shattering the glass. Jagged spears of glass rained down on the wall-mounted heater and the floor in a dazzling, reflective array. David gasped and managed to grab some air. Before Burt could drag him out into the hallway, he climbed to his feet and once again shrugged Burt off of him.

He shouted Udell's name, but it was too late: The kid had managed to hop up onto the heater, and without hesitation, leapt through the ragged hole in the window.

A wave of shrieks rose up from out in the hall. David was

crying out, too, although he wouldn't realize this until later, as he sat speaking with police and contemplated why his throat was so hoarse.

David turned and shoved through the crowd of students that had gathered in the hallway just outside the classroom. Burt followed him down the stairwell and out into the courtyard, where a sizeable crowd had already gathered. Shock registered on every face. Someone kept muttering, over and over again, "Oh my God, oh my God, oh my God . . ."

It was only a two-story drop, but Sandy Udell had swan-dived onto the stamped concrete walkway. His paper mask had come off in the fall, revealing a lacerated and glistening pulp that looked more like raw hamburger meat than someone's face. The impact with the pavement had flattened one side of Udell's skull while the glass from the window had sliced the kid's nylon jacket to ribbons.

When Udell gasped, David did, too. The kid's shoulder, which bulged from his torn jacket at an impossible angle, readjusted itself. One of Udell's arms grated along the concrete, scraping over bits of gravel and javelins of glass. He brought his hand up and out and past his head, his fingers groping for purchase on the pavement. Udell was trying to drag himself along the ground.

Jesus Christ, no, David thought.

He knelt beside the boy and said, "You're going to be okay. Just lie there and don't move. Lie there and don't move."

There was a sound like air escaping a vent. Udell's body seemed to deflate. His arm stopped moving; his fingers stopped groping. David heard the gurgle of blood at the back of the kid's throat as he died.

30

They were back on the road the following morning by the time Ellie woke up. She yawned, stretched, gazed momentarily out the passenger window at the autumn trees shuttling by, then looked at him.

"Was it a bad dream?" she said.

He didn't need her to elaborate. What happened back in Goodwin felt like a nightmare to him, too. He shook his head. Said, "I wish it was. Are you okay?"

"I guess so."

He stared at her for several heartbeats before turning back to the road.

"What?" she said.

"What you did to him," he said. "That guy Cooper. With the gun." He wanted to ask a million questions but he couldn't formulate a single one.

"It just happened," she said.

"Was it like when you were angry and you shocked me?" he asked.

"Sort of," she said. "But different, too. It was an accident with you."

"I know. But it . . . I mean, you were able to do it this time. To control it."

"I was angry," she said. "I was scared."

"Is that how it works?"

"I don't know how it works." There was a noticeable

tremor in her voice now. Her face became instantly red. She looked on the verge of tears.

"I'm sorry," he said, his voice lowered. "Does it upset you to talk about it?"

"I don't know."

"I'm just curious. I'm trying to wrap my head around it."

"I don't know how to explain it," she said. "Just like I can take the bad stuff out of you," she said, "I can put it inside someone, too. That's what I did to that man. I gave him all the bad stuff."

"You were able to will it this time," he said.

"I think so," she said. "Yeah."

"Where does it come from? The bad stuff you . . . you gave him . . ."

"I don't know. Sometimes I think maybe that's what I take out of people when they're scared or nervous or angry—all that bad stuff. I don't put anything in there to make you calm, Dad. I just take all that bad stuff away."

David's mind was racing. "So it's . . . it's like you just suck out the fear, the anxiety?"

"Yeah."

"And then where does it go?"

She seemed to consider this. "Inside me, I guess. I hadn't really thought about it until recently."

"That doesn't sound good."

Ellie didn't respond.

"How come it doesn't make you feel all those things? All the bad stuff?"

"It just doesn't," she said simply enough.

"What other people have you done this to?" he asked. "Take the bad stuff away, I mean."

She looked down at her hands twisting in her lap. It was a question he could tell that she did not want to answer.

"How many others, Ellie?"

"I don't know." It came out almost in a whisper.

"Can you think of someone else that you've . . . you've calmed down . . . other than Mom and me?"

"Mrs. Blanche," she said. Mrs. Blanche was the elderly widow who lived in their neighborhood who sometimes watched Ellie after school. Ellie had been with her the day Kathy died.

"Why Mrs. Blanche?" he asked.

"Because sometimes she gets lonely and sad and I feel bad for her."

"Did she say anything to you about it?"

"No," Ellie said. "She never noticed I was doing it."

"Who else?"

"Some kids at school. The day that girl died on the playground, everyone was so *upset*, Dad. We went inside and were watching the people who came in the ambulance from the windows, but we all knew the girl was dead. Some of the kids were very scared. I went around and touched each of them."

This can't be real, he thought. *This can't be happening. It's impossible.*

"But none of them knew I was doing it," she added quickly. "Just like Mrs. Blanche, no one noticed."

"How could they *not* notice, Ellie? It's like . . ." He tried to think about what it was like, how to describe it, having all your sorrow and fear and grief and anger siphoned from you in one fell swoop, and how it could be possible for someone not to realize something out of the ordinary was occurring . . .

"Because it's different now," she said. "It's getting stronger. Before, no one would notice. You and Mom never noticed. But now it's different."

He glanced at her. She looked on the verge of tears again. "I wonder if it's good for you to do it," he said. "It can't be good, taking in all that . . . that poison." There was no other word for it.

Ellie said nothing.

David thought of the way Cooper had screamed when she'd touched him, how his face had gone slack and terror had flooded his eyes. He wondered if he would suffer any permanent damage. But that wasn't a question he wanted to ask his daughter. She was upset enough as it was.

"You saved our lives, you know," he said.

She turned away from him and looked out the passenger window.

"Are you hungry?"

"Yes."

"Good. We can stop somewhere."

"A good place," she said, leaning forward and popping the disc from the CD player. "Not like yesterday."

"No," he agreed. "Not like yesterday." He ran a hand through her shortened hair. "I'm sorry. We don't have to talk about it if it upsets you."

"It doesn't upset me."

"Then why do you seem upset?"

"Because I don't want it to upset *you.*"

He smiled at her. He felt tired, sad, depleted. He felt like sleeping for a week straight. "I just want to be sure whatever this thing is, it doesn't hurt you to do it."

"I guess there's no way to know that," she said.

After a time, he said, "I guess not."

She unwrapped the Bananarama CD from its cellophane then poked it into the CD player. Blessedly, she kept the volume low.

"People are changing," he told her. "Times like these, it brings out the worst in some folks. What happened back there—"

"The good, too, though. Right?"

"Well, yeah." Though they hadn't come across much good lately.

"Was that a real skull, Dad?"

"Probably."

"Whose was it?"

"Couldn't say." He turned to her, cracking a smile. "Probably just someone who lost their head."

"Oh *God,*" she groaned, rolling her eyes but returning his smile. There was some of the old Ellie still in there.

"What do you feel like eating?" he asked.

Without hesitation, she said, "Pizza."

★ ★ ★

They continued across Missouri in the direction of Kansas City for much of the day. Sometimes they drove through residential neighborhoods or sleepy-looking towns, but for the most part they stuck to the highway. Twice they passed police cars waiting like crouching tigers beneath an underpass, and both times David held his breath. Neither car pursued them. He didn't think they'd get lucky again, as they had yesterday. Besides, he'd cleaned the blood from his face and changed his shirt. He was too damned presentable now to scare anyone.

He decided they should wear the face masks he'd bought at the convenience store while they drove, in hopes that any cop who might deign to pull them over would think twice after seeing their faces covered. Ellie laughed at the idea, and David had to agree that he felt foolish driving around with a paper mask over his nose and mouth, but after a while they forgot they were wearing them.

It was a risk anytime they stopped in public, but they had to eat and gas up the Olds. Ellie saw a sign for a Pizza Hut off the highway. David took the exit, and less than five minutes later they were sharing a pie. Seated at the booth, David checked his phone again. Still no response from Tim.

"They used to have a buffet where you could get anything on your pizza," Ellie said.

"Nobody's doing buffets anymore."

"Because people are afraid of getting sick?"

He smiled wanly at her. His head ached. "If you could get anything on your next slice of pizza, what would it be?"

"Noodles," she said.

"Gross."

"How's that gross?"

"Very starchy."

"It's no different than macaroni and sauce."

"On bread. But go ahead, suit yourself," he said. "I gotta find the restroom. You wanna come with me?"

"Don't have to," she said.

He didn't want to leave her sitting here alone, but he

thought it might be more suspicious taking her into the men's room with him.

"I'll be right back," he said, and got up. "You sit tight."

Thankfully, the restroom was deserted. He clutched the tiny porcelain sink and steadied himself. He'd been feeling vertigo for the past several minutes now, ever since they pulled into the restaurant parking lot. Gazing up at his reflection in the narrow rectangular mirror above the sink, some pale, wax figure version of himself stared back. There was an abrasion along the upper part of his nose already beginning to scab. He tugged down one eyelid and saw that the flesh beneath looked darker than before. Irritated. The blood vessels there had also darkened so that they resembled miniscule black hairs veining the soft tissue. It was exhaustion. Or maybe that was just his imagination.

It was then that Dr. Kapoor's voice ghosted back to him: *You're sick, David. Your last blood test. You've got it.*

But it was a scare tactic, an underhanded attempt at getting him to go running back into their hands. With Ellie. He'd know if he was really sick.

He took a few deep breaths, washed his face and hands, then returned to their table.

"Are you okay, Dad?" Ellie asked upon his return. She was scrutinizing him.

"Sure thing." He tried to sound upbeat.

"Can I ask you something?"

"Of course."

She spit a wad of food into her napkin then said, "Those people. The family back in Kentucky."

"What about them?"

"Were they bad?"

"They were confused. They were sick."

"With the Folly?"

"No, honey. They were sick with something else."

"With what?" she asked.

Sick with madness, he thought. *Which, in the end, really, is just the same thing as the Folly after all.*

"They lost touch with reality. With humanity."

"But what they wanted to do to us," she said. "Was that wrong?"

He frowned at her. "Of course."

"But they were just trying to help the boy," she said. "The boy who was sick."

"They were going to hurt us."

"You shot that man."

"Yes. To save our hides. To get us out of there." He folded his hands atop the table. "What's with all the questions?"

"I guess I just don't see the difference," she said.

"The difference in what?"

"In what they're doing from what we're doing," she said.

David shook his head. "What are you talking about?"

"They were just trying to help their kid," said Ellie. "Isn't that what you're doing for me?"

"It's different."

"How?"

"Because we're not hurting anyone. We're not killing people."

"But we sort of are," she said. Her voice was steady and her gaze stuck to him, unwavering. Almost accusatory. "We're sort of killing the whole world."

He reached across the table and touched her hand. "Hey," he said. "Listen to me. It's different."

"Tell me how."

"It just is."

"But that's not an answer. And it's really not different. It's selfish for us to watch everyone else die if I can save them."

"There's no guarantee you can save anyone."

"But there's a chance," she said.

"Ellie, I don't know if there is or not."

"Of course there is," she said. "They wouldn't be looking for us if there wasn't. You wouldn't be so scared that they'll find us and take me away if there wasn't a chance."

"The rest of the world isn't our responsibility," he said.

Her eyes narrowed almost imperceptibly. "Then how does that make us the good guys?"

He reached out, touched the top of her hand. "Can I tell you something I learned almost nine years ago? On the day you were born?"

"What's that?"

"I learned that when you become a parent, you become a secondary character in the story of your own life."

"I don't know what that means."

"It means that above all else, I'm your father. And that means my ultimate responsibility is for your well-being. That is most important above all else. You take a silent oath when you become a parent, and you pledge that, no matter what, you'll never let anything bad ever happen to your kid. Ever. Do you understand?"

"But what about all the *other* people's kids?"

"It's unfortunate, but I won't allow something bad to happen to you."

"Maybe it doesn't have to *be* bad."

He slid his hand away from hers. "Where is this going?" he said. "You want to turn yourself in? Go back to Maryland?"

"I'm not scared of going back," she said. "Not if I can help people."

"Well," he said, "that's very honorable of you. But let me ask you something."

"What?"

"Do you love me?"

She blinked at him. "Of course."

"Do you realize that if anything ever happened to you, I'd just die?"

Her lips parted but she didn't speak.

"I couldn't go on if something happened to you, Ellie," he said. "I would hurt so much that I wouldn't be able to take it. Is that something that you'd want to happen to me?"

Slowly, she shook her head. Her eyes had become glassy, filling with tears.

"I would die, Ellie. If something bad happened to you, I would die. Do you understand?"

She nodded, knocking a tear loose and sending it down her cheek.

"So if you love me," he said, "please, please stay with me on this. Please. Will you? Will you trust that I'm doing the best thing and stay with me on this?"

"I will," she whispered. "I love you, Dad."

"I love you, too, Ellie." He handed her a napkin. "Now dry your face before someone notices."

31

David continued to check his e-mail on his cell phone as they drew closer to Kansas City, but somewhere along the way he stopped receiving an Internet signal. His e-mail wouldn't refresh, and he could no longer pull up any web pages. Panic seated itself firmly at the back of his head. He began to consider the worst—that the government had zeroed in on them and were currently jamming his phone.

They crossed into a town called Harmony, which David hoped wasn't one of those ironic names. The town looked normal for the most part, much as their own hometown of Arnold, Maryland, had been up until they left. The same sign hung in a number of shop windows, large red letters on a white banner—FOLLY FREE, COME AND SEE! This sentiment struck him as both morbid and hopeful. The country had changed so goddamn quickly in the wake of this epidemic.

David negotiated the streets until he found what he was looking for: the Harmony Public Library. It looked deserted, and that was more than okay by him.

"Put your hat back on," he said, circling the block, then pulling into the library's parking lot. There were only two other cars here—a metallic red Prius and a white van whose quarter panels were speckled with mud. The windows on the van's rear doors were obscured by dark curtains. This gave David pause. He'd maintained an aversion to windowless, nondescript vans ever since he'd noticed one showing up in his neighborhood, parked across the street from their house.

Overreacting, said the head-voice. *There was no way they could anticipate you coming here.*

Yet this logic didn't make him feel any better.

"What do you think?" David said. He patted Ellie's knee. "I need to use the computer. Maybe you can read some books or something for a while."

She shrugged. "Okay."

He realized what he was doing: seeing if she'd suggest they skip the library and keep going. It was her intuition he would put his trust in, much as he should have done back in Goodwin. Perhaps her intuition was somehow related to her newly discovered ability, much as he believed the ability itself was somehow related to her immunity to the Folly. Ellie seemed okay with the suggestion, which brought him some peace of mind. God, how he needed some peace of mind . . .

He parked around back. The library was a squat brick saltbox with narrow windows of tinted glass. The mechanized doors swished open and they crossed into an air-conditioned lobby decorated with a contradictory assortment of inspirational posters and antitheft mirrors. The main floor of the library was quiet, drab, sedate. The sections were marked clearly with large signs above the aisles—ADULT FICTION; CHILDREN'S BOOKS; NONFICTION; PERIODICALS—and there was a rank of computer terminals near the DVD and CD displays. A few plush chairs had been arranged on a woven carpet on the other side of the computer terminals.

David pointed to the computers and said, "That's where I'll be. Go find a book, then sit in one of those chairs, okay?"

She nodded, then wandered toward the nonfiction aisle.

David went to one of the computers. The screen saver was on, some sort of cartoon animal in sunglasses and buckteeth bouncing around the screen. He jiggled the mouse and the screen saver vanished. Glancing over his shoulder at the two women talking behind the checkout counter—they hadn't done more than glance in his direction since he and Ellie had come in—he was satisfied that he'd be left alone, at least for a little while.

He opened the Internet browser and pulled up his e-mail account. His flesh prickled with hope. But when he saw Tim hadn't responded to his e-mail, he felt a lead weight pulling down on him, weakening his knees. It wasn't just that they had nowhere else to go; he was beginning to worry that maybe Tim was sick. Or worse.

Behind him, Ellie climbed up into one of the plush chairs with a hardcover book roughly the size of a dictionary. David turned and winked at her. He hoped he looked somewhat sane. She smiled back at him. Beyond Ellie, halfway across the library, a figure stood watching him between two book-shelves. It was a man, broad-shouldered and tall, in faded khakis and a blue chambray shirt. He wore a paper plate mask over his face. As David stared at him, the masked figure turned and disappeared behind one of the bookshelves.

Sweat wrung from David's pores.

"I'll be right back," he said, getting up from the computer terminal. He walked down the aisle in time to see the man turn behind another bookshelf, his large shape moving across the spaces between the books on the shelf.

David turned the corner and stood at the end of the aisle, looking down the rows of books that emptied out onto the lobby. There was no one there, but he saw a shadow retreat-ing along the walkway on the other side of the mechanized doors. Above his head, one of the tubed lights hissed at him then blinked out. When he glanced up, he could see the Rorschach shapes of insects skittering behind the panel of pebbled plastic that covered the fluorescent lights.

When he returned to the computer terminals, he found Ellie still seated in one of the plush armchairs with the large book opened on her lap, talking to a stout and frizzy-haired woman in her sixties. David recognized her as one of the li-brarians from behind the checkout desk. The librarian looked up at him and offered him a smile.

"Such a polite young man," the librarian said to David. He thought she was talking about him at first, but then realized Ellie's disguise had done the trick.

"You just caught him on a good day," David said.

"Most kids, they come in here and go straight for the DVDs. Not that we get many kids in here anymore. It's nice to see a child interested in books. And such an adult book, too," she added, peering over at the text. "From our reference library."

"He's a reader, all right," said David.

"Is there anything you needed help with?"

"No, ma'am. But thank you."

When the librarian left, David lowered his voice and said, "What did she say to you?"

"Nothing," said Ellie. "She just asked what I was reading."

He glanced at the large book in her lap. "What *are* you reading?"

"It's about bird eggs. All different kinds." She turned the large book around for him and pointed to a photo of whitish eggs marbled with dark brown splotches. They looked like a Jackson Pollock painting. "These are oriole eggs. They look just like mine, don't they?"

"They do," he said. "I guess that makes sense. It's Maryland's state bird, you know."

"Not anymore," Ellie said, and closed the book.

32

He decided against driving straight to Kansas City, fearful that someone might recognize them in a big city, so they remained for a while longer in Harmony. He also wanted to check his e-mail at the Harmony library one more time before moving on. He was trying desperately to remain hopeful that he'd hear back from Tim.

There was a small movie theater showing cheesy sci-fi films from the sixties, so David bought a couple of tickets and, for a few hours, he and Ellie sat in the mostly empty movie theater, cloaked in darkness. They shared a bucket of popcorn and a large cup of Sprite, and a few times Ellie laughed at the ridiculousness of what was on-screen. David laughed right along with her. Yet he couldn't help but wonder if this was the last movie they would ever watch together. He felt jittery, sweaty, constantly paranoid that someone would come into the theater and try to pry him from his daughter.

Halfway through the movie, he felt something tickling his upper lip. He touched it and, even in the darkness of the theater, he could see there was blood on his fingertips. A column of panic rose up in him.

"I need to use the restroom," he whispered in Ellie's ear. He was covering his mouth and nose with his hand. "Stay here. Don't leave the theater."

"Okay."

He hurried out into the lobby and, still covering his nose, made a beeline for the men's room. Thankfully, the place was unoccupied. He went directly to the mirror just as a streamer of blood slipped from his right nostril, cascaded over his lips, and dripped off his chin onto the floor tiles.

"Shit."

He grabbed a fistful of paper towels and pressed them to his face. He groped for the sink and turned on the water. It chugged out of the faucet in a noisy spray.

He soaked through several paper towels before the bleeding let up. He held his head back, pinching his nostrils together, while he wet a fresh wad of paper towels under the faucet. He stuck this wad into his mouth, wedging it between his gums and his upper lip, just the way his mother had done on the few occasions he'd gotten a nosebleed as a child.

Someone entered the bathroom, startling him. He glanced in the man's direction—a guy in his late twenties in a white hoodie and oversized jeans hanging halfway down his ass. The guy froze in the doorway when he saw David. Without uttering a word, the guy turned and left.

Shit shit shit shit shit—

The reflection in the mirror was now that of a vampire, a pale-faced night creature who subsisted on blood and would crumble to ash in the sunlight. The bloodied nose, he convinced himself, was from his collision with Cooper back in Goodwin, which had been the thing that had set it bleeding initially. He must have done something to rupture it all over again and—

His cell phone trilled.

He fumbled it out of his pocket and examined the screen before answering. The caller ID was blocked, which gave David pause, but in the end he decided to answer it in hopes that it might be Tim. "Hello? Hello?" His voice was panicked and throaty, and his mouth tasted like blood.

"David? You okay?" It was Tim.

"Jesus Christ," he uttered into the phone. Relief coursed through him like a narcotic. "Oh, Jesus Christ, Tim. I was starting to worry that you were . . ." He trailed off.

"I'm here. I'm here. What's wrong? Your e-mail scared me."

There was no getting around it, so he cut right to it. "Tim, Kathy's dead." And just saying the words aloud caused a sob to lurch up from his throat. His hands wouldn't stop shaking, and his vision began throbbing in sync with his pulse.

"Fuck," Tim said. "No. No, David. Ah, Jesus. How? When? What . . . what happened?"

"It was a few days ago. Tim, it's a long goddamn story and it's gonna sound crazy. I'm terrified to go into it over the phone. I'm worried someone might be tracking my cell phone."

"What the hell is going on, man?"

"Some people are after Ellie and me. Government people."

"Because of Kathy?"

"Not exactly," he said. "Kathy was in the hospital. She volunteered. Doctors, they were studying her. They thought she might be immune to what's been going on, this fucking Wanderer's Folly, but they pushed her too hard. They killed her. Now they want to take Ellie away from me and do the same thing to her."

"Where's Eleanor now?"

"She's okay. She's with me." He closed his eyes, forced himself under control. "Tim, I need your help."

"Where are you?"

For a moment, he had no clue—his brain was fuzzy, his thoughts jumbled and nonsensical. But then the confusion dissipated, revealing a sharp gleam of clarity, and he said, "I'm about an hour or so from Kansas City. I came all this way hoping I could see you, that we could talk in person—"

"Shit, David, I split KC over a year ago. I'm off the grid now. I'm in Wyoming."

David felt the floor drop out from under his feet.

"Oh," he said into the phone, but it was someone else's voice now. The ceramic tiles that formed the backsplash behind the restroom sink appeared to rearrange themselves. David squeezed his eyes shut. He braced himself against the wall with one hand so that he wouldn't topple over. "Okay. Shit. Well, how far is that?"

"From KC? Maybe ten hours. Twelve, if you're cautious about speeding and cops."

Twelve hours, David thought. *A whole day. Jesus Christ. Can we make it that far?*

"Listen," David said. "I'm going to try to get there."

"Sure, sure," Tim said, "but just hold on a sec, okay? Let me think."

David leaned against the restroom door and glanced out into the theater lobby. Two teenagers chatted behind a glass counter, a guy and a girl. They had plastic Halloween masks perched on their heads, but they didn't seem too concerned about germs, judging by the proximity of their faces. It made David think of the guy in the paper plate mask back in the library, and how he'd been staring at him from between two bookshelves.

"Okay," Tim said. "I think I've got an idea that will help you out, but I need to make a phone call first. I'm not sure how long it will take. Are you able to stay there in the city overnight? Do you have money?"

"I've got enough for a motel."

"If not, I can maybe wire you some—"

"No, I don't want to get into all that. I'm trying to lay low. I can find a motel off the highway, but I don't want to go traipsing around the city looking for a Western fucking Union or whatever. I've got enough cash on me."

"Okay, good. Meantime, I'll get things rolling on my end. You'll hear back from me as soon as possible. Just sit tight."

"Okay. And thank you."

"Stay safe."

Tim hung up.

David washed his face and hands again before hustling back out into the lobby. The place was dead, but he noticed a white van parked in a loading zone outside the theater, and the sight of it caused his bowels to clench.

No, please . . .

He hurried back inside the theater, staggering blindly down the aisle looking for the silhouette of Ellie's small head above

the seats. When he found her, he leaned over and told her
they had to leave.

"The movie's not over yet," she protested.

"Now," he said. The few other people in attendance turned
and looked in their direction.

Ellie joined him in the aisle, and he ushered her quickly out
into the lobby. The white van was still there. Scanning the
parking lot through the wall of windows, he could see a black
sedan parked in a spot beneath a lamppost. A second black car
was pulling off the highway and coming up the paved roadway that led toward the theater.

"Come on," he said, and grabbed her hand. They hurried
toward the fire exit. David leaned against the arm bar, expecting an alarm to sound, but nothing happened. They
shoved out into the side parking lot.

"What's going on?" Ellie said.

"There're people out front."

"Cops?"

"I don't know exactly who they are."

Still clutching her hand, he dragged her around the side of
the building. At the corner, he peered into the front lot. The
van was still parked out front. There was someone behind the
wheel talking into a cell phone. The sedan parked in the lot
looked empty, though it was difficult to tell because the windows were tinted. The second black vehicle turned right
toward a shopping center instead of left toward the movie theater. It could have been a ploy to disarm him or it could have
been their tactic, circling around the opposite end of the shopping center only to come at him from the rear.

The guy climbed out of the van, stuffing his cell phone in
the rear pocket of a pair of faded jeans. He looked young and
blue collar, with a ball cap tugged down low over his eyes. He
had a ponytail. When he entered the theater, David tightened
his grip on Ellie's hand and said, "Let's go."

They ran across the parking lot and made it to their car
without anyone jumping out of the shadows and grabbing
them. The engine growled to life. It was all David could do

not to slam down on the accelerator and peel out of the parking lot. But he didn't want to draw any attention to their escape. He pulled out slowly while Ellie whipped her head around, looking for signs of danger. The white van didn't move. The parked sedan remained parked. The second black vehicle did not reappear from the other side of the theater.

They pulled back out onto the highway and drove.

33

Turned out the motel room back in Virginia that first night had been a fluke. David tried two motels in the vicinity of Harmony, but neither would let him pay cash without also showing his driver's license. He might have risked it had he been in a less populated part of the country, but things in Harmony, Missouri, seemed pretty much on the ball, what with all the FOLLY FREE, COME AND SEE! signs in the shop windows. Nowadays, good, healthy places were also xenophobic places, suspicious of strangers snaking into their midst and spreading their poison. He didn't want to risk someone recognizing his name or the picture on his driver's license and putting two and two together. Instead, he drove out of the city, thinking he'd find better luck along the highway. But every place he passed was a Marriott, a Motel 6, a Residence Inn, or some similar chain where he knew he'd run into the same problem. Probably, those places wouldn't even take cash. In the end, he settled on a seedy one-story cinder-block establishment that looked like it catered to prostitutes and had probably seen its fair share of homicides within its walls. The haggard female desk jockey did not disappoint, and brandished him with a metal key dangling from a plastic fob without so much as a glance in his direction.

While Ellie slept in the small bed beside him, her shoe box of oriole eggs on the fiberboard nightstand, David sat propped up on a stack of pillows flipping through muted TV channels. His heart hadn't regained its normal rhythm since their escape from the theater.

After a time, he set the remote down on the nightstand and went into the bathroom. His hands were shaking, and his entire body ached. He still looked like death in the mirror, but he was thankful that his nose hadn't gushed any more blood since the theater restroom. Leaning close to the mirror, he examined his pupils. His eyes looked okay.

You're sick, David. Your last blood test. You've got it.

A thought occurred to him then—one worse than him dropping dead while on the road and leaving Ellie to fend for herself. He thought of Sandy Udell, the kid who had jumped out of the window of his classroom while shrieking about monsters, and of Deke Carmody's madness, which had resulted in the man setting his whole house on fire while he was inside. He thought, too, of the countless horror stories he had heard on the news and read in newspapers since the beginning of the outbreak. All those terrible things people did to themselves . . . and to others.

What if it wasn't a ruse, and that he really *was* sick?

What if he hurt his daughter?

Terror flooded through him at the notion of it. What if he awoke with his hands wrapped around his daughter's throat? What if he . . . Jesus Christ, what if he did something to her with the fucking handgun?

No. I'll keep it together. I won't let that happen.

Which was probably what everyone in the world thought . . . until it happened to them and proved them wrong.

Please don't let that happen. Please let me hand her off to Tim without a problem. After that, if I'm really, truly sick, and it wasn't just that fucking doctor messing with my head, then I'll give up the ghost. Just a little while longer . . .

As if summoned by his prayer, his cell phone vibrated in his pocket. He dug it out and saw the blocked caller ID.

"Thank God," David breathed shakily into the phone.

"You guys okay?" Tim said. "You hanging in there?"

"Yes."

"Okay, good. Listen, here's the deal. Remember the road trip from hell? The one we all took when we were kids?"

"You mean the cross-country trip in that camper?" David said. Tim's father had rented a camper and the four of them had piled inside and toured the country for five weeks. They'd visited national parks, campgrounds, various cities, and other banal landmarks of interest only to David's stepfather.

"Best left forgotten, I know," said Tim, "but do you remember the Great Vomit Fest and Mystery Fire? The one at the campsite?"

"Jesus Christ. Of course I do." To his own amazement, he felt a smile break out across his face.

"Perfect. Meet me there tomorrow night around nine. You should have plenty of time to get there if you leave early enough in the morning."

"Tim, it's not necessary for you to drive all that—"

"Quiet. Don't talk about it. You just get your butt out there."

"I will. Christ, Tim, thank you. You have no idea."

"Not a problem. You sure you don't need money?"

"I'm good."

"And how are you feeling? You holding up? Are you able to drive?"

"Yes."

"And Ellie?"

"She's amazingly okay. She's tough."

"Okay, okay. Look, we'll take care of it. In the meantime, stay off the cell phone. Those things are like hauling around a tracking device. Don't use a GPS, either. Stick to old-fashioned road maps. And try to get some sleep."

"I will. I can't thank you enough."

"Don't thank me yet, bubba," Tim said.

"Good night," David said into the phone before realizing that his stepbrother had already hung up.

Fatigue crashed down on him. Suddenly, it was all he could do to keep his eyes open. He crawled back onto the bed and switched off the lamp. He thought he could sleep for a thousand years, and imagined he was already dead. His eyelids stuttered closed. He yawned. Somewhere in the street, a car alarm blared then went silent, as though garroted. He wondered if it was real or if he was just imagining things.

After a time, he got up and gathered the Glock up from beneath the bed, where he'd wrapped it in his T-shirt. He released the magazine and racked the slide so the chambered round popped out. He stuck the gun back under the bed but hid the magazine on the shelf in the closet. In the event something terrible took hold of him in the night—in the event that Dr. Kapoor hadn't been lying to him after all—he might not retain the memory of where he'd hidden the mag, the gun, or both. He hoped so, anyway.

That night, his sleep was restless and plagued by demons.

34

Six months earlier

The day after Sandy Udell launched himself from a second-story window of the humanities building, both David and Burt Langstrom were interviewed by a police detective named Watermere. They were interviewed separately, taking turns occupying the cramped, book-laden office adjacent to the teachers' lounge, where the cloying, antiseptic smell of Watermere's aftershave was more intimidating than the police detective himself. Watermere's questions were benign and shallow little probes, and he appeared fatigued and overwhelmed by the details of it all. David described what had happened, up until the paramedics arrived on the scene.

Watermere was quick to flip his notebook closed. The whole thing seemed to David like a formality.

"He was sick," David said. It wasn't a question. And judging by the impassive look on Watermere's stony face, he did not think he was passing along any new and vital information to the police detective.

"The Folly, sure," Watermere said. His voice was rough and deeply resonant, as if he gargled with gravel instead of mouthwash in the mornings. "It's every third call I get."

"Are you—you're *serious?* Every third call you *get?*"

"It's bad and getting worse." Watermere seemed under no compunction to withhold any information. "Two days ago, fella over in Glen Burnie, black fella, went for a stroll along the Cromwell Station light-rail tracks. Witnesses said he was raving, having a conversation—heck, an argument—with himself. Nose was bleeding, eyes looking all goofy in his head. When the train appeared, a few folks tried to get him off the track. He refused to go. Then he turns to the train and just, well . . . kinda opens his arms as if to embrace it."

David said, "Jesus."

"Was a mess, that one," Watermere said with a grunt. There was a spot of mustard on his loosened necktie. "They get trapped in these hallucinations, you know? I mean, you hear about it on the news, sure, but you really don't get what it's like till you see it. Or see the aftermath of it."

"Aren't you afraid you might be exposing yourself to it, dealing with all these sick people?"

"Way I hear it, we're all fucked. If it's in the air, it's in the air. I suppose there's a chance it's by touch, by . . . what's it . . . proximity? I mean, anything's possible. But I don't think that's the case, tell you the truth."

"No?"

Watermere leaned over the table, closing the distance between them. The pungent aroma of his aftershave caused David's eyes to water. "You wanna hear something *really* fucked up?" said Watermere. "Something that tells me humanity is doomed?"

"Okay."

"I got a brother-in-law works as a prison guard at the correctional facility over in Cumberland," Watermere said. "That's the federal joint. They got a wing of inmates there done some heinous things, Mr. Arlen, and these guys, they don't get visitors, or letters, or the occasional romp in the fuck-shed, if you catch my meaning. Other than the prison guards and the other fellas who share that wing, they get exactly zero contact with the outside world. Total isolation. Yet I heard from my brother-in-law that about three or four months ago, these guys start exhibiting symptoms of Wanderer's Folly. At first, the guards didn't know what to make of it. Most of these guys are nut-balls to begin with, so how can you tell when they're hallucinating, right?" Here, Watermere tapped his temple, as if to illustrate where all the crazy was housed. "But then things got worse. One fella, he chewed right through one of his wrists until he fully amputated his hand. Another guy actually pushed his skull through the bars of his cell. Killed himself, in other words. A bunch of the others just curl up in a corner of their cell, whimper like kids who've been spanked for spilling a glass of milk."

"They're all sick," David said.

"Yep," said Watermere. "Prison doctor confirmed it with blood tests. And they all died a couple of weeks later. Hemorrhages, embolisms, aneurysms—whatever it is. But what I'm saying is, they'd been *isolated*. And none of the prison guards had any symptoms or ever got sick. No one was carrying the sickness to 'em, in other words. Yet here they are, these jailbird monsters, getting sick and droppin' dead jus' like the rest of us."

At that moment, Watermere was overcome by a coughing jag so profound it sounded painful. Still sputtering, he produced a handkerchief from the inside pocket of his sports coat and covered his mouth with it. When he finished, his eyes red and leaky, a timorous smile curling up the corners of his otherwise humorless mouth, the detective said, "Coughin' ain't a symptom of the Folly. That's the emphysema." Then he laughed, an aggravated explosion that started in his belly and volcanoed out through his gaping, spit-flecked lips. Then the laugh transitioned into another coughing fit that, once more, caused David to imagine a bottle of Listerine in Detective Watermere's bathroom filled with granulated bits of gravel.

After the interview with Watermere, David met Burt Langstrom for lunch at the campus cafeteria. David relayed to Burt what the detective had told him about the prison, and Burt just nodded and looked mostly down at his food.

"What's wrong?" David said.

Burt looked up. The smile that appeared on his face wasn't just false: It was terrifying. "Nothing, David," he said.

"Hey, man, it's cool if you're shaken up. I'm shaken up, too. Every time I close my eyes I can see that poor kid . . ."

"I don't like this," Burt said.

"What's that?"

"Any of this." He sat back in his chair and glanced around the cafeteria. It was mostly empty, which was rare for this time of day. The only noise came from the TVs bracketed to the walls and the clanging of pots and pans from the kitchen. "I'm uncomfortable here. Anyway, I heard it's only a matter of time before they shut things down completely."

"You mean here at the college? That's just a rumor."

"Is it?" Burt's eyebrows arched. All color had drained from his face. "Is that what you think? Students are dropping classes left and right. They're leaving and going back home to be with their families. They're scared, David." He lowered his voice. "I'm scared, too."

At the far end of the cafeteria, one of the lunch ladies dropped a tray of dishes; the sound of them shattering on the tiled floor was like an A-bomb barreling through the silence. Both David and Burt jerked their heads in the direction of the commotion in time to see the lunch lady, a portly woman in what resembled a starched white nurse's uniform, frowning apologetically at them. A second woman joined her, and together they began cleaning up the mess. They both looked terrified, as if the accident might get them fired. Since the Folly, every accident was suspicious, every trip of the tongue or lapse in memory a cause for concern.

"I keep watching my kids," Burt said. "I'm looking for signs of . . . I don't even know. Disassociation? Daydreaming? Some say bloody noses or burst blood vessels in the eyes or eyelids. How can you tell if a young girl's daydreams are killing her?" He laughed a little bit here, but there were tears forming in the corners of his eyes. David considered that maybe telling him about Watermere's prison story had been a bad idea. "Just look at that," Burt continued, pointing over David's shoulder to one of the wall-mounted TVs.

David turned around and saw a news report about the outbreak in China. There were people crying in front of the camera, which then cut to what appeared to be men in haz-mat suits rolling body bags into a mass grave.

"It's no better anywhere else, including here in the States," Burt said. "The Black Death wiped out an estimated two hundred million people. That was a third of the world's population back then. At this rate, we'll reach those numbers by the end of the year, or maybe early into next, if we're lucky."

"They may find a cure before that," David offered.

"Or they may not," Burt said. "Doctors don't know shit. It's fucking biblical, David. A plague manifests among the populace with no rhyme or reason, shot like a bolt of lightning straight from the finger of God."

"You don't really believe that, do you?"

"Been hearing about these people, call themselves Worlders."

"They're a cult," David said.

"They might be a cult, or they might be the only sane people left on the planet. While the world is trying to fight this thing, to understand it, to . . . to somehow annihilate it even though no one knows what the hell it even is . . . these Worlders, they're *embracing* it, David. They're saying, 'Okay, yeah, bring it on. People have been shitty to each other for so long that maybe this is the planet's way of ridding itself of us.' It's like we're fucking head lice or something."

"I'm not so sure that's the right way to look at things, either," David said.

"Listen," Burt said, lowering his voice. "I've been considering getting out of here. There's a used car lot I pass every night on my way home. They've got really low rates on RVs right now. Rentals, you know? I guess they're big in the summer, but now, they're just sitting there collecting dust."

"What are you getting at?"

"I'm thinking about renting one. Packing up my family and getting the hell out of here."

"And go where?"

"Someplace where we can all be alone. Someplace where

there aren't any other people around. It might be safer that way."

"Didn't you hear the story I just told you? What that detective said about those inmates?"

Burt was shaking his head. "He's not a doctor. What does he know?"

"I just don't want to see you make some knee-jerk reaction because of what happened to Udell or because of shit you hear on the news or read on the Internet," David said. "I'm as shaken up as you are, but we've got to keep our wits about us. And in this day and age, where in the world would you even go where you and your family could be completely alone?"

"A campground," Burt said without missing a beat. David could tell the man had been giving this plan more than just a passing consideration. "Maybe a national park somewhere out west where there's less people. Or the mountains. We could live in the RV and tuck ourselves up into the woods. It's not as impossible as it sounds. I used to go camping with my dad and brothers all the time when we were kids."

"But that's just camping. My family rented an RV and did it one summer when I was a kid, too. But that was only for a few weeks. I mean, how long are you talking here, Burt?"

"Permanently," Burt said. "Or at least until things get back to normal."

David wondered if things would ever get back to normal. He asked Burt what he would do for money in the meantime.

"Wouldn't need any," Burt said. "We'd live off the land. You're not hearing me, David."

"I hear you just fine. I just think you should take some more time and think this through. Have you discussed this with Laura?"

Burt dismissed his question with a flap of his hand. "Laura's in denial. She's petrified. Did I tell you she quit her job? She's home with the girls now. Some days she doesn't leave the bedroom."

"And you think you're just going to convince her to hop in

an RV with you and the girls and drive up to some mountain somewhere?"

"I can." The words issued out of Burt's mouth in a breathy whisper. David could tell he had already convinced himself of this point, too. "I can do it. And you should talk to your wife, too, David. You need a plan. You can't just sit here and hope that some miracle will happen and things will get better."

David turned again and glanced at the nearest TV screen. A mother with blood on her face was clutching a small child to her breast. The child's arms and legs flailed, its eyes bugging out like the eyes of a lizard. There was the absence of thought behind those eyes, replaced by nothing but hallucinatory insanity. Just when the image had grown too intense to keep watching, the TV cut to some amateur footage of people jumping off the roofs of buildings. David had to look away.

Later, David cancelled his afternoon classes and went home early. When he drove past the charred skeleton of Deke Carmody's house, he was surprised to find that the memory of that horrible night at Deke's house now seemed no more important than all the other terrible snapshots that scrolled on a nonstop loop through his head: Sandy Udell, the screaming mothers, suicidal people plummeting from rooftops to their deaths, the frequent absences of his students as well as the other deaths on campus, the ice cream man who lost his mind right there in the cul-de-sac that December night that now seemed a million years ago. There was also Kathy's increasing depression, something she freely acknowledged and accepted with inevitable finality. She had become withdrawn, and even her interactions with Ellie appeared rote and unemotional. Her blood test had come back negative for the virus, as had the tests both David and Ellie had most recently taken—the government had mandated quarterly blood tests for all citizens by this point, done alphabetically and by county—yet Kathy shambled through her days and evenings like someone sentenced to death.

When he pulled the car into the driveway, he saw Ellie on

the front lawn beside the hedgerow that ran the length of the house. At the sound of his approach, she turned and watched him shut down the car. She waved and he waved back as he got out.

"Hi, Little Spoon," he said, walking across the lawn toward her. Brown crickets springboarded into the air and rebounded off his shins while gnats clotted around his face. He swatted the gnats away. "Whatcha doing?"

"Delicate work," Ellie said. She was holding a shoe box in one hand while holding back one of the branches of the hedgerow with the other. "I'm trying to be careful, but I can't get back there to reach them."

"Reach what?"

"The eggs."

For a moment he had no idea what she was talking about. But then he recalled the bird nest below her bedroom window, and the three spotted eggs nestled within it.

"You sure that's a good idea?" he said.

"The mother never came back," Ellie advised, "and I'm not just going to let them be abandoned."

David eyed the shoe box before reaching out and shoving the branches of the hedgerow out of the way. "So, what's the plan? You're going to be their surrogate?"

"Huh?"

"Their adoptive mother."

"Oh. Yes. Of course. Why not?"

"Because they're eggs," he said. Between two prickly boughs he spied the nest—a brownish-gray meshwork of twigs and dead leaves and blades of grass and bits of paper and cellophane all meticulously knitted together. Inside, the eggs looked profoundly delicate, and it amazed David that any birds in the history of the world had ever survived.

"They're just eggs *now*," Ellie corrected.

"And they've been eggs for quite some time," David said. He gathered the nest out of the tangle of branches and handed it over to Ellie. "They aren't going to hatch, baby."

"You don't know that," she said.

"I'm pretty sure. It's been so long, they would've hatched by now."

"You don't *know* that," she insisted, holding out the shoe box with its lid open. "Besides, it isn't right that they should be abandoned like that. Someone needs to take care of them."

"All right," he acquiesced, setting the nest into the box, then brushing his hands along the legs of his trousers. "So I guess now you're the mama bird."

"What word did you say before?" she asked, peering down at the nest in the box. She cradled it against her breast.

"Surrogate," he said.

"Surrogate," she repeated. Then she frowned. "That doesn't sound nice at all," she added.

35

He woke her just before dawn, and in silence they cleaned themselves up, pulled on fresh clothes, and made their way out to the car without muttering a single word to each other. It wasn't until they were heading west on I-70 with the sun creeping up along the rear windshield that Ellie asked where they were going.

"I spoke to Uncle Tim last night," he explained. "We're supposed to meet him at a campground in Colorado. We've still got a lot of driving to do."

"Why a campground?"

"Uncle Tim's just being cautious, and I can't say I disagree with him. Also, I don't think he wanted me driving the whole way."

"Why?"

"Because he knows people are looking for the two of us."

"Did you tell him about Mom?"

"I did. Anyway, this campground," he said, quickly changing the subject, "it was a place we'd visited when we were kids. It's called Funluck Park. Some name, huh?"

"What is it?"

"Just a state park. A campground. But do you know what it used to be?"

"What?"

"An amusement park. You know, with rides and game booths and all that stuff."

"Like Disney?"

He laughed. "Not even close, sweetheart. It was just an old park when I visited as a kid. But you know what? A lot of the old amusement park rides were still there, left behind. They were sort of like run-down landmarks."

"Do you think they're still there now?"

"Could be," he said. "Hey, do you want to hear a crazy story about what happened there when I was a kid?"

For the first time in a long while, her face brightened. "Sure."

So he told her about the cross-country trip his family had taken back in the summer of David's eleventh year. Emmitt Brody had rented an RV and had shuttled his brood—Tim, David, David's mother—beneath what Woody Guthrie once proclaimed was the "endless skyway." The trip lasted about five weeks, during which time they made it all the way out to the West Coast and back.

At one point in the trip, during a stop at a gas station somewhere in Colorado, Emmitt Brody got wind of a rinky-dink amusement park that had been closed down decades earlier and now served as a local campground. The gas station attendant who imparted this bit of trivia unto David's stepfather also added that many of the rides that had serviced the amusement park had been left behind, and while they were all out of commission and beyond repair, they had become a sort of trademark for the little park and the area that surrounded it.

Munching on gas-station hot dogs, they had detoured to the park. Soon, they came upon the ancient wrought-iron fence that surrounded the wooded grounds. There was a sign out front that read FUNLUCK PARK. Within that fence stood the relics of its former incarnation—the undulating roller-coaster tracks overgrown with weeds, the Tilt-A-Whirl cars sunken partway down into the earth, the bumper cars strewn about in a distant field like a herd of buffalo that had died in the middle of some prehistoric pilgrimage, a wooden carousel horse tipped on its side, weather-faded and strangled by vines, or perhaps the garishly painted boards of a gift shop tossed about like so much driftwood washed up on a beach.

They all got sick soon after arriving at the park, undoubt-
edly the result of eating the gas-station hot dogs, and each
of them heaved repeatedly into the underbrush. David and
Tim sobbed while David's mother vomited almost politely
behind a lilac bush. Emmitt soon joined them, the sounds
of his upchucking like the uncooperative growls of a stalled
engine. In the confusion, Emmitt had dropped his lit cigar
into a nearby trash receptacle; the debris inside blossomed
into flame. After wiping his mouth on his sleeve, David rolled
over and watched the flame dancing in the barrel, tongues of
fire licking the sky, so bright it hurt his eyes to look at it, to
stare—

He stared—

So bright, he couldn't—

"Daddy." It was Ellie's voice, swimming down to him as if
from the opening in a well.

David blinked and realized he wasn't staring at a fire—or
even the memory of a fire—at all, but directly at the sun,
which filled their entire windshield. The car was positioned at
an angle off the highway, facing backward, the vehicle's nose
butted up against the guardrail. His door was open and he had
his left foot out on the ground, a cool wind blowing the damp
hair off his sweaty forehead.

He looked at Ellie, who stared at him with terror in her
eyes.

"Hey," he said, and rubbed the side of her face.

"What happened?" she asked. He voice was barely audible.
"You were talking and then . . . then . . . you just stopped and
turned the car around . . ."

He glanced down and saw the car was still in Drive. If he'd
taken his foot off the brake . . .

No.

"Jesus, kid," he said, pulling his leg back in and shutting the
door. "I guess I was daydreaming for a second there, huh? Not
enough sleep."

"You just . . . just pulled the car over and turned around
and . . ."

"Hey, everything's okay." He gave her his best smile. "Why are you so upset?"

"You scared me. You were talking, telling me a story, and then you started talking funny and then you just stopped."

"I'm tired, El. Very tired."

He could see that her eyes were searching his. In the end, he looked away.

"Let's get back on the road, okay?"

After a moment, Ellie nodded.

They got back on the road.

36

Four months earlier

As more and more students dropped their courses, the college granted the remaining students the option of completing the semester from their homes. Certain instructors lectured via Skype while others simply e-mailed assignments to their students and awaited the return e-mails with the work attached. For David, who taught English literature, the change was welcome and easy: There was little he needed to lecture on, and his students could all read the assigned work from the privacy—or safety—of their own homes. Papers were submitted to him via e-mail. When someone failed to send in a paper, David would send a follow-up e-mail as a reminder. If *that* e-mail went unanswered, David gave up. He assumed he was dealing with your basic collegiate delinquency—there were always a slim few who carried their laziness straight out of high school and into college . . . and, David supposed, throughout the rest of their lives, too—but on the chance that something more profound had come into these students' lives, he was not going to be the one to inquire about it.

He assumed a good number of them died in those final weeks before the school year ended.

The faculty was also allowed to work from home, yet David opted to come to campus at least two days out of the week. For one thing, there was little work he could get done with both Kathy and Ellie at home now. Kathy had taken to homeschooling the girl, and while Ellie had always been a good student, Kathy became frequently frustrated in her inability to get the information across to her. But it was more than this distraction that caused him to work in the English department's office these few days a week; it was Kathy's overall disposition, which seemed to be worsening with each passing day. Her eyes always looked clouded with dark morbidity; her thoughts always seemed to be elsewhere, occupied by some distant but oncoming doom that, sometimes, David could feel if he sat too close to her or stared at her long enough. If he spent too much time around her, she would inevitably lash out at him. Lately, their arguments had been frequent and fierce.

This change in Kathy terrified him. However, he didn't have the luxury of falling apart. Kathy's disposition forced him to remain falsely positive, if only around Ellie. His hours spent at the college allowed for him to release some of his own anxiety without worrying about keeping up a strong front for his family's sake. Sometimes he had to pull over on the shoulder of the road during the hour-long drive to the college, overcome by a panic attack. Sometimes he sat in the department office's lounge area with the lights off, staring off into space, terrified to talk to anyone else on campus for fear that their conversations would inevitably turn apocalyptic.

Sometimes Burt Langstrom was there, sometimes he wasn't. When he *was* there, he acknowledged David with the same detachment as Kathy. More than once David wondered if this was a sign of the illness itself—a preemptive disassociation prior to the onset of the hallucinations. Indeed, there was a fog about Burt that spoke to his mind being elsewhere. *Wandering* was the word that immediately came to David when he looked at Burt like this. *His mind is wandering.* But for obvious reasons, he didn't like to think about it in those terms.

On this particular afternoon, David arrived in the lounge to find Burt propped up on the ratty sofa, eyes glued to the television on the counter. On most channels, it was nothing but news reports now. Today, the news report was about some small island in the Pacific whose entire population had died. The newscaster kept using the term *extinct* in all its forms, which made David think of the dodo bird. And then birds in general.

"I didn't know you were here today," David said, pausing in the doorway of the lounge.

Burt did not answer.

"You look like a zombie. You shouldn't be watching this madness." He reached out to turn the TV off, but Burt barked at him. It was just that—a nonverbal bark, just like an animal might make. David froze. When he looked at his friend, he saw that Burt's eyes were bleary with tears.

David went to the fridge, stuffed his lunch bag inside, then stood there breathing heavily with his hands on his hips. He considered not coming to the college anymore, just like the students, for the sheer purpose of keeping away from Burt Langstrom. The man was setting him on edge. He no longer liked being around him. No, it was worse than that: He no longer felt *comfortable* around Burt.

"I'm no mathematician," Burt spoke up suddenly, "but they say there's a baby born somewhere in the world every eight seconds. The rate of infection from Wanderer's Folly has just surpassed that. Like I said, I'm no mathematician, but I can figure out what that means."

"I think you're driving yourself mad," David said.

"Conspiracies abound, David." Burt turned and faced him. He'd lost weight so that his cheeks hung from him like the jowls of a hound dog. His eyes were rheumy as a hound dog's, too. David didn't like the pallor of his skin. "You should read the *Nadsat Report*," Burt said.

"What's that?"

"Online newspaper. Government cover-ups and the like. They've been posting some thought-provoking articles. They've got some insight, boy. Think the government might be responsible for this whole thing."

"The government," David said.

"They've been following the birds' disappearances, too. Early on. Like, before the mainstream media. Suspected something was up from the very beginning. You know what they're talking about now?"

"What's that?"

"The quarantines. Say some are legit but others are a ruse. They think people are being taken away against their will and studied in secret hospitals."

David said nothing.

"Government thinks maybe some people out there might be immune. If you're in a quarantined zone, where pretty much the entire population has got the Folly, and you *don't*, well, maybe that's something important. What do you think about that?"

"I just don't know, Burt." He felt suddenly exhausted. These conversations made him nervous.

"The *Nadsat Report*," Burt said, still staring at the TV.

"You been eating, Burt?"

"Sure. Say, how's the family, David?"

"They're okay."

"You're not still sending that daughter of yours to school, are you?"

"Kathy's been homeschooling her."

"Sure, sure." Burt nodded. His wet eyes danced around the room. "Laura's been doing the same for our girls. Don't let their friends come over anymore, either. Moon-Bird complained on that score, but I wasn't budging." Burt turned a grim smile toward him. David imagined he could see the man's skull through the thin, transparent fabric of his flesh. "Moon-Bird's what we call our youngest. A nickname. It comes from a book of poems she likes."

"I think you should see a doctor, Burt."

"The only fellow I'm going to see, David, is the guy who rents those RVs off the beltway. Remember me talking about him?"

"Of course. That's still the plan?"

That grim smile widened. Burt's teeth looked gray. "Still the plan, Stan," he said.

"Maybe I should drive you home."

"Don't think so. Thanks, though."

"Do you even have any work to do? Papers to grade?"

"Not a one," Burt announced. He turned back to the television. There was a toothpaste commercial on now. "I'm just out here gathering my thoughts. I guess I come out of habit. It makes it easier to pretend that things are still normal by coming in here every day."

David understood. It was what he was doing, too.

"You said your little girl is all right, David? She acting fine to you?"

"She's fine, Burt."

Burt Langstrom's brow creased. "Yeah, but . . . how do you know?"

"I . . . I don't know, Burt. But she's the same. That's all. She isn't sick."

"Well, that's good, I guess. That's real good."

"Are your girls all right, Burt?"

"Oh yeah, David. They're beautiful. Just goddamn beautiful."

David left him that way, opting instead to head across campus to the administrative offices. Only one secretary was there, reading a magazine behind a screen of bulletproof glass. She wore a surgical mask over her nose and mouth.

"I need to look up a phone number of someone in my department," David said, speaking into the microphone box in the glass.

The secretary's brow creased. "Who are you?" Her voice was barely audible.

He held his faculty ID against the glass.

The secretary got up and approached the glass. Once David gave her the information, she rooted through her computer before supplying him with the telephone number. He entered it into his phone, thanked the woman—she had already gone back to her magazine—then slipped outside into the quad.

It was springtime and the afternoon was alive with the

sound of insects of all kinds. Without birds, the world was becoming choked with them, and in such a short amount of time. Long-legged things popped out of the grass, and a variety of flying thingamajigs navigated from flower to flower. It got so you couldn't open your mouth outdoors without inhaling a few.

He dialed the number, heard it ring several times. He realized he was holding his breath. It kept ringing, and he was about to hang up when a woman's voice answered.

"Is this Laura?" he said.

"Who's this?" said the woman. She sounded nervous, on edge. He'd met Laura Langstrom a number of times, at various social events at the college. David and Kathy had also been over to the Langstroms' for a cookout last summer, a hospitality David kept meaning to repay. Laura Langstrom was what someone might refer to as a hefty woman, with meaty upper arms and thighs that stretched the fabric of her pants. She had always been pleasant enough—the entire Langstrom clan had always been happy and cheerful—but now she sounded like someone who'd been holed up in a cave for half a year and had forgotten how to converse with another human being.

"This is David Arlen, Laura. From the college."

"Burt's college?" she said.

"Yes."

"Is that where he is now?"

"Yes." He thought it odd she wouldn't know where her husband was. "He's—"

"Is he okay?" she said, cutting him off. "Did something happen?"

"Well, nothing happened, but—"

"You wouldn't be calling me if something hasn't happened. Just tell me."

"Burt's okay. I've just been worried about him lately. His . . . his behavior, I guess. His . . ." His what? Attitude? Outlook? Entire persona? He didn't know how to finish the thought.

"Does he seem sick to you, David?"

"He seems severely depressed. I think he should talk to a doctor."

"We've all been to doctors. We had our quarterly test just last month. We're all clean here, David. Folly-free, as they say." She practically sang this last part, as though it was part of some advertising jingle.

"That's not the kind of doctor I'm talking about. I think he needs to see . . . well, maybe a shrink."

"We don't have a shrink."

"Maybe he should get one. Listen, I know this is coming out of left field, Laura, but I felt I should do something—"

"Tell me," Laura Langstrom said, and now her voice dropped, as if they were two criminals conspiring over the phone about an upcoming heist. "How is your family, David? How is . . . uh . . ."

"Kathy and Eleanor," he finished for her.

"Yes!" The word jolted from her. "Yes, that's right. How are they? Are they healthy? Have you gotten blood tests recently?"

"We're all clean."

"Are you *sure*?" Her words hung there, the emphasis on that final word somehow sounding perverse. As if she was taunting him.

"As sure as we can be."

"Because sometimes you can't trust them," said Laura.

"Trust what? The blood tests?"

"Yes, that's right. But not *just* the tests. *Them.* Do you understand?" She whispered this last part.

"No. Who's 'them'?"

"Them," she said. "Them. You want to know something? We don't let anyone come over anymore. I suggest you do the same."

"We're keeping to ourselves," he said, suddenly wondering how this panicked woman on the other end of the line had managed to usurp this conversation.

"And Burt and I, we keep *watching* them. Because I think

part of this whole thing—the part they don't report about on the news, I mean—is the *sneaking* part, the part that creeps up on you and gets you, infiltrates you, even when they tell you the blood tests are all fine. Fine and dandy." Again, she lowered her voice to a whisper: "But I don't believe it. Not for one goddamn second. You might think we don't notice those . . . slight changes . . . in their behavior, David, but we do. We do."

"Who are you talking about?"

Laura Langstrom's response was a single whistling exhalation.

"Are you feeling all right?" David asked.

"Me? Oh, I'm just fine, David." Her normal voice again, as if some pill had just kicked in and regulated her. "We're just all so scared, David."

"Burt mentioned something about packing up and driving off somewhere."

"Now?"

"No, not now. He said something about renting an RV and—"

"It's beyond that," Laura said flatly, once more cutting him off. "I'm afraid it's beyond all of that, David." She cleared her throat. "It's David, isn't it? I've forgotten."

"Yes," he said. *This was a bad idea.*

"Maybe," she said, "it's beyond that for all of us."

"I'm not sure I—"

Laura Langstrom hung up.

37

They stopped for milk shakes at a dusty curbside burger joint, slurping them down while seated at a picnic table, a yellow and white umbrella over their heads for shade. At one point, when Ellie got up to use the restroom, David went inside the place and bought a road map and a pen. His phone had GPS but he was reluctant to use it. Opening up the map at the picnic table, he found their current location, which was halfway across Kansas, then located the area in Colorado where he knew Funluck Park to be. He penned some calculations in the margin, estimating the time it would take to get to the park in Colorado, and then how long it would take to make it to Wyoming from there. It was a lot of driving.

A man in white shirtsleeves and dusty slacks ambled over to the Oldsmobile. David glanced up at him and watched him, unobserved. The man was spooning frozen custard from a Styrofoam cup into his mouth while he walked around the front of the Oldsmobile. He was a large fellow with an expansive midsection. Beads of perspiration stood out on his sun-pinked forehead. The man turned and saw David staring at him.

"Ninety-nine Cutlass, am I right?" said the man, jerking a thumb over his shoulder at the car.

"You're right," David said.

"Used to have one just like it, 'cept in powder blue. How many miles?"

"More than you'd think."

"Don't you know mine went for just over three hundred thousand? And she was still purring when I sold her for five hundred bucks to some teenager."

David forced a grin. He was uncomfortable talking to the man. Something about the guy reminded him of Detective Watermere.

Ellie came out of the bathroom and joined David at the table. She wasted no time popping the milk shake straw back into her mouth.

"That your boy?" the man said. David watched as the stranger shoveled another spoonful of frozen yogurt into his mouth.

David nodded, hoping the man would take the hint that he was not interested in conversation.

"Well, then. You folks have a good one." The man raised a hand and ambled off, apparently taking the hint. A minute or two later, the man pulled out onto the roadway behind the wheel of a silver Honda. He tapped the horn twice, waved at David, then motored on down the highway.

"Who was that?" Ellie asked.

"Don't know. Just a guy." But he hadn't liked his questions, hadn't liked the way he'd been looking at the car. *Scrutinizing* the car.

Midway through his milk shake—mint chocolate chip, his favorite ever since he was a kid—his cell phone trilled. He saw the blocked caller ID and worried that Tim's plans had changed.

"Yeah, hello," he said, answering the call.

"Is this David Arlen?" A man's voice, frank and clipped. He didn't wait for a confirmation. "My name's Craddock. I've taken over the CDC's northeast operations formerly overseen by Dr. Kapoor."

"You guys are relentless. You tell Kapoor he can go jump off a goddamn bridge."

"Kapoor's dead," said Craddock. "Most of his staff are, too.

I've been flown in from Atlanta to pick up where he left off. You and your daughter, Mr. Arlen, are our number-one priority at the moment."

"I don't give a shit. I'm hanging up."

"Don't be so reactionary. You and I need to talk. ASAP. Wherever you are, I'll go there and meet you, face-to-face. We don't need to involve your daughter at this point. I understand your reservations. I just want to talk with you and explain things."

David barked a laugh into the phone. "Meet me? Are you serious? You'll never find me."

"We will," Craddock said. There was not a waver in his voice. "It may take some time, but we'll find you eventually. I just hope it isn't too late by then."

"You can keep your threats."

"You keep answering your phone," Craddock said. "There must be some part of you that questions what you're doing. What happened to your wife will not happen to Eleanor."

"Empty promises," David said.

"And then there is you, Mr. Arlen. Your condition. How long do you think you can keep this up?"

David stepped away from the table, out of Ellie's earshot. She watched him go.

"Have the hallucinations started?" Craddock said. "The nosebleeds?"

"Lies," David growled into the phone. "I'm not an idiot."

"We can't help you, Mr. Arlen," Craddock said, his voice as smooth as silk sheets, "but we can help your daughter. And your daughter can help the world."

"You're just trying to trick me."

"For what purpose? Do you think my goal here is to torment you and torture your little girl? No, Mr. Arlen. My goal is to save people. I can understand why you're not convinced of that at the moment, so that is why I'm asking you to sit down and talk with me. Let's reach an agreement. An understanding. It doesn't have to be like this."

"Go to hell," David said.

"You can't run forever," Craddock said. "Based on the results of your last blood test, I can't image you have much time left at all."

"We're gone," David said into the phone. "Do you hear me? We're gone. And if you keep this up—if the cops or the CDC or the fucking FBI or whoever else continues to look for us—I will personally hunt you down and kill you. Do you hear me?"

"David—"

"Go fuck yourself." David hung up. His whole body vibrated. The milk shake in his stomach felt as if it had started to curdle.

He stood there for a moment, not trusting himself to maintain his composure if he returned to Ellie too soon. He watched the dust swirl in off the roadway. He listened to a pair of young boys playing behind the burger joint, probably the children of the proprietor. He looked in their direction and saw two dark-skinned, slender boys chasing butterflies through a field. So many butterflies. Whole regiments of them.

Beyond the boys, deeper in the field, stood a figure. It was a man, though his face was obscured by a plain white mask with two eyeholes cut into it. It looked eerily like the paper plate mask Sandy Udell had been wearing the day he threw himself from the classroom window.

Despite the distance between them, the figure appeared to be staring directly at him.

Then a sound registered in his ears. Upon hearing it, he realized he *had* been hearing it for several seconds now, but was only now realizing it. The goddamn whirring blades of a helicopter.

No sooner did he realize this than he looked up and saw the bright silvery frame of a chopper cruise out from behind the roof of the burger joint. It was much too low to the ground to be a casual flyby, and it sent dust and debris twirling like dervishes across the parking lot. The striped umbrellas above the picnic tables rattled and flapped in their frames. Ellie looked up as the helicopter rushed by overhead, its shadow momentarily darkening her as it whipped along the earth. She covered her eyes with one hand as grit whipped across the ground.

David watched it head in the direction of the setting sun. The land was flat, and he was able to watch it for a good long time before it shrank first into a pinpoint, then vanished into nothingness altogether.

"Who were they?" Ellie asked, staring out at the horizon. "Cops?"

He hadn't made out any insignia on the helicopter. "Not sure. Military, I think."

"Should we get back in the car?"

"Yes."

Before leaving, he looked back toward the field. The two boys were still frolicking in the tall grass, but the man in the mask was gone.

38

Fifteen minutes later, as they continued heading east along I-70, a police car appeared in the rearview mirror. It seemed the past couple days could be summed up by a procession of police cars in rearview mirrors. They'd passed a few on this lonely stretch of highway, either parked on the shoulder against endless fields of corn or seated behind a billboard, their windshields golden with pollen, but this was the first one on the road. David kept his eyes on it for a while, and at one point he thought that the cruiser was keeping a deliberate distance between them. When David slowed, it appeared that the police car slowed, too. For a moment, he considered pulling onto the shoulder of the road to see if the cop would pass him, but he decided that was a stupid idea. What if the cop stopped to see if he needed some assistance? He'd be inviting disaster.

After a time, his mind returned to the man back at the burger and ice cream shop, the guy who'd been appraising the Oldsmobile while spooning frozen yogurt into his gullet. *Ninety-nine Cutlass, am I right?* It wasn't a goddamn Lamborghini; why had that guy been so interested in the car?

But it wasn't really the car, was it? he thought now. *He hadn't been looking at the car; he'd been checking out the license plate.*

"Goddamn," David muttered, glancing up at the rearview again at the police car. It maintained its distance.

A Maryland license plate in Kansas was certainly unusual but not something overtly suspicious, was it? The guy had definitely been looking at the license plate . . . yet despite his friendly banter, he never once commented on the fact that David and Ellie were roughly twelve hundred miles from home. He'd commented on Ellie, though. *That your boy?*

"Back at the milk shake place, when you went to the bathroom, which restroom did you use?"

"What?"

"Which restroom, El? Do you remember? Men's or women's?"

"Oh, uh . . ." She just stared at him.

Back at the roadside joint, she'd had the baseball hat on, a boy's shirt. She had been playing her role. The stranger had recognized her as a boy, and had said as much to David—*That your boy?* Yet he realized that Ellie had come out of the goddamn *women's* restroom, and the stranger had seen it.

"I can't . . . I think . . ." Her voice trembled.

"Never mind." His eyes flitted back toward the cop car in the rearview. Suddenly his bladder felt heavy. His heart felt like a piston jackhammering against the wall of his rib cage.

Cooper's gun was under his seat.

As they approached an exit, David decided to take it. He turned onto the ramp, silently praying that the police car would not follow them, would not follow them, would not follow them.

David Arlen held his breath.

39

Ten weeks earlier

Toward the end of June, Burt Langstrom stopped showing up at the college. At first, David thought nothing of it—it was summer, after all—but then he was notified by Miriam Yoleck, the head of the English department, that Burt had turned in his resignation a week earlier and that all his summer classes (which were to be taught online) had been canceled. When David pressed Miriam for additional information, she said she knew very little except that Burt had cited "personal reasons" for his departure. And while Miriam did a good job looking disappointed at this news, David couldn't help but see through her act; if Burt Langstrom's "personal reasons" were that he had gotten sick, Miriam was more than happy—relieved, even—not to have him around.

That evening, David detoured from his usual route home, heading instead to the breezy bayside neighborhood where the Langstroms lived. As he drove down Burt's street, he began to wonder if Burt would even answer the door.

As he rolled up in front of the Langstroms' split-level house, he was distraught to find that the shades in all the windows had been pulled and that there was an overall vacant look to the house that troubled him on some gut level. Had it not been for Burt's champagne-colored Oldsmobile in the driveway, David would have suspected the family had picked up and left. For several minutes, David sat in the Bronco, listening to the radio—a classic rock station whose music was interrupted by occasional news and traffic reports. Then he got out.

He was halfway up the Langstroms' driveway when Burt came around the side of the house. David's presence must have startled the man; Burt paused in midstride, a slack expression on his face. He wore a pair of khaki shorts and a T-shirt from last year's faculty bowling tournament. His bald head was shiny with sweat.

David smiled and raised a hand as he approached. At the back of his head, he was recalling what Miriam Yoleck had said about Burt resigning for personal reasons, and wondered now if Burt had, in fact, contracted the illness. Yet as David drew closer, Burt broke out into a wide grin. David couldn't remember the last time he'd seen Burt Langstrom smile.

"David. What are you doing here?"

"Hi, Burt. I heard from Miriam that you pulled the plug. Thought I'd check in with you, see if everything was okay."

Burt shook his hand—the palm was clammy and hot—then pulled David closer for a one-armed hug. "Good to see you," Burt said into his ear, then he pulled away. Rivulets of sweat trailed down the sides of Burt's face. He smelled of perspiration. "But you didn't need to come here."

"I was worried about you. I never expected you to quit. You had summer classes."

"It doesn't matter." Burt peered over at the front of the house, and David had the peculiar feeling that he was checking to made sure the shades were still drawn and that no one was looking out. "I'm done with that job."

"What will you do for money?"

"I won't need money. I'm putting the plan into action, David."

"Renting the RV?"

"We're heading off to the woods. I stopped by this morning and forked over the first payment. I'll be picking the old girl up tomorrow morning. Then we take to the hills."

"And Laura's okay with it now?"

"She's come around. Staying cooped up in the house hasn't been healthy for her. She's been so stressed."

David recalled the way she had sounded that afternoon on the phone, when he'd called her to talk about her husband. She had sounded more than just stressed, David thought; she had spoken like someone under the influence of a hypnotist.

"Well," David said, "I'm sorry to see you go, but who knows? Maybe you're right. Maybe it's for the best."

"Of course," Burt said. "Of course it is. You should think about it yourself."

"Maybe I will. Is Laura home now?"

"Of course."

"Can I see her?"

A deep vertical crease formed between Burt's eyebrows. "Huh?" he grunted.

"Can I talk to her for a second?"

"She won't see you," Burt said. "She won't see anyone."

"What about the girls? Are they here?"

Burt planted two meaty hands on his hips. "What's this about?" he asked.

"I guess I just want to say good-bye before you all take off for the woods," David said. He offered Burt a sheepish smile and hoped he appeared genuine. The truth was, he was suddenly terrified of what might have become of Burt Langstrom's family. Something was wrong here. Something was off.

One of Burt's eyebrows arched. "Is that right?"

"Just to say good-bye."

"She won't open the door. Not even for you, David. It's nothing personal, of course. It's just . . . the way things are now."

"Then I'll wave to her from the window," David said, already moving past Burt and up the walk toward the front door. He knocked then turned that sheepish, bullshit smile back on.

"She won't answer it," Burt called, and followed him up the

walk. David stepped aside and Burt opened the door and leaned his head in. He called Laura's name while keeping a tight grip on the doorknob.

That's so I don't shove him aside and run into the house, David had time to think.

David heard movement from inside—a laborious, shuffling sound. When Laura appeared, she was mostly hidden in the gloom of the darkened foyer. All the blinds had been drawn over the windows. David caught a whiff of the air inside, and it smelled stagnant, like unused basements. Yet despite the gloom, David could still make her out . . . and he was instantly taken aback at how much weight she'd lost. Her face looked sallow, her cheeks sunken, her hair an unkempt mop piled atop her head. She was practically swimming in her clothes, which now looked several sizes too large for her. Without stepping any further, she said, "Burt? Who's there with you?"

"David Arlen," Burt said.

Laura made no comment; she only shuffled her weight from one foot to the other.

David peered over Burt's shoulder and raised a hand toward her. "Hello, Laura. How've you been?"

Laura just hugged herself with frail arms.

"Wanted to wish you and the girls luck," he added.

"It's not safe to keep the door open so long," she said to her husband. Then she turned around and zombie-walked back down the hallway until the deeper shadows swallowed her up.

Jesus, David thought. She might not have the Folly, but some other stressor had broken Laura Langstrom down until she was nothing more than the walking goddamn dead.

"And the girls?" David said.

Burt grimaced at him and pulled the front door closed. The door knocker thumped. "Look," Burt said. "I appreciate your concern. I really do, David. But I think it's time you go now."

"All right." David held out a hand for Burt to shake.

Burt glanced at David's hand, nodded once, but didn't take it. "So long, David," he said and turned down the walkway.

David watched him as he ambled around the side of the house and vanished.

David looked back up at the house. In one of the second-story windows, the two Langstrom girls were watching him from a part in the curtains. As he looked, the curtains whipped back into place, as if the children were fearful of being seen by him. Just catching a glimpse of them eased his mind considerably.

David turned and headed back down the driveway. He dragged an index finger through the layer of pollen that covered the Oldsmobile as he went.

40

The police car did not follow them; instead, it continued straight on I-70 as David negotiated the Olds off the exit ramp and onto a narrow band of blacktop.

He looked at Ellie in the passenger seat. "Are you okay?"

She nodded.

"Scared?"

"Sometimes," she said.

"Now?"

"I gotta pee too bad to be scared right now," she said.

He smiled then laughed. She smiled, too. It did his heart some good. "Yeah," he said. "I gotta pee, too. We'll stop somewhere."

But there was no place to stop for several miles. They drove, flanked on one side by acres of cornfields while tracts of dusty flat land greeted them on the other side. For a time, the only sign of civilization were the telephone poles every quarter mile.

"Scarecrow," Ellie said, pointing out the window. "See it?"

"Look at that."

The thing was close to the shoulder of the road and looming several feet above the tall green stalks of corn. It was nothing more than a sackcloth head tied to a cross from which a pair of weather-faded overalls hung like the sail of a tiny ship.

"It's silly now," Ellie said. "There aren't any birds for him to scare away."

"So much for job security," David said.

Yet as they drew closer, David realized there was something too . . . authentic . . . about the slouching human form strung up to the post in that field—the weighty slump of the head, the articulated fingers protruding from the sleeves, the bulk and musculature of the thighs in its sun-faded overalls. Beyond the scarecrow, David glimpsed several more out in the field. These others had the same distressing qualities as the first, and there were the coppery stains of blood on the clothes of a few of them. He wondered if he was seeing things accurately.

"Those scarecrows look all right to you?" he asked Ellie.

She pressed her nose against the glass of the passenger window, her breath fogging it up. "They look creepy," was all she said after a moment.

"Yeah?"

"Yeah."

He decided not to push the issue.

Ten minutes later, they drove past a succession of small farmhouses. The lawns were all overgrown and there appeared to be no livestock in any of the pens. There were vehicles in some of the driveways or parked along patches of grass behind the houses, yet David got the distinct impression that these houses were empty. This thought was only confirmed when he noted the red *X*'s painted over each front door.

The road emptied them out in the center of a small two-street town. Clapboard buildings ran the length of both streets, squalid mom-and-pop storefronts that appeared neglected and forgotten despite the OPEN signs in some of the windows. The most inviting appeared to be a small sandwich shop, so David parked the car.

"Put your hat back on," he said. "And this time, use the right bathroom." He winked at her. Then he slid the Glock out from beneath his seat and wedged it down into his pants against the small of his back.

Ellie grabbed the shoe box and opened her door.

"Wait," he said. "Leave that here."

"I won't."

"It'll look too weird, you hauling around a shoe box like that. We don't want to do anything that might cause someone to remember us later."

"I won't leave them behind again." Her tone was firm, her eyes heavy on him. He knew better than to argue with her when she had her mind set. Her mother had been the same way.

"Okay," he relented.

They entered the sandwich shop, which was no bigger than the claustrophobic little office David had shared with the other instructors in his department back at the college, and went straight to the rear. There were no tables, just a wall-length counter where two burly men sat eating sandwiches and drinking coffee. Keno played on a TV screen behind the counter. The air smelled of grease.

"Restrooms?" David asked the man in the white apron behind the counter.

"You sick?" asked the man. He was scrutinizing David's face.

"No."

"Your kid?"

"He's clean."

The man pointed to a shabby rectangular cutout in the dry-wall that couldn't precisely be called a doorway. "End of the hall," he said. "You want some menus?"

Because the tone of the man's voice suggested the bathrooms were for paying customers only, David said, "Sure."

The man placed two menus on the counter in front of two vacant stools while David led Ellie through the cutout in the wall and down a narrow, unlit corridor. There was a single door at the end of the hall with the word RESTROOM written on it in black marker.

Ellie went first, then waited out in the hall while he used the toilet. The bathroom itself was no bigger than a shower stall, the toilet—and a good section of the wall behind it—caked in black grime. There was a single window here that looked out upon the row of shops and the road they had taken coming into town. Massive black flies, each one the size of a small grape, thumped senselessly against the windowpane.

The sink looked about ready to give him tetanus, so he decided to forgo washing his hands. In the streaky mirror over the sink he glimpsed his haunted reflection—sunken eyes, poorly dyed hair, beard stubble shading the lower half of his face. The bridge of his nose was still swollen from when he'd rammed his head into Cooper's chest while trying to wrench the gun from him. But at least it hadn't started bleeding again.

Dead man walking, said the head-voice. And he wondered just how true that was.

I'm not going to let those bastards get to me. They won't trick me into having a nervous breakdown. They won't trick me into turning around and driving back to them. They won't.

He was just about to leave when he glanced back out the window again. Through the haze of flies, he saw two police cars come rolling up the street. They slowed down as they approached the front of the sandwich shop. One car braked in the middle of the street while the other pulled up alongside the Oldsmobile.

Shit . . .

Both cops got out. Their guns weren't drawn but they had their hands to their hips, ready to draw at a moment's notice. The cop who'd parked alongside the Olds—a stocky black guy with a goatee—peered in through the Oldsmobile's windshield. He said something inaudible to his partner. The partner—a young kid in mirrored sunglasses—pointed to the license plate.

Shit-shit-shit!

David opened the bathroom door. Ellie stood there, gazing up at some foul graffiti someone had scrawled on the wall in black marker. "Get in here," he said, his voice a tense whisper.

She came in and he closed and locked the door.

"What is it?"

"Cops," he said.

Through the window, he watched as the officer in the sunglasses said something into the radio he had clipped to his shoulder. Then both of them crossed onto the sidewalk toward the sandwich shop.

"We have to get out of here now," he said. He flipped the latch on the window, then pried it open. Flies tickled the tops of his hands. "Come here," he said, grabbing her beneath her armpits. She clutched the shoe box to her chest. "It's a bit of a drop but not too far."

"I don't think—"

"No time. Go."

He lifted her out and helped her over the sill. She landed on her feet outside in a cloud of rising dust. Then David scrambled out after her.

There was only one place to go: the alleyway that ran behind the stores. He snatched up Ellie's wrist and dragged her as he ran. The alleyway zagged twice, sharp right turns that, he feared, would empty back out onto the main road and into the path of more police. But he must have gotten turned around, because when they burst out of the alley they were facing a wooded embankment and, beyond, a sea of cornstalks.

"Come on." He urged her forward.

Halfway across the embankment was a chain-link fence; David slammed into it before he actually saw it. It wasn't too high. He hoisted Ellie over then he scaled it. The chains rattled.

Only when they reached the corn did he risk a look over his shoulder. He could see no one coming after them, but that didn't mean they weren't seconds behind. Just then he heard the sound of a siren.

"Daddy!" Ellie cried.

"It's okay, baby. Come on."

They ran through the corn.

41

By the time they came through the corn and saw the farm-house, David was carrying his daughter. There were bits of farming equipment scattered about the lawn here. The house itself looked deserted, and there were even a few boards nailed across some of the windows. A set of rickety wooden stairs led up to a door, the upper half of which was made of glass. A red X had been spray-painted from corner to corner.

David carried Ellie up the stairs, then set her down beside him. Without pausing to consider a better option, he elbowed the single-paned window. The glass didn't completely shatter, but he did manage to knock a rectangular section out of the way. He reached inside, fumbled for the lock, praying it was the type of dead bolt that had a knob and wouldn't require a key.

His hand found the dead bolt.

There was no knob.

He took a step back, figuring he could knock the rest of the glass out and climb in through the window and—

Ellie reached out and twisted the doorknob. The door creaked open.

"Stick to me like glue," he said, slipping inside.

The air was rancid. David wondered how long the place had been unoccupied. Shafts of daylight slid in between the boards fitted over the windows, cutting through the dimness of an outdated kitchen with cornflower wallpaper and a wall clock that had seized up at 2:18. Dust clung to every available surface, making the light bulbs in the chandelier above the kitchen table look like large gray Q-tips. Tiny footprints—rats?—had been stamped into the dust covering the countertops.

"Where are the people who live here?" Ellie whispered against his ribs.

"They're gone."

"What happened to them?"

"Anything."

"What?"

"Anything could have happened."

Along the opposite wall hung a chalkboard on which someone had kept a running grocery list. Next to the board was a wooden plaque affixed with a series of hooks. Depicted on the plaque was a cartoon pig with its hands—or hooves—on its hips. The caption above its head read DON'T HOG THE KEYS! Dangling from one of the hooks was a set of keys.

He snatched them up, saw that one was a car key with the Chevrolet emblem on it.

"You doing okay?" he said, grabbing hold of Ellie's hand. He led her out of the kitchen and down a narrow, gloomy hallway toward the front of the house.

"Y-yes," she stammered.

The front rooms were empty. Even the furniture had been removed, if there had ever been any furniture to begin with. Flies and gnats and large flying beetles crisscrossed in front of his face. David went to the front windows and saw a bright red Monte Carlo in the driveway. It was then that he considered his options—take the car and get the hell out of there, or hunker down in this abandoned farmhouse until the coast was clear. Both options had their benefits and flaws, their wins and losses. Yet in the end he decided it was easier to find a hiding man than a running man.

Ellie cried out.

"What?"

"There. There."

It was a dining room with a large oak table at the room's

center, set with what looked like good china for several people. But the meal would never come. David counted six bodies of varying sizes hanging from ropes tied to the exposed ceiling rafters. The smallest one looked like that of a child maybe no older than four or five. The air was black with flies, and the smell, which struck David instantaneously, was as thick and meaty as an abattoir's—so much so that both he and Ellie began to gag.

David cradled Ellie's head against his chest. He tried the front doorknob, found this one was locked, then fumbled through the key ring for the house key. He jabbed two different keys into the lock before finding the correct one. It turned, and David shoved open the door and dragged Ellie out onto the porch.

"Let's go, let's go!" he shouted, pulling Ellie toward the car. He unlocked the door, yanked it open, and shoved Ellie inside. He climbed in after her, and in his panic, it took him three or four attempts to jab the key into the ignition. When he finally got it, he had a moment to wonder what he would do if the goddamn car wouldn't start before he cranked it. The engine roared to life.

He reversed down the driveway and hit the road hard enough to rock the car on its shocks. Ellie cried out, "Too fast!"

He slowed down once he was cruising in a straight line toward the highway, the houses with those red X's on their doors streaming by in a blur. They drove by the field of scarecrows again, and in David's periphery, they appeared to be shambling down off their posts. David forced himself not to look.

It seemed to take forever to reach the highway. He took the exit, merged with what little traffic there was, and tried to make this shiny red car look less conspicuous by sheer force of will.

They were only on the highway for less than thirty seconds when David heard a distant drumming sound.

"Do you hear that, too?" he asked Ellie.

Ellie was hyperventilating and didn't answer. David glanced at her, gripped her knee. She just stared blankly out the windshield, her chest heaving, her respiration disconcertingly labored.

David looked due north and saw three helicopters descending in the direction of the town he and Ellie had just left. The helicopters passed directly over the highway. David could feel the choppers' rotating blades vibrating through his bones. He kept waiting for them to change course in midair. He kept waiting for them to pursue.

But they didn't.

That man at the milk shake place—*Ninety-nine Cutlass, am I right?*—had seen the Maryland tags, had seen the young "boy" coming out of the women's restroom, and he had called the police. Or maybe he had been a cop himself. A detective like Watermere.

"You're bleeding," Ellie said. She had gotten herself under control and was staring at him now with concern in her eyes.

He touched his nose but his fingers came away clean. He looked at his face in the rearview mirror.

"No," Ellie said. "There."

He glanced down. There was a swath of blood across the front of his shirt and more smeared along his left arm. His palm was sticky with it, and he had gotten some on the steering wheel. He turned his arm over and saw a gash in the flesh just above the left elbow. It must have happened when he elbowed the glass while breaking in to the house.

"I've got towels and shirts and stuff in my bag," he said.

She just stared at him.

"In the back!" he shouted.

Ellie shook her head.

"What?" he said. "What?"

"You're thinking of the wrong car," she said.

42

There were napkins in the Monte Carlo's glove compartment, which David used to staunch the bleeding. The owner's manual was in there, as well, wrapped in a plastic folder bound with a large rubber band. David used the rubber band to bind the napkins to his injured arm. The band was tight enough to slow much of the bleeding, which was good; the wound was deep enough to require stitches, but he couldn't stop and worry about something like that right now.

He repaired his arm while driving, and when he finished, the steering wheel was tacky with drying blood. He'd gotten more blood down the side of his shirt and on the inside of the door, too. When he began to feel a little light-headed, he fought to keep his gaze steady on the road ahead.

He took mental inventory of all the things they'd left behind in the Olds. *At least I've still got the gun,* he thought. *Also, the money.* How much was left? He was burning through it too quickly, and he had splurged on unnecessary purchases in an attempt to keep Ellie in a state of complacency as best he could. Milk shakes had soothed her, much as the pizza lunch. As had the motels. Had he been alone, he would have risked sleeping in the car and been frugal with every dime, but he was also trying to keep some semblance of normalcy in his daughter's life. It was a delicate balance.

Not to mention I wouldn't even be doing this if I was alone . . .

Red bands of light were stretching across the horizon while, at their back, the sky had darkened to a starry black. He had thought Ellie was sleeping all this time, but when he looked at her, he could see that her eyes were halfway open as she reclined in the passenger seat. She watched the scenery without really seeing anything, blinking languidly every once in a while like someone under the influence of a strong sedative.

She had the shoe box in her lap, and it struck him as peculiar that she had insisted on taking it into the sandwich shop with her and refusing to leave it behind. As if she had known they'd never return to the Olds. The thought caused a chill to ripple through him.

Perhaps sensing his eyes on her, Ellie rolled her head so that she faced him. Her skin looked mottled and fluid in the dusky light. For an instant, she looked so adult—so much like Kathy—that David felt a sudden ache in the center of his chest.

"What would those cops have done if they'd caught us back there?" she asked. Her voice was just barely above a whisper.

"They would have taken us into custody."

"They would have taken me away from you," she said.

"They would have tried."

"They would have hurt you to get to me," she said. It was Kathy talking now: Ellie's face looked so different in the dark.

"I'm not sure the local police know exactly how important you are," he said.

Ellie turned her head away from him.

Western Kansas had given way to the lush switchbacks of Colorado. The trees that flanked the highway were enormous black pikes driven into the earth. At the horizon, the sky continued to darken as the sun settled beyond the western hills. They were roughly two hours from Funluck Park, according to the road map he'd found in the glove compartment and the calculations he'd worked out in his head.

"How exactly did those doctors kill Mom?" she asked, still not looking at him.

"It's complicated," he said.

"Explain it to me."

"I'm not sure if it's the best thing for you to know, honey. You don't need to think of your mom that way."

"I want to know."

He considered this. Finally, he said, "Mom was okay at first. The doctors were just drawing blood. But then Mom started to get worried that she might get sick. She stopped eating and grew weaker. And the doctors, they just kept taking more blood."

"Why did you let them?"

It was like an arrow thwacking into the center of his chest. When he opened his mouth, he found it difficult to speak at first. He cleared his throat and said, "Your mother didn't want to leave at first. She was afraid of getting sick if she left the hospital."

This was close enough to the truth that he didn't feel like he was telling a lie, although it wasn't the complete truth. Ellie didn't need to hear the complete truth.

"In the end, she'd just grown too weak. Her body just gave out."

Enough silence passed between them that he thought he'd answered all Ellie's questions. But then she said, "Would I die like Mom if we gave up and went back home? If they took me to some hospital to study me and take my blood?"

"You don't have to worry about that."

"I'm just asking a question. Would I die, too?"

He slammed a palm down on the steering wheel. "I don't know, El! I can't predict the goddamn future. I'm just trying my best to keep them away from you."

"It makes me feel sick," she said. "It makes me feel like what we're doing is wrong. It makes us no different from those people back in Kentucky. Those people with the skull . . ."

"I told you already, it's not the same thing."

"Yes, it is. You can't even tell me why it's not."

"Because we're not actively hurting anyone. Those people, they were going to shoot us, kill us. Don't you see?"

"You've got a gun right now. You'd shoot somebody, too, if they tried to get me. How is that different?"

"I'm trying to protect you."

"But if I could help all those people who are sick—"

"Enough!" he shouted at her. "Okay? Enough. I'm your goddamn father and you'll do what I tell you."

She said nothing, just kept staring at him. He could feel her gaze on him, an icy javelin pressing against his flesh until it cooled his entire bloodstream. Another glance at her and he saw she had the shoe box's lid open. She was caressing the eggs inside the nest.

He turned back to the road, feeling as if he'd just sprinted a mile. He forced his breathing to calm down. When the yellow lines on the highway began to blur, he rubbed his eyes and wished he had a cup of coffee or maybe some pills to keep him awake. For whatever reason, the image of Ellie's stuffed elephant jumped into his head then—the elephant that had been her favorite toy that was now lost forever since they deserted the Oldsmobile. For whatever reason, the damn thing seated itself in the center of his brain, as if there was something vitally important about it. The more he concentrated on it, trying to figure out its significance, the more texture it took on in his head. And then it was there, a dinosaur-size elephant undulating beyond the trees at the horizon, its thick hide pink in the waning dusk, its tremendous bulk toppling trees and causing the earth to shake, its massive face turning, tusks like lances severing the treetops, the gleam of a single melancholic eye, brown-yellow, agonized, a pupil as black as ichor, as deep as space, and as it charged them, David could make out its every detail, down to the minute blond hairs in the creases of its knees, the fat white mites scuttling through the caverns of its ear canals, the dried black mucus pressurized into a pasty gruel at the corners of its mouth—

David cried out. He jerked the steering wheel sharply to the left and felt the car fishtail. He overcompensated, spinning the wheel to the right. The tires screamed and gravel peppered the windshield. Ellie screamed.

There was a loud *pop* then a shushing sound. The Monte Carlo canted to the left and the steering wheel began to vibrate. The shushing sound followed them as they bucked along the road—*shhh-fump, shhh-fump, shh-fump.*

Ellie sat up straight. "What happened, what happened?"

"Flat tire," he said. He slowed the car down and eased it to a stop on the shoulder.

"Now it's your nose," Ellie said, pointing at his face.

He glanced at himself in the rearview mirror and saw a fine thread of blood dribbling out of his left nostril.

43

Blessedly, there was a spare tire and a jack in the trunk. He changed the tire while jacked up on the shoulder of the highway, working up a sweat despite the autumn chill in the evening air. Ellie stood beside him, studying him for a time, then turning her attention toward the headlights that occasionally cruised along the road. She held the shoe box against her chest, cradling it in both arms.

"All right," he said, standing up and wiping the grease from his hands. He was out of breath and trembling, though less from exhaustion and more out of anxiety. For some reason, he felt like they were standing still while the whole world shifted beneath them. He felt as though he might be knocked flat at any moment.

He opened the passenger door for her. "Come on. Get in."

Back in the car, he cranked the ignition but nothing happened. Not a series of clicks, not a grumble from the engine, not the stubborn *rrr-rrr-rrr* of the motor struggling to turn over.

"No. Come on."

He cranked it again. Again. Again.

Dead.

"Son of a bitch!" He pounded the steering wheel with a fist. Then he ran his shaking hands through his hair. Ellie stared at him from the passenger seat. After closing his eyes and counting to ten in his head, he turned to her, forced a smile, and tried not to let her see the fear in his eyes.

"It's broken," she said. It was not a question.

"I'll have a look under the hood. Is there a flashlight in the glove compartment?"

She opened the compartment, but it was obvious there was no flashlight in there.

"Okay." David nodded at her. His arm ached. Again, he felt light-headedness threaten to overtake him. He took several deep breaths to regulate his respiration. "Just sit tight. I'll go have a look."

He climbed out of the car and pulled up the hood. His arms felt like rubber. As he stared at the assemblage of mechanical parts, his vision threatened to pixelate. He felt his respiration ratchet to a fever pitch . . . yet at the same time it seemed impossible to suck any air into his lungs.

This is it, said the head-voice. *This is the end of the road. This is as far as you were meant to go. The Night Parade stops here and death takes over. What will it be? A heart attack? Or maybe Kapoor and that Craddock guy weren't pulling your leg after all—maybe it's the Folly that's getting ready to take you down. You will die of a hemorrhage and leave your daughter stranded all alone and in the middle of the night on the shoulder of a Colorado highway.*

"Go fuck yourself," he muttered. His voice sounded hollow and tinny in his ears.

The blast of an air horn caused him to jerk upright and slam the back of his head against the hood. He twisted out from beneath it in time to see two large headlights settling behind the Monte Carlo on the shoulder of the road. The stink of diesel exhaust filled the air.

Ellie had gotten out of the car and was standing on the shoulder again, her small shape silhouetted against the approaching headlights. David winced at her, as if it hurt to see her. "I told you to stay in the car."

"Daddy?" she said, fear in her voice.

He reached out, touched her shoulder. She felt very much real. "Get back in the car, honey," he told her. Then he continued toward the truck, one arm up to shield his watery eyes from the glare of the headlamps.

He heard the hiss of air brakes and, a moment later, the sound of someone's boots crunching along the gravelly black-top. A man's hard voice said, "Shitty place for car trouble."

"Yeah," said David.

The man was nothing more than a barrel-shaped silhouette until he stepped around the side of the Monte Carlo. He was a big guy in a nylon vest and a flannel shirt, a John Deere hat pushed back on his head. He pressed his large fists on his hips as he approached David, sizing up the Monte Carlo with evident disappointment.

"Hate to say it," said the trucker, "but American-made cars ain't what they used to be." The man turned toward David, his frown brightening into a grin. In the glow of the truck's headlights, the man's teeth looked as large and as gray as tombstones. "I'm Heck. Hector." He held out one thick hand.

"Tim," David said—the first name on his mind. He shook the man's hand. "You wouldn't know how to fix it, would you?"

"That depends. What's wrong with her?"

"I don't . . . I don't know." He rubbed his eyes. "Everything was fine until we blew a tire. I changed it with no problem, but when I went to start it up again—nothing. Not a sound."

"Who's 'we'?" Heck asked while simultaneously leaning in through the open driver's window. He reached for the keys in the ignition, then saw Ellie in the passenger seat. "Well, hello, sugar."

"Hi," said Ellie.

Heck cranked the ignition a few times with nothing to show for it. "Bummer, ain't it?" he said to Ellie.

"Sucks," said Ellie.

Heck chuckled. "You said it, darling." He withdrew from the window, then went around to the open hood. David trailed behind him. Those large meathooks parked back on his hips, Heck surveyed the engine in silence. After a full minute had passed, he stared at David and said, "Can I make an admission?"

"Sure."

"At the risk of having to turn over my Man Card, and despite the fact I make a living driving that big rig back there, I really don't know piss-all about cars." He grinned, exposing those tombstone teeth again. "You and your kid live around here?"

"No. We were heading for a campground about a hundred miles northwest of here."

"Well, I'm heading in that direction myself, so I'll offer you and your girl a ride. Or if this puts a damper on your camping weekend, I can drop you someplace else. Just hate to see you folks stranded out here with night closing in."

"That's very kind. I'd appreciate it. The campground will be just fine." It wasn't lost on him that Hector was observant enough to see through Ellie's disguise and recognize her as female. It made him slightly uncomfortable, and he would have preferred to part ways with Hector right away, but they needed this man to get them to the campground.

"Wonderful," Heck said, removing his cap and sliding a thick-fingered hand through the buzzed gray bristles of his hair. "I'll give you a hand loading your stuff into the truck."

"Uh, we don't have any stuff," David said. "It's just us."

"Guess you ain't a Boy Scout. Camping with nothing more than whatever's in your wallet." Heck jerked a chin at David's bandaged arm and the blood on his shirt. "What happened there?"

David hugged the injured arm to his ribs. "Sliced my arm changing the tire."

Another whiskied chuckle rattled up out of Heck's throat. "Yeah, yeah," he said, shaking his head and moseying around the side of the car again. "No Boy Scout, all right."

44

Hector Ramirez's current gig was hauling eleven hundred cases of Valvoline motor oil from Trenton, New Jersey, to Lakewood, Colorado, a run he looked forward to because it took him through some beautiful countryside. He had been a trucker since he could vote, starting out for a small company based in Utah before cutting his corporate ties and buying his own cab. Now he worked for himself ("I'm an honest-to-God businessman," Heck said. "CEO, president, vice president, and grunt worker all rolled into one."). For his fiftieth birthday, his wife, Rita, had surprised him by having his cab airbrushed with the nighttime cityscape of Gotham City, complete with Batman swinging from his bat-rope that filled up most of the driver's door. He was a friendly enough guy whose slender wedding band seemed to be cutting off the circulation of his chubby ring finger, and he talked for nearly the entire duration of their trip like someone who'd just been rescued from a desert island and hadn't seen another living soul in several years.

Before getting back on the road, Heck insisted he have a look at David's injured arm. When David removed the wrapping—the napkins had soaked all the way through and were now as colorful as Christmas decorations—Heck whistled through his teeth, then nodded like a bobblehead doll.

"Yeah, okay. That's a gash, all right. Prob'ly needs stitches. Hold tight."

Heck slipped through a narrow opening between the front

seats that led to a small compartment in the rear of the cab. There was a cot back there, a stack of magazines and books, an open bag of Doritos. A moment later, Heck returned with a first-aid kit. Utilizing a roll of gauze and a few butterfly bandages, Heck wrapped David's arm after first cleansing the wound with peroxide. After he was done, Heck sat up straight, grinning and evidently pleased with himself.

"Not half bad for government work," Heck commented.

"Better than some Burger King napkins and a rubber band," David said.

Then they hit the road.

Heck was a talker, the kind of guy who filled the silence with anecdotes about his life and his career, or just random trivia in general—anything to keep the silence from dominating. During the only lull in the conversation, Ellie, who sat perched between them on the bench seat, pointed to a framed photo of a young, dark-haired boy that was fixed to the truck's dashboard. "Is that your son?" she asked Heck.

"Yes, ma'am."

"What's his name?"

"Benicio," Heck said. "We called him Benny."

David noted the past tense. He also noticed the rosary draped around the boy's picture. He touched one of Ellie's knees, but she didn't take the hint.

"How old is he?"

"In that photo, he's about six. Bit younger than you, my dear."

"I'm eight. But I'll be nine in a couple of days."

"That's right," David said. In all the commotion, he had forgotten.

"Well, happy birthday . . . in a couple of days," Heck said, and tipped his hat at her.

"How old is he *not* in the photo?" Ellie asked. "Like now, in real life, I mean."

"Oh, well, sweetheart," Heck said. "My boy, he ain't with us no more."

"Where did he go?"

"Ellie," David said.

"It's okay," Heck said. He smiled down at Ellie, a pleasant enough smile despite the liquid shimmer suddenly visible in his eyes. "Benny passed on."

"He died," she said.

"He got sick. Lots of people getting sick nowadays."

"I'm sorry," David said.

"He was a good boy." Heck's gruff voice hit a snag, like a piece of thread from a sweater getting caught on a hook.

"Was it the illness?" Ellie asked. "Some people call it the Folly."

"It was," said Heck. "He was one of the lucky ones. He went very quickly. I was on the road when it happened."

"He was alone?"

"Come on, Ellie," David said, squeezing her knee.

Heck raised a hand. "It's all right," he said. "No, dear, he was with his mama back home."

"Oh." She leaned forward, scrutinizing the photo of the handsome little boy. "When did it happen?"

"Last year."

"Do you have any other kids?"

"No, *pepita*. Now we're alone."

Ellie looked up at Heck. The trucker glanced down at her, smiling, his eyes glassy and red. Ellie reached up and placed a small white hand on the man's broad shoulder. David felt his heart racing a mile a minute.

The big man cleared his throat and said, "You wanna hear me blast this air horn, darling?"

"I heard it when you drove up behind us," Ellie said. "It scared me, it was so loud."

Heck chuckled. A single tear spilled down his cheek and merged with a crease at the corner of his mouth. "Well, now, I suppose that's true. You're a frank little lady, aren't you?"

"I guess so," she said.

"What you got in that shoe box?"

"Bird eggs. Three of them."

"Yeah?"

"Oriole eggs, I think."

"Now, where'd you go and find bird eggs?"

"In the bushes outside my house. The mother never came back, so I adopted them."

"Well," Heck said. "Isn't that nice. I reckon something like bird eggs is about as rare as a dinosaur fossil these days."

"I'm sorry your son got sick and died," Ellie said.

"Thank you, baby. But ain't nothin' nobody could do."

Ellie's hand slid off Heck's shoulder. She turned her gaze toward David.

45

It was ten after nine when Heck pulled his truck up the paved path that led toward the entrance of Funluck Park. David saw that condos had been built along the road leading up to the park, ugly brick buildings with only a few lights on in the windows. The surrounding forestry was overgrown and poorly maintained.

"Road's a bit narrow," Heck said. The truck's air brakes whistled.

"We can walk the rest of the way from here," David said. "Thank you so much, Heck. You were a godsend."

"One good deed, and all that." Heck tipped his hat at Ellie. "And it was a pleasure meeting you, little miss. You have fun camping with your old man, y'hear? And take care of them bird eggs!"

"Good-bye, Mr. Ramirez," Ellie said. She held out her hand and Heck laughed, but he shook it. Then he patted her head.

David climbed out of the truck, then lifted Ellie out. "Thanks again, Heck. You saved our butts."

Heck leaned across the passenger seat and said, "That really your little girl, Tim?"

David felt the hairs on the back of his neck prick up. "Yes," he said.

"I ask, because I get the sense that something's a little off-kilter with you both, if you catch my meaning. I mean no offense by it."

"I appreciate your concern, but we—"

"Campground with no camping gear," Heck went on. His tone was not accusatory; he was merely commenting on the truth as he saw it. "That gash on your arm you said you got from changing the flat. It would bother me if I didn't say something, you understand?"

"All right, Heck. Then say what's on your mind."

"For one thing, are you really that girl's daddy?"

"I am."

"It also seems like you're both in a panic to get to wherever you're going." Heck chewed on his lower lip, then added, "Or maybe you're just trying to get away from someplace fast."

"Maybe it's a little of both," David said. "But I promise you it's for the good of my daughter. I hope you can understand that."

Heck jerked a thumb over his shoulder, indicating his cargo. "Stuff back there don't mean shit, in the grand scheme of things. Hell, this'll probably be my last trip. Didn't even want to take this one, truth be told, but it's just so darned pretty out here, don't you think?"

Again, David nodded.

"It's takin' care of your family that matters," Heck said. He glanced down at the picture of his son. "I can give you both a ride to wherever you need to get. No questions asked."

"That's incredibly nice," David said, "but this is our next stop. We'll be okay from here."

"In that case, I wish you luck."

"You, too."

"Just hold up a sec." Heck leaned over the back of the seat and rummaged around in the cramped compartment in the rear of the cab. A moment later, his hand reappeared clutching a balled-up polo shirt. He tossed it out the door and David caught it. "Whatever is going on with you two," Heck said, "you won't blend in with your shirt smeared with blood like that."

David just looked down at the polo shirt he now held. When he looked back up at Heck, he said, "I'm really very sorry about your son. It's terrible. It'll haunt me."

"Nothin' you could've done."

David wiped at his eyes.

"God bless," Heck said. He reached out and pulled the passenger door closed with a squeal of hinges. As David stepped away from the truck, Heck released the brakes. The truck grumbled forward, then cut down a fork in the road. David watched its taillights slip between two of the darkened condominiums.

He wondered now if he should have asked Hector Ramirez to wait with them, just to make sure Tim showed up. They were here now at this campground with no car and it was getting cold. If Tim failed to show up, they were screwed.

When he turned back to Ellie, he was surprised to see tears standing in her eyes, too. "Hey," he said, rubbing the side of her face. "What's the matter?"

"That boy," she said. "Benny."

David smiled at her.

"Do you think Mr. Ramirez will be okay?" she said.

"Yes, hon. I think he'll be fine."

Because what was one more lie on top of all the others?

46

At the top of the hill, the fence surrounding Funluck Park arose out of the gloom—a series of iron pikes capped with spearheads at the center of which stood two wrought-iron gates. The gates stood open, though they were so entwined with vines and ivy that David doubted they'd be able to close. The sign above the gates was missing letters. It now read:

FU   CK PARK

Things arced through the air just overhead as they crossed through the open gates. When Ellie noticed, she cried out jubilantly, "Birds! Birds, Daddy! Look!"

"They're bats, hon."

The park grounds were overgrown, the grass thwacking against David's shins while coming up almost to his hips. Clouds of tiny insects billowed out of the underbrush with each step. Ellie walked behind him, allowing him to clear the way through the buggy undergrowth. When they came to a snare of thorny branches and desiccated holly bushes, David stripped off his bloodied shirt and stuffed it down within the prickly boughs. He pulled Heck's shirt on over his head and found that it was at least three sizes too big. With some irony, he wondered what proved more conspicuous—a bloodstained T-shirt or Hector Ramirez's XXL polo shirt hanging from him like a parachute. To make it appear less obvious, he tucked it into his jeans, feeling the hem of the shirt bunching up around his waist. He left only the rear untucked, so that it covered the butt of the Glock, which poked out of his waistband.

They came upon a clearing where a half-dozen picnic tables rose up out of the tall grass. The tables were empty, but David could see a few cars parked in the adjacent parking lot. Beyond the lot, he could see the flickering tongue of a bonfire and hear distant chatter. The cabins were no longer there, as they had been when he was a child, but a few tents had been erected in the nearby field, black triangles just out of reach of the sodium lampposts that lined the circumference of the parking lot.

"Where are all the old rides?" Ellie said.

David looked around. "There's some, I think," he said, pointing to a series of dark humps partially digested by the underbrush. "Come on."

He took Ellie's hand and led her over to the arrangement of shapes rising out of the ground. They were the bumper cars. Their metallic paint had faded to a dull monochromatic gray, and much of the rubber around the base had rotted away, leaving behind only black, jagged teeth of brittle rubber. He wouldn't have thought it possible that this place could fall into further disrepair, but that seemed to be the case.

David tapped the hull of one bumper car with his sneaker and something small and furry darted from it, squealing like a creaky hinge. Both David and Ellie jumped back, then laughed nervously. The overgrown grass parted as the creature—a raccoon, most likely—carved its way across the field.

He surveyed the surrounding hillside. Deadfalls blocked the path leading to the top of the hill, and much of the hilltop itself was overgrown in forestry. He decided it made more sense to wait for Tim in the parking lot.

Please show up. Please show up.

On their way back to the lot, Ellie found the plaster face of a clown in the weeds. The face held a hideous grin, all its paint having faded to various shades of gray throughout the passage of years. It looked like something that had once decorated the roof of a carousel.

"Creepy," Ellie said. She held it up over her own face. The clown mask leered at him.

"Cut it out," he said. It reminded him of his students, and those terrible masks they wore. "Let's go sit on one of those picnic tables over there."

She dropped the plaster face and followed him to the assembly of picnic tables. From this vantage, they could keep an eye on the parking lot, the campers around the bonfire in the nearby field, and the dark curtain of trees that bordered the park. Far in the distance, a few windows glowed in the façade of the condos. Otherwise, they could have been camping out in some remote and undeveloped part of the world.

As they sat on the picnic table, Ellie leaned her head against his arm and continued to stroke the bird eggs. She sang to them in a low voice, though not bereft of musicality, and although David could not recall the name of the tune, he knew it had been one of the songs Kathy had sung to Ellie when she was just a baby.

He kept an eye on the parking lot. Two teenage boys stood smoking and gabbing beneath a lamppost, and there was a woman sitting cross-legged on the hood of a prehistoric Cadillac the color of gunpowder, also smoking a cigarette. *Don't let me down, Tim.* If Tim was a no-show, he and Ellie were screwed. They had no transportation, and a guy with a bandaged left arm might draw some suspicion wandering along the shoulder of the highway with an eight-year-old girl. *Nine,* he reminded himself. *She'll be nine in a few days.*

Movement in the periphery of his vision caused him to return his attention to the other row of picnic tables, the ones standing against the backdrop of the woods. He thought it might have been the breeze stirring the leaves in the trees . . . but then he caught sight of a figure sitting on one of the picnic tables, a sizeable fellow dressed in dark, nondescript clothes. The guy had his feet planted on the bench, his buttocks on the tabletop. He was staring at David across the expanse of darkness, and David saw that there was something wrong with his face.

Not his face, he realized then. *A mask. He's wearing a mask.*

It was another plain white mask, most likely fashioned out of a paper plate, and for a moment David thought this was the same man he had glimpsed in the field behind the burger joint earlier that day. But of course that was impossible.

As David stared at the man, the man raised a hand. A solemn wave.

Tim in disguise?

Or was it?

"Hey," David said, bumping Ellie's head from his arm with a hitch of his shoulder. "Sit here for a second, will you? I'm going to talk to that man."

"Dad—"

"Just sit tight."

He got up from the table and proceeded toward the next row of tables. As David approached the halfway mark, the man in the mask got up from the table, his heavy bulk shifting beneath the patchwork fabric of his clothes—his shirt looked like checkered flannel, his pants like camouflaged BDUs. He wore large forester boots.

"Tim?" David called, his voice a half whisper so as to not draw attention from the teenagers and the woman in the parking lot.

The masked man held up that same hand in another wave—or possibly to halt David's progress—before stepping around the side of the picnic table and heading in the direction of the woods.

David glanced over his shoulder and saw Ellie still perched on the picnic table where he'd left her, half her body silvered in the glow of the lamplights coming from the parking lot. He could not make out her expression from this distance, but he could tell that she was staring straight at him, and the closed, tight shape of her body suggested she was suddenly afraid.

When he turned back around, he saw the masked man enter the woods, cutting between two large trees dense with foliage.

"Wait," David said, and hurried after him.

Yet when he crossed through the trees, he could find no sign of the masked man. It was dark enough for someone to hide from him with ease . . . yet why would someone *want* to? Who would wave to him just to get up and hide from him?

He stood there in the lightlessness of the woods, waiting for movement, for the sound of twigs crunching underfoot. But after several seconds, all he heard was his own harsh respiration.

I'm making myself crazy.

He turned around and went back through the trees. When he stepped out into the clearing, he saw someone walking toward Ellie, who still sat watching him from her seat on the picnic table.

"Ellie," he said, and broke into a run. He reached the girl and gathered her up off the table and into his arms just as the figure approached.

It was a woman—the one who had been sitting on the hood of the Cadillac, smoking. She had shoulder-length dark hair, a slender build, and was dressed in an unassuming pair of blue jeans and a luminous white tank top.

"Who are you?" he said.

"Easy, buddy. Are you David?" she asked.

He just stared at her.

"My name's Gany," she said. She had an unlit cigarette between two fingers, which she parked behind one ear now. "Your brother sent me to pick you up."

47

He thought her name was Candy, and called her as much, for the first twenty minutes of their drive. It was Ellie, seated in the backseat of the Cadillac, who ultimately corrected him. "Dad, it's *Gany*. With a *G.*"

Gany laughed. "It's short for Ganymede."

"That's a cool name," Ellie said.

"It's one of the moons of Jupiter."

"Sorry," David said. "My mistake." His head hurt.

"My parents were of the 'free love' variety. Big-time granola hippies. And my mom was something of an amateur astronomer."

"What exactly did Tim tell you?"

"He said to meet you and your little girl here around nine o'clock. I'm supposed to drive you to straight to the Fortress. No stopping."

"The Fortress?"

"Of Solitude," Gany said. "Like in the Superman comics? The ice castle in the North Pole where Supe goes when he needs a little R and R?"

David shrugged, not comprehending.

"I thought you were supposed to be an English professor or something," Gany said.

"Not much room in the curriculum to take on Superman comics, unfortunately," he said.

"Are you Uncle Tim's girlfriend?" Ellie piped up from the backseat.

"You know," Gany said, drumming fingertips on the Caddy's steering wheel, "that is a spectacular question. You should remember to ask your uncle exactly that when you see him. I'd love to hear the response."

"I don't understand you," Ellie said.

"Story of my life, dear heart," said Gany.

"What else did he say about us?" David asked.

"Nothing. He just said to take the Caddy and pick you guys up. He said if you weren't there when I got there, I should wait. Give you a few hours. He thought you might be late, but you weren't. Not *too* late, anyway. Oh—" she said, interrupting herself, "one more thing. Do you have your cell phone on you?"

"Yes."

"Let's take a peek-see."

David dug it out of his pocket and handed it to her. "I've been careful not to—"

Gany rolled down the window and flipped the phone out into the darkness.

"What the hell?" David said.

"Tim said to lose the phone. So now it's lost."

"Jesus. There might have been info on there that I needed."

"Was there?"

He considered this. "I guess not."

"Besides, I wouldn't have let you turn it on. Tim was very adamant about that—'Do not let him turn on that phone. Get rid of it. Don't fuck around with the phone.' Oops, sorry about the language, honey pie. I'm just quoting your uncle."

"I've heard 'fuck' before," said Ellie.

"Hey," David said, leering at his daughter from over his shoulder. Then he turned back to Gany. "I was careful with the phone. I figured they might be able to trace it if I was on it."

"I assume you mean the federal government," Gany said. "In that case, they don't even need for you to be using it. Just *having* it is a liability. Did you know that the Feds have a device that can turn any cell phone into a listening device? Like, an actual *microphone*?"

"Jesus," David said. "No, I didn't."

"Of course, on the other hand, you've got some things playing in your favor right now, too."

"Do I? By all means, fill me in."

She glanced at him, an expression on her face that suggested he might not fully grasp the entirety of the situation. "For one thing, David, the whole world is falling apart, in case you haven't noticed. The government has a lot more important things to worry about than to track down you and your kid, no matter what you've done."

"So Tim didn't say anything about why we needed help?" he asked.

"He didn't say and I didn't ask. That's sort of how we operate in these types of situations."

"These 'types of situations'? What's that mean? How often does something like this come up?"

Gany laughed. It was a pretty sound. David examined her profile. It was too dark to guess her age with any accuracy, but he could tell she was younger than he was. There was no glamour about her—she wore no makeup or jewelry and her fingernails had been gnawed to nubs—but there was an innate attractive quality about her that was unbridled, untamed. What some people called a natural beauty.

"Your brother's always got his mitts in something or another," Gany said. "I'd like to say this isn't the craziest thing I've ever helped him with . . ." Here, she paused. Her gaze flirted in his direction again, albeit for just a second or two this time. "Far as I can tell, anyway."

When he heard light snoring from the backseat, David turned around and found Ellie asleep, sprawled out across the seats, the shoe box wrapped in her arms.

"Your kid asleep?" Gany asked.

"Yeah."

"You get in a bar fight or something?"

"Huh?"

"Your face. And that bandage on your arm."

"What happened to asking no questions?"

"Sorry, Charlie. Was just making conversation. It's a long drive, you know."

"I know."

"So . . . bar fight? Please tell me it was an angry bar fight."

"You should see the other guy," David said.

Gany put her head back and laughed a silent laugh.

"You said we're driving straight through without stopping," David said. "To Wyoming?"

"Just sit back and enjoy the ride," Gany said.

"But you must be exhausted."

"Not yet, but I'll get there soon enough. That's when you'll take over the driving duties. In the meantime, I suggest you get some shut-eye. I'll wake you when I start feeling sleepy."

"I can't sleep. I'm too wired."

"Don't be an asshole," she said. She pushed a CD into the player and a moment later, Zeppelin issued through the Caddy's crackling, overwrought speakers. She lowered the volume so it wouldn't wake Ellie. "Close them eyes, bugaboo."

David considered protesting some more. Instead, he reclined the seat, folded his arms over his chest, and shut his eyes. Night air coming through the cracked windows, cool and fresh-smelling, coupled with the melodious caterwauling of Robert Plant, helped usher him to sleep. At one point he thought he woke up and asked Ganymede some question— what it was, he had no idea—but then he realized he was only dreaming, and so he let himself fall into it.

48

Seven weeks earlier

There was some talk about it on the radio, but before he could catch any of the details, he lost the signal completely. It was his final day at the college—the last of his students had bailed out of their summer courses this past week, a determination David made after several attempts at e-mailing those few remaining students were met with no responses—and he had been only half-listening to the radio broadcast while letting his mind wander on the drive back home. When he finally realized what had happened, he turned up the volume . . . only to lose the station completely an instant later.

He scrolled through the other radio stations, but the rest were all dead, too. However, it wasn't just static on each channel, but a high frequency trill that emanated from the Bronco's speakers, a sound that was not exclusive to any one station in particular, but to all of them. It sounded like someone was deliberately jamming the frequencies.

About a mile and a half before his exit off the beltway, traffic snarled to a stop. Up ahead, two large white vehicles with flashing orange lights on the roof were parting the traffic. David could see no windows on either vehicle, and there were large vents on the sides. Despite the nondescript whiteness of them, he could tell they were comprised of bulletproof armor. Government vehicles.

A few people got out of their cars and snapped photos of the vehicles with their cell phones. Other commuters honked and shouted out open windows. David's own vehicle came to a standstill beneath the shadow of an overpass. When he unrolled his window and craned his head out, he could see traffic on the overpass above at a standstill, too.

I don't like this.

The radio disc jockey had been saying something about an explosion, a possible terrorist attack. David had missed most of it, but seeing those roving white vehicles with the bulletproof hides caused a finger of panic to rise up in him.

More people got out of their cars and began milling about the road. Many looked stricken. David peered to his right and saw a blond woman behind the wheel of a maroon Subaru, her knuckles white as her hands clenched the steering wheel. A small child was in a car seat in the back. David caught the woman's eye and she quickly looked away, as if he was some swarthy figure eyeing her up on the subway. She said something, presumably to the child in the back, whom she kept glancing at in her rearview mirror.

When he heard the whirring blades of a helicopter, he got out of the Bronco and stared up at the sky. A chopper soared by, so low to the ground that David felt the wind from its rotors. It was a black, sleek affair with no insignia on it, as far as David could tell.

David squeezed between the Bronco and the Subaru and continued down the narrow slip between the parked cars. Horns blared and people shouted from every direction. Someone's dog was barking and someone else's baby was screaming.

"What happened?" David said, coming upon a man and a woman standing beside the open door of an F-150. The man was as thick as a construction barrel, with springy silver chest hair spooling out over the neck of his Harley-Davidson tank top, but when he turned to look at David, his was the haunted face of an asylum inmate.

"I don't know, brother," the man said.

"I heard something about an explosion just before my radio went dead," David said.

"I don't *know*, brother," the man repeated, his voice cracking. "My radio's out, too. Cops are probably using the channels."

"They can *do* that?" David said.

"They're the cops, man. They do what they want."

The woman at his side—a meaty biker gal in her midfifties with fatty forearms reddened from the sun—pressed a set of acrylic fingernails into the cleft at her chin. Her eyes cut toward David, and he could see gobs of mascara snared in her lashes. She looked like someone who'd just been told they had twenty-four hours left to live.

"Those ain't the cops," she said. "They're federal. Top-secret NSA shit."

"No Such Agency," said the man.

They heard sirens but couldn't tell where they were coming from or where they were headed. People began climbing onto the roofs of their cars for a better vantage. A second helicopter cut through the sky, this one with a TV station logo on its side.

"They're so *low*," said the biker gal. "Whatever happened must be close."

A third news chopper chased after the others. This one flew low enough to throw grit into David's eyes. The biker gal coughed and hocked phlegm onto the blacktop.

At that instant, something exploded on the far side of the beltway. The sound was like a crack of thunder, only David could feel it like an earthquake in the ground, radiating up his legs. A moment later, a black column of smoke rose up on the horizon. People started pointing and shouting.

"Jesus," David muttered.

"Jesus is right," said the biker.

A helicopter appeared in the vicinity of the smoke. Someone asked where it was coming from and someone else said it was too far away to tell.

"It was a bomb," said the biker. "Done my time with the marines. I know what a fucking bomb sounds like."

David could only shake his head and watch as the column of black smoke was slowly blown westward on the breeze.

Once the large white vehicles had exited the beltway, and as the sirens began to fade, traffic started to limp along again. David nodded at the guy and his biker gal and the guy patted him on the shoulder—they had shared some brief and confusing camaraderie, it seemed—and then he hustled back to the Bronco. More horns blared. Where did all these assholes expect people to go?

Back behind the Bronco's steering wheel, he geared it out of Park and eased forward no more than a couple of inches. The car in front of his—a sea-foam green Prius with a University of Maryland sticker on the rear windshield—seemed hesitant to make a move.

David peered out the side window again. The woman in the Subaru was frantically checking her mirrors. Clutching the steering wheel, her knuckles were white as bone. David glanced in the backseat and was startled to find the kid in the car seat looking back at him through the rear window. The kid was maybe four or five, too damn big to still be facing backward in a car seat, and he had a fresh summer crew cut. A black slick of blood trickled down from the kid's left nostril, coursed over his lips, and had been smeared in a bright crimson streak along his chin. The kid's eyes were strangely unfocused, the pupils too big, the whites a canvas of broken blood vessels. The irises themselves seemed to dance as if floating on the surface of rippling water. Yet David knew the boy was staring right at him.

Jesus, he thought, looking back at the frantic mother. Her panic seemed to be a result of the commotion on the road and the black smoke that still clung to the horizon, not because of the child in her backseat. He wondered if she even knew the kid was sick. Had the kid been facing *forward* instead of backward, she might have caught the poor kid's reflection in the rearview mirror, but as it was—

The car behind him blasted its horn and someone shouted at him to step on the fucking gas. At the same moment, the Subaru bucked forward then sped off to join the rest of the traffic. David watched it go, noting the vanity plates—

BUSYMOM—and the stick-figure family decals on the rear window, which showed she had a husband, two other kids, and a cat at home. The husband stick figure swung a golf club while the mom wielded a tennis racket.

Jesus, he thought again, his heart racing. It seemed the only thing he was capable of thinking at the moment. *Jesus Christ Almighty.*

The asshole behind him laid on his horn again. David rolled down his window, flipped the guy the bird, then shoved his foot down on the accelerator.

He arrived home two hours later than he should have, sweaty and unnerved. He realized he was speeding through his neighborhood at twice the speed limit when he reached the turn onto Columbus and he nearly lifted two tires off the ground. He slowed to a cool gallop until the Bronco jerked to a stop in the driveway.

"Kath," he said, coming into the house. His voice cracked.

Ellie appeared at the far end of the hallway. Her expression was one of confusion and fear, a mixture of emotions David so rarely saw on his daughter's face.

"What happened?" he said.

"The news," Ellie said. She pointed toward the living room. "Mom's watching it now on TV."

In the living room, Kathy was parked on the edge of the sofa staring at the television. The volume was turned way up, and the image on the screen showed a stricken male reporter standing in front of a crisscross of yellow police tape. David could tell Kathy had been crying.

"What happened?" David said.

"Explosions," Kathy said. "Bombs."

"Where?"

"One in Towson. One in downtown Baltimore."

"I heard one. I was stuck in traffic, saw trucks on the beltway. There was an explosion and there was smoke in the distance."

"It's bad," Kathy said. Her lower lip trembled. "The one in Towson was a day-care center or something."

David shook his head in disbelief. Ellie appeared at his side.

"The other was a hospital. Hopkins."

"Who did it?"

"They're not sure yet," Kathy said, "but it looks like a pair of lunatics with homemade bombs drove their cars into the buildings."

"My God."

Ellie's hand crept into one of his. Just the feel of her helped him relax. It was like a drug. He squeezed her hand gently.

"They think it was related to the virus," Kathy said.

"The bombers were sick?"

"They don't know that for sure," she said, "but that's not what they're saying. Apparently the day-care center is in an area that has the highest percentage of infected kids in the state, and it had recently been quarantined by the CDC with the kids and teachers inside. And then there's Hopkins, where they've been taking people who get sick in the city. Some reporter said the CDC has been working there, too." She looked at him, her eyes muddy and foreign. "David, there were *kids* inside. Little *kids.*"

The TV cut from the reporter to one of the scenes of the crime. At first, David couldn't tell what he was looking at. But then the camera pulled back, and David could make out the rear end of a large automobile—or what was left of it—wedged within the crumbling maw of jagged brickwork and smoldering debris. There was black smoke everywhere. A second angle showed a portion of the building blown out, debris littering the parking lot. Medics were loading small shapes buried beneath white sheets into the backs of ambulances. Men and women screamed from the street.

". . . found here at the recently quarantined Towson Day School, where the death tally has now risen to eighteen students and three instructors," the reporter said. "Eyewitnesses said there had only been one occupant in the vehicle that—"

"Go play in your room, sweetheart." He rubbed the back of Ellie's head.

"I want to see it."

"No. Do as I say."

She exhaled audibly, then turned and sulked down the hallway toward her bedroom.

"This is so messed up, David," Kathy said. She was gnawing on her thumbnail. "The whole world is falling apart."

"*We're* still here," he assured her.

She looked at him. There was something beyond fear in her eyes: There was a hopelessness so deep it looked bottomless. "For how long?" she said. "For how long, David?"

He couldn't answer her. In his mind's eye, he was back on the beltway, staring out the Bronco's window at the little boy with blood spilling from his nose while black smoke fell like a shroud over the horizon. A boy with eyes like the gray backing of a mirror.

By the close of the day, there was a total of five children and four teachers dead at the day-care center. Eleven people died at the hospital, with many more treated for injuries. The suspects, both retired toll collectors named Hamish Kasdan and William Maize, were also killed in the blasts. They'd outfitted the trunks of their cars with a mixture of ammonium nitrate and nitromethane, similar to the cocktail Timothy McVeigh had used in the Oklahoma City bombing. A search of Kasdan and Maize's Baltimore City apartment revealed suicide notes detailing their roles as "renegade saviors for the earth," here to help usher in the last days of mankind. They said they were part of the Worlders' movement, a group of radicals who praised Wanderer's Folly for bringing an end to mankind's parasitic reign over the planet. They hadn't been targeting the sick, but the doctors and nurses who were attempting to help them.

Kathy wept in her sleep that night.

David hardly slept at all.

When dawn finally cast its lurid hues through their bedroom window, David got up, went to the bathroom, then crept into the kitchen to make a pot of coffee. There was a newspaper on the kitchen counter, the front page comprised of a map of the United States with various "hot spots" where the infection was the greatest. Other cities had been completely evacuated. The report said these evacuees had been transported to one of the CDC's quarantine stations, with D.C., Philadelphia, and Newark being the closest to David's area. The report also listed the most recent estimated death toll, both domestic and global—numbers that increased daily and required decimal points. He balled up the paper and shoved in down into the kitchen trash.

In the living room, he slid a Paul Desmond CD into the stereo and turned the volume down low as to not disturb Kathy and Ellie. Back in the kitchen, he poured himself a steaming mug of Sumatran coffee, then pried open the window above the sink so he could smoke a cigarette without having to go outside on the porch. He had hoped the music might fool him into thinking things hadn't changed all that much and that they could still enjoy the simple day-to-day pleasures, but it didn't work. He couldn't trick himself into pretending that everything was normal. The music grated on him and he shut it off.

Someone knocked on the front door.

David chucked the half-smoked cigarette down the garbage disposal, then carried his coffee mug to the door. There were curtains covering the vertical strip of glass beside the door, which he pulled aside. Three figures stood on the porch. A sleek black sedan was parked out in the street by the mailbox. He thought they might be cops or federal agents.

He unlocked the door and opened it. The man in the center, flanked by two men in dark suits, wore a tweed sports coat with suede patches on the elbows and a garish pink bow tie over a blue-and-white checked shirt. He was dark-skinned, slender, nervous-looking. The man's face was narrow and pinched, though somehow not unfriendly.

"Mr. David Arlen?" the man said, extending a laminated badge with his photo on it for David's inspection. He spoke with a heavy Indian accent. "My name is Dr. Sanjay Kapoor. I am the head epidemiologist and director of the recently established Washington branch of the Centers for Disease Control and Prevention's Office of Infectious Diseases."

"The CDC?"

"You are the husband of Kathleen Arlen, is that correct? She is still located at this residence?"

"I think you'd better tell me what this is—"

"Hon?" Kathy said, coming down the hall in a pink terry-cloth bathrobe. "What's going on?"

"Mrs. Arlen?" Dr. Kapoor said, peering past David.

"Yes." She came up beside David, and he put a hand on her shoulder.

"These guys are with the CDC, hon," David said.

Dr. Kapoor repeated his introduction again, then said, "I came here to speak candidly with you, Mrs. Arlen." His dark eyes shifted toward David. "You and your husband, of course."

"What's wrong?" she said.

"You subjected to a blood test at the Spring Hill Medical Center this past quarter," Dr. Kapoor said.

"Yes," she said. "But I was told I was okay. The blood test came back negative."

"Is she sick?" David said. He pulled Kathy away from the door and took a step in front of her. She hugged his arm.

"No, Mr. Arlen." Astoundingly, Dr. Kapoor's pinched face broke into a smile. A silver incisor glittered like tinsel. "Quite the opposite, in fact. May we come in?"

49

He came awake as if pulling himself from quicksand. His head hurt and his neck was stiff. He was in a car, but he wasn't driving . . . and this realization set off his internal panic alarm, causing him to bolt upright in his seat.

"Hey," said the woman behind the wheel. "Take it easy, okay?"

Her name was Ganymede, David recalled. He rubbed his eyes, then wiped the scum from his lips. It was still dark. The glowing green numerals on the dashboard clock read 3:11. Rubbing at a kink in his neck, he turned and saw that Ellie was still asleep, sprawled out across the Caddy's backseat.

"Pleasant dreams?" Gany said. She had her window cracked and was smoking a cigarette.

"Do you think I could get one of those?"

She handed him her lit smoke, then dug a fresh one out of the pack that was wedged in the console between an empty cardboard cup and a pair of mirrored sunglasses. A road map was tucked down into the space between the console and the driver's seat.

He sucked the life out of the cig, relishing it. A sweet mentholated air permeated his lungs. "Ah, Jesus," he muttered.

"Better than sex, isn't it?" Gany said.

Again, David peered into the backseat to make sure his daughter was sleeping. Then he sighed. "Goddamn, it really is." It was almost enough to take his mind off the throbbing ache in his left arm. He extended the arm, bent it at the elbow, straightened it again. The bandage-work Heck Ramirez had done was holding up—there was no blood seeping through the gauze—but the pain, he feared, had intensified while he slept. The whole arm felt tender and hot.

"There's some Tylenol in my purse, if you need it. Back there." Gany nodded toward the backseat.

Her purse was on the floor, a slouching gray satchel that looked like the gutted carcass of an armadillo. He fumbled through it until he located the tiny white bottle of tablets. He shook three into his hand, popped them into his mouth, and dry-swallowed them.

"I'm going to need you to take over for a while," Gany said. "I'm running on fumes here. You okay with that?"

"Yeah. I gotta take a leak, though."

She pointed to the empty cardboard cup in the cup holder.

"You serious?" he said.

Gany laughed. "No. I'm messing with you."

She pulled over on some bleak and hopeless stretch of highway so they could switch seats. The air smelled of tree sap, and David could hear running water—a waterfall?—somewhere off in the distance. They hadn't passed another vehicle since he'd woken up. While he urinated in the bushes, he took his time to breathe in the air and observe the untouched, expansive surroundings. *Being out here, you could almost trick yourself into believing that the world is fine and everything is okay.*

Back on the road, David behind the wheel, he said, "How much farther do we have to go?"

"We should get there around eight in the morning or so." Gany snapped her seat belt into place, then curled onto her side so that she faced the passenger window.

"How do I know where to go?"

"There's a map stuck down by your seat." She yawned.

He tweezed the map out with a thumb and forefinger then spread it across the steering wheel. It wasn't even a MapQuest printout, but an actual *road map,* with their route highlighted in bright yellow marker. There were handwritten notes in spidery print near their destination, telling him what back roads to take once they got off the main highway.

"Tim did all this?" he asked.

"Mmm-hmmm."

"I get the sense that this is his usual MO, and not just because of . . . well, my situation."

"He's a cautious fella," Gany said. "Now, will you keep quiet so I can catch some z's?"

"Sorry."

"There's CDs in the glove compartment. Classic rock. And I don't mean the *new* classic rock, I mean the legit shit. Have at 'em. Just keep the volume down."

"I think the silence will be just fine."

Gany didn't respond. Judging by the deepening of her respiration, David guessed she had already fallen asleep.

50

According to the map, they were only about an hour from their destination—Tim's so-called Fortress of Solitude—when the early morning sunlight glinted off a collection of chrome bumpers farther up the road. David slowed down. Gany leaned forward in the passenger seat and said, "What is this, now?"

"Daddy?" Ellie said, sitting upright in the backseat.

"It's okay, hon. Looks like a fender bender, that's all."

"I don't see any fender bender," Gany said. She rolled down her window and stuck her head out. The morning air swooped into the car. It was downright *cold*.

Five or six cars stood in a queue behind a single vehicle that was parked slantways across both lanes of the road. The car—a pine-green Corolla with rusted quarter panels—did not appear disabled. Whatever had occurred, it must have just happened, because there were no police on the scene yet, and as David pulled up to the rear of the line, a few people got out of their cars and began to wander over to the Corolla.

"Should we see if they need help?" Ellie said. She was peering between the front seats now, gazing at the wreckage ahead of them.

"No," Gany said. "Tim said no stopping. We don't stop."

David looked at her. She was right; he knew that she was.

"All right," he said. He spun the steering wheel and rolled the Cadillac up onto the shoulder. There were grooves in the pavement, which caused the car to vibrate.

"But someone might be hurt, Dad."

"There's enough people around to help out," he said. His hands were tight on the wheel, the vibrations traveling up his arms. Trees encroached upon the shoulder and he brought the car nearly to a stop in order to navigate around them.

"Hey, asshole!" someone shouted at them.

"Roll your window up," David instructed.

Gany started to roll her window up . . . then paused. David eased down on the brake and followed her gaze. They were directly across from the Corolla now, and David saw that the driver's door stood open and that a slim brunette had staggered several feet from the vehicle, dragging the rigid body of a child toward the center of the road. The woman held the child under the armpits, and at first David thought the kid was unconscious or possibly even dead until he saw the face.

The child was a girl, maybe a bit older than Ellie, mousy brown hair like her mother's streaking across her pallid, sweaty face. She wore jean shorts, the hems of which were nothing but stringy white tassels. Her legs were smooth and white, the knees pink. A torrent of blood gushed from both nostrils, soaking her powder-blue shirt with a rhinestone unicorn on it. When her head lolled in David's direction, he saw that she was perfectly conscious. The girl exposed all her bloodstained teeth in a hideous grin. When her hair fell away, David saw that her eyes were blind with madness and swelling from their sockets. As if to give David a show, the girl began chattering her blood-flecked teeth, that rictus grin fixed firmly on her face.

"Drive, David. Go."

For a split second, his foot forgot which pedal was the accelerator and which was the brake.

"Daddy," Ellie said again, her voice a rising whine. She grabbed a fistful of his shirt.

The woman in the street shrieked, "My baby! My baby!"

The would-be Samaritans froze in their haste to assist the woman, quickly turning into a gaggle of gape-mouthed onlookers too terrified to get any closer.

"My baby girl!"

That bloodied rictus grin persisted. David thought he could even hear the clatter of her teeth—*clack-clack-clack-clack!* The light behind those hideous mad eyes was nearly luminous. She flailed in her mother's arms, and a too-white sneaker came off one slender foot and lay by itself now in the sun.

"Drive the *car,* man," Gany said. She whipped her head around to glare at him.

Yet before he could snap out of it and plant the accelerator on the floor, he heard the Caddy's back door pop open. A second later, he saw Ellie running across the highway toward the woman and the sick girl.

"Holy shit," Gany said.

David hopped out of the car and chased after his daughter. In the road, the mother struggled with the girl, shrieking and calling for help. The girl twisted loose and staggered like a zombie a step or two in no particular direction, her one bare foot slapping on the blacktop. Her jaw chattered like some electric machine.

"Ellie!" David cried after her.

Ellie did not stop running, did not turn to look at him. She approached the girl, who cocked her head at a terrible angle, and only then did Ellie slow down to a deliberate walk. Blood sluiced from the girl's nose. Her eyes blazed like twin moons.

"Ellie!"

Ellie reached out and grabbed one of the girl's wrists.

A second after that, David reached her. He wrapped an arm around her waist and, with his other hand, tried to break Ellie's hold on the girl's wrist. Yet, at that same moment, he was overcome by such a powerful jolt that his vision briefly flickered to darkness. A moment later, he felt all his terror drain from him, leaving behind a vast, windy cavern of peacefulness, and he felt—

(calm perfect calm you can even sleep now if you want it's so calm it's so perfect it's living up here in the cool grass and streams and the mountains and flying like a bird yes that's right you're flying you're

flying like a bird that's how calm it is how calm how calm how calm
you're flying flying)

Ellie shoved him away. He staggered backward, the panic and fear flooding back into his body like boiling water, causing sweat to burst from his pores and his heart to hammer. So overwhelmed by the abrupt shift in emotion, he found he could do nothing but stand there, helpless, terrified.

He realized at one point that Ellie and the girl were no longer standing, but that the girl was laid out supine on the blacktop with her head in Ellie's lap. Ellie had a hand on either side of the girl's head, and she was leaning forward so far that their foreheads nearly touched.

The girl had stopped chattering her teeth. Those eyes—those horrible, impossible eyes—had closed. Now her face was nothing but a smooth canvas of peace, as if she had fallen—

(you can even sleep now if you want)

—asleep.

"What is she doing?" It was Gany, speaking in a low voice very close to him, although it took him several seconds to realize this. Not that he could answer her—he no longer possessed the strength to speak.

The only other noise was the sound of the girl's mother sobbing as she stood a few paces behind Ellie, her hands over her mouth. When her daughter's body appeared to go slack, the woman issued a high-pitched whine and sank to her knees.

Gently, Ellie rested the girl's head on the pavement. She stood, and there was blood smeared on her shirt and along one pale white arm. She turned and, without hesitation, approached the mother who remained kneeling in the middle of the street. Ellie's shadow fell over the woman's face. She reached out and touched a hand to the left side of the woman's face, as if to caress her. And indeed, the action looked very much like a caress—an act of comfort, of kindness.

The woman ceased crying. Her chest hitching, her breath

coming in rapid gasps, she looked up at Ellie. David watched as the woman's eyes softened, as her respiration slowed . . . as a semblance of . . . peace . . . settled over her face.

But not just her face.

Her entire body.

When Ellie was finished, she rejoined David and Gany at the side of the road. She took both their hands and led them back to the car.

"What did you do?" Gany asked her. "What the hell just happened?" She glanced over her shoulder at the girl, who remained prostrate in the middle of the street. The girl's mother had crawled over to her and was cradling her now, weeping against her lifeless body. The crowd of onlookers stared.

51

They had driven less than three minutes from the scene with no one capable of speaking a word until Ellie said, "Pull over. I'm gonna be sick."

Gany pulled the Caddy onto the shoulder of the wooded highway. The moment the car stopped, Ellie was out the door and hurrying into the trees. She got only about five yards before she bent forward and vomited in the grass.

David got out of the car and joined his daughter. When he reached her, she had finished retching, but remained bent forward, hands on her knees, staring off at the dark, intersecting branches of the trees. David rubbed her back. He didn't say anything.

"I'm sorry," Ellie said. Then she spit on the ground several times.

"Feel better?"

"I guess so." She turned her head and looked up at him. Her face was beet red, her eyes bleary. A trail of saliva hung from her chin. "It was a lot to take in."

"I guess it was. Were you trying to save her life?"

"I'm not sure. I don't know what I was trying to do. But she died, anyway."

"Yes," David said, still rubbing her back. "But much more peacefully than she would have, I think."

"I took it all out of her and helped her get over," Ellie said.

"It was very brave," he said. "Very stupid, but very brave."

She began to cry.

"Aw, hon. Come here." He hugged her tight. "It's okay."

"I'm sorry," she said, her voice muffled against his chest.

"Shhh," he told her, squeezing her more tightly. He looked back toward the Caddy and saw Gany standing outside, leaning against the hood and smoking a cigarette. Watching them.

"What are we gonna say to her?" Ellie said. She was looking at Gany now, too.

"I'll handle it. You okay to go? Feel better?"

Swiping the tears from her face, Ellie nodded.

"Okay," he said. "Let's roll."

When they got back in the car, David expected Gany to hit them with a barrage of questions. But to his astonishment, she said nothing. Not a word. It made him uncomfortable, so he cleared his throat and proceeded to fumble through some sort of explanation that was somewhere between a half truth and a complete fabrication.

"Hey," Gany said, interrupting him. "Listen, man. You guys don't owe me an explanation. As far as I'm concerned, your girl back there's got a big heart and was trying to help someone in need. We can leave it at that."

"All right," David agreed. "Let's leave it at that."

In the backseat, Ellie fell quickly asleep.

By the time Gany left the highway and pulled onto a narrow ribbon of blacktop that wound through acres of bare-branched forest, Ellie was awake again. She stared out at the trees, not talking. All conversation had pretty much died after the highway incident.

"This place is a retired chicken farm," Gany said as she navigated the unwieldy Cadillac along the serpentine twist of roadway. "Tim's been out here for about a year, I guess. Previous owners sold it to him for a song. Not much use for a chicken farm when there aren't any more chickens."

"What exactly does he *do* out here?"

"Whatever he wants," Gany said. "He's always been a bit of a recluse, only now it's trendy."

"But what does he do for money? Does he have a job?" She looked at him. "You guys are brothers, right?"

"Well, stepbrothers. We haven't spoken in a long time."

"So, are you one of those guys who only reappears when he needs something?"

The question jarred him. About a million responses shuttled through his brain, but none of them seemed adequate enough. He opened his mouth to speak, but Gany cut him off.

"I'm just screwing with you, man," she said, smiling at him. She had a bit of an Elvis curl to her upper lip.

"I just don't want to get him in trouble," he said. Then added, "Or you."

"Tim's no dummy. He looks before he leaps." She glanced sidelong at him. "I'm no dummy, either."

After about ten minutes, the blacktop gave way to packed earth. The trees crowded in closer to the car, and a few bare branches reached out and scraped twiggy fingers along the Caddy's roof. David got the sense that they were driving gradually uphill the whole way.

The dirt road eventually emptied out onto a small sunlit glen, at the center of which was the farmhouse. It was comprised of natural, untreated wood, with a slouching cantilevered roof, green and furry with moss. A series of antennas jutted straight up from the center of the roof, forming a semicircle around a satellite dish. Running the length of the house was a wraparound porch that sagged beneath a shingled alcove. The windows were all shuttered, and there were NO TRESPASSING signs posted to the trees every few yards. A silver Tahoe was parked around one side of the house, decorated in splatters of mud.

"A deer," Ellie said. "See it?"

David looked and saw a large doe standing motionless among the foliage to one side of the house.

"It's a fake," Gany said. "A phony."

Ellie said, "Huh?"

"It's made of rubber. There's a camera in its head. Wave,

gang. We're on CCTV." Gany stuck her arm out the window and waved to the deer. The deer's head swiveled mechanically, following the vehicle's progress around the side of the house.

"You're kidding me," David said. "What's that all about?"

"Precaution," Gany said.

"Precaution from what?"

Gany eased down on the brake and shifted the car into Park. "You should really speak to your brother more often, man," she said.

They got out of the car, feeling the cool, unblemished breeze on their skin, and inhaling the scent of pinesap in the air. There was an ax-head wedged in a tree stump and a few archery targets fixed to bales of hay. A rusted artesian well jutted crookedly from the earth, looking like something that had landed there after dropping off the fuselage of a 747. Also, there were the bugs: Out here, halfway up a mountain and in the middle of the wilderness, the air was teeming with tiny, flying insects. Larger things catapulted out of the grass. Glancing around, David saw a number of gauzy webs strung up in the forks of trees. He thought of the gigantic spider on the lamppost back in Goodwin, Kentucky.

Gany pulled her hair back and tied it behind her head with a rubber band. "It's beautiful out here, isn't it?"

"The air feels thinner up here," David said. They had driven halfway up a mountain, the height nearly dizzying. He could feel the change in elevation in his bones.

"Cleaner, too." The voice was male, booming. David turned to see his stepbrother standing on the porch, a cigar parked in one corner of his mouth, his big arms, blue-gray with tattoos, folded over the porch railing.

"Holy shit," David said. He couldn't help but smile. "It's like looking at a ghost."

"Maybe you are," Tim said, returning David's smile. He had a gruff but warm face, with sharp blue eyes beneath gingery eyebrows. His hair was long and tied behind his head in a ponytail. When he stood upright off the railing, the top of his head nearly touched the sagging lip of the roof. "Maybe we're all just ghosts floating about through the ether, occasionally bumping into one another." He turned and looked at Ellie, who stood near one of the hay bales, one hand around the shaft of an arrow ready to pull it out. "My God, is that you, El? Smokes, you're a goddamn woman!"

The smile that came to her face was enough to brighten her entire being. Something within her seemed to swell. "Hi, Uncle Tim!"

"Come and give me a hug, El."

She trotted across the yard and mounted the creaking porch steps. Tim met her halfway, snatching her up off one of the risers in one muscular arm and swinging her against him. She wrapped her arms around his neck and he hugged her back. Before letting her go, he kissed the side of her face. It had been years since she had seen him, yet she went to him with familiarity. With trust.

"I thought you said kids were lampreys with legs," Gany said.

Still smiling, Tim jabbed a finger in Gany's direction. He made his way down the stairs and ambled over to David. As he approached, the smile on his face transitioned to a sympathetic firmness of the lips. His eyes softened.

"I'm sorry about Kathy," he said.

David felt something loosen inside him. Before he could embarrass himself, Tim snatched him up in a bear hug that lifted both his feet off the ground. The crook of Tim's neck smelled like cigar smoke, his flannel shirt like marijuana. David felt tears spring from his eyes; it was almost as if Tim was squeezing them out of him.

"Thank you," David said once they'd parted. "You have no idea what this means, letting us come here like this. You probably saved our lives, Tim."

Tim tucked the cigar back between his lips. He asked Gany if they'd had any trouble.

"Smooth sailing," Gany said, though her gaze darted briefly in David's direction. "I tossed his cell phone right after I picked him up."

Tim nodded, pleased. "Why don't you take Eleanor to see the rabbits?"

Ellie looked at her uncle, wide-eyed. "There's rabbits?"

"Bunnies," he said. "Newborns. A whole brood."

"Come on," Gany called to her.

Ellie went halfway down the steps, then paused and looked at David.

"Go on," he said.

Smiling, she rejoined Gany on the lawn. Gany took hold of Ellie's hand and they proceeded to trot around the side of the farmhouse.

"She's beautiful, David."

"She looks like her mother," David said.

"Come inside with me." Tim slung an arm around David's shoulder—it was like hefting a log onto his back—and led him up the porch and into the house.

David was surprised to find the interior of the farmhouse clean, organized, meticulous. The absence of personal flourishes—there were no pictures on the walls, no bric-a-brac on shelves, no homey touches—made the place seem more like a *facility* than a home. As Tim talked about how he'd purchased the property for a song, David followed him through a series of rooms that all seemed to serve their own very specific purpose—a room filled with computer equipment and two laptop monitors with activated screen savers; another room serving as a library, where hardbound books climbed the walls; a room overflowing with various ferns bursting from hanging pots lit by a regiment of solar lamps while misters breathed vapor into the air. Music issued from hidden speakers and followed them from room to room, some instrumental jazz heavy on the electric bass. The tour ended in a screened-in porch that overlooked a field of brown grass bisected by a narrow wooden structure that looked like a series of miniature boxcars shackled together. Beyond the field, a curtain of fir trees wreathed the base of a mountain range. There was snow on the peaks.

"It's beautiful out here," said David.

"Sit, sit," Tim said, waving his hands around at a group of wicker chairs. "What happened to your nose?"

"Got in a tussle with some hillbilly zealot in Kentucky."

"Broken?"

"I don't think so."

"How about your arm?"

"I cut it on some glass." David sat, the Glock jabbing him painfully in the small of his back. He withdrew it and held it out toward Tim. "Think you could stow this away somewhere?"

"Christ, man. And they say some people never change." Tim grinned, plucking the Glock from David's hand and shoving it down in the rear waistband of his own pants.

David sighed. Above his head, more potted ferns gently swayed in the breeze that came through the screens. There were birdhouses hanging from the porch on the other side of the screens, but these looked about as vacant as the houses with the X's on the doors back in Goodwin.

"Let's have a look," Tim said. He knelt beside David and proceeded to unwrap the bandaging.

"What were those aerials on the roof for?" David asked.

"I rigged them up myself. I've got a ham radio and some closed-circuit monitors in the basement. The place is outfitted with security cameras. Some other junk, too." Tim removed the bandage from the wound, then made a disapproving face. David glanced down and saw that the wound was still bleeding. He felt woozy just looking at it.

"I thought you were off the grid."

"Most grids," said Tim. "How long ago did this happen?"

"Yesterday morning, I think. I've lost track of the days."

"It's reopened. It needs stitches."

"I can't go to a doctor."

"You won't have to. I can do it here."

"Jesus," David said, looking away.

Tim squeezed the back of David's neck. "It'll be fine. Ain't my first rodeo."

Tim got up and sauntered into the next room. David heard

him rummaging through drawers. Glass bottles clinked together.

Out in the field, Gany and Ellie trudged through the tall brown grass on their way to the wooden structure that resembled a series of boxcars. David guessed they were the old chicken coops that had been modified into rabbit hutches.

"I don't understand what you're doing out here," David said.

"I'm living," Tim said from the next room.

"What happened to Kansas City?"

"I felt stifled there. It was always just a layover for me, anyhow."

"Every place is just a layover for you."

Tim laughed in the other room. When he returned, he had a black leather satchel under one arm and a lowball glass half-filled with amber liquid. "I was never one for the rat race. You know that. When they started marching the National Guard through downtown, I knew it was time to pop smoke. Hold still."

"Wha—"

Tim splashed the contents of the lowball glass onto David's wound. It was like being branded with an iron, and David half-expected the open gash to smoke and sizzle. Instead, he shouted and bolted right out of the chair.

Tim chuckled. "Relax. Sit back down."

"Son of a bitch," David gasped, though he lowered himself back into the chair.

Tim slipped back out into the adjoining room and returned with a refill. He handed the glass to David. "You can drink this one."

David sniffed it. "Moonshine?"

"Go on," Tim said, kneeling beside David's chair. He unzipped the satchel as David upended the glass, knocking the liquor to the back of his throat. It seemed to fall straight down into his stomach, unimpeded, where it detonated like an explosion.

David made a hissing sound. "Tastes like lighter fluid."

"Shit's just as flammable, too. My own personal concoction. Distilled dandelions and pinesap. I'll join you for the second round." Tim was threading a hooked needle.

Again, David averted his eyes. "What's with all the potted plants?"

"I've become something of a horticulturist. Some of the best people I know are plants."

"So you're a horticulturist and a part-time surgeon. A regular Renaissance man."

Tim grinned. "Don't look."

David turned away. He winced as Tim sank the hooked needle into his flesh. "Christ, are you *kidding* me? Goddamn it!"

"Hold still, you big sissy," Tim said. He was still grinning. "Remember that time we were roughhousing in the living room and I body-slammed you and broke your collarbone?"

"It still aches."

"I bribed you to keep your mouth shut, gave you my new baseball glove and everything."

"I never squealed," David reminded him.

"That's right. But you could only mope around the house so long with one shoulder slumped before someone started to notice. And boy, did my old man let me have it after that." Tim chuckled, and the sound of it briefly transported David back to a simpler time—a time of his youth, of family, of living in the rambling old house in the woods of rural Pennsylvania with his mother, Tim, and Tim's father. Ancient memories, buried and forgotten beneath mounds of brain dust.

Once Tim had finished stitching and bandaging his arm, he returned to the adjoining room, only to reappear with an unlabeled jug of liquor and a second lowball glass. Out in the field, Ellie was holding a large gray rabbit against her chest, the rabbit's hind legs cycling wildly in the air. David heard Ellie squeal with delight.

"I guess I should tell you what happened," David said after some silence.

"It's up to you," Tim said. "If you want to do it now, let's do it now. If you want to wait, maybe get some rest and put some food in your belly first, then it can wait."

"I want to wait, but I also want to get it out while Ellie's not sitting next to me. You know what I mean?"

Tim nodded. "Then let's do it."

David cleared his throat and said, "Kathy was working as a psychologist at a state hospital. When things got serious—when some patients and a few doctors got sick—they mandated that all staff get tested. I actually thought it would be a good thing. She had become so depressed, so unlike herself . . . and so *convinced* that she was sick . . . that I thought this would help alleviate her concerns. Sometime after that, we got a visit from the CDC, some doctor named Sanjay Kapoor, head of their Infectious Diseases office in D.C."

He was reliving it now—the conversation with Dr. Kapoor in their living room, a mixture of emotions coursing through him. He had held Kathy's hand in his as they sat together on the couch, listening to Dr. Kapoor explain the situation. Had they been pardoned or cursed? It was easy to answer that now, in hindsight, but he had been lost and confused at the time. And maybe—stupidly—a little bit hopeful.

"There was an abnormality with Kathy's blood work, something Kapoor and the CDC were very interested in. They were interested in the presence of what they called IgG antibodies in her blood. In other words, she had been exposed to Wanderer's Folly but had somehow developed antibodies to fight off the virus. Kapoor said that viruses generally rely on receptors that exist on cells within the body. Kathy had what Kapoor called a genetic mutation for that receptor, which prevented the virus from attaching to and infecting the individual cells. It was a hiccup in her DNA."

"She was immune, in other words," Tim said.

"Exactly. She'd been exposed but that genetic mutation was creating antibodies that fought off the Folly. And they were thrilled at the prospect. They wanted her to volunteer and submit herself to a battery of tests. Blood cultures, exposure to the virus, that sort of thing. There's a lot of . . . of medical jargon I can't really . . ."

"It's okay," Tim said.

"They made it sound so harmless at first. Kapoor said it was no different from donating blood to the Red Cross—those were his actual words, Tim—and that there was no way she could deny their request because she would be in no danger. Like I said, Kathy had been losing it for a time. This whole epidemic terrified her. She'd become severely depressed. She'd started seeing a shrink and was on meds for depression and anxiety. She still looked the same, but I swear to God, Tim, when she walked around the house, it was like someone else was controlling her. When she looked at me, someone else stared out from her eyes. I know how that sounds, but I swear it, Tim. I swear it."

"I understand," Tim said. "So what happened?"

"We took twenty-four hours to talk it over and make a decision. We couldn't see the risk. It sounded so simple, and it was like she'd be . . . well, she'd be helping to save the world. My God, it sounds so fucking stupid now, but it just didn't seem like that big of a deal for her to agree to it." He laughed now, a humorless bark. "We might have thought about it more clearly if it hadn't been for some nutcases blowing up a day-care center and a hospital and killing a bunch of kids up in our area. It was all over the news. She was already anticipating the end of the world, and these lunatics with two carloads of manure just so happened to solidify all her fears. She asked me what the point of living was if it was in a world as mad as this one had become. We had a daughter; we needed to make sure she grew up happy and healthy. So, yeah, in the end, it seemed like a no-brainer."

A peal of laughter drifted across the field, followed by Ellie crying out, *"Oh no!"* The rabbit had kicked its way loose and Ellie had dropped it to the ground; she scurried after it now, darting about in the long grass, while Gany laughed and tried to help her catch it. *"Oh no! Oh, you rabbit!"*

"She felt like she was doing some good," David went on.

"She felt like she was helping to find a cure. We both did. But she was giving too much of herself, and she was growing weaker and weaker. Because of all the tests, she had to stop taking her meds. Depression medication, stuff prescribed by her shrink. I can't remember now. Goddamn it. It made her anxious, paranoid. After some time, she fell back into some deep depression, too.

"A few days a week they would keep her overnight, just to keep an eye on her vitals. I'd stopped going to work—my students had all pretty much dropped out, and the college was pretty much a ghost town by this point—so I spent my days with Kathy at the facility. It wasn't even a hospital, but some retrofitted office building in Greenbelt."

"Where was Eleanor during all this?"

"In the beginning I would bring her with me. Things were okay back then, and I didn't see the harm in it. It was good for her and Kathy to be together. But as things . . . worsened . . . as Kathy's temperament continued to sour . . . I guess I thought it best that she didn't come. There's this older woman a few blocks up from our house, used to teach Ellie piano when she was younger. Mrs. Blanche. She agreed to keep Ellie during the day. They got on fine, so I was very thankful. Particularly toward the . . . well, toward the end of things."

Tim nodded.

"They asked Ellie and me to give blood samples, too. They tested our blood the same way they'd tested Kathy's. Mine was just normal." He grimaced tiredly at Tim.

"But Ellie," Tim interjected.

"Yes," David said. "Ellie has the same genetic mutation as her mother. She's immune."

"And so they wanted to study Ellie, too?"

"Dr. Kapoor suggested it. I told him I'd give it some thought. But by that time, things with Kathy had started to look grim." He lowered his head. "She was staying at the hospital around the clock by then. I decided to take her home and stop the testing—it was wasting her away, Tim—but Kathy refused. Something . . . something inside her had changed. They said they never actually injected her with the virus, but I don't believe that. I *saw* her, Tim. I saw what they did to her.

"I told her about Ellie's immunity. She cried, she was so happy. But then that didn't last long. She began to wonder what it would be like once everyone on the whole goddamn planet died except our daughter."

"I guess that didn't help her state of mind any," Tim said.

David shook his head. "And all along, they kept promising nothing would happen to her." His voice cracked, and he felt his throat tighten. In his mind, he heard Kathy's last words to him, echoing like the report of a pistol in the center of his brain: *Bring the heater closer, would you, honey? It's so cold in here.* "But it was all too much for her in the end. Her body just gave out. Those doctors had used her up, weakened her body and her mind, and she just . . . she just died, Tim."

"Were you there when it happened?"

"I had stepped out to have a cigarette and put some stuff in the car. She was dead when I went back up to the room."

"Okay. Okay. How much of this does Eleanor know?"

At the mention of her name, David looked back out through the screen at the sloping brown field and rabbit hutches. Gany and Ellie were gone. Trees sighed in the breeze.

"She knows everything," he said. "I tried lying to her at first, but Ellie, she's too goddamn perceptive for that. I mean, I didn't go into the details of Kathy's death, but she knows."

"She's a smart kid," Tim said. "She sees through the bull-shit."

"There's something else, too," David said, "and I'll be damned if I know how to even begin to explain it to you."

Just then, Ellie appeared in the doorway. She had her shoe box under one arm and a smile on her face. "Did you see me with the rabbits, Dad?"

He returned her smile with one of his own. It felt like it might crack his skull. "I sure did," he said, pawing at his eyes.

"One got loose, Uncle Tim."

Tim waved a big hand in front of his face. "They come back, you know. They've got a whole network of tunnels beneath that coop."

Gany came up behind Ellie. She put a hand on the girl's shoulder. "I'm thinking about some food, fellas."

Tim stood up. "That's a great idea." He turned to David. "In the meantime, why don't you and El get washed up? I've got some clothes for you both to wear. Have a proper shower."

David struggled out of the chair, careful not to put pressure on his freshly stitched arm. "Sounds like heaven."

Tim knocked back the last of his moonshine, then smiled at them. "So then let's hop to it," he said. Then he winked at David and said, "We'll finish our chat after we chow down."

"Works for me," David said, rubbing his eyes with the heel of his hand. He followed Tim back inside the house.

52

Tim had given them two bedrooms at one end of the farmhouse, across the hall from each other. The door to Ellie's room was cracked open, and David poked his head in while on his way to his own room. Ellie stood before an open window, absently flicking large beetles off the screen.

"Hey, you," he said, coming in.

"Hi." She didn't turn away from her bug-flicking exercise.

Folded at the foot of the bed were some clean clothes, as well as the Nike shoe box containing the bird eggs. David moved them aside and sat down. Bedsprings squeaked.

"We didn't get much of a chance to talk about what happened today," he began.

"Isn't much to talk about," she said. The screen vibrated as she flicked a beetle the size of a quarter off it.

"How did you know you could . . . ease that girl's suffering?" He didn't know how else to phrase it.

"Just something I felt."

"Can you look at me, please?"

She turned around and he saw that the reason she hadn't wanted to face him was because she had been crying.

"Hey." He got up and went to her. Put a hand on her shoulder. "What is it?"

"I wanted to save her. I thought maybe I could."

"Why did you think that?"

She looked down at her feet. "I don't know."

"You brought her peace," he said. "In the end."

Ellie looked up at him. "When I touched her, I saw what was in her head. I saw her hallucination."

"What was it?"

"It was terrible. It scared me. She wasn't just seeing things, Dad. She was hearing them, feeling them. Like her mind was someplace else and only her body had been left behind. And for a second, I was there, too, seeing and hearing and feeling all those things." She looked down at her hands, so small and pale, the fingers pink and thin. "I took all that bad stuff out of her and let the good stuff in. I tried to make her sleep."

David remembered. When he'd grabbed Ellie around the waist and tried to pull her free from the girl, he had been greeted with a shock from just touching Ellie's flesh. He recalled something about sleeping and birds flying—it had been more of an emotion than an actual image, an emotion that somehow translated into thoughts, into ideas—but he found he couldn't remember the details of it—

(calm perfect calm you can even sleep now if you want it's so calm it's so perfect it's living up here in the cool grass)

—now.

"I just wish I could have been there to do that for Mom," Ellie said.

David hugged her.

"Whatever it is inside me," Ellie said, "it's getting stronger."

"Are you scared?"

"No," she said, "but you are."

He offered her a sad smile. There was no use arguing the point. "I'm just worried about you," he said.

"Don't worry, Dad," she said. "I think it's supposed to be this way."

53

Three weeks earlier

He first noticed the van approximately two weeks prior to Kathy's death. At the time, he didn't think much of it. It was parked right there across the street from their house, a white-paneled van with no windows and PVC pipes tied to the roof rack. There were no logos on the side, and it had nondescript Maryland plates. Someone had placed a sunshade on the dash, so it was impossible to see through the windows into the cab.

David had just picked up Ellie from Mrs. Blanche's house, having spent the afternoon at the Greenbelt facility with Kathy. He turned onto Columbus Court, the daylight already draining from the sky. The trees beyond the houses had started to shed their leaves. As he always did, he glanced at the remains of Deke Carmody's house. When he looked up, he found that the otherwise inconspicuous white van was crowding the left-hand side of the street. David steered around the van, not thinking much of it . . . yet it was his first conscious sighting of it, and it would come to nestle itself into the recesses of his brain in the days to come, as things with Kathy took a quick turn for the worse.

That evening, before tucking Ellie into bed, they called Kathy on her cell phone. She answered, and despite sounding cheery for Ellie's sake, David knew she was wiped. Kathy gave the obligatory responses to all of Ellie's questions. Yes, she was fine. Yes, she would be home with them soon. Yes, this was something very special that she was doing. Yes, of course she missed her very much, but she had been too tired lately for visitors.

After they hung up, David ushered Ellie into bed. He turned off her light and kissed her good night. In the half light, he watched her roll onto her side and hug her pillow.

Before he got up from her bed, she reached out and laced her hand inside one of his. He smiled at her . . . then closed his eyes. It felt good to hold her, to touch her, just as it had when she was an infant and he'd walk the floorboards with her all night while she gazed up at him with those wide, impossible eyes. He felt calm, serene. Strangely at peace.

Once she had fallen asleep, he kissed the side of her face and got up off the bed. He closed her bedroom door, then wandered aimlessly about the house—a house that now seemed impossibly large and mazelike, a turreted castle with countless dark corners and unending corridors. He could feel his anxiety creeping slowly back into him. Since Kathy's stay at the Greenbelt facility had become permanent, David had stopped sleeping in their bedroom, opting instead for the living room couch. In fact, he found himself limiting his time spent in the master bedroom altogether, as the scent of Kathy's perfume lingered in the pillowcases, the sheets, the curtains over the windows, the clothes in their shared closet. The hairbrush she'd left on the bathroom sink made him melancholy. The unfinished Wally Lamb novel on the nightstand, propped open with its spine in the air as if it were doing push-ups, made him restless and caused his mind to wander in the direction of dark things.

Despite his nightly reassurances to his daughter, he had a bad feeling about the direction of things. He had mentioned to Kathy a few times lately that he wanted her to come home with him. But she said she was okay, that she could stick it out. She'd insisted.

Earlier that day, he'd commented to Dr. Kapoor about the pallor of Kathy's skin. She'd become jaundiced, with bruise-colored hollows under each eye. She had lost so much weight in such a brief amount of time—there was no question about that—and the result was eerie, causing the flesh of her face to stretch taut around her skull, which gave her cheekbones an unnatural emphasis. Her fingers had slimmed, and as David sat beside her bed that afternoon eating lunch, they'd both heard the clinking of her wedding band as it fell from her finger and *tink-tink-tink*ed across the floor. He'd picked it up and tried to slide it back on her finger, but she pulled her hand away, almost embarrassed, and shook her head. *No. No.* For a moment, there was a strange telescopic look in her eyes, much like the lens of a camera as it adjusts to focus on something at some great distance.

"You keep it for me," she'd said.

He had it in his pocket now. He dug it out and pushed it onto his pinkie. It fit.

"Something's wrong with her," David had expressed to Dr. Kapoor before leaving the facility that evening. They stood talking in the hallway outside Dr. Kapoor's office, their voices low although there was no one around to eavesdrop. "She doesn't look well."

"We've been taking a lot of blood," Dr. Kapoor said. "As long as we keep her on the IV, though, everything will be fine. The weight loss comes from her lack of appetite. She gives us trouble about eating."

"You've taken her off her psych meds, the antidepressants. She's distraught."

"It's necessary for the blood work, the cultures. I assure you, Mr. Arlen, that she is getting all the proper nutrients through the IV."

He took Dr. Kapoor at his word, though he didn't feel good about doing it.

That night, he drank a whole six-pack of Flying Dog while watching *Close Encounters of the Third Kind* on AMC. By the time Richard Dreyfuss found himself surrounded by those bug-eyed, long-limbed extraterrestrials, David was half in the bag. He rarely got drunk and never when he was home alone with Ellie, but he cut himself some slack tonight.

When the movie was over, he shut the TV off but remained on the couch, staring off into the darkness while the wall clock in the kitchen kept a metronomic beat. There was a drip in the kitchen sink, too, a steady and repetitive *plink!* every few seconds, and he focused on that for a while in his drunkenness. But then some nonspecific disquiet roused him just as he was about to slip into unconsciousness, and he got up, wended down the hall in the dark, and checked on Ellie. She was still sound asleep in bed. On the nightstand beside her was the shoe box containing the bird eggs. Ellie was not the source of his disquiet, he realized: It was something else. Without disturbing her, he kissed the warm and dewy side of her head, then retreated back out into the living room.

Before going to sleep, he peered out the front windows. It was as if something was beckoning to him. Across the street, the houses were dark, silent.

The white van was still parked along the curb.

And he realized it was the van that troubled him, although he had no idea why.

How do I know that van? Where have I seen it before?

In the dark, he collected the six empty beer bottles from the coffee table and carried them into the foyer. There, he set them up in a line on the floor in front of the door—an adult version of Ellie's Night Parade. When he finished, he checked the dead bolt to make sure he'd locked it before returning to the warm indentation on the couch.

54

He stood barefoot on a gravelly patch of earth, watching as a parade of impossible animals campaigned along the desolate countryside in a single-file line that stretched all the way to the horizon. They were prehistoric in their hugeness, yet there was nothing mammalian about them. Instead, they appeared insectoid, multi-legged and wielding great segmented antennae, with shimmering, chitinous carapaces and eyes like swirling, gaseous planets. Their massive, spine-laden feet punched craters in the earth, and their sheer size blocked out the sun. Massive machinelike limbs muscled over trees and brushed against the sides of shallow mountain ranges. When these monstrous creatures reached civilization, David saw that all the buildings were decimated and abandoned, like those of ancient Greece or the bombed-out cities of some Middle Eastern country, and there were no signs of human life anywhere. Or at least it appeared so, until a figure materialized from within the shadows of a crumbling brick alleyway. A ghost-shape. The figure was slight, sinewy, feminine, with long hair hanging over her face. She looked like a teenager, perhaps even older, her clothes filthy and nothing more than rags, her arms piebald with bruises and abrasions. Her bare feet left bloody footprints on the dusty pavement. As David watched, the woman's hair swung away from her face and, despite her years—despite the feral, detached look in her eyes and the broken shards of teeth that gnashed and chattered endlessly, madly—David recognized his daughter.

David awoke in a bedroom with blank alabaster walls and a single window at his back. He was sprawled out on a bed, his hair still damp from the shower he'd taken, and he was dressed in the clean clothes Tim had given him, though he could not remember getting dressed. As consciousness fell fully upon him, he was aware of a small headache jack-hammering at his right temple. He realized he had come in here to lie down for a few minutes after showering and getting dressed, but the time—and his own consciousness, apparently—had been siphoned from him. Judging by the murky seawater quality of the daylight coming through the partially shuttered bedroom window, David guessed he'd been asleep for a few hours.

The image of those insectile dinosaurs was still fresh in his mind. He could still taste the powdery air of that evacuated city at the back of his throat, could still feel the impossible vibrations of those hideous, segmented, Lovecraftian bug-legs driving themselves into the earth. He knew it was only a dream . . . yet what troubled him was the idea that it might have been a portent of things to come, too: a glimpse into a not-too-distant future when the next breed of creature ruled the earth, much as people had replaced dinosaurs. And in that future, the only living human being was his daughter.

The thought caused him to shudder.

Downstairs, he found the three of them seated around a kitchen table, a plate of overdone flank steaks on the counter. He'd caught them in the middle of their meal, Ellie's plate piled high with scalloped potatoes, green beans, applesauce, and a blackened, rigid cut of meat. He got the sense that he *also* had caught them in the middle of some private conversation, for they all ceased talking and stared at him as he approached. Ellie looked startled by his presence.

"Well," Tim proclaimed. "There he is."

"Hi, Daddy."

"Hi, sugar." He sat down, rotating his left shoulder to work the stiffness out of his injured arm. "What're you guys gabbing about?"

"We're trying to figure out what to do for this little lady's birthday," Tim said.

"We've got some cake mix in the cupboard," Gany suggested. "It's pretty old, so I can't attest for the quality. Can't mix it with eggs, either, but it should do in a pinch."

"Gonna be nine years old," Tim said, marveling at Ellie while rubbing the back of her head with one of his big hands. Ellie's gaze still clung to David, and he was certain in that moment that they hadn't been discussing Ellie's upcoming birthday when he'd come into the kitchen. It had been something else. "I remember when you were born, squirt." Tim turned to David. "Those stitches holding up, partner?"

"Feels like it. How long was I out?"

"Four hours or so," Tim said.

Gany pushed her chair back and stood up. "Hungry?"

He was ravenous. He couldn't remember the last meal he'd eaten. He found that he couldn't recall how many days he and Ellie had been on the run, either; time was beginning to come apart at the seams, unraveling like an old afghan. Each day bled into the next.

"You bet," he said. He stood to help her, but she told him to sit back down and not to be silly. She loaded a steak onto a clean plate, then piled some potatoes and green beans around it for good measure.

While they ate, Tim brought David up to speed with what he'd been doing over the past several years since they'd last seen each other and had a proper conversation. Back in Kansas City, he had started an IT consulting firm, which had become moderately successful. His clients were mostly private industry, and his advertisement was limited to word-of-mouth recommendations. At the height of the company, he'd had three employees working under him, which afforded him the opportunity to do a bit of traveling. Tim Brody had never been one to settle down in one place for very long, and even with the success of the company, he felt constricted by the responsibilities. So after about two and a half years, he sold the company and made himself a "tidy little profit," which

David suspected was a very modest statement. This was around the time the first cases of Wanderer's Folly broke out. Birds had seemingly vanished overnight, and those held in captivity in zoos, in labs, and on farms, all succumbed to the illness in a matter of weeks. Given the sudden gaping hole in the agricultural ecosystem, the price of beef, pork, and fish skyrocketed. Ever the entrepreneur, Tim decided it was time to invest in a food source that had mostly been overlooked till then, as a way to compete—and undercut—current market prices.

"Rabbits," he said, grinning.

"Oh no," David said, pausing with his fork halfway to his mouth. He glanced down at the charred bit of meat at the end of the tines, abruptly recalling the rabbit hutches out back.

"It made perfect sense. It's a very lean meat and, to speak frankly, will give you a terrible case of the runs if you eat too much of it," Tim said, "but it was basically an untapped resource. I was sitting on a cache of dough after the sale of the company and this idea just jumped into my head. When I realized I could buy an old chicken farm for pennies on the dollar—because no one's raising *chickens* anymore—I started looking around and doing some research. When I found this place, I saw that it fit my needs perfectly." He spread his arms wide. "I'm miles from nowhere in every direction. I'm basically running my own sovereign nation out here."

"Are you saying you eat those rabbits out back?" Ellie said.

"Mostly, I sell them," Tim said. "In cattle country, I'm the guy undercutting the cattle ranchers by selling rabbit meat. Not to mention the furs, which I also sell on eBay."

Ellie set her fork down in her dish.

"Honey, this is beef," Gany reassured her.

"Oh." Yet Ellie did not look convinced.

"I've spent the better part of the year working on these ferns, too," Tim went on, jerking a thumb over his shoulder toward the room with all the hanging plants and UV lamps.

"I've unlocked something in the ferns that's helped pump up the body mass of the rabbits."

"Steroids for Bugs Bunny," David said.

"In a way," said Tim, "though they're totally harmless. No chemicals, no injections. It's just been a process of trial-and-error, cross-pollenating various seeds and allowing them to germinate under different environmental conditions. It's all natural."

"You're really doing all this stuff?" David said. "I'm impressed."

"Oh, that's just two-thirds of my operation." Tim raised his glass, which contained a cocktail of fruit juice and his pungent liquor. "That moonshine you had earlier?"

"Dandelions and pinesap," David recalled.

"I've got quite the distillery set up."

"So you're bootlegging, too?"

"This isn't Prohibition, man."

"Not that he has a license," Gany added. She winked at Tim.

"What are you, the whiskey police?" Tim said. "Anyway, I'm not quite ready to roll the stuff out to consumers, not just yet. It's still a bit overpowering."

"We use it to light the bonfire in the yard," Gany commented. "Not joking."

"Yeah, it's basically pure ethanol with natural ingredients added during the distillation process," Tim said. "The first few batches were just awful."

"As opposed to that firewater you gave me earlier," David said.

Tim shrugged. "Hey," he said. "It did the trick, didn't it?"

"You make it right here in the house?"

"No. I've got a cabin a few miles farther up the mountain. It's pretty remote."

"In the event you're raided by the ATF, I suppose," David said.

Tim winked at him.

"What's the ATF?" asked Ellie.

★ ★ ★

Once their plates were cleaned, Tim and Ellie cleared the table and washed the dishes by hand in the sink. Gany remained at the table with David, speaking in broad strokes about her own life just to make conversation. When she mentioned a boyfriend in South Dakota, David said, "Oh, I just assumed you and my brother . . ."

At the sink, Tim guffawed. Gany shot him a sly glance, then reclined in her chair. She was sipping a dark red wine, having declined a glass of Tim's home brew earlier.

"Do you remember that guy Applewhite?" Gany said. "The Heaven's Gate nut who initiated that mass suicide in the nineties?"

"I remember seeing it on the news," David said.

"That's your brother."

David laughed. "A cult leader, huh?"

"Oh, he hasn't horse-whispered people into cutting their balls off and taking cyanide pills," Gany said, "but he's equally as charismatic."

"So, where's the rest of his sordid cabal?"

"Oh, they're around," Gany said. "It's not like we all live in some big commune, you know. I've got an apartment back in Colorado."

"Oh. I just assumed you both lived here."

"Your brother would lose his mind if he had to share this wonderful estate with anyone but his shadow," Gany said, shooting Tim a sidelong glance. "We've all just united in common beliefs, common thoughts. You don't need to live under the same roof to share the same ideals."

"What ideals are those?" David said. "Aside from raising rabbits and growing ferns, I mean."

"We're not afraid, for one thing," Gany said, and for the first time since he'd met her, David heard her voice turn serious.

"Afraid of what?"

"The end," said Gany.

"Hey," Tim said to her as he dried a plate with a dish towel.

Gany shrugged. "What's the big deal?" She turned back to David and said, "We're resigned to the fact that this is it. The end is nigh, and all that. You'd be amazed at the peace that overtakes you once you surrender to the inevitable."

David looked at Tim, who was staring back at him. "You're Worlders," David said.

"No," Tim said firmly. "We're not. Worlders are radicalized lunatics, bombing hospitals and praying for the annihilation of the human race. And even then, you're talking about just a small subset of a larger whole."

"But you both believe that Wanderer's Folly is some sort of penance put upon the human race," David said. "That mankind is meant to be wiped out."

Tim flipped the dish towel over his shoulder like a barkeep. "Not exactly," Tim said. "I believe that whatever is supposed to happen will happen. There's no divinity behind anything, no supernatural motive. The goddamn zodiac hasn't conspired to eliminate the human race. I just don't see much hope out there anymore, David, and I decided a long time ago not to lose sleep over it."

"So we live for each day," Gany interjected. "It's better that way. People are losing their minds over this epidemic, and it's getting so you can't tell who's got the Folly and who's just gone batshit fucking crazy worrying about it." She nodded toward Ellie and said, "Sorry for the language, sweetheart. But sometimes it's the best way to get the point across."

"I don't mind," Ellie said, drying a plate with a dish towel.

Tim snapped a dish towel at Ellie's backside. "Yeah, well, you crass ladies are making me uncomfortable," he said. "Why don't you gals go play Monopoly or something?"

Gany stood up with her wineglass and reached out over the counter for Ellie with one hand. Ellie took her hand and Gany gave her a little twirl.

"Jesus Christ," Tim grumbled, though not disapprovingly.

As Gany and Ellie danced out of the room, Tim tossed the

dish towel onto the counter, then settled himself back in his chair at the table. He patted one of David's knees. "You seem a little freaked out."

"There's a bad connotation to what you've said tonight and what they say about Worlders on the news," David told him. "I guess I'm just a little surprised."

"I'm not a terrorist, David. I'm just a man at peace with himself."

"But you think the Folly shouldn't be cured," David said.

"No, that's not what I think, not at all. If there's a cure—if your *daughter* is the cure, man—then God bless us all. I'm just saying that, until you told me about Eleanor, I didn't see any way things could get better, and I had to struggle to make my peace with that. Everybody's got their own way of handling things, and this is mine. You know, it's no coincidence that we lost touch over the past year and a half or so. It's easier to convince yourself that you're okay with the world dying when you don't have constant contact with your loved ones who'll just go ahead and die with it."

David nodded, his gaze momentarily falling to examine the wood grain of the tabletop. "Am I doing the right thing here, Tim? Hiding her away like this?"

"I guess that depends on where your greatest moral obligation lies," Tim said. "Is it to the well-being of everyone on the planet, or to your daughter?"

"She isn't some sacrificial lamb," he said. "She's my little girl."

"Then I guess you've already made up your mind on that score."

"I guess I have."

"What was that other thing you wanted to mention to me earlier?" Tim said.

David sighed. "I honestly don't know where to begin," he said. "And even after I tell you, I'm not so sure you'd believe me."

"There are very few things in this world I find hard to believe anymore."

David nodded. "It started the night we left Maryland. Well, I guess it started even before that, but I hadn't noticed it until the night we hit the road. Kathy had just died, and I picked Ellie up from her babysitter's house. I couldn't tell her about her mom, not then, not at that moment. There were people at our house waiting for us," he said, and told Tim about the white van. "Now that Kathy was dead, I knew they would come for Ellie. They wouldn't take no for an answer. So we went on the run. And I was such a mess that night, so . . . so fucked up . . . and I'm just driving, not knowing where the hell I'm going . . . and Ellie, she just reaches out and touches the back of my neck. And, man, it was like she sucked all the fear and sadness and grief right out of me."

One of Tim's eyebrows arched.

"I know, I know," David said. "Just hear me out."

He told Tim the rest of it from there—the shock she'd inadvertently given him after learning that her mother was dead and that he'd lied to her; the events that took place at Turk Powell's house in Goodwin, and how she'd . . . done something . . . to Cooper, which had enabled them to escape; and finally, he told Tim about the scene on the highway, where Ellie had calmed a young girl in the last moments of her life, and then calmed the young girl's mother, too, while several people, including Gany, looked on.

Tim listened to the whole story without an expression on his face. Once David had finished, Tim sighed, ran his fingers through his hair, and said, "Well, fuck."

"Exactly," said David.

"I'm not sure what to make of all that."

"Just please say that you believe me."

"I do," Tim said. "Of course I do."

"What do you think it means?"

Tim shook his head. "Buddy, I have no idea."

"Whatever it is," David said, "it's getting stronger."

"Are there side effects?"

"She says no. But she got sick and threw up a little after the highway incident. She said it was a lot to take in."

Tim startled David by laughing. "A lot to take in," he repeated. "Christ, you're telling me." He pitched his head back, a look of consideration on his face now. The sandy bristles along his unshaven chin and neck sparkled like flecks of mica. "So either her immunity has also given her these abilities—"

"Or these abilities have granted her immunity," David finished. "Like, whatever that mutated gene in her DNA is, it does more than ward off the Folly. Yeah, I've already considered the same thing myself."

"In that case, what about Kathy? Did she ever exhibit any—"

"No, no, nothing like this. Ellie's special."

"Is it something she can show me herself? That touching the neck thing?"

"Probably, but let's not go there. In fact, don't tell her I told you at all. She's weird about it."

"Yet she jumped out of the car in front of a handful of strangers and went straight over to that girl who was dying in the street," Tim said.

"She was trying to help her."

"Did she think she could have cured her?"

"I think so. But instead, she just wound up making her last moments more . . . bearable, I guess." He thought about adding how he had reached out and briefly touched his daughter when Ellie had first grabbed hold of the dying girl, and how he had been overcome by the swirl of emotion flooding through them, the—

(flying like flying)

—unmitigated serenity that had come over him by that brief connection with his daughter's icy flesh. In the end, he decided to keep that part to himself.

"I won't say a word." Smiling, Tim crossed his heart with one finger. "I love that kid. And I love you, too, man. You're my brother."

David returned Tim's warm smile. "Stepbrother," he corrected.

Tim shook his head. "No, man. My brother."

David nodded. "Okay. Thank you."

"Listen," Tim said. "There's something I want to talk about with you, too, but now's not the time for it. Let's do it later tonight, after the ladies have gone to bed. Okay?"

"Okay," David said.

55

That night, they grilled rabbit on the barbecue, and despite her utter refusal to eat any of it, Ellie seemed comfortable and at ease for the first time in recent memory. Tim regaled them with old folk songs, which he played on a battered acoustic guitar, his throaty singing off-key but jubilant. They lit a bonfire, too, and roasted marshmallows on the ends of long sticks. Tim and David smoked cigars and drank wine— David just couldn't stomach any more of his brother's bathtub whiskey—and Gany told a ghost story that she claimed was real and had actually happened to her when she was a young girl growing up in Iowa.

By the end of the night, as the bonfire started to dwindle and the stars appeared to burn holes in the firmament, Ellie got up from where she'd been sitting cross-legged in the grass twirling a marshmallow stick around in the air, and approached David's lawn chair.

"Hey, hon," he said, running a hand along her arm.

"I want to do something for Mom. We never did anything."

He sat up straighter in the chair. Beside him, Tim coughed in his hand and righted his posture, too.

"Like what?" David asked.

"A funeral," said Ellie.

David smiled and squeezed her hand.

Gany got up from her chaise lounge and ran her fingers

through Ellie's shortened hair. "We can certainly do something," Gany said.

"Yes, we can," Tim said, springing up from his chair. "You got it, kiddo. That's a wonderful idea."

"It's very thoughtful," David said.

"I'll be right back," said Gany, and she went off into the field toward the rabbit hutches.

"Is there a song you could sing, Uncle Tim?"

Tim gathered up his acoustic, which he'd leaned against the arm of his lawn chair, and strummed a few chords. "I sure can. What was your mama's favorite song?"

"'Hot in the City' by Billy Idol," said Ellie.

Tim laughed but his face looked sad in the firelight. His eyes appeared to moisten. "Well, heck. Lemme see if I can fumble through it." He proceeded to strum a few repetitious chords.

Gany returned with a bouquet of wildflowers clutched to her bosom. She handed them to Ellie. "We don't have any incense to burn, but I thought maybe you could throw them on the fire. They smell nice when they burn."

Ellie thanked her. Then she took one of David's hands. He stood and let her lead him over to the dying bonfire. In the background, Tim began singing the opening verse to "Hot in the City," as best he could remember it.

"Dear Mom," Ellie said, addressing the fire. "You were the best mom in the world. I think maybe you're not really gone, because it doesn't seem real to think of you not here. I know you were just trying to save the world. I think that's a good thing. I think it was *brave*. The world is messed up and it needs saving."

She began to cry, her hand slipping from David's. She sank down to her knees and David let her be.

"I'm sorry for all the times I was bad. I wish I had do-overs for all of those times. But we had a lot of fun, too, and I'm going to miss all of that. I'm going to miss *you*. So much, Mommy Spoon."

She glanced up at David, her face shiny with tears, before turning back to the fire.

"Don't worry, Mom. Dad's doing a great job taking care of me. He's a good dad. Anyway, I just wanted to say good-bye. I miss you. I love you."

She threw the flowers on the fire. The flames flared, and a banner of black smoke lifted up into the air. Gany had been right: The burning flowers smelled like perfume.

Ellie stood, wiping her nose on her arm. With a hand against his hip, she pushed David toward the bonfire. "You say something now," she told him.

I can't, he thought. *I'm afraid to open my mouth. I'll lose it.*

"I love you, babe. I'm sorry. I'm sorry. I'm—"

He went down on his knees.

56

"That was a beautiful service," he said as he tucked Ellie into bed. Ellie pulled the sheet up over her shoulders, and David leaned in and planted a kiss at her temple. "Will you be okay in here by yourself tonight?"

"Yes. Dad?"

"Yeah, hon?"

"Are *you* okay?"

He smiled at her in the darkness. "I'm fine."

She seemed like she wanted to say more. Yet in the end, she gave him a brief squeeze around the wrist, then slid her hand away. Even in the dark, he could tell she was studying him, perhaps reading him. Searching his thoughts, his emotions. Mrs. Blanche, Ellie's elderly babysitter, had called Ellie a deep and contemplative child. "She *roots*," Mrs. Blanche had told David once. "The girl, she sinks the deepest parts of herself far down into the soil and soaks up life." The elderly woman had said this with admiration and tenderness.

"If you were sick," she said, "I'd want to help you."

For several seconds he could not find his voice. "You're a sweet girl," he said finally, a coward's way of avoiding an actual response. His throat felt constricted.

"I keep thinking about that girl on the highway. I feel bad for her."

"You gave her peace in the end," David said. "That's some gift, Eleanor."

"You never call me Eleanor."

He smiled at her in the darkness.

"I keep thinking about that boy, too," she said. "Benny. The truck driver's son."

"Yeah," David said.

"I feel bad about him, too."

"It's okay to feel bad. I feel bad, too."

"And Mom," she said. "Dad, what if I was the one keeping Mom healthy while she was at home? What if she got sick when she went into the hospital because I wasn't there to keep her from getting upset?"

This jarred him, caught him off guard. He didn't know what to say. It had never even occurred to him. He smoothed the hair from her forehead and said, "Please don't be so silly and start blaming yourself for things. You can't help it."

"But I can," Ellie said, her voice perking up a notch. "I can help everybody."

"No one knows that for sure," he said. "Not one hundred percent."

"But we could try."

David's smile faded from his face. "Are we back to this again?"

"I don't want to be one of the bad guys. I want to be a good guy. Like Mom."

"I know you do."

"If I was sick and someone else was the cure, wouldn't you want them to help me?"

David exhaled—a long, shuddery, uncomfortable sound. "You think too much. Where do you get off being so smart for an eight-year-old?"

"I'm pretty much nine."

"Yeah, that's right. I keep forgetting."

"You didn't answer my question."

He tucked the bedsheet around her small body. "Honey, if you were sick or hurt or in any kind of danger whatsoever, I would do anything in the world to protect you. That's why we're here."

"Then you have to do the same thing for other people, too, Dad. All those other people who have sick kids. Or parents."

"Listen to me," he said. "You've got something amazing going on with you right now. What you can do . . . what you did for that girl today . . . that's a miracle, El. Maybe *that's* your gift to humanity. Maybe it's not that you happen to be immune, but that you can do something great with your ability once you learn what it is. But you'll be giving all that up if you turned yourself in to some doctors who just want to study your blood. You might be doing more harm than good that way. Do you understand?"

She was quiet for a while. Then, in a voice just above a whisper, she said, "I think so."

"Good. Now, give your old man a kiss."

She sat up, kissed the side of his face, hugged him hard. He tucked her back in, then pulled the bedroom door halfway closed as he stepped out into the hallway.

Gany startled him, sliding down the hall in the dark toward her own bedroom. She paused and touched his arm. "Hey," she said. "You're a good dad, you know that?"

He smiled at her in the darkness, his face feeling stiff and made of rubber. She returned his smile, though he registered something stiff and insincere about it. He wondered if she was secretly afraid of Ellie and what the girl had done on the highway. He wondered if she was really at peace with all she had claimed she was earlier at the dinner table. Most of all, he wondered if she'd just overheard their conversation.

"Good night," Gany said, and continued on down the hall.

In the kitchen he found Tim seated by himself at the table, finishing the last of the wine. Only the small light above the sink was on, leaving much of Tim's face masked in gloom. Beyond the window at Tim's back, the night sky boasted an impossible arrangement of stars.

"How's the kiddo?" Tim asked.

"Tired." David smiled wearily and sat down to join his brother at the table. "So am I."

Tim poured the remaining wine from the bottle into a fresh glass, then slid it over to David.

"You look haunted, you know," Tim said.

"I am," David replied. "She wants to turn herself in."

"Ah," Tim said. "Shame on you for raising such a conscientious child."

"She's my daughter. I'll protect her at all costs. No matter what."

Tim nodded. He knocked back the last of his wine, then said, "There's something I want to talk to you about."

"All right."

"I want you to tell me how Kathy died."

"I thought I already did."

"You said she grew weak until she just expired. But I'd like to know what was her actual cause of death."

"I don't understand," David said.

"What'd she die from, David? I want you to tell me."

David looked down at the table, then turned so that he stared down the darkened hallway that came off the kitchen. The light over the sink was causing the windows to fill up with bugs. He thought of—

(bring the heater closer, would you, honey? it's so cold in here)

—the insectoid monsters from his dream again. His whole body began to tremble.

"After I spoke with you on the phone," Tim said, "I Googled your names. I found the newspaper articles. They all said she committed—"

"Don't," David said, shaking his head. "Don't say it."

"I love you guys. You and Ellie. Kathy, too. And I'm here to help. Whatever you need, David. I just want to know what really happened. You were there. I just want you to tell me."

His skin felt hot.

"David," Tim said, his voice barely above a whisper. One of his big hands slid across the table, his palm up. Without thinking about it, David reached out and grabbed his brother's hand. Squeezed it.

"I'll tell you," David said, his eyes welling with tears. "I'll tell you what happened."

And he did.

57

Six days earlier

They kept her in a white room with a single window that looked out on a gray parking lot. She was in bed with a starched white sheet draped over her thin frame. The air was rank with medicinal smells and industrial cleaners. It made David's eyes burn each time he walked into the room.

"How's Ellie?" Kathy's voice was a sandpapery rasp. The whites of her eyes had turned a chalky gray.

"She misses you."

Kathy glanced down at the stuffed elephant propped next to her in bed.

"I'm getting you out of here," he said. "We're not doing this anymore. I've already spoken to Kapoor. You can leave with me tonight."

"I'm not sure that's a good idea, David," she said.

He brushed a strand of hair out of her face. Her hair was dry and brittle, and he imagined that if he'd wanted, he could snap that strand right in half like uncooked spaghetti.

"Tell me why," he said. "You gave it your best shot, but now we've got to get on with our own lives. You've got a little girl at home who misses you very much."

Something akin to a smile came over her face, stretching out her thin lips and protruding cheekbones. "I'm so scared for her. I'm scared that I've got something and I might be bringing it back home to her."

"You're not sick, Kath. You don't have the Folly. And Ellie's immune, anyway." He'd told her this a few days ago, when Dr. Kapoor had notified him regarding the results of their blood tests. Kathy had been elated, had broken out into tears . . . but now there was a different emotion in her eyes. Something darker.

"When I got here, I was immune, too," Kathy said. "But maybe all that has changed. My body isn't the same since I've gotten here. I feel *off*, David. What if something in this place has changed me? What if I bring that same thing home to Ellie? What if I'm carrying the thing that will hurt her?"

"I think you're overthinking this."

"No one knows anything about this disease, David. Don't tell me I'm overthinking things. She's my daughter."

"Yes," he said. "And she wants her mother back. I want you back, too, Kath."

Her hands smoothed out the bedsheet, her knuckles sharp and craggy, her fingers too damn thin.

"I had a dream last night where I came home with you, David, and Ellie was so happy that she hugged me and kissed me and wouldn't leave me be. And she crawled into bed with us and the three of us slept together like we did when she was a baby."

He smiled at the thought.

Then Kathy's face grew grim.

"And when I woke up," she said, "you were dead. And Ellie was dead. And you were both . . . stiff and gray and dead . . . because I brought something out of this place and carried it home to you. Poisoned you both. Killed you both."

He reached out and took one of her hands. Squeezed it gently. He felt the bones roll beneath the skin.

"Come home with me," he said. "Let's be a family again."

It seemed like she looked at him, smiling in an emaciated way that made the corners of her mouth protrude, for an un-measurable amount of time.

"Please, baby," he said.

Kathy's face softened. "Yes," she said finally. Tears stood out in her eyes. "All right. Let's go home together."

He closed his eyes and rested his head in her lap. Her thin fingers grazed the nape of his neck.

When he stood up, he was crying a little, but smiling at his wife. She had Ellie's stuffed elephant beside her in bed, which she picked up and looked at now.

"You know," she said, "it's funny, but when Ellie first gave me this thing, I imagined I was getting strength from it. Every time I hugged it, it was like I was hugging our daughter. It even smelled like her, for a while at least, and it was a beautiful thing."

"That's nice," David said.

"But then, after a while, it faded away," Kathy said, her smile retreating from her face. "And I wasn't strong anymore." She held the stuffed elephant out to him. "Might as well bring my things down to the car, if I'm leaving with you, Mr. Arlen."

"I'll go right now," he said.

"Just do me one favor?" she asked.

"Name it."

"Give me a kiss before you go."

Smiling, he leaned over and kissed her on the mouth. Her lips felt like burlap.

"Love you," he said.

"Love you, too," she said, and touched the side of his face.

He carried the elephant to the door, but just before he could exit out into the hallway, she called out to him.

"What is it?" he said.

"Bring the heater closer, would you, honey? It's so cold in here."

There was a portable space heater in one corner of the room, attached to an extension cord that was plugged into the wall. David rolled the unit over to her bedside and adjusted the temperature. Kathy had settled back into her pillow, her eyes closed. Tears stood out in the corners of her eyes. He decided not to say anything, and slipped out into the hallway as quiet as a ghost.

He went down the hall and the stairwell, then out into the

parking lot. It had grown cold. Darkness crept up over the horizon, and the trees that fringed the parking lot trembled in the wind. What clouds he could see moving across the face of the moon looked malicious and virulent, like a poison descending from the sky.

He went to the Bronco, popped open the door, and tucked Ellie's stuffed elephant into the duffel bag he'd brought with him. Sometimes he'd stay so long he'd need a change of clothes. A pack of cigarettes were inside the bag, only two smokes left. He lit one and sucked hard. The cold made it difficult to keep his eyes from watering. But he was standing out there alone, and so there was no need to fight them off: He wept freely if silently.

He smoked the second cigarette immediately after the first, wiping his bleary eyes with one hand now. He didn't want to go back to Kathy's room looking like he'd been out here bawling. He looked out across the parking lot, watching the sunset just beyond the facility. Most of the vehicles in this lot were black, nondescript, with tinted windows and government plates. There was also a cadre of white vans parked at the far end of the lot along a chain-link fence that appeared to shudder in the strong wind. Something about those vans bothered him.

Maybe Burt Langstrom was right. Maybe it's time I pick up my little family and we get the hell out of here. Maybe we really should go live in the mountains somewhere, a place where we can't be bothered, where it'll just be the three of us forever . . .

After he'd sucked the life from the second cigarette, he tossed it to the ground, then began the campaign back across the lot toward the building. The first-floor lobby was empty. He skipped the elevator and took the stairs to the second floor, where the CDC had set up shop. When he came out of the stairwell, he was aware of a commotion at the far end of the hall. A few voices were raised, and a woman in hospital scrubs rushed down the hall into an adjoining room. A persistent mechanical beeping could be heard somewhere close by.

David picked up his pace. A few more people crisscrossed

the hall in front of him, their white lab coats flapping, and a man's voice shouted something unintelligible but unmistakably urgent. The room they were all going into was Kathy's.

He broke into a sprint and closed the distance to Kathy's room in what seemed like the blink of an eye. Nurses crowded the doorway, but he shoved them aside and entered the room.

His first thought was that she had fallen out of bed, coming to rest half propped up against the steel legs of the bed itself, her legs folded Indian-style on the floor. But, no—her legs weren't *on* the floor, and she wasn't propped up but *held upright,* and unnaturally so, with some strange orange band around her neck—

(Bring the heater closer, would you, honey? It's so cold in here.)

The horror of it struck him all at once, a tidal wave of electric madness that siphoned the color from the world and caused his body to go numb.

(so cold)

Two large men were attempting to remove the extension cord from around her neck, while a third was hastily trying to untie it from the hook on the wall above the bed. She had tied the heater's extension cord to the hook, noosed it around her neck . . . and had simply rolled off the side of the bed, hanging herself.

Someone was shouting his name over and over again in his ear, but the voice could have traveled the distance of some long, corrugated tunnel for all David could tell. He leapt forward, shoving aside the men attempting to get the cord away from Kathy's neck, and Jesus fucking Christ, her *face*—

(cold)

—gray, dead, vacuous eyes that stared through him, impossible, all of it, this wasn't real, wasn't happening, wasn't—

Someone gripped him in a bear hug and hoisted him up off the floor. David screamed and kicked his legs. The man squeezed the air from his lungs and dragged him out the door and into the hallway. A second man—this guy in a security uniform—reached down and groped for David's ankles to stop his legs from pinwheeling.

At some point, Dr. Kapoor appeared. His brown face looked like that of a puppet carved from expensive, delicate wood. He spoke to David, but David did not register a single word he said. In the end, Dr. Kapoor withdrew a hypodermic needle from the pocket of his lab coat. Expressionlessly, he stabbed David in the forearm with it.

David continued to fight against the arms that constricted around him, and even managed to administer a swift kick to the head of the security guard who knelt on the floor groping for his feet, before whatever was in that hypodermic caused him to feel light-headed and noncombative. After a time, the man's arms loosened, and David felt his body slump to the floor. He sobbed as the two men grabbed him under the armpits and hoisted him to his feet. But his body wouldn't cooperate. They dragged him down the hall and took him into a small room where a ratty sofa stood against one wall. The men let him free-fall onto the sofa, and somewhere in the descent, David blacked out.

Whatever sedative Kapoor had pumped into his bloodstream wasn't merciful enough to grant him a few hazy moments upon waking when he held no memory of what Kathy had done to herself. Instead, the moment he regained consciousness, he did so with the face of his wife burning in his brain, the unnatural position of her as she hung there over the side of the bed, the extension cord looped around her throat.

David screamed.

His first instinct was to bolt from the room, locate Dr. Kapoor, and throttled the son of a bitch. But when he tried to stand, his legs threatened to surrender beneath him and send him toppling to the floor. He remained seated on the sofa, where he buried his head in his hands and cried.

He lost all concept of time, and didn't realize that it was fully dark until he dried his eyes and looked up at the black rectangle of a window at the opposite end of the room. Careful not to overexert himself, he rose and, somewhat unsteadily, stood up off the sofa. With one hand against the wall for support, he was able to make it around to the far side of the room, the feeling slowly creeping back into his legs. When he reached the window, he looked down at the darkened parking lot, with its matrix of bright sodium lampposts. For a long time, his gaze lingered on the collection of white vans at the far end of the lot. White vans no different from the one that had been parked on Columbus Court for the past two weeks. Right outside their house.

They've been watching our house, watching us. Because of Ellie. They're going to want Ellie.

He made it to the door with little difficulty, the control over his muscles returning to him now. He expected the door to be locked, but it wasn't. He opened it and leaned out into the hallway. The place was as silent and void of life as a mausoleum. He hurried down the hall, found the stairwell, and made his way down to the first-floor lobby.

It was as if God had felt pity for him and granted him one final wish, because as he crossed the lobby he nearly walked right into Sanjay Kapoor as the doctor turned a blind corner. Both men froze, momentarily stunned by the presence of the other.

"David." Kapoor's voice cracked. The small man shuffled back a step or two. "I'm so sorry. Let's sit down and talk. We can—"

David struck the man in the stomach. Kapoor buckled at the waist and, emitting the faintest of grunts, crumpled to the floor.

"I should fucking kill you right here," David said, standing above him.

Curled in a fetal position, Dr. Kapoor put his head back and gasped for air. His silver incisor gleamed.

David turned and rushed out into the parking lot. His heart slammed in his chest as he hurried to the Bronco. It took several attempts to fit the key into the door, but he finally got it. He climbed behind the Bronco's steering wheel, shoved the key into the ignition, cranked it. The Bronco roared to life.

Kathy's face still hung before his eyes; he couldn't blink it away. He sped through the opening in the facility's front gate and drove in a blind stupor, part of him in shock, part of him still back in that makeshift hospital room with Kathy, another part of him hovering somewhere in the stratosphere, an angel or a ghost looking down upon his mortal form. *Help me.*

He was pushing eighty miles an hour down the highway when he reached the exit for his part of town. For several seconds, he couldn't remember where Mrs. Blanche's house was. He'd been picking Ellie up there for the past two weeks or so, but right now, for the life of him, he couldn't remember how to get there. He drove in confused patterns up and down the neighborhood streets, waiting for his brain to engage. When he saw the wedge of beech trees on the corner and the mailbox shaped like a lighthouse, he breathed with a sigh of relief and pulled into the driveway.

Before he got out of the truck, he examined his reflection in the rearview mirror. At some point during the drive he'd stopped sobbing, yet his eyes still looked puffy and red. When he went to shut down the engine, his hand trembled and thumped into the switch that activated the windshield wipers; the rubber blades *reeeet-reeeted* across the dry glass.

Mrs. Blanche was in her seventies, a kindly old widow with silver hair piled into a bun atop her head like some cartoon grandmother. She was too preoccupied telling David how wonderful Ellie played the piano that afternoon to notice his distress. She invited him inside but he refused, saying it had been a long day at the hospital and he really just wanted to get home and go to sleep.

"Is Kathy all right?" she asked him, smiling, her brow creased in concern. He assumed it was the poor lighting on the porch that prevented her from seeing the devastation on his face.

"She's okay," he managed.

A television played too loudly in the background, the soundtrack replete with canned laughter and applause.

"Why don't you come in for some dinner before you go?"

"Thank you, but I'm just so tired." And this certainly was no lie; he hadn't slept at all last night, worrying about Kathy's worsening condition. That was when he'd made the decision to get her the hell out of that place. One fucking day too late.

"I can pack you some food to take home," Mrs. Blanche continued. "You'll just have to reheat it in the microwave."

He felt like screaming. "Really, no. But thank you." He leaned past the woman and called out to his daughter.

Mrs. Blanche turned and smiled down at Ellie when she came to the door. She was holding her shoe box with the bird eggs inside.

"Hey, Dad."

"Say good-bye to Mrs. Blanche."

There was a hesitation before the girl said good night to the old woman—a tentative pause, her gaze weighty on him, sensing, he deduced, the anguish, grief, and distress on him. It clung to him like a stink.

She knows. The notion struck him like a thunderbolt.

He took her hand, led her down the driveway, and helped her into the passenger seat of the Bronco.

"Mom says I have to ride in the back," Ellie said. "She says it's safer."

"It's okay this once. Just put your seat belt on." He closed the door on her and hurried around to the driver's side. When he got in behind the wheel, he saw that Ellie had climbed into the back and was buckling up behind the passenger seat.

Mrs. Blanche waved to them from the doorway. David honked his horn in return, using the sound to mask the sob that ruptured from him. When he pulled out onto the street, he turned on the radio, found an alternative rock station, and cranked the volume so his daughter wouldn't hear him cry.

58

Tim's face remained impassive throughout the whole telling of the story. When David finished, he felt spent, drained, some vital part of himself having been removed and destroyed in the process. A silence simmered between them now, and for a moment, David was grateful for it. He just hung his head and allowed his eyes to examine the wood grain of the tabletop.

Tim climbed up out of his chair and ambled over to a bottle of his moonshine that stood on the counter. He snatched up two lowball glasses and, returning to the table, poured them both two fingers each. Tim knocked his back all in one gulp. David couldn't even manage to reach out and grasp the glass, he felt so weak.

"Listen," Tim said after a time. "I love that little girl of yours. And I love you, too, man. You know that. And I'll do whatever it is you want me to do. You came here for my help, and that's what I promise to give. If you want to stay here until the end of time, then the place is yours. No one will ever find you here. But I also want you to do something for me. Okay?"

David lifted his gaze to meet Tim's. "What's that?" he said.

"I want you to consider the possibility that your grief, your pain, and your anger over what happened to Kathy might be coloring your perception of all this."

"What are you saying?"

"Kathy was on antidepressant meds, which the doctors took

her off of," Tim said. "You said she had been seeing a shrink, and then that stopped cold turkey, too. More than that, you said that she . . . well, that she'd *changed* over the past year, growing paranoid and depressed and—"

"And what?"

"She was headed down a bad path before those doctors ever got to her. Later, at the hospital, you said she'd stopped eating."

"I know what I said."

Tim held up one hand. "Please don't get defensive."

"I'd just like to know where you're going with this."

"David, Kathy killed herself. Those doctors didn't do it."

"They allowed it to happen."

"Maybe they never expected it. You didn't expect it, either. And you were her husband."

Briefly, the moths on the windowpane at Tim's back appeared to form a scowling face. Then their image blurred as David's eyes grew wet.

"What I'm saying," Tim went on, "is that there's nothing here that tells me your daughter is in any danger if she was to cooperate with that Dr. Kapoor guy and the rest of his staff."

"She's not a fucking guinea pig," David said. "Anyway, Kapoor's dead. Some other guy took over. They've been calling my phone, trying to trick me, to get me to turn her over to them."

"What about what Ellie wants?"

"What about it?"

"Earlier you told me Eleanor wants to turn herself in."

"Her opinion doesn't matter," David said flatly. "I'm her father. I call the shots. And didn't you just tell me earlier that I'm under no moral obligation to sacrifice my daughter for the rest of the world?"

"That's true," Tim said. "But it's different if it isn't a sacrifice at all. If it's just your fear—"

"I'm not turning her in. That's it, Tim. I won't do it."

"Fair enough." Tim poured himself another shot of moonshine. "Then listen closely to me, okay?" Tim leaned over the table, bringing his face closer to David's. Close enough that David could smell the moonshine on his breath. "If that's what you want, then that's what I'll do. As long as I'm alive on this planet, I will help you take care of that beautiful little girl."

"Thank you," David said.

"Drink with me," Tim said.

David picked up the glass and tossed the 'shine to the back of his throat. It felt like a fireball blasting down his esophagus.

They drank together, mostly in silence, for the next forty minutes or so. After a time, Tim stood, ambled over to where David sat, and kissed the top of David's head.

"I love you," Tim said. "Good night."

Alone now, David listened to the house settle down all around him. After a time, he got up and wended his way through the halls until he came to his bedroom door. He stood there in the hallway for some time, a headache beginning to work its way up from the base of his neck and over the top of his skull. In the end, he decided he didn't want to sleep alone.

He went into Ellie's room and found her snoring gently in the large bed, her profile silvered by the moonlight coming through the bedroom window. The window was cracked open a bit, and a chill autumn breeze filtered into the room, cooling his flesh.

Careful not to wake his daughter, David climbed into bed and curled up behind her. He closed his eyes and inhaled the smell of her.

Little Spoon, he thought, draping an arm around her.

59

He dreamed of giant bugs again, and the world was filled with their sound—an unrelenting, mechanical buzzing that followed him out of sleep and into the real world.

Tim stood above him, shaking him awake. The bedroom light was on, and the buzzing was still there. Beside David in bed, Ellie groaned and rolled away from him.

"Get up," Tim said. "Hurry."

"What's that noise?" David said.

"An alarm," said Tim. "Someone's coming."

David sat up and rolled out of bed. Ellie's eyes snapped open and found him. She asked what was going on. David said he wasn't sure. He thought he'd misheard Tim. Out in the hallway, Tim shouted for Gany, his voice loud over the buzzing alarm.

"Stay here," David told Ellie. He got up and hurried out into the hall.

Tim stood at the end of the hallway, opening a closet door. Gany appeared, pulling a sweatshirt down over her head.

"Who's coming?" David said.

"I don't know." Tim took a long gun from the closet and held it out to him. "Take it," he said.

David took it. It was heavy, cold, and smelled of oil.

Tim placed a hand on Gany's shoulder. "Go sit with Ellie. Don't come out unless I tell you to. Understand?"

"Yes," she said, and hurried down the hall, brushing by David as she went.

Tim took a second shotgun from the closet and what looked like several boxes of ammunition.

"The fuck's going on, Tim?"

"Come 'ere," Tim said, and beckoned David to follow him into the adjoining room.

It was the room with the two computer monitors, only now the screen savers were gone. David saw that each screen was divided into quadrants, each quadrant providing a live CCTV feed from various places around Tim's property, to include the exterior of the farmhouse. The digital clock on the screen told him it was 4:53 A.M.

Tim tapped the keyboard and the buzzing alarm silenced. He tapped the keyboard a second time and the images on the computer screens changed. In one of the quadrants, a pair of headlights cut swiftly through the night along an unpaved wooded road. David recognized it as the road leading up to the farmhouse.

"Shit," David said.

"They're maybe three minutes out," Tim said. "The system should have picked them up sooner. I've got an alarm system down in the foothills by the main road that never went off. They must have deactivated it somehow."

"They found us . . ."

"I don't know," Tim said. "They don't look like the government or the police. Something isn't right." His fingers danced along the keyboard, and the angle of the cameras changed yet again. This time, they were afforded a long shot of the oncoming vehicle, its dual headlamps jouncing over the rutted dirt road, the video grainy and tinted emerald green. "It's just one vehicle."

"Maybe more are on their way," David said. The idea sent his stomach into his socks.

Tim tossed him a box of ammo. "You know how to use a shotgun?"

"No."

Tim shouted for Gany, then pulled a pistol from the rear of his pants. He handed it to David. It was Cooper's Glock. "Use this, then."

Gany appeared in the doorway. Ellie clung to her hip and peered into the room. She looked frightened.

Tim handed Gany the shotgun. "Take Eleanor to the back bedroom. Barricade the door. Anyone forces their way in there, you use this."

"Yeah, okay," Gany said, breathless.

"Dad," Ellie said. Her gaze fell on the pistol in David's hand.

"It'll be okay, baby," David told her.

"Come on," Tim said, and shoved them all out into the hallway.

They split up, Gany and Ellie heading down the darkened corridor toward the rear of the house, Tim and David hurrying toward the front. Tim swung open the front door and a cold night wind accosted them. They went out onto the porch.

David couldn't see the approaching vehicle's headlights yet through the trees, but he could hear the growl of its engine. It was moving very quickly toward them.

"Go to the far end of the porch," Tim instructed. He pointed to a pitch-black corner. "I'll stand front and center. I've got floodlights on the roof," Tim said. "When the vehicle pulls up, motion sensors will turn the lights on. They'll be lit up like a football field and they won't be able to see us. But just in case, you go over there. I'll soak up their attention. They won't see you with your gun pointed at them in the dark."

David looked at the gun in his hand.

"How good of a shot are you?" Tim asked.

"Fuck if I know."

Astoundingly, Tim laughed.

Headlights appeared through the trees.

David ran to his corner, tucked himself down in the shadows. The gun felt like it suddenly weighed fifty pounds; he needed both hands to lift it up and rest his wrists along the porch railing for support.

Tim shoved a number of slugs into the shotgun, charged it, then pointed it toward the approaching vehicle as he took up position at the top of the porch steps.

He hugged my daughter on those steps, David had time to think.

The headlights broke clear of the trees, the large SUV's engine snarling like a wild animal. At the same instant, the floodlights on the roof burst on, so bright David winced and turned away, though not before he saw the white, mud-stippled SUV come burning across the lawn in a cloud of bluish exhaust.

The vehicle came to a sudden stop, its tires gouging trenches in the earth. Giant insects flitted by in the twin glow of the SUV's headlamps.

The gun shook in David's hand.

For several seconds, nothing happened. But then Tim leveled the shotgun at the vehicle and shouted for the driver to identify himself. This was greeted by more silence. "In the event that you're illiterate or maybe you just happened to miss all my fucking signs," Tim called out into the night, "you're fucking trespassing. You've got five seconds to back outta here before I blow out your tires."

No response from the driver. The glare from the floodlights on the roof of the farmhouse made it impossible to see inside the SUV's windows. There could be a small army in there, David thought.

Tim descended a single step. He raised the shotgun to eye level, still pointing it at the vehicle. From his position on the porch, David released a shuddery breath. Sweat stung his eyes. The gun was slippery with perspiration and suddenly difficult to hold.

The rear door of the SUV opened, and a man in a camouflaged jumpsuit stepped out. He was a big man, broad across the chest. He held a rifle but kept it pointed at the ground.

"No one has to die here tonight," the man announced. He

was pale-skinned and with a few days' growth of dark beard wreathing his jawline. The hair on top of his head was cut high and tight, in a military fashion.

"Who the hell are you?" Tim said.

"Doesn't matter." The man's voice was calm, the expression on his face almost friendly. "Put your gun down."

"Like hell," Tim said.

"Do it." It was a woman's voice, right at their back. David turned and saw Gany standing in the doorway, the shotgun pointing at Tim's back. "Put the gun down, Tim." She looked in David's direction. "You, too, David."

"Ah, Gany." Tim sounded like a disappointed parent. "What the hell have you gotten yourself mixed up in?"

Gany's face was firm, expressionless. "I'm not mixed up," she said. There was an edge to her tone, an apprehension. "Now, put that gun down, Tim. I'm not joking."

"Better listen to her," said the man in the jumpsuit as he closed the distance between them. A second man stepped out of the driver's side of the SUV. He sported a frizzy salt-and-pepper beard that hung down to his collarbone, and he wore a red bandanna on his head. He had a pistol in a holster at his hip.

In slow motion, Tim set the shotgun down on the porch. Then he raised both hands.

Gany swiveled her weapon in David's direction.

"Where's my daughter?"

"She's inside," said Gany. "She's fine. Now, put the gun down."

"Ellie!" he shouted. When the girl didn't respond, he called her name again.

Faintly, from within the belly of the house: *"Daddy . . ."*

"Put the gun down and you can go be with her," Gany said.

David knelt and set the pistol down at his feet.

"In the house," said Jumpsuit, coming up the porch steps.

Gany stepped aside and Tim went through the door. David followed.

They were shepherded into the living room, where Ellie

was sitting on the sofa. As David came into the room, Ellie jumped up and rushed to him, wrapping her arms around him. He kissed the top of her head.

Gany, Jumpsuit, and Bandanna came into the room. Jumpsuit handed his rifle to Bandanna, and the instant the gun was out of his hands, a broad smile filled his face. He motioned to the sofa. "Why don't the three of you have a seat."

No one moved.

Jumpsuit's smile fell away. "Sit down."

They sat, Ellie wedged between them on the sofa. David kept an arm around her.

"So, you're Tim," Jumpsuit said, the broad smile returning. "Heard a lot about you."

"Who the fuck are you?" Tim growled.

"That's not important. What's important is this little lady right here." Jumpsuit fixed his gaze on Ellie. He took a step toward her and bent at the knees to meet her eyes. "Hello, darling."

Ellie quaked and David squeezed her against him.

"I heard tell that you possess some rather unusual abilities, sweetheart," said Jumpsuit.

David looked at Gany. "What'd you tell them?"

Gany returned his stare but didn't respond. She held the shotgun on him.

"There've been rumors circulating the underground about people who've been displaying some unique talents lately," Jumpsuit continued. That smile was still firmly etched onto his face. This close, and in the soft light of the living room, David could see a puckered pink scar traversing the left side of his face, from temple to the lower corner of his jaw. "Some say there's folks out there can actually heal the sick. Can you imagine?"

Jumpsuit reached out as if to caress the side of Ellie's face, but David slapped his hand away before he could manage it. Without missing a beat, the guy in the bandanna had his pistol out of its holster and pointed it at David.

"Don't you touch her," David warned him.

Jumpsuit stood and raised both hands, as if to show that he'd meant no harm by the gesture. He kept his eyes on Ellie.

"Gany says she witnessed you doing a little magic of your own, sweetheart," Jumpsuit said. "Tried to help a dying girl out on some highway. Is this true?"

Ellie said nothing.

"You try and save some girl's life?"

"No," Ellie said curtly.

Jumpsuit's eyebrows arched. "No?" he said. "Then what was it you did out there?"

"I just made her feel better so she didn't suffer."

"She touched her," Gany said, "and the girl just calmed down. She touched the mother, too. And when we went back to the car, she held my hand and it . . . it was like I could still feel it going on inside her. It made my knees weak. It was like magic."

"Is that what you do?" Jumpsuit said. He bent down on his knees now so that he was face-to-face with Ellie. "You touch people and make them feel better?"

"Yes."

"Can you heal the sick?"

"No."

"I'll bet you can," said Jumpsuit, "only you just don't know it yet." He extended his hand, palm-up. There was grit beneath his fingernails. "Go on," he said. "Touch me. Let me see what you can do."

Ellie looked at David. Despite a sinking sensation in the pit of his stomach, he nodded for her to go ahead.

Ellie reached out and placed her hand atop Jumpsuit's open palm. Her pale flesh against his olive skin made her look like a ghost. Jumpsuit's fingers closed around Ellie's hand, his eyes locked onto hers.

At first, nothing happened. But then Jumpsuit's smile faltered. His eyes widened, as if in surprise.

"You're nervous," Ellie said. "You're acting tough on the outside, but on the inside, you're scared."

David thought he saw doubt briefly pass over Jumpsuit's face.

And then it was like some great vacuum had sucked the air out of the room. The hairs on David's arms stood up, and he could tell, judging by the looks on everyone else's faces, that they felt it, too. The air had become charged with some preternatural energy.

"Your name is Aaron Kahle," Ellie said.

"Jesus fuck," said Aaron Kahle. That smile returned, but it wasn't just for show anymore—there was genuine awe there, an unmasked incredulity. He turned to Gany and said, "Touching her, it's like a sedative. It's . . . it's almost euphoric." He turned back to Ellie. "What else can you tell just from touching me?"

"That you're not a nice man," Ellie said. "That you've hurt people. You've killed them."

Kahle quickly withdrew his hand, that wolfish smile morphing into a grimace. The moment he did so, David could suddenly breathe again; the hairs on his arms relaxed. Kahle held his hand up before his eyes, as if to see if she'd left behind any marks, any side effects. He flexed the fingers, wiggled them. Made a fist. Then he lowered his hand and leaned closer to Ellie.

"You're a very special little girl," said Kahle. "I'll bet there's a whole world of things you can do in time." That wolfish grin reappeared. "Not to mention that special blood you've got pumping through your veins." Kahle turned that grin on David. "She's immune?"

David looked at Tim.

"I never said a word to anyone," Tim said.

"I heard you talking," Gany said. "And I've read the news and know that people are after the girl."

"We've got a whole group of people who would love to meet you," Kahle said to Ellie.

"We're not going anywhere with you," David said.

Kahle stood. "What's this 'we' business?"

"We're not going to hurt her, David," Gany said. "She'll be okay."

"She isn't going with you," said David.

Tim leaned forward on the sofa and stared up at Gany. When he spoke, his voice was low, his tone compassionate. "Gany, honey, what's this all about? Who are these people?"

"We're true Worlders, Tim," she said. "But we're not just going to sit by and wait to die. Someone like Ellie—someone with her abilities—might be enough to keep us healthy. She might even learn to cure the Folly in time."

"So you're turning her in?"

Kahle laughed, a series of loud barks. "Turning her *in?* Are you kidding me? We've got no moral responsibility to the rest of the world. Let them die, for all I care. Not us, though."

"So you'll take her as a hostage," David said. "Use her like a drug and hope that she can keep you all from getting sick."

"I can't do it!" Ellie cried. "I've tried and I can't! I can't cure anybody."

"Well, maybe, sweetheart," Kahle shouted back at her, his face suddenly cold as stone, "you'll figure it out."

"You're all mad," David said.

"You're no humanitarian yourself, David." It was Gany, a trace of anger in her voice now. As if *she* had been the one be-trayed. "What difference does it make if she's *our* hostage or *yours?* You're letting the world die anyway."

"Don't do this, Gany," Tim said. "This isn't what you really believe."

"Don't tell me what I believe!" Gany shouted at him. Her eyes were fierce. "I've watched enough people die! I buried my whole goddamn family!"

"Gany—"

"Enough." Kahle reached out for Ellie. "Come on, kid. Let's go."

David wrapped her tightly in his arms.

"Don't make me kill you, Daddy-O," Kahle said. "Let her go."

David did not let her go.

The guy in the bandanna stepped forward and pressed the muzzle of his pistol against David's forehead.

"Stop this," Tim said, but even his voice was quaking now.

"Ain't got no problem opening up your head right here, Pops," Bandanna said. His voice was as deep as a drum.

"No!" Ellie sobbed, pulling free of David's arms. "Don't hurt my dad!"

"Ellie," he said.

She shook her head. There was terror in her eyes, but she wasn't crying. She looked at Kahle and said, "I'll go. Just don't hurt him."

"No, Ellie," David said.

She hugged him around the neck, kissed the side of his face, and whispered something too low for him to decipher into his ear. When she pulled away from him, it was as if something vital had extracted itself from inside his body.

Ellie took Kahle's outstretched hand and got up off the sofa.

"Ellie . . ." David said.

She glanced at him over her shoulder as Kahle hauled her toward the doorway. And then David saw it—the slight narrowing of Ellie's eyes on an otherwise impassive face. The terror was gone, replaced by a sharp calculation. It was tantamount to the look that had overtaken her just before she'd touched Cooper back in Goodwin.

"You want me to shoot 'em anyway?" Bandanna said. He'd removed the pistol from David's forehead but still had the gun trained on him, no more than two feet from his face.

"No!" Ellie shouted. She tried to pull her hand free of Kahle's, but he wouldn't release her. "I'll never do anything for any of you if you hurt them."

Kahle nodded at her. "Fair enough." He turned to Bandanna and said, "You heard the little lady. Let them be."

They marshaled out of the room, Gany bringing up the rear with the shotgun still pointed at both David and Tim.

"It isn't too late to do the right thing, Gany," Tim said.

Gany just shook her head at him. The look on her face suggested that Tim was a fool and that she pitied him. And then she was gone, moving quickly down the hallway toward the front of the house.

David got up and rushed after them.

"David!" Tim called after him.

David made it to the front porch in time to see Kahle leading Ellie across the lawn toward the SUV. Bandanna hurried ahead and opened the rear door of the SUV. He had collected David's and Tim's weapons from the porch and was sliding them into the SUV's open door now. Gany hung back, the shotgun still trained on David.

"You just stay up there," she instructed him.

"Shoot the tires out of their cars so they can't follow us," Kahle told her. "I don't want to take any—"

Kahle stopped suddenly and froze in midstride. Then he looked down at Ellie's hand, which was gripping his own so tightly now that the tips of her fingers had turned white.

"You're—" Kahle began.

Fear ghosted like a quick shadow over his face. He tried to jerk his arm away from Ellie's grip, but she did not release his hand. For a split second, it was as if Kahle was fighting off a laugh, or at least a smile . . . but then something *changed*, and that laugh, that smile, never came. Instead, his mouth stretched to an impossible length, as though his jaw had become unhinged, and then there was the sound of a teakettle whistling on a stove top. It took David a moment or two to realize that sound was coming *from* Kahle.

And then Aaron Kahle began screaming.

Gany spun around. Beside the open door of the SUV, Bandanna stood, trying to comprehend what was happening.

Ellie reached up and placed her other hand on Kahle's forehead.

"Hey!" Bandanna yelled, though he looked suddenly terrified and did not move away from the vehicle. "Hey! Aaron, what's—"

Kahle began thrashing his head from side to side, though whether this was to loosen Ellie's grip on him or simply out of sheer pain, David could not be sure.

Bright red blood burst from Kahle's right nostril. A second later, crimson tendrils spilled out of his mouth and dribbled down his chin. The high-pitched keening that was emanating from his throat suddenly took on a wet, clotted sound before dying out altogether.

Ellie kept her hand firmly against Kahle's forehead, her other hand still clutching one of his, as Kahle dropped to his knees. He was shrieking and tearing at his hair now, his eyes rolled back to their whites. Blood whipped from his nose and spattered across Ellie's face.

She didn't even blink.

Gany suddenly broke her stupor and ran toward Kahle and Ellie. At the same time, Bandanna peeled himself off the SUV and took a few timid steps in their direction, too.

David sprung up and jumped over the porch railing.

Gany reached out, grabbed Ellie's wrist, and tried to wrench the girl's hand off of Kahle's face. A second later, Gany withdrew her hand, recoiling as if shocked by a jolt of electricity. Ellie whipped her head around to watch Gany take a step backward, a look of abject horror now etched across Gany's face.

Suddenly, the air was sucked from David's lungs again. He froze, his sneakers skidding in the dirt. His flesh began to tingle.

Ellie released her hold on Kahle; the second she did so, Kahle's body dropped face-first into the dirt. She turned and clamped both hands overtop Gany's, which were still clutching the shotgun. Gany screamed and the shotgun went off, blowing a crater into the earth at their feet. She tried to wrench her hands free, but Ellie wouldn't let her go. She fell quickly to her knees while simultaneously throwing her head back. Her screams became operatic, taking on a frequency David would have thought impossible for human vocal cords. Blood began streaming out of Gany's ears.

A second gunshot rang through the air. David turned and saw Bandanna firing his pistol at Ellie. He was shooting erratically, his face full of terror. David rushed him, and Bandanna swiveled and got off one more shot before David collided with him and they both went crashing to the ground. The pistol exploded again, the blast so close to David's left ear that all sound was instantaneously sucked out of the world. Bandanna struck him in the face, knocking him onto his side in the dirt. David rolled over and climbed to his feet, the absence of sound quickly replaced by a shrill, sonorous whistle. He tripped over his feet and fell backward onto the ground, his teeth gnashing together in his skull.

Bandanna loomed above him, a shifting silhouette against the row of floodlights that now partially blinded David, a silhouette that swung its pistol toward him. Faintly, over the ringing in his ears, David heard the roar of a gunshot . . . and in that same instant, his attacker's silhouette was swept away from the floodlights. David felt no pain.

(sleep you can sleep you can fly you can sleep)

(so cold)

Consciousness threatened to leave him, but he fought to hold on to it. There was nothing but the burning stench of gunpowder in the air, the blinding floodlights that were rapidly pixelating, and the incessant tonal ringing at the center of his head. Even when the smell of gunpowder faded and the floodlights turned dark, he could still hear that ringing, ringing, ringing.

60

He wasn't sure if he ever truly lost consciousness, though he was aware of his senses rushing back to him at one point, so he must have been close. He smelled the burning early morning air and heard the ringing in his ears. He sat up and saw a dead man with a red bandanna askew on his head not two yards from him, a gaping, sodden wound in his chest.

David crawled to his feet and stood there, wavering like a drunk.

Ellie stood facing him, her eyes wide, her lower lip trembling. She held her arms away from her body, like a child pretending to have airplane wings, and there was blood on her nightshirt, her arms, her face. She wore no expression, as if a part of her mind had fled during the melee. Only her eyes showed any sign of life—two blazing orbs that seemed to be seeing everything and nothing all at once.

Kahle's body lay at Ellie's feet, the twisted agony on his face and his swollen, bloodied eyes all David needed to see to know he was dead. Gany's shotgun lay beside Kahle, but Gany herself was nowhere in sight.

David staggered toward his daughter, and it seemed to take forever to close the distance. When he reached her, he pulled her against him and hugged her hard. She felt as stiff as petrified lumber, and for one terrible second, he couldn't even feel her heart beating through her chest, couldn't hear whether she was breathing or not.

"Are you okay?" he said, his face pressed against hers. Her

face was hot and moist with tears. When she didn't answer, he held her out at arm's length and spoke directly into that blank, unregistering face. "Are you okay, Eleanor?"

"*Yessss,*" she said, her stare jittering in his direction. The word sounded like the perfect hybrid of a child's sob and a serpent's hiss.

Dawn broke fifteen minutes later. To the east, fingers of daylight crept over the horizon and threw javelins of pink light through the trees. The forest insects continued their chorus, unabated and unafraid of the encroaching daylight.

Back in the house, David helped Ellie clean up, washing the blood from her face and arms in the bathroom sink while she stood there, her face registering no emotion, the pupils of her eyes tiny and insignificant black dots. Something inside her had changed.

"Baby," he said, using a warm washcloth to rub away the streaks of blood from her arm. "Talk to me."

"It's getting stronger," she said. Her voice sounded different, although he couldn't tell why. Something about her was different now.

"Are you gonna be sick?"

"No. Not this time. Not anymore."

"Are you afraid?"

She looked directly at him. Her pupils widened. "No," she said simply enough. "Are you?"

He summoned a smile for her, though he felt devoid of any good feelings. He was terrified. The blood did not want to wash off Ellie's face.

"Dad . . ."

"Yeah, baby?"

"I killed those people." That flat, toneless voice. He could see himself reflected in the dark pools of her eyes.

"Shhh," he told her, and brought her close against him. Hugged her.

He wished she would cry on his shoulder, would open up

and let it all out. But she didn't. It felt like hugging a wooden puppet.

Afterward, he carried her back to her room and laid her in the large bed. She was already asleep before her head hit the pillow. David stared at her impassive face for countless minutes, studying her, hoping he'd be able to discern what had changed inside her by such superficial scrutiny. He even touched her, gently and on the side of her face, and closed his eyes. Concentrated. Tried to suck all the bad out of her just as she had done to him. But he couldn't. He was helpless.

Before leaving the room, David kissed her forehead. Her flesh was cold against his lips.

Tim was standing at the far end of the property, at the cusp of the dark woods that swelled up the mountainside, looking down at something on the ground. In the light of morning, the bodies of Kahle and Bandanna looked surreal.

David climbed down the porch steps, and started across the yard to join Tim at the edge of the woods. At one point, he saw pieces of the ground move—small mounds of dirt appearing to respire, to swell up in a mound then collapse again. He paused and examined one such area, a crumbly molehill surrounded by a patch of dark grass. The mound bulged one last time, and something began to emerge from the apex. It emerged headfirst, its head outfitted in oversized, multifaceted red eyes. Its body was ashy white, bullet-shaped, with two translucent, ovoid wings fixed to its back. Once it was fully free of the dirt, it scuttled halfway down the side of the mound, then paused. David got the sense that this large insect—roughly the size of a mouse—was staring up at him. The thing emitted a machinelike buzzing sound that David felt vibrate in his back teeth before it flared its wings—they were as decorative as stained glass—and lifted off into the air. It moved with the labored, weighty lassitude of a carpenter bee. David watched it climb in the air until it disappeared over the roof of the farmhouse.

Moments later, he joined Tim at the edge of the woods. He realized Tim was staring down at Gany's body. In the stark light of morning, she was almost unrecognizable. A network of black blood vessels had burst along both of her cheeks. The tendons in her neck stood out like hydraulic cables. It looked as though she had screamed with such force that her lower jaw had actually come loose. Blood had spurted from her nose, mouth, and ears, and was now smeared across half her face. And her eyes . . . Christ, her *eyes* . . . The irises were no larger than pinpricks, the sclera filled with blood.

Insects were already working her over . . .

"After Ellie touched her, she ran off toward the woods," Tim said. "She was screaming like a madwoman."

"So then it lingered," David said. "Even after Ellie stopped touching her."

Tim looked at him. "Is Ellie okay?"

It took him a while to answer, unsure of the right words. "I don't know, Tim. She's changed."

"I'm sorry about this. Jesus Christ, David, I'm so sorry about this."

"There's no way you could've known."

"I don't know what happened to her," Tim said, and he bent down before Gany's twisted body. He looked like he might reach out and touch her—perhaps attempt to slide her eyelids down over those bulging, bloodied orbs—but he didn't.

"Sometimes people lose their way," David said. He was thinking of Kathy as he said it. "I just hope she didn't tell anyone else that we were up here."

Tim glanced up in his direction. The expression on his face suggested he had already considered this. Then he looked back down at Gany's body and said, "Let's clean this shit up." He rubbed at one moist eye with the heel of his hand, then stood up.

David agreed.

They dragged the bodies deep into the woods and buried them in shallow graves. David only gagged and vomited on the ground once, when a large brown beetle trundled out of Gany's distorted mouth and clattered into the underbrush. He was grateful when the chore was done and they finally returned back to the farmhouse.

For several minutes, they sat on the porch steps smoking cigarettes. When they were done, Tim said he was taking the Tahoe down to the main road to see if he could reset the alarm.

"What should I do?" David asked.

"Get some sleep," Tim told him.

David showered, dressed in clean clothes, and crawled into bed next to his daughter, where exhaustion wasted no time dragging him into unconsciousness.

61

He roused to a soft cooing somewhere nearby. And for a time, he allowed the sound to be incorporated into his dream. But when his eyes opened and he rolled over in bed, Ellie's slight form pressed up against him, he turned toward the partially opened window. A pale block of daylight stood against the windowpane, nearly iridescent. Listening, it took him several seconds to place the sound.

Birdsong.

He sat up, his neck aching, his headache throbbing steadily in the center of his skull. He crawled over Ellie and slipped off the bed, crossing to the window while shielding his eyes from the early morning light. The cool air pricked at his flesh. The sound had vanished, but there was no denying what it had been.

Impossible, he thought.

"Ellie. Ellie."

The girl did not stir.

He crept down the hall in silence. He crossed into the kitchen and saw dishes and glasses on the counter and in the sink. The bottle of moonshine and the lowball glasses were still on the table. Through the wall of windows that looked out onto the screened-in porch, he could see the remnants of last night's bonfire. In the distance, the fir trees swayed in the wind.

He went out through the back porch, descended the few steps, and walked backward through the tall, colorless grass.

He was looking up toward the peaked roof, at the peeling black shingles and the clumps of bright green moss. There was the bedroom window, partially opened.

And then he saw it: a sleek black bird with oily feathers perched on the cusp of the eave. It was a blackbird, a raven, with oil-spot eyes and a tapered beak like the blade of a pocketknife. As David stared at it in disbelief, the bird cocked its head so that one of its eyes focused on him. It unleashed a shrill caw, then cranked open its wings. Its feathers were so black and slick and iridescent, they were practically blue.

He took another step backward, unable to pull his gaze from the bird.

The bird cawed a second time, the sound of its cry echoing out over the valley, and then its wings began to flap. It lifted off the roof and coasted clear across the field, cutting over David's head, its shadow passing quickly over his face.

He found himself laughing at the sight of the creature.

He followed it with his eyes as it darted over the field and vanished among the branches of the nearest trees.

A figure stood in the middle of the field. It was a man, and he was wearing the same mask that he'd worn when David had first glimpsed him in the library in Missouri, then in the field beyond the burger joint in Kansas, and then later at Funluck Park in Colorado.

The figure did not move; he simply stood there, the broad shoulders silvered with early morning daylight, the querying cock of his head reminiscent of a curious dog. The blank white mask had been outfitted with eyeholes that resembled empty sockets in a skull.

It took David a moment to find his voice. Once he did, he managed to eke out, "Who are you?"

The figure said nothing. The head cranked toward one shoulder incrementally, the movement that of a somnambulist.

David took a step toward the figure.

"Who are you? What are you doing here? What do you want?"

The figure reached up and removed the mask, revealing a

round and doughy face reddened by the sun and glistening with perspiration. The top of the head was hairless and shiny, like a globe slickened with petroleum jelly.

It was Burt Langstrom.

62

Six days earlier

Something inside him—some animal instinct—caused him to slow almost to a stop at the top of their street. Everything was as it should be—the soft lights in the windows of his neighbors' houses, the radiant white glow of the street lamps, the cars parked silently in driveways—but he was overcome with such apprehension that he began to clench his jaw. At the far end of Columbus Court, the white van was still parked against the curb, just as it had been for the past several nights. He had inquired about the van to some of his neighbors, but no one had claimed it, nor had they any idea to whom it belonged.

But *he* knew. How he hadn't pieced it together sooner, he had no idea. He'd seen this van parked here every morning when he departed for the hospital to be with Kathy . . . and he'd seen its counterparts parked in the CDC parking lot in Greenbelt among those dark, pantherlike sedans with the government plates.

His gaze flicked over toward Ellie, who had fallen asleep in the backseat.

Is this really happening? Or am I caught in the middle of some terrible dream?

He reversed, spinning the steering wheel, then pulled back out onto the main road. He headed north toward the highway, but in truth, he had no real destination in mind. As it turned out, he drove around for a good thirty-five minutes with no game plan whatsoever while continuing to check his mirrors to see if the white van—or maybe a whole cadre of those sleek black sedans—followed him. It wasn't until he passed the RV rental place off the highway that he thought of Burt Langstrom, and of Burt's empty house and abandoned car. It was an Oldsmobile, if he remembered correctly.

The Langstrom house was dark, all lights off. In fact, the entire *street* was dark, with all the streetlights blown out and very few lights on in the neighboring windows. The Olds wasn't in the driveway, and for a second, David felt a sinking in his gut. But unlike his own house, the Langstroms' place had a *garage,* so he might still be in luck.

He shut the Bronco's headlights but kept the engine running. Turning around in his seat, he watched Ellie sleep for a few seconds while he contemplated waking her. In the end, he thought it best to leave her be and hope she didn't wake up to find him gone, their truck parked in front of some stranger's house. He would just have to be quick.

He got out, careful not to make any noise closing the door, and hurried around the side of the house. He didn't bother with the front door, opting instead to try the back door. There was a sliding-glass door off the back deck, if he remembered correctly. He didn't think Burt would have left it unlocked, even if he never planned to return to this place, but it was worth a shot. And if it *was* locked, well, he'd just have to be real quiet breaking in.

The door was unlocked.

He tugged it open, the rollers squealing, and hurried inside.

There was a panel of light switches on the opposite wall, but the room extended into another that faced the front of the house, and he did not want to turn on any lights that could be seen from the street. Instead, he crept through the darkened hallway in the approximate direction of the garage. He opened one door to find it was a closet chock-full of fall jackets and winter coats. The next door opened up on a black cave, the air rich with the smell of motor oil. When David turned on the light switch, he saw the Oldsmobile right there, shiny beneath the light of the mechanized garage door opener.

Keys.

He scoured the front hall, a credenza, the hall closet, every single drawer in the kitchen, but he couldn't find the car keys.

Maybe Burt took them with him.

Yet he'd left the back door unlocked . . .

Maybe there's a spare somewhere.

He went back out into the hall and glanced up the flight of stairs to the second floor. It was like looking up at the bridge of a ghost ship sliding off in misty waters.

The steps creaked as he ascended. The handrail felt cold. He'd never been upstairs in the Langstroms' house before, but he surmised that the master bedroom was at the far end of the hall, so he went there. The only other place he thought he might find the car keys was in the bedroom, perhaps in the drawer of a nightstand or maybe atop a dresser or bureau.

The bedroom door was closed. He eased it open, then felt around the wall for the light switch. This side of the house faced the backyard, which was mostly concealed from the neighbors by large Douglas firs along three quarters of the perimeter.

The lights came on.

David froze in the doorway.

In that instant, he knew exactly what he was seeing, yet it took his brain a few seconds to catch up.

They were all laid out on the large king-size bed—father, mother, both daughters. Three of them had been configured to suggest peacefulness, with their hands folded neatly atop their abdomens—a grotesque juxtaposition to the bullet holes in the center of their foreheads. The final figure—Burt himself—was the only one caught in the candid act of his suicide, with his head jerked unnaturally to the left (as though even in death he meant to kiss the side of his dead wife's pale, waxen face), his chin jutting toward the ceiling. His bulging Adam's apple looked tremendous and severe, almost like an elbow thrusting up from the center of his neck. There was an opening at Burt's right temple—a congealed, muddy porthole ringed with dried blood and cluttered with brain matter and startling white bits of skull—and a backsplash of dried blood and snotty globs of brain along the headboard. Burt's left hand clutched his wife's forearm; his right arm dangled over the side of the bed. On the floor was a pistol.

How long David stood there staring at this scene, he would never be able to say; it could have been seconds, it could have been a quarter of an hour. It was as if someone else had slipped inside his body and was using his eyes, reporting all the information back to him in a string of Morse code.

Were you even sick, Burt? You or anyone in your family? Or did you just lose it and freak out? Jesus Christ, Burt, how were you able to line them all up like that and shoot them in the head? How the fuck could you have done it?

Yet something about this monstrous scene drove home the frailty of his own situation. *That van has been parked there, watching us for how long now? When they realized I'd left the hospital with no intention of coming back—with no intention of speaking to them about Ellie and all she holds inside her—would people have poured from that van, entered our home, taken my daughter from me? Have they been planning this from the very beginning?*

He'd never held a gun before in his life, yet seeing it there on the floor beside the bed, he suddenly knew that his whole life had *changed*, and he would have to change with it. For Ellie's sake.

In the end, he took the gun. He found two boxes of ammo in a sock drawer and he took those, too.

We'll run. We'll hide. We'll get far enough away from this place before they even realize we're gone. They'll never know where to find us.

But he would have to take heed not to upset Ellie. She was the most important thing to him, and he would have to concoct some story that wouldn't frighten her.

She already knows something is wrong, he thought, opening the jewelry box on the dresser. *She's a smart kid. Too damn smart.* There was nothing but costume jewelry in there. He closed the lid and noticed a black leather wallet tucked behind the box. He opened it and saw Burt's face smiling up at him from his driver's license behind a clear plastic window. David split the wallet and saw that it was choked with bills.

Were you planning to take off in that RV after all? Was this cash your reserve, Burt? A quickie withdrawal from the nearest ATM before you and your family hit the road? And if that was the case, what stopped you? What changed your plans so drastically that you decided this horrible madness was the better option? A quartet of dead bodies lined up on a bed, holes in their heads, a Night Parade of the damned . . .

It was anger that he felt, and try as he might to convince himself it was directed at Burt for his terrible acts, he knew it wasn't. It was Kathy he was thinking of, Kathy's terrible face he couldn't get out of his mind.

Fuckfuckfuck—

He didn't bother counting the money, though at a glance it looked like nearly six hundred bucks. David stuffed the cash in the back pocket of his pants.

Why, Kathy? Goddamn you, why?

(bring the heater closer, would you, honey? it's so cold in here)

He tossed the wallet back on the dresser, then opened the dresser drawer. More costume jewelry, some brooches that looked like antiques, a hairbrush, some other random things. And a set of car keys.

Thank you, God.

He took the keys and stuffed them in his pocket before heading back out into the hall and into another bedroom. This one had belonged to one of Burt's daughters, judging by the overabundance of *pinkness,* and although he couldn't remember either of the Langstrom girls' names, this child's nickname was stenciled on the wall over her bed in great swooping script: *Moon-Bird.*

You said your little girl is all right, David? She acting fine to you?

Burt's daughter had gotten sick. One . . . or possibly both of them. Or maybe they hadn't. Maybe, given his unstable state and increasing paranoia, Burt had just *thought* they had. Some-

how that was even worse. Either way, he had done the un-
thinkable . . .

(so cold)

(why?)

David went straight to the closet, grabbed some clothes,
some board games from a shelf, a book or two. On the floor
of the closet was a little pink suitcase with a rubber handle.
David slid this out into the center of the floor, popped it open,
and filled it with these random items. He dropped the two
boxes of ammo and the handgun inside it, as well.

Back downstairs, he rifled through the kitchen cupboard,
which was mostly empty. He surmised that the Langstroms
had been holed up here for some time, eating all the food they
had on hand until it dwindled down to practically nothing. In
the end, David settled for some granola bars and a few warm
cans of soda from the cupboard.

In the garage, he opened the Oldsmobile's trunk and tossed
the pink suitcase inside. Then he went back through the house
and out the sliding glass door to the front, where he opened
the rear door of the Bronco and felt around on the floor for
his duffel bag.

Ellie stirred and woke. She never woke like a regular
child—all sleepy-lidded, muzzy, blustery like a winter snow-
storm. Instead, she always came *instantly* awake, as if she'd
been faking her slumber all along.

"What are you doing?" she said.

"Something's happened. We can't go home right now.
We're at a friend's house and we're going to use his car."

"Why can't we go home?"

"It's all very complicated," he said. He grabbed the duffel
bag and yanked it out. He motioned for her to follow, too.

She shook her head.

"Let's *go,* Ellie. *Now.*"

She gathered up the shoe box, then slid along the seat and
dropped down onto the driveway.

David slung the duffel bag over one shoulder, then grabbed

hold of his daughter's hand. "Come on," he said, and dragged her back around to the rear of the house.

"Whose house is this?"

"A friend. He's away. We're taking his car."

"Why?"

He pulled her in through the open door.

"We need a different car."

"Why? Where are we going? Why can't we go home?"

"Just give me a goddamn minute, will you?" he said, half-shouting. His voice cracked midway through and he struggled not to burst into tears.

He hauled her out to the garage. "Get in," he said, going around to the open trunk of the Oldsmobile. He dumped the duffel bag inside. His hands were shaking and his nose was running.

When he slammed the trunk's lid, he saw that Ellie hadn't moved from the doorway.

"Get in the goddamn car, Eleanor," he said.

She just stared at him.

His eyelids fluttered closed. In his head, he counted to ten, taking deep breaths. When he opened his eyes again, he said, more calmly, "Please, baby. I need you to get in the car."

She pointed at him. "Your nose is bleeding."

He touched two fingers to the divot above his upper lip. The fingers came away slick with blood. *What the fuck?* He looked up at her again and tried to smile. Said, "Baby, *please*."

She carried her shoe box to the rear door of the Olds, opened it, climbed inside. The sound of the door slamming shut was like the report of a starter's pistol.

It's a nosebleed from overexertion, he told himself. *That's all it is. It's a wonder I'm not having a heart attack right now.*

Before leaving, he stowed the Bronco in the Langstroms' garage and shut the door. When he reversed the Oldsmobile out onto the street, it took him a few moments fumbling with gauges and buttons and switches to find the headlights. And then another few seconds to turn the high beams off.

"Why can't we go home?" she asked from the backseat.

"Because," he said, his mind racing. "Because. Because we're not allowed. Some doctors and police came and shut down our street. People were getting sick, and they had to come in and close it off."

"Just like on the news," Ellie said.

"Yes. Just like on the news."

"It's because of the sickness."

"Yes."

"Are we okay?"

"Yes, baby."

"I mean, we aren't sick, are we?"

"No."

"Did everyone on our street get sick?"

"No, honey. It's just a precaution."

"So where are we going now?"

"Away."

"Why?"

"Because, Ellie, we were not supposed to leave the house. But we did. So now we can't go back." His mind was reeling.

"That doesn't sound like a good idea."

"Just give me a few minutes to relax, okay? Why don't you close your eyes and try to get some sleep? I'll explain it all to you later."

"We always call Mom before bedtime."

He closed his eyes for a moment, imagining the roadway a hundred miles wide. "We can't right now. So just get some rest."

"Later?" she said.

"Yes. Later."

"Promise?"

He promised.

Several seconds later, he felt her cold fingers touch the back of his neck.

They drove south.

63

When he opened his eyes, he found the sky cloudless, pure blue. There were no sounds except for the wind sighing in the trees and the bugs chattering away in the tall grass. He ran his palms overtop a fringe of wildflowers.

The headache claimed him the moment he sat up. It slammed around in the center of his brain, ricocheting like buckshot off the walls of his skull. Wincing, he pressed the heels of his hands into his eye sockets. When he touched beneath his nose, he felt the warm slickness and saw the bright red blood on his fingertips. There were streamers of red running down the front of his shirt, too.

Before he could stand, he was alerted to a tickling sensation along his left arm. When he looked at the bandage Tim had applied, he could see specks of blood blossoming up to the surface. And then the bandage *bulged,* swelling momentarily before sinking back down. The tickling turned to a frantic itch. The bandage—or, more accurately, whatever was *beneath* the bandage—swelled like a balloon before deflating again.

He tore the bandage off and stared in abject horror at the avalanche of small black beetles that spilled out from his perforated wound. He shrieked, swatted at the wound, feeling no pain, feeling nothing except the sensation of those bugs crawling all over his flesh. It wasn't until he'd torn open a number of stitches that he realized there were no bugs there. And he was left bleeding freely from the reopened wound.

He reached out and used the leg of the nearest rabbit hutch

to hoist himself to his feet. Behind the meshwork, large gray rabbits scampered about, panicked. One of them roared at him like a lion. On closer inspection, he saw that they weren't rabbits at all, but alien creatures with slender, segmented legs and bodies comprised of thick, iridescent shells. Their heads were mainly a system of eyes of varying sizes, some of them mirrored so that David could see his own terrified reflection in them.

He staggered back to the house, up the steps, in through the porch. It seemed to take a great effort, as if he was doing this simple exercise on a planet with a stronger gravitational pull and less oxygen.

When he came in through the kitchen door, he saw Tim standing there, tugging on a lightweight jacket. Ellie stood beside him. At the sight of David, a shadow darkened her features.

"Dad," Ellie said, her voice low.

"I was just coming out to look for you," Tim said. He stood frozen in the middle of pulling on his jacket.

"I think I'm sick," David said.

"Yeah," Tim said, finally shrugging off his jacket and folding it over one of the kitchen chairs. "We know."

David shook his head. "How . . . ?"

"I could tell the moment I laid eyes on you," Tim said, "right when I came up and hugged you outside. Ellie told us when you guys got here. *She* knew."

Their secret conversation at the breakfast table, David thought, his mind racing. *Their secret birds at the breakfast car.* His head pounded and his thoughts were muddled.

He looked at Ellie. "I'm sorry, baby. I'm so sorry."

"I didn't want to believe it," she said, "but I knew. I could feel it in you." She was fighting off tears. He wanted to go to her, comfort her, lie and tell her it would be okay. But at that moment he didn't trust himself to move.

"Sit down, David." Tim moved toward him, pulling out a kitchen chair.

"No," David said. He took a step in Ellie's direction but the world seemed to cant, the floor sliding out from beneath him.

"Whoa, whoa, whoa," Tim said, and hurried to his side. He grabbed David beneath the armpits and helped lower him onto the kitchen chair. He went down like wet laundry.

David's gaze lowered to the table. Three perfect circles of blood, each one smaller than a dime, formed a constellation on the tabletop. He turned his hands over, examined his palms, and thought he saw the ghostly impressions of the wildflowers hidden there among the whorls and creases and cross-hatches.

Ellie took a single step toward him. She seemed hesitant to approach him, though he knew she wasn't afraid of touching him, of getting sick. She was *seeing* him, and in perfect clarity, from where she stood, and she was reluctant to move from her vantage because she was digesting every bit of him.

She's a special one, Kathy said in his ear.

"Yes," he said aloud. "She is."

And then she was just Ellie again, Eleanor Elizabeth Arlen, his Little Spoon, the delicate spray of freckles across the saddle of her nose, her eyes impossibly filled with so much intuition and wisdom and understanding that she looked like an old soul in the body of a young child, and she came to him with economical footsteps, a firm expression of both compassion and sadness—

(cold it's so cold)

—and when she reached out and hugged him about the shoulders, he found himself desperate to inhale her every scent, embrace every molecule of her, terrified at the prospect of his traitorous brain dismissing all his best memories of this wonderful, impossible, fierce, loving, inimitable girl, and their brief time together on this planet.

"I want to save you," she whispered in his ear.

"It's too late for me," he said.

Gently, Ellie pulled away from his embrace. He expected her to be crying, but she wasn't. She was her mother again in that instant, so clearly Kathy that David had to wonder if he wasn't suffering another hallucination.

"How bad is it, David?" Tim asked.

David looked at his brother but didn't respond. Tim nodded; David's look spoke volumes.

"Could you give us a minute, Uncle Tim?"

"Sure thing, El." Tim smiled at them both, then left the room, his heavy footfalls receding down the hall until David heard the front door squeal open.

Ellie turned back to him, not speaking right away. Her eyes scrutinized him. "Does it hurt?" she said.

"Not really. Just here." He pointed to his heart.

Ellie nodded. "Me, too," she said. A tear rolled down the side of her nose. "I tried to make you better. While you slept, I tried to take it all out of you. I thought maybe . . . maybe the stronger I got, I might be able to do it. But I just couldn't do it. I'm not strong enough. Not yet. I can't get the sickness out of you."

"It's okay, baby. It's okay," he said. "That power of yours is meant for something. Do good with it, Ellie, but be careful with it, too. Do you understand?"

She lowered her gaze and nodded.

Gently, she pulled away from him so that she could see his face. Then Ellie did a strange thing—she reached out and caressed the side of his face. It was something Kathy had done a million times in their marriage. "Daddy Spoon," she said. Just as he closed his eyes, he heard Ellie say, "You've been a good dad. You've done your best. I love you."

"I love you, baby."

He tried to wrap her up in his arms, but his body refused to obey him all of a sudden. Perceptive as always, Ellie intuited his intention, lifted his arms for him, and wrapped them around her waist. He drew her into a hug.

"I don't want to keep running and hiding," she said into his ear. "I want to help the good people, not hurt the bad ones. I want you to let me go. I want you to let me do it."

He managed to summon enough strength to squeeze her tightly. He could instruct Tim that she was to stay here in the farmhouse and remain hidden, and Tim had already agreed to do whatever David thought was best . . . but then what would

happen if Tim got sick? Ellie would be left alone. He thought
of those terrible bugs that had uprooted themselves from the
molehills in the yard—and even now, he wondered if they had
been real or merely a hallucination brought on by the Folly
and his own deteriorating brain—and imagined the farmhouse
surrounded by them, swarmed by them, and Ellie trapped inside. Alone.

We have come to the end of the line, said the head-voice. Bright
swirls capered behind his eyelids. *This is it, David.*

When they separated, he kissed her on the forehead. Her
eyes were planets, her eyelashes like butterfly wings.

"All right," he said. "You're a big girl. You make your own
decision. I trust you."

She squeezed his hand in hers.

"I don't want to go to those doctors who have been looking for us," she said.

"No?" This surprised him.

"No," she said. "I want us to go back to Goodwin. I want
to find those people living in the firehouse, and the man who
can heal the sick. Do you remember that story the man Turk
told us about those people?"

"Yes," David said.

"I don't know why, but I think that story is true, and that
there is a man there who has abilities like mine. Only he's
older and his powers are . . . stronger. I don't know how I
know this, but I do. I think I even saw him that morning in
the street, and it was like he wanted me to follow him, to go
find him. And I think maybe he can show me what I need to
do to make my powers stronger, too, and use them the right
way. There might even be other people out there like me and
him, too."

"How do you know all this?"

"I don't know. I just do. I feel like I might be part of a puzzle, one piece that needs to come together with other pieces
to stop the world from dying." She looked down at her hands
and said, "Maybe it's not the cure in my blood that's supposed
to save the world, but the mystery of my power."

"You're such a smart and wonderful girl," he said.

"And this man, whoever he is," she said. "He can help you, Dad. I can't cure you, but he can. I *know* he can."

He just smiled wanly at his daughter, taking both of her hands in his. He brought her hands to his mouth, kissed her knuckles.

"What?" Ellie said. "What is it?"

"Ellie, I'll never make it back to Kentucky. I'm very sick."

Her face seemed to change in subtle increments before his eyes until she was crying again. She withdrew her hands from his. "No," she said, her voice barely above a whisper.

"It's okay," David said. "I'll talk with Uncle Tim. He'll take you. It's a good plan, Ellie. You need to do it. And you need to get on the road right away."

She shook her head. "No. No, Dad."

"It'll be okay."

"No," she said.

"I can't make the trip, Ellie. I'm at the end here, sweetheart."

"Then I'll stay with you until the end. I'll make it better for you in the end."

"No. I don't want you to see me like that. I don't want your last memory of me to be . . . to be whatever is going to happen."

"I can make it better for you," she sobbed. "Like I did with the girl on the highway."

"I don't want you to do that," he said. He leaned toward her so that their foreheads touched. "Now, you go and save the world. You hear me? You go and save the world, Eleanor Arlen."

She closed her eyes and nodded, her forehead still against his.

"That's my girl," he said, closing his eyes and smiling to himself.

His head was full of locusts.

64

David watched as Ellie and Tim loaded the Tahoe with some snacks, fresh clothes, and a few jugs of water. Tim also packed the two shotguns and the pistol in the back of the Tahoe, along with several boxes of ammunition. Tim estimated they could make it back to Kentucky in two days, unless they ran into trouble on the road. He had been apprised of Ellie's plan and had agreed to see it through. "I'll take care of her like she's my own daughter," Tim assured him. "Don't you worry about that, David."

David hugged his brother and kissed the scruffy side of his face.

He managed to make it out into the yard as they finished packing the Tahoe. Ellie stood beside the Tahoe's open rear door, hands in her pockets, her face emotionless. She stared at him as he crossed the yard. And she hugged him when he reached her.

He knelt down so that they were eye to eye.

"I've been meaning to give this to you for a few days now," he said. "It was Mom's." He twisted Kathy's wedding band off his pinkie and held it out to his daughter. "It's too big for you now, but you'll grow into it."

Ellie took it between two fingers, holding it up so that the sunlight caused it to sparkle.

"Happy birthday," David said.

She hugged him around the neck. Cried against him.

"I love you," he said, and kissed the burning hot side of her face. He braced her head in both hands and pressed the tip of his nose against hers. "Listen to me. Listen to me."

She nodded.

"I'm so proud of you. Your mom and I, we've always been so proud of you."

"I don't want to leave you."

"It'll be okay."

He kissed her forehead, the side of her face. Said, "*Shhh, shhh,*" over and over to her until her sobs tapered off, leaving only the sharp hitching of her chest in their place.

"Okay," she told him, once she'd gotten herself under control. "I'll be brave. I'm okay."

"That's my girl."

"Little Spoon," she managed.

David smiled. "That's right," he said. "My Little Spoon. Don't you forget it."

His brain must have shut down for a few seconds then, for when he regained consciousness, he was watching the Tahoe drive away, Ellie's small silhouette framed in the rear window. She had one palm pressed against the glass, Kathy's wedding band shining on her finger. She was crying.

65

It took him several attempts before he made it up the front porch. Beneath him, the steps seemed to melt and grow soft, and he kept losing his footing. At one point, the handrail turned into a large millipede, its countless legs thrashing, its body undulating beneath his hand, causing him to scream, lose his balance, and tumble down the stairs. Several times he nearly gave up, and curled up on the ground. But the sound of the bugs in the grass began to drive him mad.

When he finally made it inside, he found that the sky outside the windows was a hellish black, even though he knew it was still midday. He progressed down the hallway, one hand on the wall for support. When he passed the open bathroom door, he saw Burt Langstrom standing there, his face half gone, a fireworks display of blood sprayed along the bathroom mirror. When David blinked again, Burt was no longer there.

In the kitchen, Dr. Kapoor was seated in a chair, his face as expressionless as a cadaver's. The charred remains of Deke Carmody appeared beside David at that moment, not even startling him. David could smell Deke's burned flesh, and when Deke grinned, it was the grin of a skull covered in flaking black chips.

Go on, Deke said, acknowledging Kapoor propped up in the chair. *Grab some of that moonshine, a match, and burn the motherfucker. In fact, go ahead and burn down the whole house. Hell, that's what I did.*

But when he turned to respond, Deke was gone. So was Kapoor. The house was empty.

Yet when he turned back to the wall of windows, he saw that a figure stood outside, peering in at him. It was a dark-skinned little boy with rosary beads around his neck. As David stared at him, the boy's mouth unhinged and a catlike hiss ratcheted up his throat.

David turned away, his heart thumping. The periphery of his vision was breaking apart, leaving a border of blackness around everything. It was like looking through binoculars.

Ellie stood in the doorway.

"Are . . . are you real?" David managed.

"I couldn't leave you like this," she said, crossing the kitchen and coming over to him. He knelt down, wrapped her in his arms, and indeed she felt solid. Real.

"They don't have to be bad," Ellie said into his ear. "Some of them are beautiful. Some of them are the most beautiful things you can imagine. I think that if you hold on to beauti-ful things when the end comes, then that's what you'll see. It'll be like walking into a wonderful dream."

From over Ellie's shoulder, David could see the shoe box sitting on the kitchen table. The lid was open, the three eggs, impossibly delicate yet somehow quite formidable, corralled together in that skilled construction of twigs and leaves and bits of paper.

He smiled, his vision growing blurry with tears.

One of the eggs rolled onto its side. A second egg rocked. A third jumped. One shell appeared to bulge just the slightest bit . . . and then it cracked, a section of it falling away, a dark triangle left in its wake. One of the other eggs cracked down the middle, splitting open. The thing inside the shell was fully feathered, alive, wide-eyed, chirping.

David laughed. The tears were coming freely now. So was the trickle of blood from his nose. Ellie's arms grew tighter around him.

(it's like flying you can fly now you can fly)

The birds zigzagged around the room, frantic and beautiful, their birdsong soothing the throb of his headache.

"Let me take you there," Ellie whispered to him.

Just a little while, he told himself, closing his eyes and inhaling the scent of his daughter. *Just rest here a little while . . .*

The pressure in his head grew. Blurry smears of dazzling lights projected against his eyelids. Still, he heard the birdsong.

It'll be like walking into a wonderful dream.

Let me take you there.

66

And he woke up on a patch of green grass, staring at the sky. The air smelled fresh and clouds chugged lazily across the bright blue heavens. As he watched, a single bird darted across the sky, small and sharp and fast, like an arrow fired from a bow. Two more birds followed it . . . and then three, five, nine, twenty more . . .

A moment later, the whole sky was infused with birds—small ones, large ones, countless varieties, shapes, colors—their birdsong a radiant cacophony that seemed to impart wisdom, grant wishes, make dreams come true, the flutter of their wings a chorus of rustling velvet drapes.

David stood up. He found he was home, standing on his own front lawn. He turned and hurried up the walkway to the front door. He gripped the knob, cool to the touch, and turned it. When he eased the door open, he heard a sound like falling typewriter keys or distant tap dancing—toys lined up on the other side of the door, little plastic figurines, a Night Parade in broad daylight announcing his presence.

He entered the house, crossed down the hall, and froze when he came through the kitchen doorway.

Kathy and Ellie were seated at the kitchen table. There was a birthday cake with a waxy number 9 candle on it. Ellie's stuffed elephant was propped up beside the cake, a pointed party hat fastened to its head. There was also an empty seat waiting for him.

Kathy waved him over. Laughed beautifully.

Ellie brightened, just as she used to when she was a little girl. "Daddy," she said.

"Little Spoon," he said.

And he went to them.

ACKNOWLEDGMENTS

It's romantic to think of a story as a found thing, a relic unearthed. Some say stories have always existed, and it's the author's job to bring them out into the light of day, much like some sculptors believe their artwork is hidden within the confines of a block of stone. Others believe that you trip over a story, much like you'd trip over a rock half-buried in the earth, and all that is required is for the author to dig it out. And maybe sometimes all of that is true. Other times, it takes the input and counsel of a great many people.

Many thanks to my agent, Cameron McClure, whose finger rested firmly on the pulse of this novel from the very beginning and whose guidance helped me shape it. Thanks to my editor, Peter Senftleben, whose suggestions raised this tale to the next level. My undying gratitude to my own personal savior, Dr. Charles J. Sailey, MD, MS, for his input on all things medical, and for the generosity of his valuable time and even more valuable knowledge. A tip of the hat to Jim Braswell, my brother in words, for his insight and faith, and to the inimitable Kristopher Rufty for his friendship, input, and at least one late-night phone call when I thought all was lost and he showed me how to find it again. Thank you to my wife, Debra, who remains my strongest critic (as all wives are) and my most reliable sounding board (as all wives should be), and to my dad, who's got a good sense of story and an even better sense for telling me when I've gone off the rails. Lastly, thanks to my daughters, Madison and Hayden, without whom this book would not exist. You rock Dad's world.

If you liked *The Night Parade*, be sure to read *Little Girls*, available now!

From Bram Stoker Award nominee Ronald Malfi comes a brilliantly chilling novel of childhood revisited, memories resurrected, and fears reborn . . .

When Laurie was a little girl, she was forbidden to enter the room at the top of the stairs. It was one of many rules imposed by her cold, distant father. Now, in a final act of desperation, her father has exorcised his demons. But when Laurie returns to claim the estate with her husband and ten-year-old daughter, it's as if the past refuses to die. She feels it lurking in the broken moldings, sees it staring from an empty picture frame, hears it laughing in the moldy greenhouse deep in the woods . . .

At first, Laurie thinks she's imagining things. But when she meets her daughter's new playmate, Abigail, she can't help but notice her uncanny resemblance to another little girl who used to live next door. Who *died* next door. With each passing day, Laurie's uneasiness grows stronger, her thoughts more disturbing. Like her father, is she slowly losing her mind? Or is something truly unspeakable happening to those sweet little girls?

Chapter 1

They had been expecting a woman, Dora Lorton, to greet them upon their arrival, but as Ted finessed the Volvo station wagon up the long driveway toward the house, they could see there was a man on the porch. Tall and gaunt, he had a face like a withered apple core and wore a long black overcoat that looked incongruous in the stirrings of an early summer. The man watched them as Ted pulled the station wagon up beside a dusty gray Cadillac that was parked in front of the porch. For one perplexing instant, Laurie Genarro thought the man on the porch was her father, so newly dead that his orphaned spirit still lingered at the house on Annapolis Road.

"Glad to see Lurch from *The Addams Family* has found work," Ted commented as he shut off the car.

"It looks like a haunted house," Susan spoke up from the backseat, a comment that seemed to underscore Laurie's initial impression of the ghostlike man who stood beneath the partial shade of the porch alcove. Susan was ten and had just begun vocalizing her critical observations to anyone within earshot. "And who's Lurch?"

"Ah," said Ted. "When did popular culture cease being popular?"

"I'm only ten," Susan reminded him, closing the Harry Potter book she had been reading for much of the drive down from Connecticut. She had been brooding and sullen for the majority of the trip, having already pitched a fit back in Hartford about having to spend summer vacation away from her friends and in a strange city, all of it because of a grandfather she had never known.

Who could blame her? Laurie thought now, still staring out the passenger window at the man on the porch. *I'd pitch a fit, too. In fact, I just might do it yet.*

Ted cupped his hands around his mouth. "Thank you for flying Genarro Airlines! Please make sure your tray tables are up before debarking."

Susan giggled, her mood having changed for the better somewhere along Interstate 95. "Barking!" she cried happily, misinterpreting her father's comment, then proceeded to bark like a dog. Ted wasted no time barking right along with her.

Laurie got out of the car and shivered despite the afternoon's mild temperature. In the wake of her father's passing, and for no grounded reason, she had expected her old childhood home to look different—empty, perhaps, like the molted skin of a reptile left behind in the dirt, as if the old house had nothing left to do but wither and die just as its master had done. But no, it was still the same house it had always been: the redbrick frame beneath a slouching mansard roof; Italianate cornices of a design suggestive of great pinwheels cleaved in half; a trio of arched windows on either side of the buckling front porch; all of which was capped by a functional belvedere that stood up against the cloudy June sky like the turret of a tiny castle. *That's where it happened,* Laurie thought with a chill as her eyes clung to the belvedere. It looked like a tiny bell tower sans bell, but was really a little room with windows on all four sides. Her parents had used it mostly for storage back when they had all still lived here together, before her parents' separation. Laurie had been forbidden to go up there as a child.

Trees crowded close to the house and intermittent slashes of sunlight came through the branches and danced along the east wall. The lawn was unruly and thick cords of ivy climbed the brickwork. Many windows on the ground floor stood open, perhaps to air out the old house, and the darkness inside looked cold and bottomless.

Laurie waved timidly at the man on the porch. She thought

she saw his head bow to her. Images of old gothic horrors bombarded her head. Then she looked over her shoulder to where Ted and Susan stood at the edge of a small stone well that rose up nearly a foot from a wild patch of grass and early summer flowers on the front lawn. *Yes, I remember the well.* Back when she had been a child, the well had been housed beneath a wooden portico where, in the springtime, sparrows nested. She recalled tossing stones into its murky depths and how it sometimes smelled funny in the dead heat of late summer. Now, the wooden portico was gone and the well was nothing but a crumbling stone pit in the earth, covered by a large plank of wood.

Without waiting for Ted and Susan to catch up, Laurie climbed the creaky steps of the porch, a firm smile already on her face. The ride down to Maryland from Connecticut had exhausted her and the prospect of all that lay ahead in the house and with the lawyer left her empty and unfeeling. She extended one hand to the man in the black overcoat and tried not to let her emotions show. "Hello. I'm Laurie Genarro."

A pale hand with very long fingers withdrew from one of the pockets of the overcoat. The hand was cold and smooth in Laurie's own. "The daughter," the man said. His face was narrow but large, with a great prognathous jaw, a jutting chin, and the rheumy, downturned eyes of a basset hound. With the exception of a wispy sweep of colorless hair across the forehead, his scalp was bald. Laurie thought him to be in his late sixties.

"Yes," Laurie said. "Mr. Brashear was my father."

"I'm sorry for your loss."

"Thank you." She withdrew her hand from his, thankful to be rid of the cold, bloodless grasp. "I was expecting Ms. Lorton. . . ."

"I'm Dora's brother, Felix Lorton. Dora's inside, straightening up the place for you and your family. She was uncomfortable returning here alone after . . . well, after what happened. My sister can be foolishly superstitious. I apologize if I've frightened you."

"Not at all. Don't be silly." But he *had* frightened her, if just a little.

Across the front yard, Susan squealed with pleasure. Ted had lifted the corner of the plank of wood covering the well, and they were both peering down into it. Susan said something inaudible and Ted put back his head and laughed.

"My husband and daughter," Laurie said. She recognized a curious hint of apology in her tone and was quickly embarrassed by it.

"Splendid," Felix Lorton said with little emotion. Then he held out a brass key for her.

"I have my own." David Cushing, her father's lawyer, had mailed her a copy of the key along with the paperwork last week.

"The locks have been changed recently," said Felix Lorton.

"Oh." She extended her hand and opened it, allowing Lorton to drop the key onto her palm. She was silently thankful she didn't have to touch the older man's flesh again. It had been like touching the flesh of a corpse.

"Hi, there!" It was Ted, peering up at them through the slats in the porch railing while sliding his hands into the pockets of his linen trousers. There was the old heartiness in Ted's voice now. It was something he affected when in the company of a stranger whom he'd had scarce little time to assess. Ted was two years past his fortieth birthday but could pass for nearly a full decade younger. His teeth were white and straight, his skin unblemished and healthy-looking, and his eyes were both youthful and soulful at the same time, a combination many would have deemed otherwise incompatible. He kept himself in good shape, running a few miles every morning before retiring to his home office for the bulk of the afternoon where he worked. He could work for hours upon end in that home office back in Hartford without becoming fidgety or agitated, classical music issuing from the Bose speakers his only companion. Laurie envied his discipline.

"That's my husband, Ted," Laurie said, "and our daughter, Susan."

Susan sidled up beside her father, her sneakers crunching over loose gravel. Her big hearty smile was eerily similar to his.

She had on a long-sleeved cotton jersey and lacrosse shorts. At ten, her legs were already slim and bronze, and she liked to run and play sports and had many friends back in Hartford. She was certainly her father's daughter.

"Nice to meet you folks. I'm Felix Lorton."

"There are frogs in the well," Susan said excitedly.

Lorton smiled. It was like watching a cadaver come alive on an autopsy table, and the sight of that smile chilled Laurie's bones. "I suppose there are," Lorton said to Susan. He leaned over the railing to address the girl, his profile stark and angular and suggestive of some predatory bird peering down from a tree branch at some blissfully unaware prey. "Snakes, sometimes, too."

Susan's eyes widened. "Snakes?"

"Oh, yes. After a heavy rain, and if it's not covered properly, that well fills up and it's possible to see all sorts of critters moving about down there."

"Neat!" Susan chirped. "Do they bite?"

"Only if you bite first." Lorton chomped his teeth hollowly. Then he turned his cadaverous grin onto Laurie. "I suppose I should take you folks inside now and introduce you to Dora."